The
Heart
Denied

The Heart Denied

Linda Anne Wulf

Hydra Publications

Printed in the United States of America

First Printing, 2010

ISBN 978-0615432427

Hydra Publications
337 Clifty Dr
Madison, IN 47250

www.hydrapublications.com

With love to Mark and the boys for all your patience and encouragement;
to Janet Schmidt for reading the original manuscript;
and to Karen Rhoads, Nita Eick, the late Victoria Koenig, Bud Wulf, Sharon Wulf,
Lois Wulf, Irma Young, Nita West, Kathy Adams Manning, Shannon Dunnagan,
Vickie Marise, Brenda Hartman, Cindi Kuebler, Rosemary Haydock, Dr. Patty
Thompson, Adrian Anderson, the late Pat Becker, Laura Corey, and James C. Vines,
for reading the book before its final edit.

Your support is amazing, my appreciation boundless.
Bless you all.

PROLOGUE

London
June 28, 1728

Bed curtains?

Thorne Neville rolled over with a groan, only to see the deep cleft in a plump bosom. Six inches closer, he might have smothered.

There were worse ways to die.

"Sleep, Mister Adams," said a drowsy voice at his ear. "'Tis barely dawn."

Mister Adams. His alias. That explained the bed curtains. "You sleep," he mumbled. "I'll be off."

"So early?"

"Aye." He sat up and feigned a yawn to make his next words sound casual. "I'm going home."

He tensed as the mattress shifted and flint struck behind him. Candlelight bathed the bed, revealing his stray clothing--which he gathered with unusual haste while Katy Devlin's stare seared his back.

"Home? You're leaving Oxford?"

Dread slowed Thorne's heart. Must she make this more difficult than it already was? He tugged on his stockings and tied the garters, jammed his arms into his shirtsleeves. "Do you not think four years at university enough?" Turning, he pinned Katy with the unnatural brilliance of his blue eyes, an intimidating maneuver he'd often used to his advantage, though never on a woman.

She didn't flinch. "Then you'll be leaving London, too, Mister Adams. And me."

It was Thorne who flinched, dropping his gaze. "I...I'm not 'leaving London,' nor anyone in particular." He freed his black mane from inside the shirt and smoothed the wrinkled linen into his breeches. "I merely return to my ancestral home to take up the reins where my father left off."

"And would that be, sir, the very place you've avoided like the plague, since he died? Where you've not ventured in four years, neither at Yuletide nor harvest?"

The barb pierced its target. In return, Thorne pierced Katy with a silent glare.

"Well then, be off, Mister Adams!" She rolled out of bed and flung on a wrapper, swiping a sleeve across her eyes in the same motion. "I've other gentleman callers to see today."

"Aye," Thorne muttered. "We've each our obligations, however less than noble." He fastened his waistcoat, yanking at the mother-of-pearl buttons.

"But you know mine. I know naught of yours."

So the fight wasn't over. "Nor would you care to," he said shortly, hoping to put an end to it.

"You think not?" Katy sashayed toward him, fists planted firmly on her ample hips. "Then all you know of me is that I sleep with men for my keep."

"And that it was not by your choosing," he said quickly--too quickly.

"Och, defending me against myself now, are you? And what does it matter how I got here? I am who I am, Mister Adams, and I'll be begging no pardons, even from you. Who the deuce *are* you this morn, by the by? Where's the man who's bedded me every se'nnight for four years? *He's* never judged me."

"Nor shall he." A snap of his wrist shook the folds from his neckcloth. He looped it around his throat, briefly considering hanging himself with it.

"Then look at me," Katy pleaded, tears constricting her words, "and tell me what summons you home with such haste you cannot linger another hour."

Thorne swallowed a sudden tightness in his own throat. "You ask too much of me," he said, fumbling with the long ends of his neckcloth.

"Och, sir, I've never so much as asked your true name, or whence you come. Here, let me." She brushed his hands aside and tied the linen with deft fingers. "All I know is that someone holds stewardship of your lands in your absence...has he died, that person? Is that why you must go?"

Thorne looked into her eyes--those emerald wells of compassion from which he'd drunk for four years now, believing that as long as he paid for the privilege, there would be no demand for his heart--long ago stolen and buried.

He'd been wrong. Wrong to think Katy's profession made her invulnerable. Wrong to keep calling here after he saw the signs. And wrong to confess to her that she was his first and only lover.

But he hadn't been wrong about his heart. Years ago gone with a young woman to her grave, its resurrection was out of the question.

The sun's first pale rays rippled over Katy's hair. Unable to help himself, Thorne touched an auburn lock before going on to trace the rose-petal softness of her lips. His pulse quickened as she caught his fingertip between gentle teeth.

Silently cursing fate, he hauled Katy to him, slipping her wrapper and shift off one shoulder to caress its smooth roundness. Rebelling suddenly at the passing time, as well as at other growing constraints, he slid his hand down to cup a full, firm breast. He encountered Katy's open palm instead.

He smiled into her eyes; he knew this game. "You would bargain your favors with me, Miss Devlin?"

"They are my stock in trade," she said, irony lacing her words.

Thorne's smile froze. "So they are--as you seem bloody bent upon reminding me this morning." He snagged his tricorne from the hat stand and strode toward the door. "I should have gone before sunup, at any rate."

"Mister Adams."

So grim was the note in her voice that he halted in his tracks and turned to meet her unblinking regard. Her tears were wiped dry.

"If you pass through that door, sir, without telling me who or what summons you away-" Katy took a deep, tremulous breath and squared her shoulders. "Then I shan't receive you again."

I won't be calling here again, Katy. He knew he should say it, but the words stuck in his throat.

Awash in the rosy light of dawn, she stood with her gaze unwavering, hands loosely clasped, mussed hair tumbling to her waist over the nightclothes still drooping from one shoulder. That she made no move to rearrange herself only added to her dignity.

But Thorne feared that the anguished pride in those dry, green eyes would forever haunt his dreams.

In three strides he had her by the shoulders. He pressed his lips to her pale brow, then took a deep breath and drew back to look her in the eye. He owed her at least that much.

You owe her the truth. Every rotting word of it.

"I've a promise to keep," he heard himself say in a low, taut voice. "An obligation to fulfill." He firmed his hold on her shoulders and shook his head, scarcely able to believe it himself.

"I *must* go home, Katy...to meet my bride."

ONE

Wycliffe Hall
June 29, 1728

Behind a desk that nearly dwarfed her, Dame Priscilla Carswell shot to her feet. "How *dare* you barge in here unannounced."

"I dare," Tobias Hobbs fired back, "the way the Combs wench dared barge into my stables this morn." He slapped his cap against his thigh. "Keep your fool maids in the Hall where they belong, Carswell. I'm stable master, not a bloody nursemaid. I've no time for their bawling."

"Yet you've ample time for their deflowering," the housekeeper retorted, blushing to the roots of her perfect white coif.

Hobbs smirked. "They come to me, and I'm not one to refuse. But I've my hands full just now-"

"And you think I don't?" Dame Carswell folded scrawny arms over her pleated stomacher. "With his lordship to arrive from University in two days, his guests even sooner, and my best maid sick as a pup over the way you've used her? Twice this morn I've sent her topstairs to collect herself!" The housekeeper's beady eyes flashed as she rapped a finger on the desk blotter. "Elaine Combs is not your common trollop, and 'twas *you* hounding *her* a month ago. So you've brass, Toby Hobbs, marching into my office with your dung stench and acting my superior! I shall speak to Pennington straightaway-"

"You do that, you old crow. He doesn't want her in the stables any more than I do." Hobbs turned on a mud-caked heel and, stealing a backward glance at the housekeeper's livid expression, sauntered across the great hall and out through the kitchen, tipping his hat to blushing maids all the way.

* * *

Thorne stared out the coach window, his gut tightening as Wycliffe Hall slid into view. A jewel, some called the huge Tudor hall with the flagged terraces and sloping gardens, faceted as it was by numerous oriels and gables and set in such lush Northamptonshire countryside. But the jewel had a flaw. Meant to save lives, the towering stone keep at its northeast corner had so far only taken one.

The coach ascended the winding flagstone drive. Reaching the terrace, Thorne watched paneled-oak doors with leaded lights swing wide on the portico.

A tall, white-haired man in gray livery stood framed in the doorway, looking so confounded that Thorne had to chuckle. "Steady, Jennings," he said, alighting from the coach. "I'm two days early, not back from the dead."

A snap of the old butler's bony fingers brought two footmen scurrying out for Thorne's trunk. "Welcome home, M'lord," Jennings croaked, bowing as Thorne doffed his tricorne and ascended the portico. "Though 'tis rather topsy-turvy just now."

Thorne crossed the threshold and peered between the carved-oak panels of the draft screen. "I quite see what you mean."

Gray-frocked women swarmed the great hall, some polishing glass chimneys, others waxing the parquet flooring, still others remounting the tapestry over the massive mantelpiece. Several footmen hauled a settee and some rolled carpets from the east wing into the west.

All this, for me and two guests? Perhaps word had leaked that one of his guests would soon be mistress of Wycliffe Hall?

Behind him, Jennings cleared his throat. "We'd have gathered to greet you properly, had we known-"

"Then I've spared the lot of us, haven't I." Dodging the commotion, Thorne walked the great hall of his ancestors, reacquainting his gaze with the carved-oak wainscoting, the arched braces and blackened collar-beams high overhead. The old oak trestle table stood, newly sanded and waxed to a shine, on the dais with twenty chairs at either side, all under the same three-tiered chandelier from which he'd once managed a swing and gotten baptized with hot wax for his trouble.

He smiled inwardly to see the servants going about their work as if he wasn't there; Carswell had always run a tight ship. "Where is the old dame?" he muttered over his shoulder.

"She's been fetched, M'lord," Jennings said, predictably at Thorne's heels.

"His lordship's chambers are not readied." Dame Carswell's steel-velvet voice accompanied a staccato step that double-timed Thorne's easy stride. "Leave his trunk outside my office."

The footmen hauling the trunk nearly fell down the stairs in their haste to obey. The housekeeper turned to Thorne and curtseyed. "M'lord, what a pleasant surprise." Swathed in black bombazine, her white cuffs and cap as starched as her backbone, Dame Carswell spared him a tight-lipped smile. "We might have been prepared for your early arrival if not for Tobias Hobbs' meddling."

Thorne arched one eyebrow. "A matter for Pennington, surely."

"I have informed him, M'lord."

"And my guests, have they arrived early as well?"

"No, M'lord."

"Thank Providence for small favors, eh Carswell?"

Her mouth only grew more pinched.

"Never mind, you'll soon have everything to rights." Teasing her had amused him when he was a pup and his father had left the discipline to her; now it seemed tiresome. He gazed easily over her head. "Where is Pennington?"

"In the south pasture, M'lord. Some ewes are down, I believe."

Thorne's pulse tripped. "*There's* a welcome home." With a cursory nod for Carswell, he strode toward the kitchen and the nearest rear exit.

Suddenly he slowed his pace, his eye catching a movement on the musicians' gallery. No one had been up there in the eighteen years since his mother died. His father had forbidden it, along with music in general. As Thorne gazed up intently, a figure stepped back into the shadows, its slender gray sleeve and pale hand disappearing as the narrow gap in the curtains closed.

He thought about slipping up the service stairs to catch the servant red-handed, but he had reached the kitchen door by then. He opened it to a blast of steam, smelling of onions, thyme, and roasted meat. Chatter died, replaced by gasps from the scullery maids. A kettle lid clattered on the stone floor.

"Have a care, Hillary. Bless ye, Master Thorne...M'lord...ye're home!" A frowsy-haired woman materialized from the haze, her flour-covered hands clasped to her bosom, her old eyes misting. "Och, and look what a man ye've growed into!"

"A man indeed," someone exclaimed, prompting a whispered "whusht" and a giggle. Thorne paused to give the cook a courtly bow and a droll wink, and then turned and strode backward as he headed for the rear entry. "'Tis grand to see you, Mistress MacBride," he called out over the sounds of hissing steam, sizzling meat and popping coals. "Of all I missed at University, 'twas you I missed most."

"Ha! More likely ye missed my scones," she crowed back at him, her ruddy cheeks turning redder.

Thorne halted in the doorway, grinning. "Any fresh?"

"Maids or scones, M'lord?" Mistress MacBride countered, with a wry glance at her scullery crew. "Aye, we'll have them in a trice." She shook a finger at Thorne. "But only if ye call me 'Bridey,' like ye've always done."

He chuckled. "Very well, Bridey. Send the scones 'round to the library with a pot of tea in an hour. With two cups."

He saw her sudden consternation, and heard it when she must have thought he was out of earshot.

"Eating in the old baron's reading room," she fussed; but then she cautioned her giggling maids. "Mind ye've no fool notions, he's not Young Master anymore. He's our lord and liege now, and I'd best remember it quick as any of ye."

Out in the foyer, Thorne smiled to himself. If only Carswell were so adaptable.

* * *

"Aye. Two of Graham's ewes were found dead this morn," Arthur Pennington, longtime steward of Wycliffe Hall, replied with a grim nod.

"Anthrax?" Thorne held his breath.

"God willing, no. Kendall's having a look. He'll send word."

Thorne nodded, treading carefully over the herders' rutted path in the buckled shoes he had not bothered to change. Arthur was his mentor, but he tended to put more stock in God than Thorne was willing to invest. He only hoped his arrival home didn't mark the loss of their entire flock--a sorry way to carry on his father's decades of hard work.

Thorne stared off at the manor church, nestled in a hollow near a copse of trees. Arthur must have noticed the direction of that stare.

"He's missed by all," the steward said quietly. "Parson finds a fresh posy on the gravestone every Sunday. Hasn't a notion who's leaving it there."

Shame, and something close to rebellion, twisted Thorne's belly, with the thought that, while he was hiding away at Oxford, someone who wasn't even kin had paid regular tribute at his father's grave.

"And the salmon?" He gazed at the stone bridge over the deep, silent currents of the beck. An approaching cloudband shadowed its gray waters.

"A good haul. Thirty stone or better," Arthur replied. They had reached the rear gardens, where the steward leaned against the gatepost and lit his brier pipe. "When will your guests arrive?" he asked after a few puffs.

"Any hour now. Best not tell Carswell, though."

Unsmiling, Arthur drew on his pipe again and said casually, "No doubt you're looking forward to meeting Radleigh's daughter."

"Aye, considering she's to be my wife." Thorne frowned. "What's on your mind, Arthur?"

"Thought you might have heard. Rumor has it Radleigh is in financial trouble." Arthur quietly cleared his throat. "Gaming debts."

With a warning rumble, clouds broke overhead. An omen? Thorne turned his face in defiance to the cold rain and forced some cheer into his voice. "Come inside and join me for tea."

"Tea, M'lord?"

"An Eastern ritual I've got used to with friends in Chigwell. You'll like it, I think." Holding the gate wide for Arthur, he winked. "Better than drowning, at any rate."

* * *

Hunkered down in a velvet wingback chair, breathing the perfume of leather-bound books and burning apple-wood, Thorne watched through the wavy glass of the library solar as the rain pelted smiling stone cherubs in the garden. He felt oddly content. If his bride proved sensible, he could imagine a pleasant enough future at Wycliffe Hall.

In another chair, Arthur sat with his gray head bowed, his teacup dangling from one finger. Thorne's mouth twitched. "So, what's Carswell's gripe with Hobbs?"

Arthur jerked upright. "Glory, but you've your father's way of catching me off guard." He set the cup in its saucer as Thorne grinned. "Toby, aye. Seems Carswell's pet maid took a shine to him, and whatever he did - or didn't do - the wench took it to heart. Combs is her name. Elaine Combs."

Thorne unbuckled a shoe and tossed it aside. "Hobbs is roughly twenty now?"

"Aye, five years younger than your lordship."

Thorne winced. "Spare me the lordship drivel, Arthur, at least when we're alone." He aimed for the first shoe with the second, nailed his target, and propped his stocking-feet on an ottoman. "If Hobbs can't sow his oats elsewhere, we'd best find a new stableman."

"Stable master," Arthur reminded him. "And first-rate with the horses. He's quite impressed with the Arabian you sent ahead from Chigwell, by the by. Gone to great lengths to make him feel at home."

Buttering a scone, Thorne grunted. "Could be a waste of time. My friend Townsend will demand a rematch. He was well into his cups that eve, and royally

- 13 -

brassed off at himself come morn. But as long as the stallion is here, I intend to ride for all it's worth.

"And then there's Henry."

"Who?"

"Little Henry Pitts. Stable lad," Arthur explained, seeing Thorne's blank look. "Our Toby found him starving in London and took him to apprentice. Hard-working lad, good disposition."

"So, you're telling me Hobbs has a heart...yes, Jennings?" Thorne said, looking past Arthur with arched brow. The head-footman had just flung open the library doors.

"Begging your pardon, M'lord." Color spotted Jennings's gaunt cheeks; he seemed to relish his role after four years with no one to announce but agents and tax collectors. "Lord Radleigh and The Honourable Miss Stowington await you in the great hall."

* * *

Caught in a hearty embrace by his father's oldest and dearest friend, Thorne first glimpsed his bride-to-be over the big man's shoulder.

What irony that her eyes were green, the second pair to pierce his heart today. As they widened at the sight of him, he wondered if she'd ever seen a man at close range, other than her father. And her priest. She was, after all, fresh from the convent.

"May I present my daughter, Gwynneth." Perspiration coated Radleigh's brow as if he'd endured some ordeal. "Gwynneth, this is Thorneton Neville, Baron Neville of Wycliffe."

Thorne bowed. "I'm most honored, Miss Stowington."

Gold-dusted eyelashes fell on persimmon cheeks in a Devonshire-cream complexion. Long, strawberry-gold hair rippled forward as Gwynneth Stowington felled her green-velvet hood and executed a flawless curtsey. "My lord."

Her pout might have discouraged Thorne if it weren't for her blush--the mark of a true ingenue. It reminded him that the pleasure of initiating her into secular life would be his. And hers, if she proved willing. His smile warmed along with his blood. "Welcome to my home, Miss Stowington." *And to yours*, he was about to add, when the door burst open again.

A tall, slender maid bustled into the room--the infamous Elaine Combs, Thorne suspected, judging by the tear-swollen eyes she kept so doggedly on her task, which was to deliver two more teacups. His odd pang of sympathy died as she hurried away without tending the fire.

Suddenly he knew, for no apparent reason, that she was the young woman who'd spied upon him from the gallery yesterday. Carswell's favorite maid, Arthur had said. Strange. She seemed less than industrious, perhaps too distracted by her troubles with Hobbs.

Thorne stirred the fire while his guests took seats. He chose a chair where he could observe Radleigh's daughter without staring. Gwynneth gazed at the rows of books.

"You must find it strange, Miss Stowington, to be out in the world after" - Thorne glanced at Radleigh - "ten years?"

Radleigh nodded, splaying beefy hands on his spread knees. "She was eight when her mother died and I sent her to the sisters of Saint Mary, but deuced if I'd bargained on her wishing to take their *vows*! Not to worry," he added hastily, seeing Thorne's consternation, "I talked her out of it."

"Bullied me out of it," Gwynneth said coolly, ending her perusal of the bookshelves with a hostile look at her father. "And bribed the prioress to say there wasn't room for me in the novitiate."

Radleigh's eyebrows gathered like thunderheads. Thorne tried to disperse them while soothing the girl and reassuring himself. "Do you find your father's plans for you so objectionable, Miss Stowington?"

"I do." Gwynneth kept her gaze on Radleigh. "He has ripped me from the bosom of divinity, and for what? To go and keep house at Radleigh Hall and wait on his every whim."

Thorne bit off an exclamation as Radleigh shot him a warning look. Obviously Gwynneth knew nothing of the plan her father and Thorne's father had hatched years ago.

Thorne arched an eybrow at Radleigh. "In your letter, my lord, you promised a long visit here at Wycliffe Hall."

The older man fidgeted, scratching his head and knocking his wig cockeyed. "Aye, but the girl has only her convent rags. I've scheduled fittings with a dressmaker in London. We'll depart day after tomorrow, and stop here again on our way to Radleigh Hall." *I need time*, his eyes pleaded.

"Then I'll look forward to it." Thorne regarded Radleigh narrowly over the rim of his cup. "I trust I'll not be disappointed again."

* * *

"Well, you'd best *take* an interest," Radleigh groused at Gwynneth over supper. "You're to be the lady of the manor, after all, so by God, you'll dress like one."

"'Tis a sin to take the Lord's name in vain," Gwynneth snapped. "And who's to see me at Radleigh Hall but the servants? It isn't as if you entertain. I'm to be your housekeeper and nursemaid, is what it boils down to. So my convent frocks and pinafores will be more than adequate." She speared a juicy bit of capon.

Radleigh flushed scarlet. "You'll wear what I pay for in London, and that's the end of it. I've recruited Caroline Sutherland to oversee your fittings. No small *coup d'état*, I can tell you."

"I've heard her name," Thorne broke in, trying to keep peace. "Much sought after in London society, isn't she?"

"Relentlessly." Radleigh glowered at Gwynneth. "You should be grateful for her help."

Gwynneth shrugged. "London society and its clucking hens mean nothing to me."

Thorne tried not to laugh. "Isn't she the wife of Horace Sutherland, of Sutherland Apothecaries?"

"Aye, and quite the beauty. No, 'beauty' doesn't begin to tell it. She's devastating, a goddess...tall, buxom, wide shouldered. Skin like gold, hair as dark as a rook's wing. One glance from her black-velvet eyes will melt you to a puddle."

"Or nail you to the wall?" Thorne ventured with a wry smile.

"Aye, that too," Radleigh said, chewing with gusto, "and you'll be thanking her all the while you're dangling there."

"Well she has at least one admirer," Gwynneth said sourly.

Radleigh shook a finger. "And she'll have one in you, just wait and see."

"So," Thorne said to Gwynneth, "you're not weary of convent attire?"

She met Thorne's curious gaze without blinking. "*Nothing* about the convent wearies me, my lord. And as for couture-" Shrugging, she dipped a piece of meat into the sauce. "I have lived a secluded life. One seldom covets what one never sees."

"And when at last one *does* see..." Stroking the stem of his wine goblet with languid deliberation, Thorne watched Gwynneth halt her knife in mid-cut to follow the movement of his finger. "Does one then begin to covet?" he finished softly.

Gwynneth tore her gaze away and finished cutting her meat, cheeks blooming with color. "You speak in riddles, my lord."

Thorne acknowledged Radleigh's wink with a slight nod. The Honourable Miss Stowington might well have made a proper little nun, but she wasn't entirely invulnerable to the charms of mortal man.

* * *

Thorne ushered Arthur into the study and closed the door. "'Tis late, you should be home by now. Is the news that bad?"

"Kendall's just come from Graham's place."

"Bad news indeed, if Kendall brought it himself."

Arthur nodded gravely. "The sheep were poisoned, M'lord. Deliberately poisoned. All the signs were there, inflamed stomach linings, swollen lungs."

"So, the pasture was powdered."

"Likely more than once, though not so as the sheep noticed. The effects were cumulative."

"Then I dare not open that pasture, despite the rain."

"Risky at best, I think."

Thorne eyed his steward grimly. "What do you make of this?"

Arthur shook his head. "I don't know what to make of it. But pray God it will end with your homecoming. If it doesn't, I fear someone is out to bleed you dry."

TWO

Elaine Combs clutched a tray in white-knuckled hands and stood rooted to the floor, her heartbeat pounding in her ears.

She had not prepared for this encounter, hadn't expected to find the curtained archway between the master sitting room and bedchamber wide open. Hadn't expected to see, stretching in front of an open window, the master himself.

Her wide eyes darted from his chamois breeches and scuffed jackboots up to his thick black mane, unbound from its queue and cascading a quarter of the way down his bare, taut-muscled back.

He turned before she could avert her gaze, and reached for the cambric shirt on the bedpost. He froze.

Elaine forgot to breathe. Mesmerized by the blue fire in Lord Neville's eyes, she gave a startled gasp as he snapped the shirt off the post and slid it over his head.

He emerged with arched brow. "You might try knocking."

"Begging your pardon, M'lord. I-I thought the archway curtains would be closed and I could leave this without disturbing you."

"'Tis you who seems disturbed...Combs, is it?" He laced the neck of his shirt, eyeing her burning cheeks all the while.

"Aye, M'lord. Elaine Combs." Of course he knew. Tongues were still wagging over her humiliating confrontation with Hobbs in the stables yesterday. She set the tray on a mahogany blanket-chest before the silver and china could start rattling.

"All this?" Eyeing the porridge, meat-pies, scones and jam, he chortled. "By tomorrow she'll have me filching in the larder for a crust of bread."

Elaine filled his teacup with miraculous control. "I daresay you might expect a feast every morn, M'lord. Mistress MacBride is that pleased to have you home."

"Ha." He rolled his sleeves to his elbows. "I'll lay ten to one that before the week is out, she'll have her broom at my backside."

Elaine's burst of nervous laughter died as his eyes pierced her through.

"I've seen you before," he said. "Before yesterday, when you spied upon me from the gallery."

Dear God. His eyesight was as extraordinary as his eye color. Elaine wanted to crawl under the Aubusson rug.

"Were you in service here when I left for University?"

She managed to keep her voice steady. "No, M'lord. Dame Carswell took me on while you were away." She dropped a hasty curtsey. "I shall return later to see to your chambers-"

"You may see to them now."

Heaven help me. With another curtsey, she turned to make up the bed. A soft exclamation escaped her.

"Is there something wrong, Combs?"

"No, M'lord, just...odd."

"'Tis rather skeletal, isn't it?"

"Sir?"

"My bed, Combs. You were staring at my bed."

Heat flooded her face again. "I was staring at what is *missing* from your bed, sir." She turned to see his shrug.

"I like light, though I'm quite comfortable in the dark. Nor do I mind a bit of a chill in the winter." Settling on a window seat, he slathered butter over a scone. "So I've no use for bed hangings. You'll notice the window draperies are open as well. They're to remain so."

"Aye, M'lord. Until nightfall, of course."

"Until Kingdom Come, Combs." He cocked an eyebrow. "Frown away. Carswell thinks me a heathen, why shouldn't you?"

Turning back to her task, Elaine suppressed a smile. She plumped the pillows, resisting a mad urge to bury her nose in them, then hurried to set them aside and haul the top sheet up over the bed. The scent that wafted from the billowing linen rocked her back on her heels.

Sandalwood.

She clutched the counterpane until a wave of dizziness passed, all the while steeling herself for a comment from behind. It was not long in coming.

"Damnation!" China rattled on the tray.

Elaine turned with wide eyes to find her employer staring not at her, but out the window. She moved behind him to peer through the mist. Barely visible in the misty distance, a boy herded sheep through a pair of wooden gates.

"Doesn't the fool know the bloody pasture's contaminated?" Lord Neville swiped a napkin across his lips, threw it down on the tray and sprang from the window seat.

Elaine had no time to move. Her mobcap flew off as she collided with her master, hairpins raining around them. She stumbled backward.

He caught her swiftly by the shoulders, then froze as a lock of her chestnut-colored hair fell over his forearm. For the space of Elaine's missed heartbeat, he stared at the silky length, then met her gaze. "Beg your pardon," he muttered. "No harm done?"

"None," she breathed.

"Then I dare not tarry. My apologies." He squeezed her shoulders as if to steady her again, then bounded from the chamber.

Elaine reached the gallery in time to see him fly down the steps and vault the railing mid-way, career across the great hall and crash through the kitchen door. "Saints preserve us, what ails ye, M'lord?" she heard Mistress MacBride cry just before it banged shut.

Elaine scooted across the gallery to an empty chamber. Through a window she watched Lord Neville sprint to the stables and leap onto the bare back of a filly just come from morning paces. Little Henry Pitts appeared, waving his arms in the doorway, but to no avail. Dirt clods spewed from under the filly's hooves as she shot across the stable yard with her unwelcome rider, who jumped her over one drystone wall and headed for another.

"God save him, he's got no saddle!" Elaine heard the cook wail in the garden below. "He'll get himself killed!"

"Aye," came the voice of Hillary, one of her maids. "Bit of a tear, ain't he, our master? Best get himself an heir, I'd say, and the sooner the better!"

Elaine's stomach lurched. Tears stung her eyes, though she'd promised herself she'd never shed another. After all of her weeping yesterday, she'd thought the well dry at any rate.

But *these* tears, she reminded herself bitterly, sprang from a different well altogether.

* * *

"Do you ride, Miss Stowington?" Delighted to find Gwynneth in the stall of a dappled-gray mare, Thorne turned the panting filly over to Henry Pitts.

Gwynneth stroked the mare as it nuzzled her other hand. "Only on holiday with my Aunt Evelyn, in Seagrave. She breeds prize steeds." Gwynneth brushed sugar from her palm. "Tobias kindly gave me a sweet for Abigail here."

Only then did Thorne see the man crouched behind the mare. No longer a gangly lad of sixteen, Tobias Hobbs had developed a physique to complement the face and seductive charm that even then had won him more than his share of conquests.

"M'lord," he grunted, with a stiff nod.

"Tobias offered to saddle her and ride with me. He was just looking over her shoes." Gwynneth glanced from one man to the other. "He said you wouldn't object."

"Hobbs," Thorne said, still eyeing the stable master, "is quite right. I don't object, on one condition--that I accompany you myself. There are ruts in the road and burrows in the meadow. Exposed roots in the forest." He narrowed his eyes on Hobbs. "Not to mention the occasional wild beast."

Hobbs expression turned sullen. He went back to his inspection.

"I've a new stallion to try this morn," Thorne told his guest, "a Darley Arabian named 'Raven.' My winnings in a lucky billiard match."

Alight with excitement, Gwynneth's heart-shaped face fell. "You wagered for him."

"I did. And I'll wager that once you've seen him you'll agree he's quite a prize."

Gwynneth elevated her chin. "I daresay, my lord, that when you confess to your priest, he will quite likely instruct you to return your 'prize' to its rightful owner."

"I daresay he would, Miss Stowington. If I had a priest."

Her mouth opened, then shut without a sound.

Thorne smiled crookedly. "Ride with me," he said, and saw the pulse quicken in her slender throat. "Let's see if we can find something redeeming about my heathen soul."

* * *

"Beck's Hollow," Thorne said with a nod, pride in his voice.

Gwynneth looked from the towering oaks across the ravine to the mossy granite boulders mirrored in the beck. "Such sanctuary," she breathed.

Thorne's heart leapt as he eyed her delicate profile. "I couldn't have said it better."

Dismounting, they left the horses to graze in the heath. Thorne bent down at one boulder's jutting tip and retrieved a corked bottle from a rocky cache in the water. "Nicely chilled," he remarked, taking a corkscrew, two glasses, and a linen-wrapped flatbread from Raven's cantle pouch and setting them down. He broke off some gorse and swept a section of boulder clean.

"Wine," Gwynneth announced, arranging her skirts and shaking her head at the glass Thorne offered, "is for priests, and only at Holy Mass."

He smiled. "And I am no priest, am I, Miss Stowington? Nor saint, like your beloved Sister Theresa Bernard at the convent." He handed Gwynneth the flatbread. "I did notice your glass went untouched at supper last night. Yet Christ himself drank wine." He took a drink from the bottle now that there was to be no sharing.

"Won't you tell me about your home?" Gwynneth said in a brittle voice.

Thorne shrugged, then stretched out and propped himself on an elbow. "Not much to tell, I fear. Old, drafty. Built by my fourth great-grandfather, Thomas Thorneton Neville."

"Has it some history of note?"

"Some. A tragedy, really. Though somewhat indelicate for a young lady's ears."

Gwynneth elevated her chin. "I am no child, my lord."

"Indeed you are not," Thorne agreed quietly, resisting a glance at her high-necked but shapely bodice. Her sudden blush quickened his blood. He took another drink of wine to gather his wits. "Then prepare to be scandalized," he said, corking the bottle and setting it beside the untouched flatbread Gwynneth had put between them. "It began with my great-great-Aunt Agnes conceiving a child at the age of eight-and-twenty."

Gwynneth shrugged. "Older women have borne children."

"Aye, but Agnes was a spinster."

"Oh!" Gwynneth's cheeks turned scarlet. "Wh-who was the father?"

"The village vicar."

Gwynneth gasped. "A man of God? What became of them?"

"The vicar disappeared soon after poor Agnes gave him the news. Abandoned his wife, as well."

"His w-" Gwynneth broke off, her shocked expression turning indignant. "Then I should hope Agnes was shut away, or came to some other such end."

"Another end altogether. She died of a crushed skull and broken neck, after leaping from the battlements atop the tower."

Gwynneth slid her horrified gaze to the east. "*That* tower?"

Thorne nodded.

"She took her own life and the babe's with it?"

"Sadly, yes."

"Where was she buried?"

"In the manor church yard."

"In hallowed ground?" Gwynneth cried.

"Yes, along with all the other imperfect folk whose lives have graced the Hall, may God rest her soul along with theirs." He felt his heart sink as Gwynneth's expression hardened.

"Be assured," she said coolly, "that adultery, fornication, and suicide sent your Aunt Agnes' soul to a place entirely bereft of God, where she is more likely writhing in flames than resting. At least," she added with an air of grim satisfaction, "the vicar's wife was avenged for her husband's sin." Turning her palms upward, she shrugged, then smiled as if pleased with her conclusion.

That childish gesture thawed the ice forming in Thorne's veins. Surely time and gentle guidance would temper Gwynneth's narrow, convent views.

Or so he hoped. "If you can forgive Wycliffe Hall its one scandal, what would you say to a long visit when you return from London?"

A small furrow formed in Gwynneth's brow as she finally tore a piece off the flatbread. "You are inviting us to stay at Wycliffe Hall indefinitely?"

Thorne chortled. "Wild horses couldn't keep your father away from Radleigh Hall. I was referring to you."

The furrow in Gwynneth's brow deepened while she chewed the bread, which went down with an audible swallow. "And just what would you intend, my lord, seeing my father off to his home and lodging me under your roof?"

"My intentions are honorable, that I can tell you." He heard her breath catch as he took her hand and brushed his lips over the back of it. Damn Radleigh for his spinelessness! Gwynneth Stowington was ripe and so obviously and ready for plucking.

A crumb of flatbread clung to her lower lip. Unable to resist, Thorne let go her hand to brush it away--and unexpectedly had his middle finger branded by a single, searing flick of Gwynneth's tongue.

A jolt of exquisite pain struck him in the groin. His finger stayed as if melded to her lip, for though he knew her touch was only a reflex, the innocent eroticism of the gesture had paralyzed his entire body.

Except for one appendage. Thorne suddenly wished he'd worn a waistcoat. Pushing himself up off the boulder, he rose on unsteady legs. *No fault of the wine*, he thought with a wince.

"My lord?" Her voice sounded far away. "What is it, what ails you?"

Barely able to speak, Thorne held up a hand, then hobbled down the bank until he recovered his normal gait. He returned to find Gwynneth tucking the half-empty bottle into his cantle pouch.

"Why-" she began, but broke off as Thorne shook his head. He boosted her onto Abigail.

"Forgive me, Miss Stowington." Tightening the mare's girth, he gave Gwynneth a rueful smile. "But you are an angel in a woman's body...and the devil stands ready to take me to hell."

* * *

Thorne marked his place in the ledger on his desk, then glanced up from under his brow. "Why don't you inquire, Arthur? Instead of staring holes in my face."

"Forgive me, M'lord, I'd no idea I was staring. Quite rude of me."

Thorne slammed the ledger shut. "Yes, rude, you old fox. Are you not the least bit curious about the lady?"

"I'd quite forgotten her, M'lord, having seen neither hide nor hair of her. Perhaps she's of a more spiritual breed?"

Thorne pulled a wry face. "Very clever. Well I've seen both, though more hair than hide." He shoved the ledger aside and crossed his feet upon the desk. "And you *would* have seen her, had you not ducked out the instant Jennings announced them."

"I was better attired to greet their horses," Arthur reminded him wryly. "At any rate, should you insist upon discussing the lady, I'm game to listen."

"Oh, I insist. But I want more than your ear. Will a Scotch whiskey loosen your tongue? There's a fresh decanter on the way."

As if on cue, Elaine Combs knocked upon the door, which Thorne had left ajar. He waved her in. She set the decanter on the desk, curtseyed, and turned to go.

"'Tis your eyes, Combs."

She halted in her tracks, then turned slowly to face him. "M'lord?" she said faintly.

"I've decided it is your eyes that seem familiar."

"M-my...eyes?" The orbs in question widened.

"Yes. They're the queerest gray, like doves. Almost silver."

Suddenly Thorne felt foolish. Arthur was staring at him as warily as Combs was.

"You may go, Combs." He'd meant to sound brusque, not harsh. Yet she looked relieved. Irritated and befuddled, Thorne turned his back on her exit, and poured the liquor into two glasses.

An unexpected wave of nostalgia struck him as he recalled his father doing the same for the steward from behind this very desk. Passing Arthur a glass, Thorne saw his thoughts reflected in the old brown eyes. "To my father," he murmured, raising his glass.

"To Lord Neville," Arthur agreed, doing likewise. "Past and present."

Thorne's glass stayed high. "And to Arthur Pennington, our loyal steward and friend. How long has it been?"

"Thirty years, M'lord. Yet even now I can picture your father sitting in that chair and looking as young as you."

The whiskey sent flames coursing down Thorne's throat and into his belly, where it settled in a pleasant pool of warmth. Turning his glass to and fro in his fingers, he watched the amber liquid swirl and shift. "I find myself in a quandary, Arthur."

"Over what, sir?"

Thorne grimaced. "You'll not make this any easier, will you."

"Nothing involving a woman is easy," Arthur said with a lopsided smile.

Thorne knocked back the rest of the dram and set the glass down. "She's a bold one, to be so young."

A flicker of concern crossed Arthur's face. "There's something to be said for boldness," he allowed, "within reason."

Thorne chuckled. "She is Radleigh's daughter, after all."

"Aye. And hence rather homely, I'd guess."

"No, quite comely. And well-schooled, and most virtuous." Thorne poured a second glass with a flourish and extended the bottle.

Arthur held out his glass. "Well, you'd expect virtue, wouldn't you, what with her being raised in a convent and all?"

"Yes. But once we're wed, she'll surely shed some of her more rigid notions."

Arthur's mouth opened and closed.

"What? If you've something to say, then say it."

Cupping the glass of whiskey in his hands, Arthur sat back in the chair. "Very well. Where's the need for haste? You're young, and whatever attraction you feel for the girl is merely carnal at this stage." Arthur's leathery cheeks turned ruddy. "Courtship is no luxury, M'lord, 'tis a necessity. Love requires time to grow. My Anna and I-"

"I see no point in waiting. 'Twas my father's wish that I marry Radleigh's daughter. Little enough for me to promise a dying man."

Arthur leaned forward in his chair. "Little? And your loyalty is commendable, but what of the rumors? What if Radleigh *has* gambled away his fortune, perhaps even his daughter's dowry? Would your father hold you to your promise, knowing that?"

Thorne gave a snort. "Any decline in Radleigh's finances is likely due to the bloody taxes the Crown levies on him for his Roman Catholic loyalties. At any rate, he's given up the tables. He told me so over brandy last eve."

"Thorne--M'lord." Arthur shook his head with an air of weary patience. "You know as well as I that if Radleigh has forsworn the gaming tables, he's likely up to his eyeballs in debt."

"Time will tell."

"Aye, I fear it will. Meanwhile, what of love? *There's* a debt that won't go unpaid, I assure you."

Thorne sighed, dragging his feet off the desk. "Marriages are made every day for naught but fortune, pedigree and politics, Arthur. And what bloody good has love ever done anyone?"

Arthur looked aggrieved. "Your parents-"

"Were fools."

Arthur recoiled in his seat. "I was about to say they loved one another dearly!"

"Yes, and all the more suffered for it! And lest you think me a blathering idiot, I have it on my father's dying word." Thorne tossed the whiskey down his gullet as he rose, then slammed the glass down and paced to a window. He stared out at the sparkling beck and the field of young wheat beyond, seeing none of it.

Arthur sounded quiet but insistent. "Whatever his lordship said, 'twas likely the laudanum talking. Delirium at best."

"'Twas my father." Thorne turned a hard stare on the steward. "*His* voice, *his* eyes. *His* hand that gripped my arm with more strength than he'd shown in months. 'Twas he who warned me to guard my heart from anything the least akin to love. 'Marry the girl, as I've promised her father, and sire a family,' he told me. 'But never let your heart be taken. Love, my son, is naught but sweet, slow poison.' *That* is what he told me, Arthur. And I haven't forgotten one bloody word of it."

Tears shone in Arthur's eyes. "Yet he loved your mother, heart and soul."

"*Precisely.*" Thorne gave him a chilling smile. "And for nearly two decades, I watched him walk as a dead man among the living. He could no longer be Catherine Neville's husband, nor could he be a father to me, because when she died, she took his bleeding heart with her to the grave." Despising the sudden thickness in his voice, Thorne turned abruptly to the window. When the beech trees across the road swam back into focus, he said more calmly, "So you'll understand why I don't for a moment take 'love' into account when reckoning Miss Stowington's suitability as a wife."

Arthur sighed. "I might understand, M'lord. But I'll never agree."

* * *

Elaine Combs looked up as Lord Radleigh poked his head around the door. "Gwynneth?"

The Honourable Miss Stowington opened one green eye and sighed. "What is it, Father? I told you I've a dreadful headache. I must rest."

Chuckling, Lord Radleigh entered and drew near the bed, where Elaine sat cooling his daughter's brow with a damp cloth. "I saw the half-empty bottle Lord Neville brought back today. There's a price to drinking fermented beverages, Daughter."

"You should know. But I did not imbibe. Never have, and never shall."

His smile disappeared. "I'll let that first remark pass, 'tis the pain talking. You'll be glad to know that Lord Neville has informed his cook of your aching head. She's brewing a potent lavender-rosemary tea for it as we speak."

Miss Stowington opened her other eye. "She's an herbalist? I thought I smelled thyme and mint outdoors. No roses, though." She sighed. "I adore roses, we'd hundreds at Saint Mary's."

Her father leaned over her, a twinkle in his gaze. "If there aren't any now, I'd wager there soon will be." His eyes widened as soon as he said it; harrumphing, he pounded his chest and straightened, then asked hastily, "Are you up to traveling tomorrow, Daughter? We could stay an extra day if you like."

Elaine hastily lifted the cloth, as Miss Stowington started to raise her head but then winced and fell back onto the pillow. "*You*," the girl accused her father with a gasp, "are scheming to marry me off!"

Elaine's stomach flipped as she saw the flustered look on Lord Radleigh's face. The rumors she had so despaired of must be true.

"I'm doing no such thing!" he protested. "But now that you mention it"--he lowered his hulk onto the side of the bed and leaned toward his daughter--"'twould benefit all concerned were you to marry Lord Neville, yourself as well. He's a very generous and just man, much respected-"

"And far too astute to be manipulated by *you*."

Lord Radleigh's face flushed. "Hold your tongue, girl, and think on it! This grand Hall"--his hand swept the air in a wide arc--"and all its gardens would be yours to oversee, with some two-score of servants under your command."

Tasting gall, Elaine hastily rinsed out the cloth, then rose and busied herself brushing the dusty hem of the convent frock Miss Stowington had laid over a chair.

"But I'm needed at Radleigh Hall! Or so you said."

"'Twould be too much to ask, now that I ponder it again," Lord Radleigh said with a sigh. "The Hall is in disrepair and my servants are fleeing like rats from a sinking ship. And caring for me might prove a hardship for you, what with my gout and all."

He lowered his voice, but not enough, further amazing Elaine with what gentry would say in front of servants.

- 24 -

"You'd be set for life here at Wycliffe Hall, Gwynneth. So would your children. And Thorne would see to my comfort in my old age, and to Radleigh Hall's restoration and maintenance. After all, the place would be his upon my passing."

His daughter's tone turned brittle. "Where has your fortune gone, Father? Have I a dowry to offer?"

Glancing sidelong, Elaine saw the viscount's shoulders sag.

"I've incurred a sizeable debt to the Earl of...a certain earl," he confessed. "I'd no choice but to use a part of your dowry as collateral."

"Then Lord Neville will not want me," his daughter retorted, making Elaine's heart skip a beat. "You might as well send me back to the convent."

"Ha! You'd like that, wouldn't you?" Another glance showed the viscount wagging a finger near the girl's face. "You'll have your dowry, never fear," he assured her. "You're quite the catch at any rate, with your beauty and virtue and skills." Elaine pictured a wink with his next words. "Lord Neville's not so hard on the eyes, either, eh?"

Elaine's heart sank as she saw the virtuous young "catch" blush and trace a finger over the moiré silk counterpane.

"He is a handsome enough man," was the girl's soft admission. "Kind, as well."

Radleigh chuckled. "He'd get a house full of children on you, girl. He's a vigorous man. He'd seek your bed often."

"Stop, Father!"

Elaine silently echoed the plea, her stomach twisting. Yet she could not resist another glance. Eyes closed, Miss Stowington had pressed a hand to her heart and taken a fan from her sleeve. Her father promptly confiscated it to wave gusts of air onto her burning face.

"Well, Daughter?"

"I shall think about it," she conceded breathlessly, opening glazed eyes. "But not a word to *him*, I warn you. I've no idea whether he desires-"

"Oh, he desires all right," Radleigh cut in, sounding smug. "I've seen how he looks at you. He desires wholeheartedly."

Elaine covertly clutched her midsection, trying not to bend double.

"I meant *marriage*, not *me*."

Turning her head slightly, Elaine saw all trace of the blushing virgin vanish as Gwynneth Stowington reached out and stilled the fan in her father's hand.

"For I can tell you this, Father," she vowed grimly. "I shan't marry anyone just to repay your gambling debts. *Never* shall I enter the sacrament of marriage to pay for a sin."

THREE

From a window of her Georgian mansion, Caroline Sutherland stared across the brick-paved street at the greensward, where a duck had just waded from the pond to follow a big-breasted dowager walking a terrier. No doubt the bird mistook the waddling woman for his mother.

Caroline felt relieved to hear Marsh trudging up the stairs--until the old servant, huffing and puffing in the doorway, spoke in her graveled voice. "Mistress, that Mister Hobbs is come calling again."

"Bloody hell," Caroline muttered, then raised her voice. "Send him up, then."

"Aye, Mistress." Marsh shuffled away.

"For shame, Mistress Sutherland. You should be pleased to see your only kin."

Despite its mocking tone, his voice could melt a glacier. Caroline hadn't even heard him on the steps. And though Marsh was too deaf to hear her cursing, Tobias Hobbs was not.

Suppressing a shiver, Caroline turned to see him leaning against the doorframe, one fist braced against her glossy-white door casing, the other crumpling his woolen cap. Sweat spiked his cropped hair and glued his shirt to his chest. Mud and dung flecked his boots. "Get your grubby mitts off my woodwork," she ordered him through her teeth, "and close the door behind you."

Without budging a finger from the door casing, Hobbs flashed his own teeth in a mirthless smile. "What a gracious hostess you are, Caroline. A true credit to London society. Or so I hear."

"And *you* are utterly repulsive. How *dare* you come to my home looking and smelling the way you do? What must my servants think?"

His amber eyes narrowed. "At least my stench is that of an honest day's work. 'Tis more than I can say for yours."

"Mind your tongue," she warned him. "Is it money again? Neville isn't paying you enough to shovel horseshite?"

Hobbs stepped into the room, hooked a boot on the edge of the door, and slammed it behind him. "No hands." Sneer turned to scowl. "I'm here to see Horace."

"He's in Birmingham," Caroline hedged, scowling as well. "Why do you want to see him? And why the deuce would he care to see you?"

"When do you expect him?"

"I don't know. He didn't say, exactly." It was the humiliating truth.

"Well, tell him *I said exactly* that he'd best contact me when he returns. It takes too bloody long to ride to London from Wycliffe, and I'll not do it again lest I know he's home." He gave her a leering smile. "Or if I need money. You'll do for that."

"The devil I will!" Caroline stamped her foot and pointed at the door. "Get your buggering, stableman's arse out of my house! This minute!"

"Don't look now, sweeting, but your pedigree is showing."

"Hush! Shut your filthy mouth, you stinking son of a b-"

"*Baron*?" Hobbs supplied with an unpleasant smile. "Was that the word poised on those luscious lips, my beautiful base-born half-sister?" His smile fled. "Because I am, you know. The son of a baron."

"Mother should never have told you." Caroline's voice trembled with fury. "And dead or not, I'll never forgive her for it."

"I'd as much right to know of my father as you did yours."

"And what good has it done you? Who'd believe you?" Scorn sharpened Caroline's hoot of laughter. "He'd fetch you straightaway to Bedlam, your Lord Neville, and who'd blame him? For all the good your knowing does, Toby Hobbs, you might as well have had no sire at all!"

He drew a ragged breath. "And *you*, Mistress Sutherland, might have married well, but deep down in your rotten core where none but you and I can see, you're naught but a whoring, mongrel *bitch*. Nor will you ever be."

He slammed his hat on his head, then yanked the door open and strode onto the gallery, missing the awesome sight of tawny skin gone pale.

* * *

"It's happened again, M'lord. This time McQuillen's ewes in the north pasture, four down and one ailing. Kendall's been and gone. 'Tis arsenic, he says. Where the deuce does one fetch powdered arsenic?"

"From a chemist." Thorne opened his desk drawer, took out a gold-plated humidor and flipped the top, then held it out to Arthur.

"The nearest we'll come to a chemist in Wycliffe," the steward mumbled as he lit the cigar, "is the good Doctor Hodges."

Thorne lit one and took a few puffs, then laid it down in the ash-receiver and squinted through the smoke. "Why should anyone want to kill off my stock?"

Arthur exhaled a cloud of blue smoke and shook his head. "'Tis beyond my reckoning."

Thorne drew hard on the cigar, then tamped it out. "Accounts are in good standing, cash reserves ample?"

"Aye." Arthur sat forward as his employer took up quill and parchment, scrawled a brief note, blotted it, and shoved it across the desk.

"Show this to Graham and McQuillen. I'll see to the other three. I want two men riding watch in three shifts from dusk to dawn. With lanterns, mind you. There'll be no moon tonight. Assign Graham and McQuillen first watch, I'll pair up with the odd man on second. The other two get third. We'll keep vigil nightly 'til we deem it unnecessary. And for now, the north pasture lies fallow.

Arthur nodded. "Will there be-"

"Hire two villagers," Thorne went on, "men that can be trusted to stay sober and awake, to watch from atop the tower in separate shifts. Compensation, you were going to say?" He nodded toward the paper in Arthur's hand. "More than adequate, I think."

Arthur glanced down, then cocked an eyebrow. "Adequate? You make it more profitable to let the vandal go unapprehended."

"A reward of five pounds in gold should hasten things along," Thorne countered. "Want of sleep will do the rest."

* * *

The sun dropped below the horizon, leaving wide slashes of tangerine and crimson in its wake. The beck turned to liquid topaz, the air to a haze of copper as the sheep kicked up dust on homeward-bound paths.

Henry Pitts turned at the stable doorway to see Tobias Hobbs galloping Bartholomew down the Northampton road. He set down his pails of water and hurried into the yard. Hoping for a stick of candy from the London apothecary, he was handed two shillings instead. He grinned. "Thank ye, Master Hobbs!"

Hobbs nodded. "All's well?"

"Aye, sir. The viscount's daughter was here again! His lordship rode with her to Wycliffe to show her the church." Henry's eyes shone. "She's a beauty, ain't she, sir?"

"She's a lady, not a filly. Keep your tongue in your head, boy, your eyes, too. I saw a rider in the southwest pasture. Any notion why?"

"Aye! There's a watch out this eve, for vandals!"

Hobbs frowned. "What the devil are you prattling about?"

Henry told him what he'd heard.

"Never mind, I'll get to the bottom of it." Hobbs patted Bartholomew. "I've run him too hard, poor chap. Rub him down before he catches his death." He strode toward the stables. "Vandals," he said with a snort, then spat in the dirt. "Shite!"

* * *

"Forgive the delay," Thorne said, straddling the trestle opposite Arthur at Duncan's public alehouse. "One of Milby's bitches had a devil of a time whelping."

"Aye." Arthur nodded Thorne's shirtfront. "You've the proof to show for it. Ever a trial for the poor washerwomen, weren't you? So, what say the herders?"

"All champing at the bit. The others?"

Arthur nodded. "And the young lady? You seem to have misplaced her."

"I left her at the church. She and the good vicar were deep in theology. He'll escort her back to the Hall for supper."

A woman set a pint of Kentish ale in front of Thorne, then curtsied. "Good eve, M'lord, will ye take some victuals? I've just took out a steak-and-kidney pie." She flashed a gap-toothed grin.

"No, Lizzie, thank you all the same." Thorne lowered his voice as she bustled away. "Milby says the north pasture had lain fallow for three days, so there's no telling what night the deed was done."

"When's your watch?"

"At two, with Timmons. I should get some sleep."

"You won't want to miss supper." Arthur's brown eyes twinkled in the light of the sputtering tallow flame. "Aren't Radleigh and his daughter bound for London tomorrow?"

Thorne grimaced. "Carswell will convey my apologies. I'm not up to dining with either of them, but the vicar will keep them entertained. I'll see them off come morn."

"You're that anxious to have her away, then?"

"I'm that anxious to have her. Period."

"Ah." Arthur looked down at his tankard. "You need some, ah, diversion. Is there someone you might...visit?"

Thorne envisioned a pair of emerald eyes and a cascade of auburn hair. "There was someone until recently. I've severed ties with her."

"Only one woman?" Obviously trying to cover his surprise, Arthur cleared his throat, then murmured as his face flushed a shade darker, "'Tis rumored there's an uncommonly clean, pox-free place just outside London."

Thorne decided against validating that rumor.

Arthur signaled for another pint, then leaned in on his elbows. "With all due respect, M'lord, and in the absence of your father, I'll inqire--was this woman a virgin when you met her?"

Thorne nearly choked on the dregs of his ale. "Hardly."

"Ah, a widow." Arthur nodded sagely. "Different breed altogether. No wonder you're avoiding Miss Stowington. Breaking a virgin is not a race, nor can you afford to be a loose cannon, even after you're wed. My Anna surrendered her maidenhead on our wedding night, but some women are more skittish, and might require a se'nnight, even a fortnight or more." Hearing Thorne's soft groan, Arthur smiled. "Patience is the test of true manhood, M'lord. Dig your heels in and grit your teeth. 'Tis well worth the torment in the end, when your bride is at last willing, perhaps even eager-"

"There, that will do." Thorne dropped his head into his hands and pressed hard on his temples. "Damn it, Pennington, I was under tight rein when I walked in here, and at this rate I'll not be able to walk out. Not without embarrassing myself, at any rate. Bloody hell."

Chuckling, Arthur reminded him another pint was on the way.

Conversation reverted to the watch, but Thorne's mind was only half there. *Patience be damned. I'll at least know Gwynneth's mind on the prospect of a betrothal.*

When Lizzie had come and gone, Thorne tapped his brimming tankard against Arthur's, and with a "bottoms up" quaffed his ale. "Fortification," he explained, seeing the steward's bewilderment. He lay coin on the table and rose from the trestle. "For what lies ahead."

"Your two o'clock watch?"

Thorne grinned. "Aye, that too."

* * *

Standing in the Wycliffe road next morning, one hand on a flank of Arthur's horse, Thorne watched Radleigh's coach round the bend. "Yonder she goes, Arthur. The future Lady Neville."

"You're betrothed, then, ring and all?"

"I am. You'll be glad to know I proposed on bent knee, and with a heartfelt speech."

"Caught you in a weak moment, did she?"

Thorne smiled. "I won't deny my libido was involved. But the fondness I professed was no less sincere for it."

Arthur snorted. "No doubt. And how does the Honourable Miss Stowington take to being the pawn in a predetermined match?"

Thorne's smile faded. "She doesn't know. Radleigh thinks it best she never know this was our plan."

"Never?"

"She believes he hatched it alone. She would have taken the vows at Saint Mary's, you see. 'Twas her life's wish."

"Sweet Jesu." Arthur shook his head.

"Be glad she's out of earshot, oh thou blasphemer," Thorne said wryly, taking hold of the bridle. "Come, let me get horsed. You might have to nudge me awake now and then. I didn't see my bed last night." He chuckled at Arthur's inquiring look. "No, my friend, nor did I see hers."

FOUR

Even for a Saturday night, Duncan's public alehouse seemed particularly rowdy. Maneuvering a tray of empty pewter tankards past the crowded trestle tables, Lizzie barely dodged a stream of spittle intended for the nearest cuspidor.

"I hope you've better aim in the privy closet, mister!" she scolded over the din. A shout of laughter went up, while the guilty party blushed and choked on his ale as his mates slapped him on the back.

"Here now, leave the lad alone, he's a bit green is all." The new arrival was a regular patron. "Lizzie, dearling, bring us a round...*on me*."

The ensuing catcalls and jeers didn't faze Tom Barker. He sat down on the trestle with uncustomary dignity.

"Perchance ye've come into some inheritance?" mocked one crony.

"Same as." Looking smug, Barker plunked a leather pounch down on the table and opened it to display a pile of shillings topped with several crinkled pound-notes and two gold sovereigns.

A low whistle broke the sudden silence. "Where'd ye fetch a purse like that, Tommy? Been grave robbing, have ye?"

Nervous laughter ended almost as soon as it began. Barker leaned in over the table, a leer on his face. "I been telling all of ye for years I'd find me a lady who'd pay what I'm worth."

Amid guffaws, the man who'd challenged Tom said with a sneer, "Come on, Barker, ye ol' blowhard! Tell us who's lying in the gutter with an empty purse now't ye've gone and cold-cocked him."

Like a shot, Barker dove across the table, overturning ale tankards to grasp the man's shirtfront with a beefy hand and twist it toward him. "Mind your manners, Jakey boy, 'cause *ye're* the only blowhard 'round here!" His rheumy eyes bored into Jake's, whose own began to bulge. Barker shoved him back on the trestle, then sat down and mopped his forehead with a sleeve. "I earned this pot fair and square," he said, focusing his indignant look on each man in turn. "And if ye're smart as ye *think* ye be," he went on, voice rising as a titter of laughter threatened the tense silence, "ye'll hold your tongues and enjoy what it buys. 'Cause after all, me boys," --he winked, a gap-toothed grin folding his jowls-- "I be a sharing man!" He seized a foaming tankard from Lizzie's tray and held it in the air.

"Hear, hear!" some shouted, and the rest joined in as Lizzie set full tankards all around the table.

The door to the street swung wide. Barker squinted through a pall of smoke at two new arrivals, his expression turning surly as he saw Duncan slip from behind the bar to lead them past the gaming and the empty hearth to a quiet corner. "Since when does Duncan give escort? Who does Neville think he is, the bloody king hisself?"

A couple of Barker's mates tried to hush him.

"I ain't going to be quiet if I don't want to be," he blustered, belching before he continued. "Look at his lordship's fine linen" --he belched again, pointing a stubby finger-- "shirt, aye, and them fine leather boots, will ye. Now there's a man what's never been hungry! *He* don't fret for his next pence." He banged a ham-like fist on the table. "I'll wager nobody ever asked *him* whence his purse come! Never mind it come from the sweat of poor working folk, likely their blood as well-"

"Shut your foul mouth, Tom Barker, ere I shut it for ye!"

Apparently awed by Lizzie's rare temper, every man at the table fell silent.

"His lordship is a good man, a decent and just man," she scolded, her nose just inches from Barker's bulbous snout. "He'd give a body the shirt off his back if 'twas needed--and ye *know* that, Tom Barker, ye know it well. 'Twasn't yourself that kept your mother out of the poorhouse them two bad years, now was it?"

Barker's eyes fell, then rose to see Lizzie holding a fresh pint just out of reach.

"So if ye've any more foolishness to speak on his lordship, ye'll have to say it elsewhere, do ye hear me, Tom Barker? And just ye try finding another of *these* within a twelve-league!"

She glared at him until he dropped his gaze again; then she set the tankard down with a slosh.

Far to the rear, oblivious of the little drama, Arthur Pennington rested his elbows on the table and covered a yawn.

"William, much to Bridey's distress, has volunteered to watch in your place," Thorne told the steward. "You're needed closer to home."

"You mean I should be home in bed," Arthur countered. "Aye, and you'd best be snatching some rest yourself. Your young lady will be disappointed if you can't stay on your feet to dance."

Thorne groaned. "I may be *bored* into sleep at this soirée or whatever the deuce it is the Sutherlands are hosting for us. Gwynneth is no more enthusiastic about it than I. She's used to a quiet, country life."

"Aye, but a cloistered one. How will she adapt to being lady of the manor?"

"Well enough, I think. She's no shy violet, despite her piety." Refilling the glasses, Thorne pulled a wry face. "Which is the one thing about her that grates upon me."

Arthur shrugged. "Let her have her piety, it needn't affect your habits. Most women are taught to keep their opinions of men's ways to themselves at any rate--at least 'til they're wed," he said with a wink.

Thorne chuckled. "Not at Saint Mary's, apprarently. You should hear Gwynneth's opinion on wagering."

"I'll pass," Arthur said soberly. "Perhaps you should, too."

"No." Thorne gave him an affectionate smile. "No, my friend. As I see it, the winds are favorable enough. My course is set, and I embark happily on life's journey, my mate at my side through fair weather and foul, for as long as she'll have me."

Arthur regarded him silently, then lifted his glass. "Then bon voyage, my friend and liege...and may God go with you."

FIVE

In the drawing room of his Covent Garden town house, Radleigh eased aside the chess board with its jade and rose quartz pieces poised in mid-match, and untied the ribbon around a sheaf of vellums.

"Gwynneth's dowry," he said, pride in his voice.

Thorne hesitated, then flattened the sheets on the table, then glanced over the list. Young ewes, beef cattle and dairy cows, oxen and horses appealed to him as a land baron and husbandman. For the Hall itself there was a Boulle cabinet inlaid with tortoiseshell and copper, two Carracci oils, a Cellini vase, a pewter table service for twenty, a full set of Meissen china, and sterling flatware. Then came bed linens, table linens, and tapestries, all either inherited or among Gwynneth's own handiwork, along with lace she'd tatted and blankets she'd woven. For Thorne personally, a gold-hilted rapier in a gem-encrusted scabbard was catalogued, followed by a carved-ivory snuffbox and a sapphire-and-diamond brooch. Halfway down the second page, he encountered a sum of cash to be transferred into his holdings.

"This is more than generous," he said, careful not to show his surprise. Apparently the viscount's finances were in better condition than rumor had it.

Radleigh's gaze sidled to Gwynneth, then back to Thorne. "Has the dispensation come through?"

Thorne kept his game-face; Radleigh knew very well that he'd obtained the *mixtae religionis* in his last days at Oxford. The charade was for Gwynneth's sake, and he must play along. "It has. Banns are posted. The wedding mass will be a *Missa Contata,* as we haven't enough clergy for a High Mass."

"Well, then!" Radleigh slapped the arms of his chair. "Shall we set the date?"

"August," Thorne said without hesitation, accepting a cup of tea from his unsuspecting fiancé. "Late August. I'll post the banns upon my return."

Radleigh took the cup Gwynneth held out to him and raised it, his broad face beaming. "Then August it is."

* * *

The Sutherlands' London mansion blazed with lights. Plumed horses drew coach after coach into the semicircular brick drive, laughter floating across the greensward as footmen danced attendance on the confections of perfumed silk, satin, taffeta and lace that spilled from the shining black conveyances. Through the open windows drifted chamber music, a prelude to the minuets and quadrilles that would follow a lavish buffet supper.

Caroline Sutherland held court in the in the wide foyer, her husband in the receiving line beside her. Next to Horace Sutherland stood Radleigh, then Gwynneth and Lord Neville, each nodding or bowing according to protocol as a stream of titled folk and wealthy merchants wished the couple well.

"You've done well by the girl," a friend told Caroline later as they watched the dancers from the gallery. "One would never guess she was a convent mouse."

Caroline eyed Gwynneth--radiant in a décolleté apple-green gown trimmed in emerald lace, hair shimmering in a gold filigree chignon studded with tiny emeralds and diamonds, teardrop emeralds adorning her ears and neck, and a large table-cut emerald--the Neville betrothal ring--on one stubby finger. "Still is, I fear. Despite appearances."

"How do you mean?"

"Her first allegiance was to religion, and from what I've seen, it will always be." Caroline's gaze slid to her friend. "A man such as Lord Neville quickly tires of porridge. He'll soon seek heartier fare."

"Caroline!"

"You needn't act so shocked. Look at him. Can't you see it in those extraordinary eyes?"

"See what?"

"Appetites. God's teeth, you can be so obtuse. The man has *appetites*."

Her friend shivered, observing Thorne Neville over her fan. "You make him sound like a ravenous beast."

Caroline smiled. At that moment, the ravenous beast looked up and locked eyes with her. Her fingers tightened on the balustrade.

"Oh, Caroline, he's smiling at us! He cannot be the ogre you make him out to be. You're too fanciful," chided her friend, rapping Caroline's arm with her open fan.

"I, fanciful? Hardly. I never said the man was an ogre, I simply said he has appetites." Caroline's gaze lingered on Lord Neville as Gwynneth reclaimed his attention with a tentative touch on his sleeve.

Her friend tugged at her arm. "Let's go down and join the dancing. You've been out of Horace's company for so long, he's likely fit to be tied."

Caroline's smile thinned. "No doubt his companions are binding him at this very moment."

Her friend giggled. "Sometimes you are as droll as he."

The eyes of her male guests followed her descent, but for once the attention left Caroline cold. Just months ago, Horace would have awaited her at the foot of the stairs, eager and impatient to have her on his arm again. Now he was nowhere in sight.

Hence it happened that as Thorne lost Gwynneth to another eager dance partner, he found himself face to face with his hostess.

* * *

Thorne had formed no opinion of Caroline Sutherland. Radleigh had scarcely introduced them before she was called away to oversee some matter. But her presence had been impossible to ignore. Everyone else literally paled in comparison to the tawny-skinned beauty.

And here she stood before him. She'd ordered a waltz, judging by the hesitant opening strains coming from the gallery. Few English women would have had the nerve to suggest it, much less the finesse to execute it, without fear of censure.

But this woman knew no fear. Thorne could see that in her bearing, and in the depths of her disturbingly intuitive eyes.

She spread the wide skirts of her coral-colored gown in a low curtsey, jet-black eyelashes briefly touching her high cheeks. When she rose, her dark eyes met Thorne's in wordless invitation.

He bowed and extended his arms, keeping his face blank for fear of betraying his fascination. It was a useless ruse, judging by the way his hostess caught her luscious lower lip between her small teeth, if to hide amusement.

Heads turned as they whirled about the floor. Fingers pointed; fans spread below watchful eyes. Usually one to avoid public scenes, Thorne discovered to his amazement and dismay that he didn't give a damn.

Caroline Sutherland's movements flowed, her body agile as a young stag but exuding a feminine sensuality and an exotic fragrance the likes of which Thorne had never encountered. He glanced at the slope of her golden shoulders, a wide expanse that gracefully bore the weight of a magnificent bosom. Observing her hair, he imagined freeing the ebony mass of waves from its pins and threading his fingers through it, wrapping the luxurious length around his growing hardness as she leaned over him...her lush lips rounding and readying, her smoky gaze promising him more than he could possibly endure...

The dance had ended. When, Thorne wondered bewilderedly, had the music? He found his hostess studying his face before he could attempt to disguise his torturous musings...and smiling.

She knew. God help him, she knew.

* * *

Near midnight, Tom Barker stumbled out of Duncan's alehouse and headed for home. He fumbled in his pocket for the flask of whiskey, hoping to rinse the sour taste of ale from his furred tongue, but then squinted up at the full moon and stopped in his tracks, swaying.

"'Tis a night for beasties on the prowl," he muttered. Leaning back, he let go a howl that ended in a hacking cough. He spat with remarkable accuracy at the horseshoe on the smithy's door. Chuckling, he staggered past the tanner's, the miller's, the mercantile, and the baker's shop. He was just beyond the cobbler's shed when he heard footsteps.

He whirled about, whiskey flask in hand.

The Wycliffe road lay empty and pale under the moon, a ragged lace of tree shadows edging one side, the shops between Barker and the alehouse lining the other. He frowned at the occasional corridor between buildings, his myopic eyes searching each shadowy break but detecting nothing. All he heard, besides a chorus of tree frogs and insects, was the distant hoot of an owl.

Moving on down the rutted road, he bolstered his courage by singing a tune his old mother often warbled about a lover's moon. He stumbled now and then, twice falling down only to pick himself up and go on. The cottage he and his mother shared was a good sixteen furlongs from the village, but he'd made the trek many a night before, and every bit as drunk.

He'd gone several paces before he heard the footsteps again. He lurched to a stop, his song trailing off into wary silence, and listened.

Nothing.

Gathering what bravado he possessed, he cupped his hands at his mouth and bellowed, "See here, now, don't go a-messing with ol' Tom Barker--leastways, not if ye know what's good for ye! I be a good twenty-stone, and many's the man what wished he'd never crossed me. Some even lived to tell it!"

The words had scarcely left his mouth when he heard a noise directly behind him. Hands of steel gripped his throat.

He dropped the flask and clawed at the vise-like constriction, but in his drunken state was helpless against such strength. He managed to pull his dirk from his breechwaist, only to have it struck from his hand by his attacker's knee. With sinking heart and hopes, he gagged and gasped, as his captor, like a cat playing with a mouse, cut off all but a tiny influx of precious air. Through the dull roar in his ears, Barker heard a voice like a low growl.

"You've loosed your tongue once too often, Tommy Barker, spending your ill-earned coin in the alehouse and bragging to anyone who'll listen that there's more whence it came. Well, I hate to be the bearer of bad news, old boy, but your spending days are over."

Barker's only reply was a ghastly gurgle as the iron grip tightened, sealing off his windpipe.

Moments later he was released with a shove, his limp body falling into the road atop his precious flask, his bulging eyes staring blankly at the lover's moon.

* * *

Gwynneth smiled up at the moon. "What a beautiful evening it has been. The Sutherlands are such kind people."

Thorne said nothing as he helped her into the coach and climbed up to sit beside her.

"Horace seems a bit distant, but Caroline helped me with all my fittings and the wedding preparations. She is like a sister."

Radleigh poked his head in the doorway. "'Tis too fair a night to be riding in here." He winked at Thorne. "The fresh air will do me good."

Thorne promptly rose to take the empty seat, but Gwynneth laid a gloved hand on his sleeve. "You needn't move," she said softly.

Surprised, he reclaimed the space beside her with some misgiving. Radleigh couldn't have chosen a worse night to leave them alone.

"You were a smashing success," Thorne told her, hoping to change the direction his thoughts kept taking. "You stole the hearts of every man there, young and old."

Gwynneth's pale brow furrowed. "Perhaps I was too merry."

"You were charming." He squeezed her hand.

He should have drunk more of the costly spirits the Sutherlands had served. Perhaps sleep would come then, unlike last night. And perhaps in sleep he could forget the Sutherland vixen. Forget her dark eyes, her velvet voice, her voluptuous form and golden skin. Forget her supple movements, so matched to his own that the two of them might have been coupling instead of dancing. Forget...forget? Who was he trying to fool? *She will haunt me in my dreams, God help me.* It galled him to be so affected. Lust was a familiar antagonist, but he could not tolerate obsession. He despised such weakness in a man.

And she had known. He had a foreboding feeling that, for a woman like Caroline Sutherland, knowledge was power.

"The hour is late, I should be more tired," Gwynneth was saying. "How did you sleep last night?"

He tried to gather his thoughts. "I'm always restless the first night in a strange bed." He smiled an apology--far less than he'd owe her if she knew how he'd tossed and turned all night, tormented by the knowledge that she was just two rooms away in her bed.

"I nearly knocked upon your door last night."

And now you knock the breath out of me! Sweet Christ.

"Sleep wouldn't come," she was explaining. "And knowing that Father had a bottle of brandy put in your room yesterday, I thought I might try some...I...I've heard it brings on slumber," she finished, faltering under Thorne's intent stare.

Why did her parted lips seem fuller, redder, in the moonlight? Were her nether lips, the ones no man had ever seen between her lily-white thighs, swelling and parting as well, preparing to receive him? Liquid fire surged through Thorne's loins, and under fortuitous cover of his waistcoat he hardened so fast it alarmed him. He should insist on trading places with Radleigh, indeed should signal the driver to stop this very instant.

Gwynneth offered no resistance as Thorne gathered her to him and tipped her chin upward. Gazing at him with a charming mixture of reluctance and longing, she whispered, "Are you going to kiss me now?"

He traced her bow-shaped mouth with his thumb, his nostrils flaring at the innocent fragrance of castile soap and lemon verbena. "Yes, sweeting," he said huskily, then added as a caution to himself, "but no more than you like, I promise."

With a trusting nod, Gwynneth offered him her lips.

* * *

Morning found Thorne up well before the sun without having slept, and in no mood for polite society or wedding talk--or any further dalliance with his libido, which had been tested to the point of pain as he kissed Gwynneth at length in the coach. He'd been a fool to think he could give her a taste of intimacy without wanting more for himself.

He scrawled a credible note of apology for his early departure, adding that he looked forward to Radleigh's and Gwynneth's arrival at Wycliffe Hall a few days before the wedding. He hired Radleigh's driver to take him into the heart of town, but once the coach had disappeared down Oxford Street, Thorne walked briskly past the livery stable and headed toward the park district. It was nearly sunrise. He kept his head down and his tricorne pulled low, although few souls were about so early on a Sunday morning.

Some thirty minutes later he dashed up the steps of a well-appointed mansion, set his valise down and dropped the brass knocker twice, silently thanking Providence for the tall hedgerows surrounding the place. He had never been desperate enough to come here without cover of darkness.

Until today.

A craggy-faced woman in a white cap cracked the door open and looked him up and down with a frown. "Well? State your business."

"I beg your pardon for the early hour, but I must speak with Madame Claire."

The frown turned to a glower. "She don't conduct business at this hour, 'specially on Sunday, which is why Bess ain't around to answer the door. Bloomin' gall you got! Come back after noon." Closing the door, the woman spotted the folded pound note in Thorne's extended fingers, glanced over her shoulder, and snatched it from him. "And who might you be?" she murmured.

"Adams. Tell your mistress that Adams has come from Oxford."

"Wait here." She shut the door.

Thorne leaned against the portico and watched the eastern sky turn a brazen pink. There would be rain today. He hoped Wycliffe was in its path, the herdsmen needing a night off their watch and the fields needing water.

The door flew open. The same servant gave him a simpering smile. "Do come in, Mister Adams. Madame will be with you straightaway."

"Madame" appeared without her usual mask of kohl, rouge, and powder, but was no less gracious for having to rise so early. "I've taken the *liberté* of waking our Katy, Monsieur Adams...I hope I was not *présomptueux*." She arched over-plucked eyebrows.

"You presume correctly, Madame. I shall be more than happy to see Katy."

She seemed amused. "Katy will be more than happy to see *you*, monsieur." Her nod indicated the curved staircase. "I expect she is ready for you now. Come."

The provocative words seemed to hang in the air. By the time Thorne followed Madame Claire's swaying skirts to the top of the stairs, the mere sight of Katy's chamber door was enough to stir his blood.

He entered the dim room and quietly closed the door, then stood still, his back to the bed, and drew a deep, silent breath.

"Would you mind opening the draperies, Mister Adams?" Her voice sounded light and melodic on the surface, but Thorne detected an underlying tremor. "I know how you fancy the light," she added, reminding him he was no stranger to her.

The bed linens rustled. Thorne's nostrils flared. He spoke without turning around. "You've changed your perfume."

"Do you not like it?"

"'Tis just that I've a particular fondness for the other." He moved to a window and began fastening the velvet panels aside, taking his time, then turned, hands clasped behind him, to see the vision awaiting him in the bed.

"Aye, well, we all have to accept change now and then, don't we." It was not a question, but a soft rebuke. Awash in dawn's blushing light amid sumptuous bed-linens and ruffled pillows, Katy sat with her mouth curved in a smile of sweet irony, her eyes heavy-lidded from slumber, her hair cascading like dark fire over her porcelain skin and pooling on the sheets around her.

And Thorne knew that if he had any reservations about being here, it was too late now.

* * *

Braced on all fours, Thorne surfaced from the tumultuous tide of his release and opened his eyes to the voluptuous satiety of Katy's smile. He leaned down to touch his dripping forehead to hers, acknowledging the tempest they'd just weathered together.

Lying in her embrace, he let his mind float away on the sweet Gaelic words she murmured as she smoothed sweat-plastered strands of hair from his brow.

"You've not yet wed," she said softly.

The transition to English startled him into opening his eyes. "No," he murmured.

"But you will."

"Yes." His mouth felt suddenly dry.

"Soon?"

He nodded.

She closed her eyes, but opened them again as Thorne kissed her nose. She watched without comment as he wound an auburn lock around his finger and brought it to his lips in wordless salute.

His eyes closed as she kissed first one lid and then the other.

They did not open again for nearly nine hours.

* * *

Katy kept vigil over her Mister Adams throughout the day, only one intrusion arriving as a servant left a tray of victuals outside the room with a discreet knock.

Watching her lover sleep, she recommitted every detail of his angular face to memory, knowing she might never see it again. As she dashed unbidden tears away, her mind cried out the one question she hadn't dared ask.

Do you love her?

The answer came immediately, as if he'd heard her in his sleep.

I would not be here if I did.

Late in the afternoon, he woke and ate, then sat patiently while Katy smoothed the tangles from his hair and fastened his garters.

"You'd make some man a good wife," he told her, as she turned his cuffs and buttoned his waistcoat.

Her laugh sounded brittle. "Would have made, you mean. Aye, well, fate and me mum chose otherwise for me, Mister Adams, and I'll not be crying over spilt milk." Bending over him to tie his neckcloth, she blew a tendril of hair off her brow and looked him in the eye. "Besides, your decision to travel the rutty road of holy matrimony wouldn't necessarily be mine."

When the time came for him to go, he pressed folded currency into her hand, closing her fingers on it for her when she made no move to hold it.

She stared blindly at his waistcoat. "I'd not accept this but for Madame Claire." Her eyes rose to meet his. "Do you understand, Mister Adams?"

Without replying, he drew her to him and pressed his lips into her hair.

She watched him walk to the door, her energy ebbing with each step he took, her face a mask with a plastered-on smile.

Stepping onto the gallery, he returned only the ghost of a smile, then slowly and quietly shut the door.

Katy gazed numbly at the closed portal. After a long while, she opened her hand and unfolded the crinkled currency. She stared at it for a moment, then fell to her knees on the rug, and was sitting there when Madame Claire knocked at the door and let herself in. Without a word, Katy handed her the money.

The madam stared at it, then at Katy, and shook her head, her smile nearly cracking her rouged face. "*Mon Dieu*, girl...he left us *fifty pounds*!"

"Aye. A farewell gift," Katy said tonelessly, and burst into tears.

SIX

Thorne's pre-dawn arrival at Wycliffe Hall guaranteed a cold hearth in his study. Crouched there with the bellows, he heard something clatter on the desk behind him.

"Bloody hell!" He shot up from the hearth.

"Pardon, M'lord." The maid clutched hard at her skirts and curtsied, then turned to flee.

"Combs."

She halted, facing the door.

Thorne went to the desk, where a tray lay on the blotter. A puddle of tea surrounded a cup in its saucer. He looked at the maid's rigid back. "This will never do, Combs. Perhaps if you weren't always in a hell-for-leather hurry to leave my proximity...Combs?"

"Aye, M'lord?"

"While there's nothing objectionable about your aft exposure, I prefer seeing your face when I speak to you."

Squaring her shoulders, she turned around, then dropped a stiff curtsey. "Begging your pardon, M'lord."

Thorne regretted detaining her the instant he saw her pale cheeks and puffy eyes. He decided to berate her for her carelessness and pretend not to notice anything amiss.

"Your demeanor, Combs, suggests something amiss...some tragedy in your family, perhaps?" *Ah, Neville, you've flipped your nonexistent wig!*

"No, M'lord."

"Has some wrong been done you?"

"No, M'lord."

Belatedly, he tried to distance himself. "No doubt Dame Carswell can assist."

An anguished look crossed the maid's face. She dropped her head into her hands.

Distance was forgotten as Thorne came around the desk and offered his handkerchief. "Here now, no need for tears. Sit down for a moment." *Daft, Neville. You're well and truly daft!*

He shut the door and guided her to a chair, noticing that she dabbed at her tears with the square of linen but refrained from blowing her nose into it. Very dainty, this one.

Her sniffling quieted. Thorne sat down at his desk and regarded her warily. "I assume from your reaction that Dame Carswell cannot be of help in the matter."

The maid took a deep breath. "She is part of the matter, sir. You see, I was ill this morn, as I have been several mornings of late. Dame Carswell has noticed, and today made some very intimate inquiries of me. She thinks"--Combs swallowed audibly--"that I am with child."

Thorne grappled with inexplicable dismay. "And the father?"

Looking as surprised as he at the question, Combs closed her eyes. Tears seeped from under her eyelids and slid down scarlet cheeks. "Toby. Mister Hobbs."

Thorne's stomach knotted. He tried to keep his voice even. "And what has he to say? Have you told him?"

She shook her head. "I dare not. He'll be angry. He'll deny it at any rate."

"Why?" Thorne demanded, scarcely believing he'd asked, or what he was about to ask. "Is there some possibility he is *not* the father?"

Combs stared at him, a hollow look in her dove-gray eyes. "I swear to you, M'lord, with God as my witness, I have never been with another man."

Thorne looked away, then rose from his chair and strode to the window, hands clasped behind him. "Then Hobbs knew."

"Knew what, M'lord?"

He quietly cleared his throat. "Knew that you were still...a maiden." He could feel Combs' hot blush as if it were his, and wondered again why he'd felt compelled to make such an inquiry.

"Y-yes, he knew," she stammered softly.

"How long ago did he seduce you?" Again he could hardly believe the question had passed his unaccountably dry lips.

"'Twas a fortnight before you returned from university, M'lord."

It was the first time Thorne had detected any bitterness in her voice. He assumed she resented his prying--and why not? He was quite disgruntled by it himself. He turned to face her.

"Please understand, Combs, that my inquiries are not of a seedy nature. I'm neither deviant nor voyeuristic. Nor am I busybody or gossipmonger, in fact I rather pride myself on minding my own affairs and giving those of others a wide berth. I simply ask in the interest of a man who has served my family well for more than half his life." There, that should do. But no, he wasn't finished--and she knew it, judging by the sudden steel in her bearing.

"Were you forced?" he asked, his voice going hoarse. "And was it just the one time? Sorry, Combs, but I must have the lay of the land before charging in"--*on your white steed*? sneered his conscience--"with indictments," he finished, snapping his mouth shut.

"I consented." Despite her flaming cheeks, she spoke with no shame. "I have not been with him since. I did try to speak with him, but that made him angry. It seems I was mere diversion, despite his endless attempts to woo me and his hints at marriage." She swiped at a fresh tear with the balled handkerchief in her fist. "Begging your pardon, M'lord, I was a fool, and I've no right to self-pity, much less to indulge it in your presence. By your leave, I shall get on with my duties now."

"In a moment, Combs. I'd be remiss in my own duty to let this go unsaid." Thorne rounded the desk and perched on its edge. "Hobbs," he said grimly, "has a reputation for breaking hearts and maidenheads from Northampton to London and back again. Several times over." There, that was turning the knife, but Combs didn't flinch. Thorne paused, unnerved by her guileless gaze, then made his voice brusque. "Nonetheless, Hobbs is a top-notch stableman, the *creme de la creme* of horsemen. I cannot afford to lose him."

Nodding, Combs looked away.

"However, I shall speak with him."

Her eyes flew to him and widened. "No, M'lord, you mustn't, I...I cannot ask that of you."

"You didn't ask. Humor me, Combs. I've my own reasons for wishing to talk to Hobbs. You may go now."

She rose from the chair and curtsied. "I shall fetch another tray, M'lord. Your breakfast is cold, thanks to me."

"I didn't ring for breakfast, Combs. And 'twas I who detained you." He sat down behind the desk. "Bring it, then. Try not to sneak by me this time."

"Yes, M'lord."

Glimpsing a smile as she turned to go, Thorne regretted having to ask one more question. "What has Dame Carswell to say of your situation?"

Combs turned to him, her smile faltering. "She says, M'lord, that if I am *enceinte*, I shall have to seek employment elsewhere."

Thorne observed the maid silently for a moment, then said, "We shall see about that."

* * *

"Murdered?" Thorne echoed in disbelief. "Tom Barker had a way of offending, but I can't say he deserved strangling, at least not to the death."

"Whoever killed him didn't profit," Arthur said. "He was bellyaching over his empty purse when he left Duncan's that night."

"Tom's mates knew his well only ran dry when the coin ran out. So if robbery was the intent, 'twas likely a stranger. Has Smythe sent for the constable?"

Arthur nodded.

"And our vigils?"

"Ongoing, 'til last night. The mists were so bloody thick a *score* of lanterns would have been of no use. I trust you enjoyed your stay in London?"

Thorne's gaze fell to his paperwork. "'Twas pleasant enough. Radleigh and Gwynneth will arrive in a fortnight or so. I understand preparations are already underway." He raised his eyes inquiringly.

"Aye." Arthur looked chagrined. "Bridey and Carswell are nearing full tilt."

Thorne chuckled. "Never mind, they'll see it through to the finish, and things will be all the better for their scrapping."

* * *

Hobbs' ropy sinew rippled with each stroke of the curry brush. "He's a fine animal," he said without looking up. "As partial as I am to Bartholomew, this one nigh puts him to shame."

Raven stood unmoved by the praise except for an impatient swipe of his tail, his coat glistening blue-black in a shaft of sunlight.

"Put to it, I'd have to agree," Thorne said, glancing at the big red gelding, his father's favorite. He watched Hobbs at work for a few more minutes, then broke the awkward silence. "I've spoken this morn with one of the maids. Combs by name."

Hobbs' hesitation was barely noticeable as he knelt to brush Raven's foreleg. "And why should that interest me, M'lord?"

"Only because it seems she's with child, and you are the father."

Hobbs turned, amber eyes narrowing. "Never one to mince words, were you, M'lord." He tossed the curry brush into a pail of soapy water. "She'll have to prove it to me," he flung over his shoulder. "If she can." He led Raven to his stall.

Thorne kept his voice level. "She claims she was a virgin when you bedded her."

"True." Hobbs shut the stall gate and leaned against it, eyeing Thorne with frowning curiosity.

"She also says it happened only once."

"Aye. Your point, M'lord?"

Thorne could barely contain his sarcasm. "Once is enough, if I remember my biology correctly."

"True, but the sword was out of the scabbard when...well, you catch my drift. Let's just say I kept my wits about me. See here, M'lord, I've admitted to bedding the woman. She's easy on the eyes, and eager enough between the sheets. Unfortunately she was besotted with me, as happens particularly with women newly broken, and when she realized I'd no intention of wedding her, she was outraged."

"You mean devastated."

Hobbs shrugged. "Call it what you will. At any rate, she likely sought consolation elsewhere and got a bit more than she bargained for. And now she seeks revenge by pointing the finger at me! Well, it won't work, I tell you." He snatched up a tack rag and began shining a saddle on the workbench.

Recognizing Robert Neville's saddle, Thorne felt a grudging appreciation that Hobbs had enough respect for him to maintain it.

"By your leave, M'lord, I've work to do."

"Hobbs."

The stable master looked up to meet Thorne's piercing regard.

"Combs vows you're the only man who's ever bedded her. I believe her. And if you're half the man I'm told you are, you'll do what is right."

Hobbs boldly returned Thorne's stare. "As I said, M'lord--she'll have to prove it."

SEVEN

I must apologize for my unladylike behavior in the coach. I have since made confession and through proper penance am absolved. You shall never again witness such a shameful display of boldness from me.

I look forward to our arrival at Wycliffe Hall in August, where I hope I am still welcome.

Father has stepped out again tonight. I fear he is at the gaming tables and will arrive home inebriated as he does often here in London. God be thanked, our coachman stays at the ready to take him home.

Today Caroline Sutherland escorted me to Madame Charlotte's shop in Regent Street for my fittings. Caroline's husband is often away, and I think she is lonely, so I am glad to keep her company.

In closing, I ask that you think of me kindly, as I think of you.

I remain your betrothed,
Gwynneth Lynnette Stowington.

Baffled, Thorne scanned the letter once more. He and Gwynneth had shared a mere kiss. Confession! Would she run to the priest with an account of their every intimacy? Surely not after they wed.

The library door opened; Elaine Combs entered with tea. Thorne folded Gwynneth's letter and slipped it into a pocket. "Sit for a moment, Combs, please."

Her quickly masked relief at getting off her feet did not escape Thorne. He wished he could offer her a biscuit and some tea without her thinking it odd or improper. "I've spoken to Hobbs," he told her quietly. "The result was not what I'd hoped."

"He denied it, didn't he." She bit her lip. "Forgive me, M'lord. I've forgotten my manners again."

"I can't say I blame you...and your manners are fine." He studied the face of this woman whose beauty seemed refined and classic instead of striking, and whose speech oddly lacked slurred vowels or truncated suffixes. "So fine," he murmured, "that I have wondered just how and where you acquired them."

Her hands tightened in her lap. "Thank you, M'lord."

Damnation, would she reveal *nothing* about herself? He couldn't just come out and ask, and she knew it. He decided to be blunt. "Hobbs wants proof he is the father."

The maid stared at him blankly.

"Combs?" Sweet Jesu, he was *too* blunt; she was going to faint.

She blinked. "Forgive me, M'lord. I was trying to think how I might possibly prove such a thing."

Thorne slowly let out his breath.

"By your leave, M'lord"--the maid abruptly rose and curtsied--"I shan't take up any more of your time. Dame Carswell will be looking for me. But I appreciate what you did for me."

"I did nothing for you, Combs." Thorne felt suddenly glum. "At least nothing to appreciate."

She looked indignant. "You saved me certain humiliation and perhaps abuse, for I hear Hobbs has a fearsome temper."

"Then avoid him."

Her startled expression told him how imperious he'd sounded. "I shall, M'lord." She hurried toward the door.

But he couldn't let her go, not yet. "I told you in our last meeting, Combs, that I couldn't afford to lose Hobbs."

She stopped and turned to look at him, her expression inscrutable. "Aye, M'lord, I remember."

"I tell you now," he said, his throat tightening, "that if the man ever lays a hand on you, I will personally thrash the devil out of him and then throw him out on his ear, *sans* letters of recommendation, and it will be arranged so that he can find no better situation than that of groom, shoveling dung in only the poorest of stables without any prospect of advancement."

They stared at one another, servant and master--she looking startled, he stunned by his own intensity.

"You may go," he said presently. His voice had nearly recovered its normal timbre.

A while later, after a double shot of whiskey, his heart recovered its normal rhythm.

* * *

6 August, 1728

> *My dearest lord,*
> *I received your letter today. You say you have a surprise for me. Might it be you have given some thought to conversion? The thought of attending Holy Mass and taking Holy Communion with you gives me great pleasure. Of course such a decision is entirely yours, for only you can know your heart in such matters.*
> *My wedding frock is nearly finished. Madame Charlotte has outdone herself, from all accounts. My*

trousseau is complete as well. I shall certainly bring
more than the one trunk with me this time!
I shall close now, and courier this today.
Fondly,
Gwynneth Lynette Stowington

Arthur looked down into his ale. "And so it begins," he said with a snort.

"What begins?" Seated across a table at Duncan's, Thorne tucked the letter away.

The steward took a long draught before replying. "Wycliffe Hall's transformation."

"Into what?"

"A deuced nunnery."

Thorne chortled. "Then I'll be its priest and we'll *all* go to the devil." Seeing Arthur wasn't amused, he sobered. "Bear up, my friend. True fanaticism would put me off, but this smacks more of sentimentality--attending church together and so on. Gwynneth isn't about to convert my household." Thorne grinned. "Though Bridey would prove an easy mark. She's forever begging the saints to preserve her."

Arthur smile looked uneasy.

"'Tis *my* conversion Gwynneth wants," Thorne assured him, "and damned if I'm willing to pay the Crown double taxes for the privilege."

"Any more than you're willing to pay to keep a priest in the village?"

Thorne narrowed his eyes. "You're a shrewd one, Pennington, never let it be said otherwise. But roughly a third of our tenants are dyed-in-the-wool Catholics, say what they will. And happy tenants mean larger profit. You know it, and so did my father."

"Aye, but not to the tune of forty pounds per annum. For a papist stipend, at that." Arthur shook his head. "And once you've joined Radleigh's family, Parliament may well view you as a subversive-"

"Bollocks. Radleigh's family is joining mine, and my family has been allied with the Anglican Church since its inception. What my wife does upon her knees is of no interest to me, much less to His Majesty." Arthur pressed his lips together, and Thorne held back a smile. "There, that was rather badly worded--but we digress. I was about to say that Gwynneth's suggestion is no surprise to me. She's lived among devoted Roman Catholics for ten years now, following their rituals and saying their prayers-"

"And wishing to take their vows."

"Yes, but now she wishes to be my wife."

"She's trading her dream for that, M'lord, and it will take much love to balance the scales."

"Bloody hell." Scowling, Thorne pushed his trestle bench back from the table. "Why the devil do you persist in this? I'm quite fond of the lady, Arthur. I want to be with her, protect her. I want her to bear my children. And I believe with all my heart--my head as well--that those things constitute a firm foundation for marriage." He gulped down some of his ale and set the tankard down hard, unable to conceal his wounded pride. "I'd hoped for your blessing before now, but I see you still have your doubts."

Arthur's brief smile did not patronize. "You have my blessing, M'lord, if you truly want it. As for my doubts" --he touched his tankard to Thorne's-- "here's hoping you'll prove me wrong."

EIGHT

"There it is, Caroline! There is Wycliffe Hall. Oh, and look! There, alongside the road!"

Caroline leaned forward to look out the coach window, but saw nothing to warrant squealing like a peasant.

"The roses...oh, Caroline, the roses!" Gwynneth clutched at the curtain. "I smelled them, but I thought it *must* be my imagination. 'Tis the surprise he promised me. There must be thousands of them!"

"Well, hundreds, at any rate." Caroline hoped her disparaging sniff passed for a sampling of the floral perfume pervading the coach interior. For her, the profusion of pink, red, yellow and white blossoms lining the drystone wall only served as a bitter reminder that Horace used to weekly send her enough roses to fill every vase in their home.

"'Tis rather like a bridal path, isn't it?" Gwynneth clasped her lace-gloved hands under her chin and inhaled with the serene rapture of a yogin.

Caroline fought an urge to slap her. "A thoughtful man, your Lord Neville." *And if there is any justice in the world, one of those bloody bees will fly in here and sting your lily-white skin right through those pastel silks.*

"He is very considerate," Gwynneth allowed with a blush. "And quite romantic, I think."

Caroline dug her nails into her palm. "I do hope my presence won't foil his romantic bent," she said smoothly.

"Oh, Caroline, don't be absurd!" Gwynneth's laugh sounded sweetly indulgent. "I know his lordship will want you here."

Yes...here and anywhere else he might have me! Caroline feigned an apprehensive smile. "I hope so, Gwynneth. I truly hope so."

* * *

Thorne and Arthur watched two coaches and three drays tarpaulined in oiled canvas roll to a stop. As footmen and maids streamed down the steps of the terraced lawn to take numerous trunks and bags, William the kitchen-boy and young Henry unhitched the horses to lead them in pairs to the beck. Thorne waved Radleigh's coachman aside to open the door himself.

"Thank God. My bones have turned to powder." The portly man heaved a sigh as his future son-in-law helped him down with a chuckle.

"Come now, Radleigh, we've filled in ruts and potholes nearly all the way to Northampton--what more could you ask?"

"Paving," Radleigh grumbled, his breath reeking of brandy fumes. "The Romans weren't entirely barbaric, you know. Just wait 'til you're my age, Neville, and see how well *you* travel these bloody country roads."

Thorne clapped a hand over a big shoulder. "A bath and a cool mug await you, my friend, but first I must greet my bride."

Gwynneth nearly melted into his embrace, crying out softly, "Oh, my lord, the roses, they're beautiful! Where did you get them, and however did you plant so many?"

He smiled down at her, his loins stirring at the worship in her eyes; his costly gift had paid off. "They came from the finest hothouses in London, along with a team of horti-" he broke off, his attention suddenly riveted beyond Gwynneth, his pulse slowing to an erratic thud. The extra coach. Of course. Monogrammed for *Sutherland*, not Stowington. "-culturists," he finished, his mouth snapping shut.

Caroline stepped down with queenly grace, her gloved hand sliding off the footman's arm as she reached the ground and smiled, first at Gwynneth with a conspirator's air, then at Thorne with perfect aplomb.

Gwynneth looked gleeful. "Are you surprised, my lord?"

"Utterly," he muttered, extending his hand. Caroline's hand slid into it as she curtseyed, her exotic scent wafting upward and bringing with it a keen recall of the waltz they'd shared. Thorne's tongue knotted along with his stomach.

"Caroline feared she mightn't be welcome at Wycliffe Hall," Gwynneth scoffed.

"Nonsense, you are quite welcome," Thorne said to Caroline. "My home's ambiance can only be enriched by your presence."

A smile played about Caroine's lips. "You are as gracious a man as Gwynneth claims, my lord, but your home isn't likely to be improved upon in any fashion by my presence." *Your person, however,* her eyes told him, *might benefit immensely.*

"We've brought Ashby, Caroline's maid," Gwynneth was saying, nodding toward a young woman William was helping down from the driver's seat. "Caroline has agreed to share her with me."

Thorne drew Gwynneth's arm through his. "But I've taken the liberty of appointing a lady's maid for you. She's waited upon you before. Do you remember Combs?"

"Yes, she seemed quite capable," Gwynneth recalled as they lagged behind the others, Radleigh following Jennings to the library and its well-stocked liquor cabinet, Dame Carswell leading Caroline and Ashby on up the stairs.

"I'm glad you agree. I've sent her ahead to your chambers, where you can begin a life of leisure by instructing her in the matter of unpacking your trunks."

Gwynneth sighed. "I think you will be a perfect husband."

"Perfect?" Smiling ruefully, Thorne shook his head. "Harbor no such delusion, dear lady. I shall, however, try my best to be the husband you deserve."

Her answering smile was so sweetly radiant that after a moment Thorne muttered, "Hang convention!" and leaned down to steal a kiss. As her lips lingered willingly under his, he drew away. "Go," he said gruffly, "while you can."

Laughing, Gwynneth ran up the steps. Thorne's smile felt more like a grimace as his loins tightened again. *Dear God, get this interminable wedding behind us.*

Turning from the newel post, he saw his housekeeper paused at the mouth of the west hall, her stony gaze upon the stairs where Gwynneth had just disappeared from view.

"Buck up, Carswell." A hint of warning lurked behind his teasing tone. "Yonder goes your new mistress."

* * *

"Am I late?"

Gwynneth's question trailed away as she paused in the open doorway of the dining room, her eye skimming the long table for the first time from a viewpoint as lady of the house. The service of china, crystal and ivory-handled sterling gleamed in the halo of tall candelabras, every precious piece set out with faultless precision on cream-colored Belfast linen.

Across the room, Thorne looked up from an aperitif.

"Late, my lady?" Setting his glass on the mantel, he turned his back on Radleigh and Caroline to approach Gwynneth. "Your father might complain," he murmured as he took her hand, "but the devil take me if I care. You're a vision to behold, and well worth the wait."

Gwynneth could hardly question his sincerity. The looking glass in her chambers had revealed a beauty rendered almost ethereal by her shoulder-baring frock, a creation of pale-pink cabbage roses on a background of ivory covered by a gauzy overskirt. But oh, how Sister Theresa Bernard would frown at the décolleté neckline, and especially the display of plump bosom it offered to Thorne's appreciative glance.

"Sweet," Caroline murmured as she joined the couple, her eyes narrowing.

Radleigh followed, strutting like a rooster. "Thorne, I must congratulate you on your choice of lady's maid for my daughter. What a transformation!"

Thorne shook his head, his eyes still on his fiancé. "Radleigh, your daughter would be a beauty even in rags."

Gwynneth touched Thorne's arm as he took his seat next to her, the heat in her cheeks rivaling the slow fire that banished all tendrils of fog daring to enter the open windows. "I've told Caroline the tragic story of your Aunt Agnes," she said hastily. "Will you show us inside the tower?"

Hesitating, Thorne shrugged. "Very well, but I must warn you and Mistress Sutherland that nothing save for spiders and bats has entered the place for decades."

"My lord?" Caroline spoke up in a velvet voice.

"Ma'am?" was Thorne's polite reply.

She smiled. "Not being particularly bound by convention, I should be pleased if you would call me by my Christian name."

"If you insist, ma'am." Looking down at his plate, Thorne picked up his spoon.

While Caroline spooned the consommé as casually as their host did, Gwynneth looked from friend to fiancé with a frown. Only Radleigh seemed unaware of Thorne's subtle refusal to grant Caroline first-name privilege.

* * *

Halfway through supper, Jennings announced a caller. Thorne put down his napkin and followed the head-footman to the great hall, but passed him as he recognized the man who'd just doffed his hat to expose an impossibly curly mass of bright-red hair.

"Townsend!" Thorne grabbed his hand and pumped it delightedly.

His visitor grinned. "Good God, Neville, I've never seen you looking so hale and hearty, the country quite agrees with you!" Richard Townsend handed his cloak and tricorne to Jennings. "Your man tells me I've interrupted supper."

"We've just finished," Thorne assured him, shooting Jennings a jaundiced look.

"Well, I should at least apologize for showing up five days too soon."

Thorne clapped him on the shoulder. "Townsend, you'd be welcome here no matter how early. My bride-to-be has just arrived this afternoon. Leave your bag for Jennings, and come meet my guests."

Thorne first introduced his friend to Radleigh. Presented to Gwynneth, Townsend bowed and pledged his undying loyalty. As he turned to Caroline, his hazel eyes brightened. "We've met before, ma'am, though I can't for the life of me remember where."

"Surely not, sir." Caroline looked at him from under her long eyelashes. "'Tis not likely I'd forget."

Thorne clenched his jaw as Townsend's face turned scarlet. Radleigh chuckled.

Gwynneth smiled. "Another heart won, Caroline."

"The first today, then," Caroline murmured, and Thorne suddenly felt Gwynneth's eyes on him, taking a long, speculative look at the only man who seemed invulnerable to her friend's considerable charms.

NINE

"The stable master?" Caroline scoffed, every nerve in her body suddenly on edge.

"Yes. Tobias--or I should say Hobbs, could not take his eyes off you." Gwynneth sounded oddly vexed.

Caroline kept her eyes on the root-ridden path on the ridge above Beck's Hollow. "I didn't notice," she said with a shrug. "I'm not in the habit of ogling strange men, particularly stablemen, though the one time I did glance his way he seemed quite attentive to *you*." She turned her head to see Gwynneth's simpering smile.

"Don't be silly. He's merely protective of me. I'm to be his master's wife, after all."

Envy pierced Caroline in the gut. "Yes, I'd nearly forgotten," she lied. "The master's wife. It sounds so...submissive."

"I wish you hadn't said that. Oh, Caroline, I think I shall go mad."

Slowing their pace, Caroline glanced at Townsend and Lord Neville, yards ahead and deep in conversation. "Whatever do you mean?" she said in a low voice.

"I cannot get Sister Theresa Bernard's warning out of my head."

Caroline reined in Bartholomew. "What warning?"

Gwynneth drew Abigail alongside the gelding and leaned toward Caroline. "That many men spill their seed, not for procreation as *God* intended, but"--she broke off with a gulp--"*for pleasure.*"

Caroline arched her brow. "And how would she know?"

"Is it true? You're married, and surely you hear tales from other wives. Tell me."

"And what if it is?" Caroline hedged, her heart beating faster. "Did your Sister Theresa Bernard say what might come of such pleasure?"

"Don't you know? Oh, Caroline, we are daughters of Eve, hence vulnerable to temptation. But if we allow a man to touch us in any way that is unnecessary for the sowing of his seed--or worse yet, allow *ourselves* to feel pleasure at a man's hands-" Gwynneth lowered her gaze, her gloved fists twisting the reins.

"What then?" Caroline prompted, then held her breath.

Gwynneth raised wide, tearful eyes. "Then we shall burn for all eternity in the fires of hell," she whispered tautly, "where Satan will take his own selfish pleasure with us, and debase us in ways beyond imagining."

Caroline fought off a hysterical peal of laughter. "And you believe that?"

"Beyond a doubt. Sister Theresa Bernard is as near to God as a person can be, and knows such things. Oh, Caroline, do you think Lord Neville is one of those men? I know he wants children...but do you think he seeks carnal pleasure in a wife?"

"I think," Caroline said cautiously, "that Lord Neville will respect your feelings." *And seek his pleasure elsewhere.*

"I hope so." Gwynneth's pale mouth trembled. "A kiss is all the satisfaction I shall ever need from my husband."

Caroline squelched her bubbling mirth with a coughing spell. When Gwynneth regained her own composure, the two women urged their mounts onward, a thrill of excitement coursing Caroline's spine as they approached the men riding ahead.

Lord Neville was a handsome, vigorous man--and, if their waltz together was any indication, a hot-blooded one as well. Wedding or no wedding, he would surely take a lover.

And how very convenient should that lover happen to be a frequent visitor in his own home.

* * *

Slipping the well-oiled bolt at the west entry, Caroline stepped into the unfamiliar nighttime landscape of Wycliffe Hall.

Ghostly tendrils of mist floated by as the clouds thinned under a waning moon. An owl hooted above the raucous chant of insects, while something splashed in the beck. Caroline's shiver had little to do with the clammy chill, as she'd fastened her wool cardinal over her shift and wrapper the moment she decided upon her reckless venture.

Treading carefully to avoid the dung heaps she'd spotted from the lane that afternoon, she hissed an expletive as a wooden heel rocked on uneven terrain. A horse whinnied inside the low building. Flattening herself against the wall, Caroline crept alongside the rough fieldstone until she reached the doorway, then peered inside. Surely that lantern wasn't burning unattended. Fearing she'd lose her nerve, she slipped inside and latched the door behind her, then on second thought unlatched it in case a speedy exit proved necessary.

A horse nickered. Recognizing Bartholomew in the dimness, Caroline stroked his muzzle and soothed him with soft words.

"Who's there?"

She whirled around to see Tobias Hobbs standing in the shadows of a narrow passageway.

"You," he said, his upper lip curling.

She stepped toward him, but stopped short as he spat on the straw-strewn floor. She gathered her cardinal protectively about her.

Hobbs approached her, a predatory gleam in his eyes. "A trifle far from home, aren't you, even for a woman on the prowl? Surely you're not here for *my* company. Though I'd bloody-well serve better than old Horace--who was conspicuously absent from your riding party this morning."

"Horace will join us on Friday," Caroline said, gritting her teeth. "As if 'tis any of *your* concern."

"Pity." Hobbs' voice was like drawn butter. "Who'll warm your bed 'til then? Five nights is a lifetime for a bitch in permanent heat." He smiled as he heard her gasp, his glittering gaze taking her in from head to toe. "Not to fret, love, you can't help what you are any more than I can. We are Cornelia Hobbs' children, after all, a wanton herself." He eyed Caroline's bosom, which had begun to heave. "Remember, too," he said huskily, "we are siblings only by half, so we shouldn't be entirely condemned for sharing a bed. And that little blond slip of a maid you have--Ashby, is it?--would be more than welcome to join-"

A choked sound escaped Caroline as she lunged for him through a red haze of rage, but her fist struck his face so hard she felt a shock go up her arm. The roar inside her head died away. Feeling something warm dribble down her fingers, she stared in mute fascination at the blood on her hand.

* * *

Lying in the straw, Hobbs felt his jaw go numb. A coppery taste filled his mouth. As his eyes focused, he saw Caroline retreating, massaging her knuckles. He spat blood and charged to his feet.

In three long strides was upon her. He swatted the hood off her head and grabbed a hank of hair.

She cried out. He clamped a hand over her mouth; she promptly sank her teeth into it.

"God rot you, you cock-teasing bitch," he snarled, not daring to shout with Henry Pitts sleeping nearby. He shoved Caroline backward.

She stumbled but regained her footing, then gasped as he pulled a knife from his pocket. "You wouldn't dare-"

"Don't tempt me." He jerked a kerchief from another pocket, then ripped the cloth in two and held the blade over a flame. Eyeing Caroline fiercely, he sliced into the bite she'd inflicted and bled it into one half of the kerchief, then seized a bottle of gin from a high shelf and splashed some over the wound before wrapping his hand with the clean piece of cloth.

"Now." He strode to within an arm's length of her; she stood her ground. "Tell me why you're here. Then get the devil out of my stables."

She dared give him a malicious smile. "*Your* stables, Toby? Has Lord Neville expired after naming you his heir in a fit of madness? He was quite alive when I saw him two hours ago."

"Answer me," Hobbs hissed through his teeth, "before I kick you out on your sweet arse!"

Her eyes narrowed. "Take care, Toby. I am a wedding guest, here by invitation and hence under protection of Lord Neville. Yes, dear brother, it so happens the Honourable Miss Stowington and I are dear friends, indeed I am her closest confidant. 'Twas I who debuted her into London society."

Staring at his sister, Hobbs struggled to assimilate this startling news. "As if I give a rat's prick," he countered. "All I want to know is why you're in these stables at this hour."

"Only to warn you that you had better keep our kinship to yourself. Otherwise, you'll not see another shilling from *my* purse."

He grinned.

Caroline stomped her booted foot. "'Tis not in the least amusing, Toby Hobbs! I am quite in earnest."

He touched a finger to his lips, then pointed down a dim passageway. "One of my grooms sleeps yonder."

Caroline's hand flew to her mouth. "Dear God--do you think we woke him?"

Enjoying her alarm, Hobbs grinned again. "Henry sleeps like the dead. Your secret is safe."

"And yours," she reminded him tartly. "You'd be out on your bum if Lord Neville got wind of it. So 'tis agreed? You won't betray me? And you'll treat me as others do--as a lady--for the duration of my stay?"

Gone was the haughty society lady. In her place stood the beautiful, spirited girl who'd cared for him while their mother labored long hours in a seamstress' shop. The girl who'd so fiercely defended him when others had dubbed him "bastard-boy."

His animosity fled, leaving him disgruntled. "Agreed."

Caroline eyed him dubiously.

"Agreed, I say!"

"Very well, then." Watching him, she tugged a boot off and pulled something from the toe. Hobbs kept a bland expression as she opened an embroidered handkerchief to display a wad of currency. "Here." Her nose was in the air again. "Take it. For the remainder of my visit, I shall have no further dealings with you, nor shall we speak to one another. Understood?"

"Quite, dear sister. You needn't nag." Pocketing the money, Hobbs dangled the dainty square of cloth in front of her. "Don't drop it. Monograms are like calling cards." He grinned. "Wouldn't want anyone to think we've had a roll in the hay, would we?"

Tight-lipped, Caroline jerked the linen from his callused hand and strode toward the door.

"Better hope the wind hasn't shifted, either," he called after her in a low voice. "The hounds are just up the lane. Oh, and one thing more..."

Caroline halted in the doorway, her back stiffening, but did not turn around.

"When dear old Horace arrives, tell him I've business with him in the stables."

"You know he doesn't ride," she snapped.

"No matter," Hobbs drawled softly. "I'll be doing the riding."

TEN

"The stables are packed and the coach house crammed full!" Elaine heard William tell Bridey. Guests had arrived with maids and manservants since Monday morning. Elaine had lost count of the extra servants hired in from the village.

While William and the footmen hauled sides of beef, joints of mutton, bacon slabs and yards of Bridey's linked sausages from the smokehouse, and crates of her crocked preserves from the cellar, Elaine helped Janey, Susan, and Hillary unload a cartload of fresh produce just in from the manor farms and orchards. Watching Arthur head happily away from the fuss and into the forest with his musket and sack, Elaine supposed she'd soon be plucking feathers while Hillary roasting partridge, pheasant, and quail alongside the lambs and suckling pigs on the spit in the cavernous kitchen hearth.

Instead, Dame Carswell gave her full charge of the wedding gifts, though under the housekeeper's own eagle eye. Displayed in the day room, formerly Catherine Neville's domain and soon to be that of Gwynneth Neville, Elaine arranged the sumptuous items for display and then cataloged them along with their givers' names in her meticulous hand.

Because Dame Carswell worked the rest of the staff relentlessly and at odd times to avoid inconveniencing anyone, the guests seemed to come and go at all hours. Elaine heard tell of picnics in Beck's Hollow, strolls in the formal gardens, Pall Mall and archery competitions on the terraced lawn. Hired coaches drove daily into Northampton for anyone inclined to buy elsewhere than the open market and quaint shops of Wycliffe. A company of musicians played in the gallery evenings after supper, when footmen removed the Aubusson rugs for dancing and then stood guard at the great hearth with bellows and waterpails for sudden drafts, flying embers, and skirt hems too near the fire screen. Elaine saw the guests at their most elegant then, as their jewels, velvets, silks and brocades transformed Wycliffe Hall into a small-scale replica of the king's Court.

* * *

It seemed to Thorne that supper's din and duration increased each evening, ale and wine flowing freely, conversation ranging from the latest fashions and Court gossip to rising taxes and denouncement of King George's latest and longest stay in Hanover. To Bridey's credit, mouthwatering aromas pervaded the Hall long before the meal, and heaping platters of puddings, meats and gravies, vegetables, fruits, and sweetmeats streamed steadily from the kitchen as it progressed.

Now and then a lady's perfume wafted under Thorne's nose, provoking thoughts of pleasures other than dining. It was at one such moment on Wednesday evening that he glanced down the table and locked eyes with Caroline Sutherland, who acknowledged him with the slightest of nods.

It was easy enough to shift his impenetrable gaze along to the next guest, and the next. But it was impossible to keep the color out of his burning face, and from the corner of his eye he glimpsed Caroline's little smile.

* * *

"Pardon, M'lord."

Leaning against doorjamb and listening to Gwynneth's Aunt Evelyn play the harp, Thorne turned to find a pair of dove-gray eyes upon him.

"M'lord, please, you must come to the kitchen."

"What, have Dame Carswell and Mistress MacBride finally come to fisticuffs?" His smile faded as he noted the maid's pallor and trembling lips. "What is it, Combs?" His hand moved to touch her face; he brought it sharply to his side.

"Please, you must come straightaway."

A glance assured him their exchange had drawn no attention. He followed her into the east hall, then laid hold of her arm from behind. "Tarry a moment, Combs, tell me what's the matter."

She stopped and shook her head, her shoulders beginning to heave with silent sobs.

Torn between a powerful desire to comfort her and the need to know what caused her distress, Thorne let go her arm. His long strides quickly putting her behind him.

Charging through the kitchen door, he was met with a gaggle of weeping women, Bridey's wavering wail rising over her maids' muffled sobs. Seeing Thorne, she pressed a trembling hand to her mouth and pointed to a small chalk-white figure laid out upon the worktable.

Beside the unnaturally still figure stood Arthur, head bowed and hat in hand.

Thorne slowly circled the table, where drying rivulets of blood trailed from young Henry Pitts' mouth and nose onto the scarred wooden surface. Colorful bruises marked his face and neck. His vacant stare and the absence of a pulse in his thin little throat left no doubt he was beyond saving.

Jaws clenching, Thorne gently closed the boy's eyes. "He's been trampled," he said gruffly. "Who found him?"

"I did." Arthur's voice shook. "By the time I reached him, there was nothing I could do. 'Twas Raven, M'lord."

Thorne felt the blood drain from his face. "How? What happened? Where the hell was Hobbs?"

"I...might we talk quietly in your study, M'lord?"

"Very well." Thorne turned to the blubbering cook. "Fetch clean linen to cover the boy. Then leave him be, and rally your maids." Beckoning Arthur, he strode from the kitchen.

Laughter drifted from the game room, punctuated by a roll of dice and the clack of wooden balls, while from the east wing, the tinkle of glasses and the drone of conversation floated up the hall on a whimsical tune from the pianoforte. Suddenly it all seemed barbaric, even blasphemous, and in the study Thorne turned a face dark with helpless anger on his steward. "Well?"

Arthur shut the door. "'Twas my fault, I gave Hobbs leave for Northampton this eve. He said he needed some leisure, what with all the extra work of late..." He twisted his hat in his hands.

"Go on."

"I'd an errand in the coach house, and was halfway there when I heard the sound." Arthur winced. "He was mad, M'lord, Raven was. From what, I don't know, I only know I've never heard such accursed cries from a horse, and God willing, I shall never again." He drew a shuddering breath. "I hurried to the stables, but by the time-" He broke off, choking back a sob.

Thorne poured a dram of Scotch and gently slid it across the desk to him.

"Henry was lying there with his body bent so unnatural," Arthur said after downing the bracing liquor, "that I knew he was dead. And Raven..." He shook his head. "'Twas as if demons had set upon him, M'lord. All a-tremble and frothing at the mouth, nostrils flaring, eyes rolled back in his head. I took the boy up and ran. Why the gate was open, I'll never know. All I know is that poor Henry was alone against the beast, and the fault is mine."

Thorne stirred from his own horrific trance and came to lay a hand on the steward's shoulder. "You're not to blame, Arthur. You must know that."

Arthur only shook his head.

"We'll investigate," Thorne said with a calm he didn't feel. "Raven should have been inside his stall, and something provoked him to trample Henry, who probably did no more than try to settle him and put him up." He poured another generous dram for Arthur and one for himself. "We'll wait for Hobbs' return and try to reconstruct events. Meanwhile, send William for the undertaker. Fetch Kendall, too. If the horse is mad, we'll put him down. If 'twas something beyond his control, and he isn't ailing, we'll let him be for now."

Arthur nodded, then set his glass down and turned to go, clutching his cap to his chest as if to a bleeding wound. His face seemed to have aged a decade. The sight of it only compounded Thorne's sorrow.

"Arthur, I would have given Hobbs leave tonight myself. He's bound to be bone-tired from this chaotic week. So stop blaming yourself." Thorne's tone brooked no argument.

Arthur paused at the door, his voice near breaking. "He was a good boy, was Henry."

Thorne swallowed hard. "Yes, that he was."

* * *

Shortly after midnight, Dylan Smythe carried Henry's shrouded body to his cart and laid it gently on a blanket. Thorne stepped back as Hobbs placed a hand upon the little form and lowered his head.

"Go," Hobbs told the undertaker abruptly, his voice thick, and headed for the stables as Smythe drove the cart away.

Thorne trekked past the dark hulk of the smokehouse and through Bridey's herb garden, hoping the scents of lavender and chamomille might soothe his troubled mind. His household had adopted Henry Pitts as readily as Hobbs had, with the exception of Dame Carswell, who'd "no truck with vagabonds and urchins."

His heart skipped a beat as he entered the great hall and spotted Elaine Combs alone on a hearthside bench. She rose hastily and curtseyed. Approaching her, Thorne detected traces of dried tears. "You should be abed," he chided.

"I've kept an ear open," she said, and he knew she meant for Carswell, which was not what he'd meant at all. "*Was* the horse mad, M'lord?"

"No." He sighed, suddenly wishing for nothing more than to sit down and have Elaine Combs sit beside him. "Kendall found nothing wrong with the poor beast," he told her, "nor was there anything amiss in the stall area. The gate had to have been open, but no one knows why. Henry might have opened it himself...but again, why?"

Combs shook her head, looking into the fire. "Mister Hobbs must be inconsolable. Henry was like a son to him."

Surprised she could be so magnanimous toward the man who'd used her, Thorne replied a bit gruffly. "More like angry, whether at me--'twas my horse, after all--or at himself for being away when it happened." He watched Combs closely, trying without success to gauge the depth of her feelings for his stable master. "There will be a small service tomorrow," he informed her, though she was bound to know already.

She thanked him as if it was news to her, then dipped her knee. "Good night, M'lord. May you rest well."

"Wait, don't go yet, Combs."

She showed no surprise. She was becoming accustomed to his waylaying tactics, Thorne realized wryly, as he groped for the right words. "Your situation," he said at last. "Is Dame Carswell still-" He broke off, struggling with the real question, and the sudden shy glow in Combs' eyes made it imperative for him to avert his own.

"Aye, M'lord," she said softly. "My situation is yet in jeopardy."

For some reason his heart sank--anxiety about her impending dismissal? Ultimately that was up to him, if he so chose, however unconventional it might be. Envious, then, of Hobbs' part in her dilemma? Perhaps even jealous?

Suddenly annoyed with her, himself, and the entire scenario, Thorne said curtly, "Well, good night, Combs," then turned on his heel and walked away, unwilling to witness yet another damnable curtsey.

* * *

Hobbs stood still as a statue; indeed his face might have been carved from stone.

As Parson Thomas Carey brought the short service to a close, Thorne signaled Hillary to escort a weeping Bridey ahead of the other servants, before the gravediggers could begin lowering the small coffin into the gaping maw of wet earth. Hobbs himself threw in the first spade full of mud.

The small horde of sniffling mourners trickled from the manor churchyard, heads bowed under hoods and hats. Thorne kept his tricorne in hand, the cold morning drizzle a blessed distraction from the gnawing in his gut. He still knew no cause for Raven's attack, and at graveside had silently sworn to find it himself.

Turning to go, he spotted a wilted posy lying next to his father's gravestone. Who, he wondered for at least the hundredth time, felt inclined to pay regular tribute to Robert Neville?

Lagging behind the other servants, Elaine Combs sank her shoe-heel in the mud. Thorne had to resist an urge to bound forward and take her arm. Deliberately slowing his pace, he nonetheless kept a covert eye on her progress.

When some way up the road she glanced back at the churchyard and stopped to stare, he turned to look as well.

The gravediggers stood off to the side, hats in hand. Alone on the soaked, matted grass beside the open grave, Hobbs sat with his head bowed over bent knees, his broad shoulders quaking with sobs.

ELEVEN

"'Tis cold and quiet as death," Gwynneth observed with a shiver. "Why was it built?"

"Defense, my lady." Thorne stood at the base of the stone steps that spiraled up the interior wall of the tower keep, his oil lantern casting grotesque shadows of himself, Gwynneth, Townsend and Caroline. They had come through a hidden door in a carved oak-paneled wall of the archive room, which doubled as Arthur's office. Just beyond the panel door, double doors of studded oak nearly a half-yard thick and hinged by one piece from top to bottom in forged iron had required all of Thorne's and Townsend's might before opening with an unearthly groan.

"It may seem folly now," Thorne admitted, "but Queen Bess conferred the barony on Thomas Neville for his help in destroying the Armada, and Thomas could not forget how Spain's army was rumored to have been marching overland to meet the fleet on shore of the Channel."

"First the army. Then the Inquisition would have returned for an encore," Townsend quipped. "And none of us would be here now, what with our ancestors having been killed in the march or burned as heretics."

"None but Gwynneth," Thorne countered, grinning as Townsend winced at the reminder of Gwynneth's original avocation. "At any rate," Thorne teased, "a manor lord never knows when the villeins might rise against him, forcing his family into the tower for survival."

"Heaven forbid." Gwynneth shivered again, rubbing her arms.

Thorne indicated the massive square timber leaning against the wall. "Lifted into those iron brackets by a half-dozen men, that barricade turns this place into a fortress." He held up the lantern, illuminating a wooden disk in the stone floor, with a thick iron ring in its center. "And this would be our water."

"None too fresh, from the smell of it," Townsend observed.

They climbed the narrow steps with caution, using handholds cut into the stone. On the second floor, meager light stabbed through small iron-barred windows in three of four separate chambers. There was no sign of use, not even a dried rush on the stone floor. There was only the smell--something besides the stagnant water in the old well below--and the chilly, tomb-like silence.

The third floor proved the source of the unpleasant odor, as arrow loops cut through the thickness of the wall admitted thin crosses of light, revealing animal droppings in partially slimy but mostly hardened heaps. As the women gasped, Thorne put a finger to his lips and pointed upward.

Four pairs of eyes rose to peer into the shadows of the heavy ceiling beams. Townsend spoke first. "'Twould seem we're not alone."

"Bats," Caroline breathed.

"God help us," Gwynneth whispered, looking ready to fly down the steps.

Thorne reached out to steady her. "We've only to be quiet and move slowly. They're sleeping. And harmless, I promise. They're of tremendous value to the livelihood of this estate, and I dare not begrudge them shelter in an otherwise useless structure." He smiled. "That said, watch your step."

Leaving the ammonia-laden fumes of the bats' lair behind with a collective sigh of relief, the party emerged onto the battlements.

While Thorne and Townsend walked around to the southern view, Gwynneth followed Caroline to the parapet's nearest crenel, a waist-high gap for an average man. "It looks like patchwork," Caroline said of the four hundred eighty hectares of pasture, crop fields, orchards, meadows, forest and beck spread out around them.

Gwynneth shuddered, staring at the flagged terrace far below. "Agnes," she said faintly, "must surely have crushed her skull on those stones. How long, I wonder, could the abominable life inside her have survived..."

It was Caroline's turn to shiver. "I imagine the poor babe died on impact as well...Gwynneth, are you ill?"

A visible tremor had seized Gwynneth, yet her focus stayed on the terrace, her words sounding slurred as she spoke through chattering teeth. "'Tis but a chill. 'Twill soon be over. Everything...will soon be over..."

"Gwynneth!" Caroline shook her arm. "Gwynneth, look at me. Let go the parapet, why do you cling so? Look at me!" She wrenched one of Gwynneth's hands loose. Slowly, Gwynneth turned to face her.

"God's blood--Lord Neville!" Caroline cried out. "Come quickly!"

Both men came on a run. At the sight of Gwynneth's glassy eyes and sickly pallor, Thorne seized her icy hands and rubbed them between his. "Christ, sweeting, what's the matter?"

His hands went still as Gwynneth's blue-tinged lips curved into a slow smile, at once seductive and contemptuous.

Caroline gasped, lurching backward into Townsend.

The ghastly smile thinned to a grim slash as Gwynneth's eyes acquired a sulphurous hue. She curled her lip at Thorne. *"You were a coward to leave,"* she rasped in a voice not her own. *"Better our child should die, than to know its father was less than a man."*

Caroline screamed and Townsend shouted as Thorne was suddenly straining to pull Gwynneth off the parapet. One leg up, foot braced against the wall, she seemed to try with all her might to climb up and over the crenel.

As Townsend joined Thorne's efforts, Gwynneth fought them off like a she-cat. Most terrifying of all was that she uttered no sound during her struggle, but only stared with savage ferocity at Thorne.

"Townsend, leave off, she's tiring!" Thorne held Gwynneth fast, looking stunned at her tenacious strength.

Townsend let go, wide-eyed. "What the devil ails her, has she gone mad?" He retreated to join Caroline, who had flattened herself against the parapet.

"Be still, Gwynneth," Thorne soothed, with a withering glance at Townsend. "That's it, sweeting. Breathe now. Deeply, slowly...speak to me when you can."

Panting for air, she looked suddenly dazed, then went limp in his arms.

"She's fainted." Relief flooded Thorne's voice; this he could handle. "Caroline, pull yourself together and find my housekeeper. Tell her to send for the doctor immediately, and have Bridey hurry tea." Lifting Gwynneth, he winced as Caroline rushed toward the tower door. "Take the lantern and leave it at the bottom of the steps for Townsend to fetch so he can bring us down--and for God's sake, Caroline, tread slowly!"

Once out of the keep and through the steward's office, Caroline took the east hall on a run, Lord Neville's terse baritone echoing inside her head.

Caroline, pull yourself together....for God's sake, Caroline, tread slowly!

Even in her heart-pounding haste to reach Dame Carswell's office, Caroline smiled.

Thorne Neville had used her Christian name.

* * *

"She simply fainted," Thorne told John Hodges before anyone could say otherwise. "We were atop the tower, and the height must have made her dizzy."

"When did she last eat?"

"Late this morning."

"Has she fainted before in your company?"

Thorne gave the doctor a wry look. "She has not."

"The morrow is your wedding, mightn't it be nerves?"

"Possible, but not probable. She seems quite prepared."

The doctor lowered his voice. "Is there any chance at all...what I mean to say is, might she be...with child?"

"Hodges!"

"Forgive me, but I'm obliged to ask."

"No, she is not with child."

"Very well. Now, if you'll kindly go and disperse her attendants, I shall examine the young lady."

Gathering Radleigh, Townsend and Caroline, Thorne took them from the study out into the gallery, where they could hear only the faint drone of Hodges' voice through the heavy door.

"What happened up there?" Townsend burst out.

"I was a fool, is what happened," Thorne said hastily, with a glance at Radleigh. "I told her that accursed story of my aunt, and she took it to heart."

Townsend stared at the floor. Caroline spoke soothingly. "She would have heard it eventually. She'll be fine, you'll see, my lord. Tomorrow she'll stand hale and hearty by your side at the altar."

"Amen," Radleigh muttered, and Thorne shot Caroline a grateful look.

The study door opened; Hodges motioned them in. Gwynneth, pale but no more than normal, was drinking tea on the settee.

"She is in fine form," the doctor assured them, returning medical instruments to his bag. "Merely took a chill. The fire and the tea and the blankets were just what she needed." Aside to Thorne, he muttered, "Those damned stays, you know. Women can scarcely breathe sitting still, let alone climbing steep steps."

He turned back to Gwynneth with a solicitous expression. "None of this 'ladylike' skimping on meals, Miss Stowington," he chided gently. "And plenty of rest tonight, early to bed." He looked squarely at Thorne, who arched his brow.

"I'll see to it," Radleigh blustered, patting Gwynneth's hand. Her answering scowl proved she was herself again.

"Doctor Hodges," she called after him as he was leaving.

The palace guards couldn't have about-faced more promptly. "Yes, my lady?"

"Will you be at our wedding?"

The doctor's long face beamed. "Barring emergencies, I most certainly will."

"Such a gentleman," Gwynneth remarked when he'd gone. "Has he a wife, Thorne?"

"No, poor chap. Not many are up to his profession--off at all hours of the day or night to visit the sick and dying." Thorne sat down and took hold of Gwynneth's hand.

"He's a lovesick pup," Caroline said dryly, "but he left us with good news, did he not?" Bending to take Gwynneth's other hand, she nearly spilled her bounteous décolletage in Thorne's face. "You had us worried, my dear," she purred. "I'll leave you now, you need your rest."

"You rest, too. You must be exhausted from all this foolishness," Gwynneth told her, smiling gratefully and squeezing her hand. "We shall see you at supper."

Struggling to ignore Caroline's blatant display, Thorne eyed the emerald betrothal ring on Gwynneth's finger. "Do you remember what happened before you fainted?" he asked after the others left the room.

"I know I grew quite cold. So you see, it *was* a chill."

Throw it off, Thorne told himself, silently vowing never to let her on the battlements again. "Let me take you to your chambers," he murmured. "You must rest, our day dawns just hours from now."

"Oh, my lord," she breathed. "I am glad, but I must know..."

"Anything, my lady." Cupping her heart-shaped face in one hand, Thorne brushed his fingertips over a peach-blushed cheek and gazed into her beseeching eyes. "What is it?"

"Do you find my kiss...satisfactory?"

Half chuckling, half groaning, he pulled her close. "Your kiss is more than satisfactory, Gwynneth...it drives me mad." He pressed his lips to her throat. "Hang the wedding, the witnesses too," he murmured at her ear, and heard her breathing quicken. "Say the word. We'll go and fetch the priest now if you-"

He broke off with a muttered curse as a knock came at the door.

Jennings spoke quietly, a jerk of his head indicating the great hall. "Sorry to intrude, M'lord, but another guest has arrived...Mister Horace Sutherland of London." He blinked then, startled at Thorne's hoarse reply.

"Thank God in his ever-belated mercy."

TWELVE

"All is in place," Arthur assured Thorne in the early evening quiet of the study--their only refuge since the guests had descended upon the Hall. "The church is polished and bedecked from chancel to nave to entry. I'd a look for myself."

Thorne's sudden cough disguised a snicker. The thought of Arthur stepping foot in a "papist" church was too much for his composure.

"There's enough food for all of London," the steward went on. "The coaches are shining inside and out, the horses are curried and new-shod, and from what I saw in the village this afternoon, labors have been cut short and shops closed early--although Duncan can't *begin* to close his door. Heard him singing at the top of his lungs over the din. The celebration has begun."

"Sweet Jesu," Thorne mumbled around the cheroot he was lighting, and handed the humidor to Arthur. "Just what we need to top off this damnable week, a pack of rowdies in their cups at the fes-"

He broke off as a shrill feminine voice rang out above stairs but was curtailed by the low, harsh tones of a man--which ended with the sound of an open-handed slap.

Silence, utter and absolute, settled over the Hall, as if the place and everyone in it were waiting, listening.

A door slammed. Thorne sprang from behind the desk to the study door and opened it a crack. Arthur twisted in his seat, his brow elevated at the unprecedented disruption of decorum.

Rapid footsteps coursed the great stairway. Caroline Sutherland moved into Thorne's limited view, her long, lustrous locks tumbling to her waist. A lace mantel draped her shoulders. She used a corner of it to dab at her streaming eyes.

"Mistress, wait!" hissed Ashby, chasing Caroline down the steps with hairbrush in hand. Caroline did not pause, and both women were quickly out of view. Soon the heavy door to the west hall thudded closed.

Thorne eased the study door shut and met Arthur's shocked look with one of bemusement. "Our Mistress Sutherland."

"No doubt her husband has arrived?"

"An hour ago. He was shown to chambers and I haven't seen him since, poor fellow."

Arthur grunted.

Thorne tamped out the cigar. "If you and I've finished our business, I believe I'll see to our guests."

"Looking forward to supper, are we?"

Thorne grinned. "We are indeed."

"I see you wasted no time getting here," Hobbs said, watching his visitor from the stable doorway. Comically out of place in his velvet breeches and powdered wig, Horace Sutherland picked his way across the stable yard, trying in vain to keep his silver-buckled shoes out of scattered piles of dung.

Horace strode past Hobbs into the dim stable, then turned and bared his teeth. "My wife is in a fine temper because I put your bloody *summons* before her *needs*, so state your business. I intend to be punctual for supper."

"Oh, by all means, we mustn't keep the great Lord Neville and his blushing virgin bride waiting." Hobbs spat in the straw, then dipped a wooden scoop into a sack of oats and carried it into a stall.

"See here," Horace sputtered, following at a distance, "you tell me what you want, now, or I shall leave immediately. Don't think I won't."

Hobbs stopped him with a glare. "What I *want*? What in bloody hell do you *think* I want?" He strode back to stand nose to nose with Horace. "Deuced if I'll beg for it, either."

Wrinkling his nose in distaste, Horace dug hastily into a pocket as Hobbs stepped back with a snort.

Pausing, Horace narrowed his eyes. "Perhaps you're not referring to money. Perhaps you need more of the-"

"Watch your tongue, old man!" The stable master jabbed a finger into Horace's chest and shoved. "You're in *my* house, now. I want money and you bloody well know it! Only one time did I ask for the other--and I've done with that." Hobbs gave him a cunning look. "Some of us aren't nearly as needy as others, my friend. God help you if *Caroline* ever discovers your little habit."

"She won't." Horace's swarthy face flushed, sweat beading on his brow and upper lip. "She's curious about our meetings, but I can satisfy her with a bauble or two. Here." He slapped a thick roll of currency into Hobbs' hand, then mopped his face with a kerchief while the stable master counted.

"All here." Hobbs patted his bulging pocket. "Pleasure doing business with you, Sutherland."

Horace turned on his heel and strode out into the sunset.

Hobbs lingered to hear Horace cursing his way back through the stable yard, then headed to his own quarters in the rear of the stables, where he stashed his new-made fortune under a loose floorboard. Covering it with a threadbare rug, he felt his hackles rise.

"Tell me."

Behind him, the voice sounded so harsh and guttural he hardly recognized it. He turned to see Caroline standing in the doorway, her unbound hair telling him she'd abandoned her little blond maid mid-toilette.

His sagging mouth thinned to a smirk as he rose. "I see you're as much Horace's nursemaid as his wife."

Caroline's voice shook. *"Tell...me...now."*

"Lower your voice."

"Lower my voice?" She nearly choked on the words.

"Get in here." Grabbing her by the wrist, Hobbs yanked her into the room and kicked the door shut. "Easy...easy," he said, realizing she was trembling like a skittish mare. He guided her to the solitary chair in his tiny room. "You'll get nothing from me 'til you've calmed yourself." Bending down to rub her icy hands between his sweating ones, he kept his voice even. "How long were you spying? What did you hear?"

"Stop it." Caroline's look branded him with shame. "I'm all the family you have-- or I might as well be--and I deserve better." She jerked her hands from his. "Now talk. And so help me, Toby, if I smell a lie, I'll gouge your eyes out."

Observing her long, manicured nails, Hobbs sat down just out of striking distance on his cot. "Your husband," he confessed grudgingly, "is paying me for my silence."

"The deuce you say!" Caroline's laugh bordered on hysteria. "Do you take me for a fool? I could have told *you* that much!"

"He's an addict," Hobbs said flatly. "Opium."

Caroline's face registered horror, denial, and finally acceptance. "I should have known," she murmured. "The extended travels, the vacant stares. His apathy for everything that used to bring him pleasure, including me..."

Eyes darting about the room, she shot up from the chair, swayed on her feet, and then crumpled into a heap on the floor, where she lay her head in her skirts and burst into wracking sobs.

It was too much. Hobbs could take her abuse, her haughtiness and her anger-- anything but her grief. Cursing, he slammed his fist into the oak planks, but the pain only fueled his anger. A powerful kick rewarded him with the sound of splintering wood. He kicked again. Surveying the damage with fierce satisfaction, he rubbed his throbbing knuckles.

Caroline's bawling ceased. With an expression that dared him to assist, she came to her feet and gathered her skirts up off the stable floor. Sweeping past him, she jerked the door open, then paused to glare at him over her shoulder.

"There will be no more money from Horace. Henceforth you've only one cash cow. I shall pay for your silence now, regarding our kinship and my background. But the sum will be determined by *me*--do you hear?" As Hobbs nodded, she took a deep, quavering breath. "I shall apprise you of that sum at a later date."

With grudging admiration, Hobbs watched her depart in the settling dusk. He almost pitied Horace for what was surely to come.

The sun slipped out of sight, leaving streaks of violet-red beneath a wash of indigo. Tomorrow's weather would be perfect for a wedding.

And not just any wedding. A *perfect* wedding. For a perfect man and his perfect virgin bride. And they would live in their perfect house, and raise their perfect children--while he, Tobias Hobbs, continued to take care of their perfect horses.

Perfect.

* * *

"Mister Sutherland remembered some urgent business in London to which he'd no choice but to immediately attend," Dame Carswell informed Thorne in a single breath. "*Mistress* Sutherland sends her apologies...she is indisposed by an insufferable headache."

"Tell Mistress Sutherland she will be missed this evening, and that I am sorry her husband was called away." *Sorrier than she could ever know.* "Have Bridey prepare a herbal remedy straightaway."

Thorne passed Caroline's message on to Gwynneth.

"I think I heard them quarreling," she said, her brow creasing. "I shall go and see to Caroline, perhaps lend an ear."

Thorne tried to hide his disappointment. "Take what time you need. I'll make excuses at supper. But remember your rest, my lady. Doctor's orders."

"Please forget this afternoon's nonsense, I'm quite myself now." Gwynneth surprised him by standing on tiptoe to buss his jaw.

"Then kiss me," he teased, and she offered her lips with a little smile. Thorne kissed her lightly at first, but as her lips parted, he cupped the back of her head and plied her sweet mouth with deliberate, tantalizing strokes of his tongue. Her soft moan was both reward and punishment as his member reached full arousal. "Tomorrow, when night falls, my lady," he murmured thickly near her ear, "I shall pleasure you to the point of exhaustion."

She began to pull away. "I assure you, my lord," she said in a breathless whisper, "that your kiss is all the pleasure I shall ever need."

"No, Gwynneth," he murmured, holding her fast to nibble at her earlobe and hearing her sensual gasp. "Your kiss tells me you want more, far more. And you shall have it. Your budding womanhood," he vowed under his breath, "will bloom full like the rose under the hands of this gardener."

Gwynneth clutched at him and shivered, then drew a deep breath and backed out of his embrace. "I must go to Caroline now," she mumbled, turning to run up the stairs as if her life--or Caroline's--depended upon it.

Frowning, Thorne watched her go. If only Horace Sutherland would return and set things right with his wife. Perhaps then Gwynneth could concentrate on being one herself.

* * *

One glance at Gwynneth's face as she took her place at table later told Thorne there would be a conference. He hoped it was short. Will had already ridden to tell Duncan that most of Wycliffe Hall's male guests would descend upon the alehouse later that evening. Thorne, along with Arthur, planned to be among them.

"Opium, Thorne, can you believe it?" Gwynneth demanded, pacing in the privacy of his study. "Horace begged her to forgive him, told her he would try to give it up. But she simply cannot endure his presence just now."

Halting, she laid a hand on Thorne's sleeve. "I realize our wedding is tomorrow, and that Caroline would have departed soon after, but mightn't she stay a bit longer?" Gwynneth's green eyes shone with tears. "Perhaps a se'nnight, or even a fortnight?"

Thorne's jaw clenched involuntarily.

"I know you aren't particularly fond of her," Gwynneth said with a sniffle, "but she is my friend and she's endured a terrible shock. She would do the same for me, wedding or no. And it isn't as if we'll be traveling soon. You said we must be here for harvest, that Parliament's opening will commence our wedding trip...please, Thorne, let her stay. For me?"

Her small fingers clutched like talons through his velvet sleeve, but she let go as he rose to stand with his back to her before the fire. He felt a strong need to warm himself. The prospect of having Caroline Sutherland underfoot in the first days of his marriage made his blood run cold.

"Very well then," he said in a toneless voice. "Let her stay."

* * *

By Thorne's pocket-watch, it was just past midnight when Arthur leaned over the dice table and spoke at his ear.

Thorne let go a colorful expletive. First splitting his winnings with Radleigh, he left the table and made his way slowly through the rowdy throng, exchanging greetings but keeping an eye out for his objective.

She was alone at a table near the door. Her cardinal was clasped at her throat, the hood crushed under a sea of blue-black hair. She cradled a dram of whisky in her hands, her stare fixed on a point beyond the room, a trace of tears marking her unusually pale cheeks.

"Friend of yours, M'lord?" Duncan's low voice gave him a start.

"A guest," Thorne said shortly.

Duncan nodded toward a crowded table against the front wall. "She's been spotted." He moved on.

Thorne recognized five of the six men ogling the lone woman. The stranger stood up on unsteady legs while two of his mates slapped his back in apparent encouragement.

Thorne timed his own casual gait to reach the woman's table just ahead of the stranger.

"Here, watch your manners, mate!" the man groused, lurching into Thorne and stumbling backward. "I've a mind to introduce meself to the lady!"

Slowly, Thorne turned to face him. "And I've a mind to toss you out into the road on your drunken ass."

"Ha!" The man stepped back, sizing him up. "You and ten other hearty chaps, mayhap!"

He shrank back as Thorne's eyes pierced him through, but offered a tentative fist until one of his tablemates bellowed, "Keep it to yourself, Fletch! 'Tis late, and your pint's a-wasting, come back and sit down."

Thorne held his stare. "A wise man, your friend."

'Fletch' grunted, stealing one more glance at the prize he coveted before looking back at his companions. The movement threw him off balance. He staggered back to fall into his seat.

Thorne faced the woman again. She'd yet to acknowledge him. *Let her be.* The thought was so distinct that it seemed for a moment Duncan had spoken again.

Thorne sat on the trestle opposite the woman. She flinched, then dragged her gaze upward to meet his own, her expression unchanging--dull, devoid of emotion, the fire gone out of her eyes. He wondered if she even recognized him.

"Caroline."

She did not reply. He saw a flicker in her eyes--pain? He'd always thought women such as she only inflicted pain.

He watched his hand move. Watched it slide unbidden across the table to envelop those cold, pale fingers in the warmth of his palms.

"Caroline."

This time she looked at him, her eyes as eloquent as they had been empty moments ago. *Why*, they asked. *Why?*

He lifted her glass of whiskey, helped her wrap her fingers around it. "Drink," he said, and gently withdrew his hand.

She did as he bade her, holding the glass in both hands like a child might, her dark eyes fixed on his face. In four little gulps she finished the whiskey, a tremor seizing her during its final burning descent.

Thorne signaled Duncan for two more.

This time Caroline drank the entire contents of her glass without putting it down, swallowing hard and fast, an erratic pulse beating in her golden throat. Color crept into her cheeks. Her eyes, dark bottomless pools, never left him.

A man could dive deep into those eyes, Thorne mused. Could swim in their depths for days, weeks, perhaps even years, without surfacing for air...

And could just as well drown.

He found his voice, hoarse though it was. "'Tis late, Mistress Sutherland. I shall escort you home."

"I rode, my lord." Her throaty tones nearly sucked the breath from his lungs. "The bay roan. He is quite gentle, just as Toby said he'd be."

"Toby." Thorne frowned. "My stableman? You're acquainted?"

Her hands, trying to corral her raven locks and pull up her hood, went still. "Not personally, of course, but"--she hiccuped--"we've all ridden a great deal, and it is his name, after all-"

"His name is Hobbs. Has he been presumptuous, tried to take liberties?"

"Heavens, no! Oh no, no, no." Caroline giggled, an odd sound coming from her, and then hiccuped again. The whiskey had done its work.

"Arthur will settle my account and see to your horse. You're riding with me."

* * *

Leaning against the stable doorway, Hobbs looked out into the night, ostensibly keeping vigil, along with the groom slouched against the wall, for returning guests. But it was Caroline for whom he watched.

Lights twinkled on the hill, the kitchen fire burning well past the usual hour as footmen waited in the great hall. Up the lane, lantern light glowed in the open doorway of the coach house.

The beat of hooves intruded on the soft night sounds; Hobbs recognized the canter of the Arabian. He nudged the dozing groom with the toe of his boot. "Nate, look lively." Nate shot to his feet as Raven rounded the bend with not one, but two, riders.

Watching them dismount, Hobbs narrowed his eyes and shook his head. Leave it to Caroline. Not only had she returned safe and sound, but with Neville himself. As Nate brought the horse in, Hobbs lingered to watch the couple cross the lane and enter the south gardens, Caroline's elbow resting in Neville's hand. At her first little stumble, he tucked her arm firmly through his.

Hobbs darted his eyes to the second-story window at the northeast corner of the Hall. Was <u>she</u> watching? He knew those were her chambers. He'd made it his business to know.

Seeing the draperies shift ever so slightly, he smiled.

* * *

Two maids met Thorne in the kitchen, their eyes widening for an unguarded moment to see Caroline "on the arm of the master with her hair unbound like a wild thing," as Ashby later heard one of them tell a scullery maid named Janie.

"Susan, Hillary, help me with Mistress Sutherland's cardinal," Thorne ordered the maids brusquely, dispelling any notion of impropriety, then nodded toward the table, where food lay waiting for the returning revelers. "Send some of that bread and broth to her chambers straightaway. And wake her maid."

As Caroline allowed Thorne to guide her up the stairs, a wave of exhaustion washed over her. With it came the terrible emptiness she'd felt after Horace's departure this afternoon. To her horror, tears rolled down her cheeks. She tried to swallow her sobs, but a tremor gave her away. Suddenly the stairsteps loomed frightfully close.

In one dizzying moment she felt herself swept up and cradled by a pair of unyielding arms. Held fast against the firm breadth of Lord Neville's chest, she was carried to her chambers, her silent tears spotting his velvet waistcoat.

Her maid cried out as Lord Neville brought Caroline through the door.

"Hush," he told the girl. "She's conscious, just unsteady on her feet. Ashby, is it?"

"Aye, M'lord." Ashby stepped back as Lord Neville crossed the bedchamber and eased Caroline onto the canopied four-poster.

He gestured toward the tray. "Your mistress needs rest, but first she needs strength. Do not let her sleep 'til she eats."

Ashby bobbed her head. "Aye, M'lord, I'll see she swallows every morsel."

"Mind you don't force it down her gullet," he said mildly. "Be gentle with her. She's had a bad shock today."

"Aye, M'lord, I know."

He turned to Caroline. "Rest well. Should you need anything during the night, send Ashby to my--to Dame Carswell's chambers, topstairs, first door to the right."

Caroline managed a wan smile. "Thank you. My apologies for disrupting your evening."

"'Twas no trouble," he said. As Ashby approached with the tray of victuals, Caroline watched Lord Neville stride to the curtained archway.

Suddenly he paused, then turned around, his eyes piercing hers through the dimness. "As I am to be married today," he said, "to a lady who considers you her dearest friend, 'twould seem odd for you to continue addressing me by my formal name."

As late as the hour was and as poorly as Caroline felt, she did not miss a single one of the three implicit messages Thorne Neville had just delivered while giving her first-name privilege.

I am to be married. Gwynneth is a lady. She believes you to be her friend.

Caroline nodded. "Goodnight, then...Thorne."

He seemed to study her. She made her expression inscrutable.

"Good night," he said at last, and moments later closed the door with quiet finality.

THIRTEEN

"Milady?"

Elaine heard no reply. Yet the flickering firelight under the door indicated her mistress was up and about. *As I would be*, she thought glumly, *were I to marry Thorne Neville today.*

She touched the handle, then recoiled as she heard the drone of a voice inside. She clutched at her middle, sickened by the thought that Lord Neville could be in his fiancé's chambers at this hour.

Her dismay vanished at the sound of a door closing on the west gallery. Even at that distance and through the murky light, she sensed Lord Neville's eyes upon her. She dipped her knee and saw him nod as he headed for the stairs.

Slowly, Elaine eased her mistress' latch open and pushed the door ajar.

The Honourable Miss Stowington knelt not on the rug but on the bare oak floorboards, her head bowed and her eyes closed, a string of beads threaded taut through her fingers. "Holy Mary, mother of God," she intoned, "pray for us sinners..."

The prayer died on her lips. Elaine watched, first in bewilderment as her mistress' pale face crumpled, then in growing horror as the prayer took a new direction.

"Pray for me," the young woman pleaded through soft sobs, "for absolution for the sin I must commit, the Original Sin of carnal knowledge, which you yourself were mercifully spared, Virgin Mother, but which I must commit for the man that is to be my husband. Please, Holy Mother, entreat our Father to strengthen me and give me fortitude to endure such pain and abasement!"

Elaine brought a shaking hand to her mouth.

The bride-to-be opened her eyes as the sun broke over the horizon, one pale beam lancing a window and striking the rumpled bed directly in front of her.

Clutching her beads to her chest, she astounded Elaine by smiling through her tears.

"Thank thee, Blessed Mother," she said fervently, "for hearing my prayer."

* * *

The Church of Saint Michael reeked of roses, incense, and tallow. With every seat filled, villagers stood five deep in the vestibule and spilled out into the churchyard.

Gwynneth floated up the nave on her proud father's arm, looking like a hesitant angel in a gown of satin, lace, and seed pearls, her trembling hands clutching a Venetian glass bead rosary and a posy of roses plucked from the very hedgerows planted in her honor. Rosebuds and baby's breath wove through her hair, while her veiled headdress displayed the traditional sprig of rosemary for keeping one's husband faithful. Her wedding gift from Thorne, a circlet of matched pearls imported from the Arabian coast, adorned her slender throat.

The shine of tears through her veil surprised Thorne. Sentimentality wasn't a trait he would have ascribed to her.

Arthur was soon handing Thorne a gold-and-emerald band to be joined to the emerald solitaire on Gwynneth's finger. "With this ring, I thee wed," Thorne repeated after Father Chandler, "and I plight unto thee my troth."

Standing behind Gwynneth and lacking her usual golden glow, Caroline stoically held the bride's posy and wedding gift to the groom, a gold signet ring featuring the couple's initials entertwined with a rose vine on a background of jet. She passed the latter to the priest.

Gwynneth took the ring from Father Chandler. As she slid the unaccountably cold metal onto Thorne's finger, Thorne caught himself gazing at Caroline instead of his bride.

The awkward moment passed into a guilty memory as Father Chandler signed the cross. "In nomine Patris," he intoned, "et Filii, et Spiritus Sancti...Amen."

Forty long minutes later, the *Missa Contata* was over.

* * *

Regaled by a crowd waving streamers and tossing flowers along the way, the newlyweds rode to the village green in a coach drawn by four plumed Percherons. Lizzie and Duncan tapped a dozen kegs of ale, and when everyone had eaten their fill of roast capons and suckling pig, the dancing began. The first dance, a reel, started off to an uproarious cheer as the bride partnered her groom and then her strutting father.

Watching Radleigh and Gwynneth, Thorne looked up to see John Hodges wending his way through the throng.

"A word, sir?" the doctor murmured when he reached him. At Thorne's nod, he led him away from the noise of pipe and fiddle to the edge of the green, and fell into step beside him. "Yesterday at the Hall, I sensed something more than a fainting spell had occurred. I thought perhaps with a day's passing, you might be more inclined to confide."

Hesitating at first, Thorne related his ancestor's tragic fate, then quoted Gwynneth's chilling words and told the doctor of her demented struggle to mount the parapet.

"Well I've something to tell you," Hodges said, breaking stride to face him. "Some weeks ago, I believe you hired a man or two from the village to keep watch from that very tower."

"I did."

"Well, one of them came to me with what I thought was a tale conceived at the bottom of a bottle, but now I wonder."

"Go on."

"He told me he had become 'infernally cold', if you'll pardon the paradox, on his third watch, colder than he'd ever been in his life. No reason for it, he said, as it was a balmy enough night in these parts. Thinking he'd caught a chill, he relied on his wife's care but, as he needed the compensation, returned to his post for the next three watches." Hodges eyed Thorne intently. "Following the sixth watch, he came to me and said he'd not go up there again."

"Why?" Thorne made his tone flat, his expression stony.

"It seems the night before, during his watch, he was...well there's no other way to put it. He was shoved from behind."

"What the deuce?"

"Indeed, shoved hard enough to lay him flat on his belly across the parapet. He said it quite knocked the breath out of him, but he'd the presence of mind to twist himself right 'round to see who'd done it."

"And?"

"No one."

"What do you mean, no one?" Thorne demanded with a growl in his voice.

"He said there was 'nary a soul in sight', and that 'no one but the devil hisself' could have reached the stairs before he turned 'round to see. Claims the door at the top of the stairs was shut tight at any rate."

"Bollocks. He was three sheets to the wind, as you first suspected--though how he smuggled a flask past Pennington is beyond me."

"There, you see? And why come to *me* with such a tale? His wife nagged him to see me on account of his sore belly, but I'd the distinct impression he was more desperate to confide."

"Desperate to convince his wife he wasn't tippling on the job, you mean. Look, Hodges, I'll admit to feeling out of sorts yesterday, hearing such words from Gwynneth in that strange voice. But you're not a fool, doctor. Surely you can see that Gwynneth fell victim to her own sensitivity. And to my lack of it."

Hodges looked unconvinced. "Well I'm glad you 'fessed up, as I can best treat my patients when I know something of their proclivities. But just for my own senseless curiosity, how long had it been, before these night watches, since anyone was atop that tower?"

"Your curiosity is more than senseless, 'tis ridiculous," Thorne said dryly. "But to humor you, not in years. As a lad I was permitted a look with my tutor, and once I took a young lady out on the battlements, to impress her..." His voice faded away. If only the memory would, as well.

"But that was fifteen years ago," he resumed abruptly. "Until the watch, no one had been up since. And I have never," he scoffed, "felt an odd chill there, nor was I ever 'pushed' by anything but a gust of wind."

The two men strolled back toward the revelers. "You should be dancing," Thorne chided Hodges, "not chasing ghosts. Do you not see that bevy of unattached young ladies looking our way?"

The doctor chuckled. "I see a new wife awaiting her wandering husband."

Thorne grinned as Gwynneth, tapping her foot with the commencement of another reel, waved at him.

"Well, M'lord," Hodges said, "send at any time, should you or your lovely wife require my services." Watching Gwynneth, he failed to see the smile his remark prompted.

"I sincerely hope, Doctor, we shall have need of you before the year is out."

* * *

Leaving the villagers to carry on the celebration, the wedding party and guests returned to the Hall for a late supper, some to depart that evening, others the next morning.

Caroline Sutherland would be among the latter. To Thorne's relief, she'd declined the invitation to stay, saying the sooner she faced Horace and their difficulties, the better. She promised Gwynneth to visit in the near future.

Escorting Gwynneth to her chambers before supper, Thorne felt his blood quicken. Although they would maintain separate chambers for awhile, he now had all rights to enter hers at any hour. "I shall be in the study when you come down," he told her, hoping to relieve any anxiety she might feel, even as he lingered on the chance she might invite him in.

"I shan't be long," she said shyly, dashing his hopes, and then glanced behind her.

Only then did Thorne see Elaine Combs. Looking pale and somehow resolute, she stood waiting to either serve or be dismissed.

And service it was. Standing out in the gallery, Thorne closed the door, but not before seeing what could only be relief in the maid's dove-gray eyes.

* * *

The door stood ajar. All tapers were extinguished. Only a small fire vied with the light of the rising moon.

Halting just inside the curtained archway, Thorne observed his bride sitting in a window seat, her posture predictably tense, her profile pensive and pale.

Her eyes widened as she turned to see him. He'd tied the sash closed on his black silk dressing gown after his bath, leaving a triangle of dark-furred chest exposed and his long, damp hair unbound.

She stood up from the window seat. With the moonlight behind her and the fire to the side, she presented a breathtaking display as she approached, her full-breasted slenderness undulating beneath a cloud of embroidered lawn and Battenberg lace.

Thorne's heart skipped a beat.

She stopped two paces away. Slowly, Thorne began to circle her, and she to turn with him. His eyes rose, from the shadowy peaks of her breasts to her slender throat, where her pulse beat like tiny bird's wings frantically seeking escape--and then to her face, at last fully illumed by the moon.

There the spell was broken. Never mind the rose-petal bath he could smell on her skin, or the lily-of-the-valley woven into hair that was brushed to spun gold. It was her eyes. He'd seen that look on a hare as he stared down his flintlock at it. A look that said *I'm done for, and I've nowhere to run.*

"You look...beautiful." He ran a hand over his fresh-shaven jaw to cover a rueful smile. "Let's have a brandy, shall we?"

"Yes, let's," she said hastily. "I shall pour it, like a good wife."

And a very nervous one, he mused, seeing her hand shake as she poured a generous measure into each snifter. Seated in the oriel window with her, his bent knee nearly touching hers, Thorne raised his glass. Gwynneth touched hers to it with a tentative smile. Together they sipped the fiery liqueur and gazed across the shadowy landscape.

"We're in for a storm," he observed, watching the stars disappear one-by-one. A faint rumble reached his ears.

"Yes, I smell it in the air." Gwynneth gripped the sill as the beeches across the road began swaying and waves scuttled across the moonlit beck. Strands of her hair fluttered on the first cool gust of air. "Shall we close the sash?"

Thorne shook his head as Gwynneth made to rise. "Not yet."

"I'll close the others." She sprang from the window seat and flew about the chamber, pulling in sashes and fastening shutters. Thorne saw her glance longingly at the fireside chairs before she returned to the window seat, where she huddled in the corner and hugged her knees to her chest beneath her shift and wrapper.

"Do you mind not going abroad just now?" he asked, hoping conversation might relax her.

"Not at all. I'm quite content here. And I am glad that your home-"

"Our home," Thorne broke in gently.

"Glad that our home," Gwynneth amended, "is the place which holds your heart."

He smiled. "I suppose it does rather hold my heart."

"As opposed to your heart being held by a person," she said, eyeing him closely for the first time all evening.

It was his turn to look away. "'Tis a dangerous thing, Gwynneth, giving someone your heart. People are careless, fickle...and they've a tendency to die."

Thunder rumbled. The moon's halo began to disappear. Gwynneth looked out at the blackening sky and then turned wide eyes on Thorne.

"Are you afraid of storms?" he asked, surprised.

"A little."

"Are you afraid of me?"

She shook her head.

"Then come to me," he said gently, extending a hand. "We'll ride this one out together."

Gwynneth hesitantly took his hand. Thorne drew her into his lap, first tucking a small cushion beneath her hips for her "comfort," as he told her, his smile going somewhat awry. Innocently accepting the explanation, his bride leaned back against him.

Lightning split the sky, thunder on its heels. Feeling Gwynneth stiffen in his arms, Thorne gathered her close and pressed his lips to her temple.

Blinding-white light speared the bedchamber, an ear-splitting crack and explosion of thunder on its heels. Gwynneth ducked her head and squealed, clapping a hand over one ear and pressing the other other against Thorne's chest.

With a soft chuckle, he pulled in the window sash. He gazed tenderly at Gwynneth as she opened her eyes. "You've nothing to fear, sweeting," he murmured, and felt her shiver as he brushed his lips against her ear. "Neither from the storm...nor me."

As if to mock him, the heavens roared again, this time rattling the casements and vibrating the window seat beneath them. As Gwynneth cried out, her body going rigid in Thorne's arms, he knew it was time...time to make her forget the storm and everything around them.

* * *

Terrified by the storm's rage, Gwynneth turned gladly to the distraction of Thorne's kiss, moving her lips against his with an urgency that defied the elements. Wrapping her arms about Thorne's neck, she desperately breached his lips and drew him inside her mouth.

His appreciative groan should have brought her up short, but the heat in her belly had quickly spread to that place she'd explored as a child and then later learned to ignore while praying feverishly to the Blessed Virgin.

Gwynneth moaned like a wanton into her husband's mouth.

Dragging his lips from hers with another groan, he tongued a river of fire down her neck, making her gasp with pleasure. But her heart leapt in warning as nimble fingers began loosening the ribbon ties at her throat. Squeezing her eyes shut, she felt the gossamer fabric of her wrapper slide off one shoulder. Warm lips followed its descent, sending wave after wave of chills over her body before backtracking to tickle her nape.

She heard Thorne's breath catch and quicken as he encountered a well-placed dab of lemon verbena. Her tension fled, her entire body thrilling to the touch of his agile tongue and lips as he forged a steaming trail to the notch in her collarbone. Caught up in the headiest sensation she had ever experienced, she could not utter a word of objection as he went on to lay one round breast, its peak painfully taut, bare to his gaze. The weak sound she did manage was drowned out by another clap of thunder. The sound did not faze her, as Thorne chose that moment to close his mouth over her virgin nipple and suckle like a starvling.

Gasping and moaning, Gwynneth arched her back in shameless entreaty, her ears roaring, not with the fury of the storm, but with the hot blood of lust rushing through her veins. A tug-o-war raged between her lavishly tended nipple and that mysterious core of fire inside her, making her thighs clench unaccountably as if to take something within their grasp. Failing to find it, they writhed against one another while she squirmed in Thorne's embrace and cried out for a relief she couldn't name.

A warm hand slid up her thigh. Her protest died as Thorne lifted his head from her breast and nibbled her lower lip between husky-voiced words that eventually penetrated her fogged consciousness.

"I beg my lady's permission," he murmured, stroking her bare bottom with a reverence that eased her initial shock.

"For what?" she asked breathlessly.

"To pleasure her to exhaustion."

Gwynneth forced her eyes open, and through a haze of passion beheld the burning blue gaze and sensual smile of her husband.

Just as Satan smiles on you from the fiery depths, hissed a voice in her head. The voice of Sister Theresa Bernard.

* * *

Thorne's smile and gentle patience were a bluff, his self-control flagging fast. The cushion he'd tucked between himself and his bride served its purpose all too well. He wished he could hurl it out the window.

"No!" Gwynneth cried with a gasp, her eyes widening.

"What?" His smile faltered.

"No!" She struggled to sit upright, levering against her husband's chest with hands that only moments ago had clutched him to her in a death grip.

As Thorne met her fearful gaze with a bewildered stare, a shrill scream rose above the waning storm. Gwynneth sprang from his lap like a serving wench caught with her master.

Outside the chamber, voices hummed and exclaimed. "Wait here," Thorne muttered. He threw the bolt back and stepped out in the gallery, where a sea of ruffled nightcaps, frowzy heads and pale but excited faces greeted him. He closed the door behind him.

"Come now, ladies, gentlemen. Someone has either suffered a nightmare or discovered a mouse. Never mind," he said hastily at the women's collective gasp. "We'll find the poor rodent and make fast work of him."

"The scream came from there, I'm certain!" Gwynneth's cousin, Aunt Evelyn's son, pointed eagerly at a door on the upper west gallery.

Thorne's heartbeat slowed, his eyes scanning the throng but failing to find one guest in particular. Encouraging everyone to return to bed before catching cold, he sounded overly hearty to his own ears. "Besides, ladies, a mouse is about to meet its end. An ugly scene, I warn you."

The crowd quickly disbanded. Thorne took the gallery on wooden legs, apprehension mounting with every step. Glancing back, he spied one lingering guest.

"May I assist?" Townsend called out softly.

The way you did on the battlements? "Not this time," Thorne replied dryly. "The next rodent is yours, I promise." But there was no rodent, and he knew it.

His hand weighed like stone as he lifted it to knock.

The door opened immediately, confronting Thorne with the wet-eyed, stricken face of Caroline's maid.

"What the devil is wrong?" He was nowhere near as annoyed as he sounded, but annoyance served to mask other emotions he'd no business feeling.

"Oh, M'lord," Ashby cried out, "'tis my mistress, she's had a terrible blow, sir, a dreadful shock!"

"Take me to her." Thorne's eyes were already searching the gloomy interior. Pushing past the maid, he bounded toward the inner chamber, where Caroline Sutherland lay motionless on the floor.

FOURTEEN

"Shut the door and stoke the fire," Thorne ordered Ashby over his shoulder. She hurried to obey. The storm had forced an unseasonable chill through a few hidden chinks in the old wattle-and-daub masonry, and Caroline badly needed warmth.

Kneeling over her, Thorne pressed two fingers to her golden throat, his shoulders sagging in relief as he found a faint pulse. Lifting Caroline, he watched the thick fringe of her lashes for any sign of movement, and carried her to the bed. Still warm from her sleep, the sheets gave off her scent as he laid her down. Thorne felt himself harden beneath his dressing gown.

Aye, no doubt even dead she'd arouse you. He yanked the bedclothes up to her neck. "Fetch her salts," he ordered Ashby, and was soon passing the vial beneath Caroline's nose.

Caroline winced, turning away from the caustic fumes with a cough. She opened bewildered eyes to Thorne's frown, then weakly waved a hand toward the bedside candle.

Next to it lay a folded piece of parchment, the sort upon which official messages were conveyed at any and all hours. Thorne picked it up with a sense of dread, smoothed out the folds, and read the message therein.

> *23 August 1728*
> *Mistress Horace Sutherland*
> *in care of The Right Honourable Lord Neville*
> *Wycliffe Hall, Northamptonshire*
>
> *Mistress Sutherland,*
> *I regret to inform you that your husband passed away this morning in the vicinity of six of the clock. The body is held herewith in custody of the London coroner, who upon your orders alone will proceed with a post-mortem to determine cause of death. Extenuating circumstances require your immediate return. I await your instructions.*
>
> *Yours in sympathy,*
> *Frederick Holstaad*
> *Holstaad, Camdenfield,*
> *and Griggs, Solicitors*

Minutes ticked by on an open watch locket on the table, accompanied by Ashby's muffled sobbing at the hearth. Caroline had lost consciousness again at sight of the paper in Thorne's hand.

"Ashby." He was taken aback by the huskiness of his voice. The maid stepped into the archway and dragged her sleeve across her dripping nose. "Mistress MacBride sleeps next to the larder," Thorne told her. "Go and knock sharply. Say that your mistress sleeps poorly and needs an herbal, but reveal no more. Do you understand?"

She did, she told him with a curtsey, and he soon heard the latch click.

He used the smelling salts again. Caroline came around immediately. Seeing him, she closed her eyes with a sigh, tears trickling from their corners.

Without a second thought, Thorne gently stemmed the warm flow with his fingers.

"I wondered what had become of you," said a cool voice behind him.

He jerked his hand back as if stung, then swept the bed hangings aside to meet the steady stare of his wife. Putting a finger to his lips, he rose and showed her the courier's message.

Gwynneth stifled a cry, then shook off Thorne's solicitous hand and took up his post at Caroline's bedside.

The chamber door opened. Ashby entered, Bridey behind her bearing a tray, and Elaine Combs bringing up the rear.

Thorne turned a withering look on Caroline's maid. "No doubt the rest of the household will be along shortly?"

Ashby shrank back, her sniffles resuming.

"Must you be so harsh, my lord?" Gwynneth arched her brow at him as she took the tray from Bridey. Thorne saw Elaine Combs' furtive glance from him to his wife as she turned to assist Ashby. Gwynneth sat down at bedside again to hold Caroline's hand and offer comforting words.

"My lady."

Gwynneth turned her cool gaze on him. "My lord?"

"As I suddenly find myself in a hen house, I shall take my leave. When you've done here, come to my chambers, please. I require a word with you."

* * *

An hour before dawn, Gwynneth crossed Thorne's threshold without a word, only gazing pointedly at his open windows and rubbing her arms.

"Sit by the fire, my lady, please." He closed the door and the sashes. Leaning against the mantel, he silently marveled that the young woman perched so primly on his settee had, scant hours ago, writhed with passion in his arms.

"Gwynneth, I'm aware you've lived more than half your life without servants."

"I *was* a servant," she said tartly. "A servant of God."

"Let's leave God out of this, shall we?" He saw her frown. "Domestic servants are a fickle lot," he went on. "Even the most loyal keep their eyes peeled and their ears to the ground. Any discord sensed between master and mistress will set tongues to wagging."

Gwynneth cocked a delicate eyebrow.

"When a wife chastises her husband in the presence of servants," Thorne explained patiently, "their respect for his authority is quite naturally diminished. And without his servants' respect, a man's household is soon in chaos."

"You refer to my chiding you for your harshness with Caroline's maid."

"I do indeed."

"I should hardly call it chastisement. Very well, then I apologize, but I've never heard you speak so to any of *your* servants."

"Gwynneth, I ordered the girl not to say a word of circumstances, only to bring the items I'd requested. Yet she returned with the cook--and your maid!"

"Combs happened to be in the larder. *Eating*, would you believe, at such an hour! No wonder she's plumped up since my first visit. Never mind, I've put a stop to it. But I've half a mind to tell Dame Carswell."

"No need, I'll do it myself," Thorne lied, knowing it would be the last straw. Combs' morning bouts with nausea seemed to have passed, but eventually--sooner than Thorne cared to admit even to himself, for some odd reason--the maid's predicament would be general knowledge. What then?

"My lord." Gwynneth's sharp tone told him she'd said it once already. "I am concerned for Caroline," she told him as his startled gaze met hers.

"So am I."

"Yes, I could see that you were. I must ask a favor of you."

Masking his trepidation, Thorne sat down beside her and dared take her hand. She didn't resist. "Ask away, then."

"I'd like you to accompany Caroline to London tomorrow."

Dumbfounded, Thorne could only stare at his wife.

"I can be of no use to her," Gwynneth explained hastily. "She will need assistance in legal matters, and a strong shoulder to lean upon when the situation is unbearable. You of all people would be of great help to her."

"For how long?" Thorne rasped, finding his voice.

Gwynneth shrugged. "However long she needs you."

He slowly shook his head. "My lady, another man in my position might wonder if you intend to rid yourself of a husband."

Gwynneth's chuckle sounded forced. "You've a droll sense of humor, my lord."

"Unfortunately it escapes me at the moment."

"Please, my lord, Caroline has been such a friend to me. Surely you can at least escort her home and help her with the property settlement!"

"Her husband's solicitor will manage the latter."

"But he won't give her moral support, and comfort, during what is certain to be a grievous and trying time."

"Your father would gladly go with her."

"Yes, all too gladly. Like as not, he'd get a bellyful of whiskey and propose to her!"

Thorne tossed her hand aside and launched himself from the settee. "God's blood," he groused, "has the woman no family?" He took a cigar from the drawer and lit it with a piece of kindling.

"You needn't swear...and must you smoke now?" Gwynneth wrinkled her nose. "The only family Caroline has is an estranged half-brother who lives somewhere in the countryside."

Thorne exhaled a cloud of blue. "Friends, then...has she no friends in London?"

"Yes." Grimacing, Gwynneth swatted at a puff of smoke. "But none educated in law, or whose title and connections could serve as well as yours. Horace's estate is very likely unstable at the moment."

Taking a long draw and tossing the cigar into the fire, Thorne regarded his wife with a mixture of annoyance and admiration. "Well, my lady, Mistress Sutherland certainly has an ally in you! So, you think I'm her only hope of survival? I wonder what *she'd* say to your lack of faith in her ability to manage her own affairs."

"She knows what I'm asking of you."

"Does she." Thorne took up the fire iron and stabbed at white-hot coals of applewood. "And what was her reaction to your magnanimous offer?"

"She seemed quite receptive."

"Yes, people in shock rarely protest." Thorne dropped the fire iron into its caddy and brushed off his hands. "And what gives you the notion her husband's estate is unstable? Have you taken up law instead of religious dogma?"

"Horace," Gwynneth said, her lip curling, "apparently spent a small fortune for his habit. I suppose I should count myself fortunate that smoking *tobacco* is *your* preferred vice. And gaming." Her eyes narrowed. "I believe your purse was fattened the night before last."

"*Our* purse."

"*Your* purse. I want none of it, for I'll not profit by the carelessness and stupidity of others. Keep it if you will."

"Gwynneth," Thorne said shortly, "I vowed just yesterday before God, a priest and an entire village to cherish you until death, but I did *not* vow to change my ways." Sitting down beside her again, he took her hand in his. "I warned you that perfection eludes me...but I also told you I'd strive to be the husband you deserve."

She eyed him intently. "Then you'll take Caroline to London?"

With a sigh of exasperation, he stood and held out a hand to this persistent woman who was now his wife for better or for worse. "I'll go," he groused, tipping her chin up as she came to her feet and looking her sternly in the eye. "But not for her. Only for you."

Looking pleased at last, Gwynneth nodded.

Thorne managed a crooked smile. "Well, my lady, we've just had our first row. I say we make a gesture of peace and good will. Something quite conventional, perhaps a kiss between husband and wife.

"Yes," she agreed readily. "'Tis a pleasant thing, kissing."

Despite her willingness, Thorne kissed her with caution, denying himself the slightest spark of passion for fear that any rekindled fires would only be doused again.

Her next words affirmed his wisdom. "I must go now and tell Caroline you're going to London with her," Gwynneth said, pulling away breathlessly. "She'll sleep all the better for it."

"Shall I wait up for you?" Thorne felt little real hope.

Gwynneth had the grace to blush. "I think I should stay what little time is left with Caroline.

Masking his disappointment with a smile, he nodded. "Then I'll see you come morn."

When Gwynneth had closed the door behind her, Thorne stared glumly at the high four-poster, the bed he'd thought would remain empty on his first night of newly wedded bliss. "Bloody hell," he muttered, flipping back the counterpane and sheet. He lay on the bed and stared at the oak-paneled ceiling.

Very well, Gwynneth. You stay with her tonight, and tomorrow I'll take up your charity. Thorne's mouth took a grim set. *And God help me, my lady...I only hope my charity proves as innocent as yours.*

FIFTEEN

London stewed in a late-summer heat wave, steam rising off the slop in the gutters, slack-tongued dogs lazing on shaded stoops, and wilted shopkeepers poking their heads through open doorways in hopes of a putrid breeze off the Thames. Exiting an establishment on Fleet Street, Thorne doffed his waistcoat and cast a hopeful eye toward the afternoon sky for any sign of an approaching storm. Giving that up, he sought out the Sutherland coach waiting among others at the curb, where Caroline's driver sat mopping his forehead, and her horses whipped their tails at the relentless, tormenting flies.

No wonder he hadn't missed the city.

Inside the coach, he wiped his sweating brow and loosened his neckcloth, then leaned back against the upholstered velvet. How he longed to be home. Barring that, he'd settle for a dunk in yonder horse trough and a pint of ale.

In the last seven hours, he had identified Horace's body at the mortuary, authorized the post-mortem, arranged the memorial and interment, and met with the man's solicitors to begin assessing real property and inventory. A thorough audit of all accounts was begun, its result to reveal the extent of damage inflicted by the funding of Horace's drug habit. Thorne absently patted his valise, the documents therein requiring only Caroline's signature to transfer assets once they were determined.

Secluded in her room, the new widow had vowed to refuse all callers and not to appear until the funeral. She'd said little throughout the close, sticky journey from Wycliffe yesterday, for the most part staring blindly through the coach window, which had suited Thorne fine.

And so he was surprised, after an interminable half-hour ride from Fleet Street to her mansion, to find her waiting for him. He saw strain about her eyes, shadows Ashby had tried to conceal with powder. Mourning hadn't affected her grooming, though, he noted wryly. With her hair sleekly coifed, her black moiré silk frock fresh and crisp, and black opals shining softly at her throat and earlobes, she seemed unaffected by the heat. He felt all the more disheveled by contrast.

After promising her a full account of the day's events, he returned to the guest room, where his needs, right down to the tankard of ale, had been faultlessly foreseen. A copper tub practically overflowed with sandalwood-scented water, a pressed white bath-sheet draped over its side. Should ale not be his preference, a glass and a crystal decanter of Scotch whiskey sat next to a linen cloth on the sideboard.

Sunk chin-deep in the bath water, Thorne drifted off to sleep. The maid's sharp rap on the door to inquire if all was well roused him a half-hour later.

In deference to his liking for a late-afternoon repast, Caroline served tea in the library, a cool enough room under its high molded-plaster medallion ceiling and the dense shade of an oak in the rear garden. Brandy was brought in as well, and Thorne watched Caroline pour two glasses. "Not particularly a habit of mine," she said, glancing at him from under long lashes. "But just now I could use some fortification."

He suppressed a smile. Neither was it her habit to justify her actions.

She seemed pleased at his assessment of the manner in which Horace's affairs were being handled, distressed when Thorne confirmed that accounts had suffered some tampering.

"Don't fret," he advised her gently, "at least, not 'til you've heard from Holstaad. The man is working tirelessly with the accounting house. Tomorrow you've the service to endure, 'tis more than enough to weigh on your mind just now."

She smiled then, a wistful, bearing-up gesture in which Thorne saw no trace of the woman who'd repeatedly held him hostage with little more than a glance, a word, or a languid movement. Instead he saw a woman who had sincerely loved her husband. For the first time since Gwynneth had begged him to come to London, he began to relax.

"You are an extraordinary man, my lord." Caroline's pensive smile lingered as she poured the tea.

"And why is that, Mistress Sutherland?"

"Not many men would have agreed to do as you've done for me. Or rather, for your wife." Handing over his cup, she eyed him keenly and, when he made no denial, sighed. "A poor state of affairs for your first days of marriage, isn't it?"

"My wife," Thorne said after sampling the tea, "has prodigious powers of persuasion."

"I tried, you know."

"Tried?"

Caroline put her cup aside and settled with feline grace into her chair. "I tried very hard to dissuade Gwynneth from asking such an outrageous favor of you."

"Did you."

"Yes, but she was quite determined to see it through. God knows I hadn't the strength to argue at the time."

"Meaning I should have?"

Caroline shrugged.

"I argued," Thorne admitted.

Eyes twinkling, Caroline bit her lip. "For how long?"

He could not keep a smile in check. "Half the night, it seemed."

Both of them laughed, then Thorne put a finger to his lips.

"Yes, you're right," Caroline said, sobering. "Talk will be all over town that the Widow Sutherland had a wonderful time with Neville of Wycliffe-"

"And did she?"

"-on the eve of her husband's burial," she finished.

Thorne froze, then shook his head. "God only knows what made me ask that. I am truly sorry, I must be half out of my mind."

Caroline waved a dismissive hand. "You probably *are* half out of your mind, with exhaustion and hunger. Excuse me, I'll see if supper can be served shortly. It might do us both good to retire early."

As she passed him, skirts rustling, Thorne impulsively caught her hand. She stopped, making no move to wrest it away, and looked down at him. "Say you forgive me," he said. "For my rudeness. Past and present."

The clock struck the hour, making the moment more awkward for him, especially as it wasn't until the last stroke died away that Caroline finally slid her long fingers out of his grasp, her shapely mouth wrapping words around a velvet voice.

"You are quite forgiven, my lord."

* * *

With the last of the mourners gone, Marsh cleared the cups and plates away. Thorne and Caroline lingered, seated near an open window, a small table between them.

"You should rest," he said. "It's been a full day for you, and not yet mid-afternoon."

Studying his face, Caroline waved her fan lazily to and fro, stirring little tendrils of hair on her forehead. "You won't rid yourself of me that easily. Besides, I've a reply for you."

"A reply? I don't recall asking-"

"You're wondering why I've produced no flood of tears, no histrionics."

God's bones, am I that transparent? "It has crossed my mind," he admitted.

"The tears will come." She shrugged. "And when they do, they shall pass unmarked."

"Meaning?"

"Meaning that I always weep alone."

"You wept in my arms Friday night," he countered before he could stop himself.

"I was inebriated, thanks to you. People in their cups will cry over anything."

"And were you inebriated in the wee hours of Sunday morn?"

Caroline's eyes narrowed. "I'd just had Holstaad's letter."

"Yes, and you were not alone. I was there. I wiped your tears with my own hand."

Stop. Stop now.

"Your point?" Her voice had grown dangerously soft.

"Only that your toughness, the self-reliance on which you seem to pride yourself, is a façade. A defense, if you will."

"Said by a man who has put up a defense or two himself."

Touché. Thorne tried not to glower.

"So," Caroline said, lightening her tone, "tomorrow, you'll return to your new bride."

"After you and I've met with your solicitors. And perhaps visited the cemetery afterward?"

She looked surprised, then touched. "I'd like that very much, thank you."

Marsh brought in brandy and a cache of cigars. "You may as well take them all," Caroline told Thorne, briefly catching her lip between her teeth before going on. "Horace never smoked...not cigars, at any rate," she amended with a grimace. "But he always kept a fresh supply for guests."

"Perhaps your half-brother will want them."

She nearly dropped her glass. "I never see the man," she said hastily. "We're not on such terms, and I seldom hear of his whereabouts or his welfare. Have you any siblings, Thorne?"

He suppressed a smile. "No. Though as a boy I often wished I had."

"Why?"

He shrugged. "The country is beautiful, but it can be lonely for a solitary child."

"Your mother died when you were young?"

"I was three. She contracted an ague in London. She was there with my father for the opening of Parliament. He never forgave himself. Buried her in the churchyard, and buried himself in business."

"You'd no nurse?"

Thorne shook his head. "My mother was my nurse--at her insistence, I'm told. Later I'd a tutor six mornings out of seven. Sundays and afternoons I roamed the manor or explored the house and generally got underfoot. The servants dared not complain-- save for one."

"Dame Carswell," Caroline guessed, and laughed at the confirmation in Thorne's rueful expression. "No friends, then, no visiting cousins?"

Thorne fell silent, debating a reply that could open old wounds. "There was one," he said at last. "A young girl who used to visit with her father--an earl or a viscount, some such title or other, a friend of my father's. At any rate, she was a good companion, and my age or thereabouts. Always willing to assist me in my pranks and share in my adventures."

"Don't you remember her name?"

He fought to keep the knot in his stomach from rising into his throat. "I could never forget it." *Try though I have.* " Madelena. 'Maddie' to her doting father, but she refused to answer when I addressed her so. Bade me call her 'Lena'. At the moment her surname escapes me."

"Were the two of you close?"

He shrugged, trying to appear casual. "As close as thirteen-year-olds can become during the course of two years. She and her father visited nearly every month for days at a time."

Caroline settled back in the stuffed brocade chair, her face in shadow and her ample décolletage in the direct light of the fire. Thorne wondered if the distraction was deliberate. He tried to focus on her face.

"So, Lena was your first love?"

"I suppose."

"But only because she was in the vicinity?"

Irritated with Caroline's persistence, Thorne still felt strangely compelled to confide in her now that she'd unlocked old memories. He drew a long breath, knowing he would have to steel himself in the end.

"Lena and I had each lost our mothers at a young age, and both our fathers grappled with grief and matters of business. They'd little time for us. She was without siblings, too. An extraordinary girl, not at all like the ones I'd seen in London, with their endless simpering and giggling and primping. She liked nothing more than to hitch up her skirts and ride hell-for-leather astride any one of the horses, the wilder the better. We'd mad races through the forests and meadows, sometimes nearly killing ourselves *and* our mounts." Thorne faltered, surprised to find a poignant smile forming on his lips. "Sometimes we'd sneak through the north end of the forest and make off with melons from a tenant's field--I could barely outrun Lena, she was every bit as reedy and leggy as I was at the time--then we'd chill the melons in the beck and bathe while we waited. She swam like a fish, and could hook them as well. Baited her own lines, too."

"Ah, the ultimate qualification for the perfect mate," Caroline said, chuckling.

"Let's say I thought it an admirable talent."

"And was this Lena pretty?"

"By whose standards?"

"Yours, of course."

He frowned. "Why is physical beauty such a point with women?"

"Because men have made it so."

"Very well then, I thought she was pretty. But my exposure to women was limited."

"Rubbish. There were maids aplenty in your house, and you've knocked about since. So, *was* she pretty?"

"Probably." Thorne frowned. "Has anyone ever told you you're quite bold?"

"Bold as brass." She shifted in her chair, allowing the firelight to reveal an impish smile on her lush lips.

"Well, whoever said it was bloody well on the mark."

Caroline scrunched up her perfect nose at him. "So, Lena visited regularly for two years. What happened then?"

Thorne took a fiery gulp of brandy and stared into his glass. "For a long while, I didn't know. They stopped coming. When I asked my father why, he put me off, something about a disagreement with Lena's father. I learned the truth much later. Lena died of malaria, on one of their more exotic travels."

"First your mother, and then Lena," Caroline said softly.

"Aye." Thorne downed the rest of his brandy, grateful for the fire in his throat and the warm coals in his belly. "From then on, my boyhood pursuits paled."

"A pity. But there'd been no romance, no hand-holding, that sort of thing, with Lena?"

"You *will* have it all, won't you? I kissed her twice. Once in the larder and again at Beck's Hollow, when she followed me up a tree--later I carved our initials inside a heart on the trunk of that old ash. We never embraced. Awkward business at that age. I did present her with a tiny vial of my father's sandalwood oil, it being the closest thing I could find to perfume, and though she laughed, I think she rather liked it."

"So, Lena was your first love as a youth...who was your first as an adult?"

He considered lying, but something about Caroline encouraged the bald truth no matter how unpleasant or difficult to tell. Her own candor, no doubt. But there was something more. He could not put his finger on it.

"I've never experienced an all-consuming passion for anyone," he admitted. "Flirtations, yes, but none that made me forget myself." He smiled grimly. "I observed early on that 'love' is ultimately self-destructive. I acquired my education in the art of seduction through a more readily available means...one on which many university men rely."

Caroline's mouth twitched. "I see. Then you were never in love."

"Alas," Thorne said, feigning a tragic expression, "I fear not.

"Until you met Gwynneth."

The few beats of silence he let go by were too many, he knew; she was clever, this woman, and he'd best not forget it. "Yes, until I met Gwynneth. Different for you, I suppose," he said evenly. "No doubt Horace was merely the last in a long line of lov-" He broke off. *Bloody hell.* He'd only meant to turn the tables, not to commit another unpardonable blunder. She did seem to bring out the worst in him. "Damn my churlishness," he muttered, his face growing warm. "I shan't blame you for giving me the boot."

"No," Caroline said quietly. "No, I think perhaps I dug too deeply. Besides, I'd like to talk about Horace, if you don't mind listening."

"Not at all," he assured her, relieved.

"Thank you." She sighed, sadly but without self-pity. "He was not my first husband. I was married once before, to a man who wooed me, showered me with gifts and, I'm sorry to say, impressed me with his title and connections"--she nodded as Thorne looked surprised--"until I was legally his. Then his true nature surfaced.

"Suffice it to say," she went on wryly, "that I endured a few bruises and sprains before I gathered my wits and fled. I supported myself and avoided him by assuming an alias and finding a situation in a tavern off Fleet Street--not the sort of establishment he frequented, or the kind of company he kept, but that's another matter. At any rate, Horace turned up frequently with his solicitor in that tavern, and a kinder man I'd never met. We wed soon after he helped me extricate myself from my sham of a marriage."

She stared into the fire, a vague smile on her exquisite face. "Horace was smitten with me, and seldom let me out of his sight. Together we feted London society. He often said that without me he could never have been the success he was. He lavished me with extravagant tokens of his affection...and was more than generous with affection itself."

There was no blush with that last revelation, Thorne noticed.

"It was only in this last year, the fourth of our marriage, that Horace became a different man--distant, short-tempered, and terribly apathetic. It frightened me," Caroline confessed. "It seemed my past had come back to haunt me, only in a different manner and with a different man.

"So you see, I've mourned for the past six months or more for the Horace I once knew, the Horace that loved me and made it obvious. And call it intuition or what you will, but at times I've the odd sense that my first husband might have had a hand in Horace's dependency."

"What do you mean?"

"Just...nothing. Nothing at all." She looked cornered, a bit wild-eyed. "You must never repeat what I've just said, not to anyone. My first husband is powerful, evil, and vicious when crossed. He has allies everywhere, those beholden to him for various reasons--henchmen, if you will. I must bind you to secrecy, Thorne, or I shall end up in the Thames, and that is no exaggeration. Please, give me your word on it."

"God's bones, who the devil is this blackguard?" Thorne rose, extending a hand to Caroline, which she readily took. "You won't tell me," he guessed, scowling.

She shook her head. "'Tis in both our best interests."

"Never mind, you've my oath." He gently squeezed her fingers. "I shan't breathe a word to a soul...no, not even to her," he said, reading the question on Caroline's face.

Tears welled in her eyes. She tried to wrest her hand from him.

I weep alone, she'd said. And no wonder, Thorne mused. Had she any choice, alone as she'd been in her troubles? Even Horace, her rescuer and protector, had become her abuser in the end.

"Let me go," she was murmuring.

"No. Not this time." Thorne gripped her hand, pulling steadily upward.

"Leave me!" came her choked whisper, but already he had her up out of the chair.

"I won't leave you. Look at me."

She jerked her head aside.

"*Look* at me, Caroline."

Slowly she obeyed, and in those dark wet orbs Thorne saw not only her pain, but also the shame she felt for letting it be seen.

"You've naught of which to be ashamed," he muttered fiercely. "And you'll *not* weep alone this time, by God. I won't let you."

A sob wrenched free from Caroline's lips; she bowed her head, and the dam broke.

Thorne slid an arm about her waist and gently pressed her cheek against his shoulder, feeling the warmth of his own breath as he sank his lips into her hair. Her sobs strengthened, her body trembling and convulsing in his grasp. His breathing grew uneven as he steadied her by clasping her more firmly against him.

But almost as suddenly as she'd lost it, Caroline regained her composure, pulling away from his embrace and accepting the handkerchief he offered her.

"Take a deep breath," he told her, his voice husky, "and let it out slowly." Silently he did the same, hoping to clear his head. Caroline took another long gulp of air as he guided her to the doorway.

"There, how do you feel?"

"Utterly exhausted," she confessed, and blew her nose.

"Good."

"What?" She scowled at him over the handkerchief.

"You'll sleep all the better for it." On the gallery outside her boudoir, he squeezed her hand and turned it loose. "Goodnight, Caroline."

"Goodnight, Thorne." The black pools of her eyes shimmered in the sconcelight. "You're a good friend."

As Gwynneth hoped I'd be. Inwardly he winced, wondering if he would prove as good a husband.

SIXTEEN

"Master's home," the cook told the steward.

"Aye," Arthur replied, tapping a keg of cider in the larder. "Saw his boots in the entry. He needs a manservant, they're a mess. Where's he gotten to?"

"Likely in his study, I've heard naught on the stairs." Bridey set a plate of oat cakes before Arthur as he sat down at the worktable, keeping hold of it until he looked up at her.

"Will you tell him?" she asked, her expression grim.

"'Tis not my concern, Bridey, or any of yours."

"Humph!" She snatched up the plate of cakes; it was only Arthur's quick reflexes that snagged one before she took them away.

He ate it hastily, rinsing it down with the cider, then rose, hat in hand. "You'll have a cartload of kitchen produce in this afternoon from Rawlings's fields."

"Humph!" she said again.

Arthur found the study door ajar.

"Good morning," Thorne said without turning from the window. "I see harvest has begun."

"Aye, started without you. Brought you some cider." Arthur came to stand beside him, where they watched the hypnotic yet jarring rhythm of the scythes the workers swung in the rippling field across the beck.

Thorne took the mug of cider. "Well, what dreadful news this time?"

The steward chuckled. "None, I'm happy to say. Harvest is coming along splendidly, the sheep and the dairy herd are quite healthy, and no one died while you were away."

"And Lady Neville...how fares she?"

"Well enough, I think."

"Meaning?"

Arthur looked slightly pained. "She's taken on her role as lady of the house with...enthusiasm."

"To her credit, I should hope?"

"To some dissatisfaction among the servants."

Thorne cocked an eyebrow. "And yourself?"

"'Tis naught to do with me," Arthur assured him hastily. "Carswell is the one to ask."

"I shall ask my wife, thank you. Is that all?"

Arthur softly cleared his throat. "You might want to know, they're saying in the village that there's a curse upon this house and its lands--aye, I know," he said, hearing Thorne swear quietly in exasperation. "'Twas bad enough the sheep were dying. Then came Barker's murder and Henry's trampling. Now 'tis said the old tower is haunted. Worse yet, word got 'round that Mister Sutherland died just hours after leaving here in a huff. You know how superstitious folk can-"

"Rubbish," Thorne interrupted, and started for door. "They need something to gossip about, is all. So, where to this morn?"

"All about. Fields and orchards."

Thorne nodded. "I'll find you later. Depending," he added under his breath, "on what I find here."

* * *

Just outside Gwynneth's chambers, Thorne heard the drone of her voice, but found the door bolted. A sharp rap brought an answer.

"Thorne!"

"My lady. I hope I'm not interrupting?"

"No, of course not." She clutched the door with one hand, the front edges of her wrapper with the other. "I've only just risen, so I'm a bit scattered. Come, sit." She led the way into her bedchamber and settled at her dressing table. "How was your journey?" She cast furtive glances at him in the mirror as she brushed her hair. "Did you ride all night? How fares Caroline?"

Thorne touched her shoulder. "One at a time, my lady. Might you welcome me home first with a kiss?"

Gwynneth offered her lips like an obedient child, looking surprised when her husband only grazed them. Surprise turned to astonishment as he took the brush from her and proceeded to run the boar bristles through her hair with smooth, practiced strokes.

"I heard your voice just before I knocked. Yet we're alone. Are you in the habit of talking to yourself?" His eyes followed hers to the dressing table, and he had his answer.

"I was saying my Rosary." She picked up the linked beads. "A long-standing habit. It gives me comfort and strength for the day ahead."

"Then I apologize for intruding. It hadn't occurred to me. I thought you were confiding your heart's secrets to your maid."

Their eyes met in the mirror. Gwynneth looked wary, watchful, as if gauging his mood. "Has Dame Carswell spoken to you?" she asked after a moment.

"No. Should she have?"

Gwynneth sighed and shook her head. "You won't believe what has happened, Thorne. I hardly know how to tell you, but you should have it from me. And you did broach the subject, after all."

"The subject?"

"My maid. Combs."

Thorne halted the brush in mid-stroke, his blood going cold. "What about her?"

"She...she...oh, I can hardly say the words...Thorne, the woman is with *child*!" Gwynneth's cheeks flamed.

Mechanically, he resumed brushing.

"Thorne, did you hear me?"

"Distinctly, my lady."

"Then you mustn't have understood. Combs is *unwed*."

"I quite understood."

Gwynneth stared incredulously at him in the mirror. "She's carrying a *bastard* in her belly...she is a *fornicator*!"

Gently, deliberately, Thorne laid the brush on the dressing table, and crossed to the fire.

"My lord?"

Hearing the rustle of her skirts as she rose, he stopped her in her tracks with a harsh demand. "What's to be her fate, then, my lady?"

"Why, I...I've already taken action. I dismissed her, of course. What would *you* have me do?"

Thorne's long black mane whipped through the air as he turned to confront Gwynneth.

She stumbled backward. "You *knew*!" she cried, her eyes widening. "You already knew! Did you know it when you appointed her my maid?"

"I did."

Gwynneth clutched the neck of her wrapper with white-knuckled fingers. "You chose her to attend *your own wife*? Sir, have you no *shame*?"

"When was she dismissed?"

"Yestereve, just before I retired. What of it?"

Thorne advanced, jaws clenched, blue eyes drilling into green. "Did she name the father?"

"Hobbs denies it!" Gwynneth scurried backward a few steps.

"Where is Carswell in all this?"

"She is with *me*." Gwynneth's voice trembled. "We dismissed Combs *together*. So, did I act through proper channels? Am I not permitted to dismiss a servant by my own power? Especially one who has committed such a grievous and wicked sin?"

"Her 'sin'," Thorne snapped, "was equally shared by another, almost certainly my stableman. Have you dismissed him as well, my lady? Are you a *fair* judge and executioner?"

Gwynneth gaped at him, then burst into tears.

Swearing through his teeth, Thorne paced before the fire, twice reaching to pull a handkerchief from his pocket, but each time finding compassion beyond him.

"How can you be so cold?" Gwynneth wailed. "I, a new bride in a new home, facing an abominable circumstance in your absence, acted in what I deemed a responsible manner--by denying an evil woman the privilege of serving in a God-fearing house!" Gwynneth stamped her foot, her usually pale face as florid as that of her father. "And I believe her allegations against Hobbs to be false. He is an *honorable* man!"

Thorne stopped his pacing to scowl at her. "Combs is no more evil than you or I, she's merely human--which is more than I can say for Carswell and her ilk. And do tell, my lady, how you know Hobbs is an honorable man."

"I've ridden with him. He kindly showed me some bridle paths in the forest."

"If you had only waited, I'd have gladly shown you whatever you wanted to see."

"I needed *something* to occupy my time," Gwynneth countered peevishly. "I'd no idea how long you might be away!"

She blanched at the ferocity of Thorne's glare.

"I was not away by choice, my lady--you dispatched me there! And I worked like a madman to get home to you as soon as possible."

Like sunlight bursting through clouds, Gwynneth's face transformed. "You were anxious to return?"

Thorne's scowl softened as he took Gwynneth gently by the shoulders. "My lady, have you forgotten how disturbed I was at the notion of leaving you so soon? You had to beg me to go."

She had the grace to look ashamed. "I did plead," she admitted, as he blotted her tears with his handkerchief. "How is Caroline?"

"She'll manage quite well, I think."

"You see?" Gwynneth's tone sounded oddly dull. "You *were* a help to her, as I knew you'd be." Thorne had slid his hands down her arms and was eyeing the ribbons of her wrapper; she clutched it to her neck again. "I must get dressed."

"You'll need help."

"No! No, please, I shall manage."

Thorne's voice turned dry. "I only meant I'd have Carswell send assistance directly, my lady."

Gwynneth blushed--embarrassed she'd mistaken his intention? Or ashamed he'd guessed her fears? Or both? God's blood, how long would this nonsense go on? The wave of despair that assailed Thorne threatened to suck him under.

"Thank you, my lord," Gwynneth was saying faintly.

"No trouble, my lady. Good day."

* * *

"But M'lord!" The housekeeper's voice trilled with indignation.

"Dame Carswell."

Her mouth snapped shut.

"I've high regard for your opinion, but in the end my own opinion will out. Always." Thorne arched his brow. "Need I say more?"

"No, M'lord." Her lips barely moved. "I quite understand."

"Tell me then, what other gainful employment Combs might find in this house. Something more reclusive."

"She might perhaps assist Markham, the seamstress. Her eyesight has grown poor."

"Can Combs sew?"

"She has mended altar cloths for St. Michael's," was the grudging reply.

"Is she Roman Catholic?" The inappropriateness of the question only struck Thorne as Carswell stared at him in startled silence.

"No, M'lord," she said, finding her voice. "Combs attends the manor church."

"No matter. She'll work topstairs with Markham, then. Tell Bridey to have her meals sent up."

The housekeeper stiffened--as if she wasn't already an utter stick already--and Thorne's left eyebrow took wing again. "Something else, Dame Carswell?"

"Only, M'lord, that the kitchen maids might balk at bringing her meals."

Thorne smacked his forehead. "What in God's name was I thinking? We gentlefolk mustn't feed such hardened criminals as she!" Giving up the charade, he scowled at the housekeeper. "Would you have the woman parade belowstairs thrice a day in her condition?"

The housekeeper's chin nearly thumped her chest. "Heavens, *no*, M'lord!"

"Then tell Combs of her change in situation. I trust you and Lady Neville did not turn her immediately out of the Hall yesterday?"

"No, M'lord." Dame Carswell looked both infuriated and relieved by the fact. "I shall inform her of your decision straightaway. Markham, too."

"It pleases me," Thorne said, his penetrating gaze fastened on the housekeeper, "to know I can depend upon you to carry out orders, and that I needn't concern myself further with the matter."

"I shall see to it immediately, M'lord."

Her deep curtsey gave him pause, not for the first time, to reflect that the more ruffled Dame Carswell's feelings, the lower she dipped her knee.

He nearly smiled. Perhaps someday her ass would hit the floor.

* * *

"Good day, Milady." Hobbs bowed with a flourish. "I thought nothing could surpass the beauty of this day. I see I was quite wrong."

Gwynneth blushed from the Kelly-green ruff of her riding frock to the roots of her hair. "You are very kind, Hobbs."

"Kindness has nothing to do with it." He boosted her into the saddle and watched her hook her right knee over the pommel, then secured the stirrup under the arch of her boot.

Arranging her skirts, Gwynneth glancing shyly at him from under the brim of her veiled riding bonnet, and blushed anew at the frank admiration in his gaze.

"Will you need a guide today, Milady? I should be honored to serve."

"Thank you, Hobbs, but not today."

"Off to meet his lordship, then." The words sounded more clipped than he'd intended.

Gwynneth gazed westward. "Perhaps later," she murmured. "Just now I want to ride to Beck's Hollow."

"Then take care on the ridge paths, Milady. Give Abigail her head. She's cautious and canny. Enjoy your ride!" He slapped Abigail lightly on the flank, then watched horse and rider trot down the curving drive toward the road.

The perfume of roses wafted his way on a western breeze. At times their scent actually quelled the stable odors of sweat, dung and leather--much like thoughts of Lady Neville quelled, for hours at a time, the stench of Hobbs' bitterness at his lot in life. With each passing day, he found himself glancing more frequently toward the Hall in hopes of seeing Thorne Neville's bride.

As Hobbs watched her ride Abigail down the Northampton road toward Beck's Hollow, an idea struck him. He was an excellent tracker, stealthy and keenly observant, on horseback as well as on foot.

He would follow her.

* * *

Descending the ridge, Gwynneth let Abigail pick her way at leisure over roots and stones, then brought the mare to an abrupt halt just inside the tree line.

Not more than a hundred yards to the west, Thorne Neville stood with his back to her. He appeared to be examining the trunk of an old ash tree.

Frowning, Gwynneth backed Abigail deeper into the woods and dismounted. First looping the reins over a decaying tree stump, she kept her eyes on the ground and headed for the boulder she and Thorne had used for their picnic. Pretending not to have spotted him, she doffed hat, boots, stockings and hairpins.

It was the sensual shake of her head that caught Thorne's eye. Watching her red-gold hair fan out over her back and shoulders, he stood rooted to the spot. Concealing himself was a lost option as Raven picked up Abigail's scent and neighed. Slowly, Gwynneth turned to meet her husband's gaze.

Thorne's mind raced as he strolled along the grassy bank. Reaching the boulder, he tried to sound casual. "Good morning, my lady. What brings you here?"

She hesitated. "A memory."

Thorne lowered his eyes. A memory had brought him here, too, though likely a very different one. He lifted Gwynneth's hand, fingered the rings on her limp fingers. "A pleasant memory, I hope?" He looked up to see her sulky expression.

"Quite pleasant--until you became angry with me."

"Angry?" Thorne frowned, perplexed.

"Yes. Just as you were that night in London, after you kissed me in the coach."

"You thought me angry?"

"Do not patronize me, my lord."

Thorne gazed into eyes as green as the moss on the boulder and as limpid as the beck waters, and shook his head. "If anger had any place in it, 'twas only at myself for nearly letting my feelings overcome my good sense."

"What feelings? Tell me. Don't leave me mystified again."

Thorne eyed her silently for a moment. "Very well, my lady, you asked, and I shall answer. I wanted you. I wanted you enough to take you there and then--in the carriage, and again on this very boulder."

Scarlet flooded Gwynneth's cheeks. She averted her eyes. "And what hindered you?" she asked, her voice barely audible.

"You were not mine for the taking," Thorne said quietly.

Her eyes darted to his, then away again. Watching the tip of her tongue slide nervously over her lower lip, Thorne recalled with jolting clarity how those lips had closed so innocently around his finger that day, how hotly that small pink tongue had branded him with a single, reflexive flick. His groin tightened.

Gwynneth's shoulders lifted with an indrawn breath. "And now..." she began, a tremor entering her voice. "Now that I *am* yours for the taking, do you want me still?"

Thorne nearly laughed aloud at the sweet absurdity of her question, his manhood already straining against the confines of his breeches. "Aye, my lady," he said huskily, brushing his lips over her ear again. "I want you still." Feeling her shiver, he pressed the small hand adorned with the Neville ancestral emerald to his heart. "Do you not feel my life's blood pounding through my veins, Gwynneth? 'Tis stirred to boiling, here...and here," he said, lowering her hand and laying it over his hardness. "You, and only you, my lady, have the power to cool it."

He saw her lips part, heard her sharp little intake of breath, and felt his turgid shaft extend even more beneath her fingers. "Aye," he said, his voice thickening, "feel what you've done to me, Lady Neville. Feel what you've done more times than you know."

Affixing wide eyes on their joined hands, Gwynneth gave the bulge beneath them a tentative squeeze.

Thorne groaned, hips flexing involuntarily. Nibbling the velvet shell of Gwynneth's ear, he felt her hand go still upon him, but sensed no objection. Slowly, he traced the tip of his tongue over the delicate whorls of her ear, then touched it to the small opening. Hearing her gasp, he turned her face toward him.

In the brief glance they exchanged just before she closed her eyes in surrender, Thorne saw something he had only suspected until now--Gwynneth Stowington Wycliffe was a passionate woman.

He had only to convince her.

She whimpered as he slanted his mouth over hers, her body rising like an ocean wave against the rigid dune of his shores. As she slid her arms about his neck, Thorne slowly went to his knees, bringing her down with him, and stretched out with her on the boulder. There was no place on earth, he realized, where he'd rather make Gwynneth his wife.

A fierce, sweet joy replaced the caution he'd felt of late toward his new bride. Reveling in her scent and threading his fingers through her silken hair, he tasted the dewy skin at her nape before delving again into the warm honey of her mouth. One hand cupping her head, he let the other roam the planes of her back and the dip of her waist before slipping it between them, where it moved to cover one full breast through her frock.

Gwynneth's earthy moan nearly unmanned him. As her lithe body began undulating against his own hard angles and sinew, Thorne gritted his teeth, feeling the moist precursor of a much-anticipated climax. It had been so long.

He slid her fock down one shoulder, tasted the curve between it and the slender column of her neck. Gwynneth threaded her fingers through his hair and gripped the back of his head--which swam with near delirioum as she guided it down, down to the damp valley between her breasts. Freeing one supple breast from her bodice, Thorne fastened his mouth over the puckered peak.

Gwynneth clutched him to her as he suckled, her breath coming in gasps, her back arching and hips writhing as she mutely begged for completion.

And this time, Thorne swore to himself, she would have it. As would he.

* * *

Halfway up the ridge, Tobias Hobbs dropped to his knees.

The lying little whore.

Moaning, he deliberately struck his forehead against the trunk of the oak beside him, but nothing could match the pain in his loins.

If the girl had said she was meeting her husband, he would never have followed her. The sight of Neville's hands on her, was more than he could bear. Why, why had she lied to him?

Leave! But he couldn't move. Oblivious to the ropy roots and broken acorns pressing through the worn knees of his buckskin breeches, he stayed, his burning eyes riveted on the lovers.

But when Neville freed the other breast from the girl's velvet bodice, and she herself cupped the firm, round, taut-tipped globe in her hand to offer it up to him, Hobbs could watch no longer. Gripping rough bark, he arose with a groan, then realigned the throbbing appendage in his breeches and forced his trembling limbs to climb to where Bartholomew waited high on the ridge. After three curse-filled attempts to mount the big gelding, who shied away from his master's unusual clumsiness, Hobbs heaved himself onto the saddle and gave the horse a desperate kick.

* * *

"My lord!" Thrusting Thorne away, Gwynneth clutched her wadded bodice to her breasts and catapulted to a sitting position.

Groaning, he rolled onto his back and shielded his eyes against the sunlight. "God have mercy, what is it now?"

"I heard something." Ignoring his swearing, Gwynneth searched the wooded ridge with her eyes.

"The horses, no doubt."

"No. 'Twas a person, I'm certain!" She yanked her bodice up over her bosom and shoulders.

With a sigh, Thorne rose on an elbow and perused the ridge, but even Gwynneth saw nothing but the dense foliage of late summer. Only birdsong and babbling beck intruded on the peaceful stillness.

Hiding her flaming cheeks behind a curtain of hair, Gwynneth donned her stockings and boots, keeping her skirts down as much as possible. "I must get back to the Hall." For what, she couldn't have said. She hoped he wouldn't ask.

"I'll ride with you."

Gwynneth darted her eyes at her husband. Seeing his pleasant expression, she nearly sighed with relief. How close she had come to trading her soul for the temptations of carnal pleasure! But he had caught her off-guard today. Next time she would be prepared.

She gave no thought to Thorne's escorting her up the stairs when they returned, or even to his opening her chamber door for her. Realization did not strike until the bolt slid into the jamb and she heard his long, easy stride behind her.

Dear God. So *that* was the reason for his patience--he'd only the ride home to endure! Now he would exact his due.

She whirled about, hoping she'd only imagined his step, but there he was--and behind him, the closed portal, bolted tight against prying eyes.

Denying the thrill of fear that surged through her veins, Gwynneth stalked into her bedchamber and tossed her bonnet onto the bed.

But when Thorne sauntered to the curtained archway, her resolve wavered. No pirate could have looked more dangerously dashing--black hair falling over his unlaced shirt, razor stubble shadowing his jaw and upper lip, his eyes as blue as the Caribbean in a painting she'd once seen, and bathing her with a heat to rival that of its tropics. All he needed was a cutlass between those impossibly white teeth.

She shivered as she imagined him slicing off her buttons with one precise flick of his gleaming blade. Her buttons! Holy Mary, she'd never manage the tiny loops at her back alone.

She tried to sound firm. "My lord, I require a maid."

"Yes, and we shall find one presently."

Her heartbeat quickened at the smooth readiness of his reply. "I...I meant just now." She swallowed hard. "Can you please have Carswell send someone up?"

Smiling, Thorne shook his head. "I shall be your maid this afternoon." He cocked an eyebrow at her soft gasp, adding in a low drawl, "I assure you, my lady, I can get you out of that riding frock faster than any maid from here to London."

Gwynneth's mouth went dry.

Abandoning the archway, her husband approached with the feral grace of a stalking panther, his eyes burning hotter into hers with each step. Paralyzed at first, Gwynneth sprang into motion--only to be reminded the bed was just behind her.

She veered to her right and positioned herself between the hearth and the fireside chairs.

Thorne halted, his smile going awry. "Am I reduced to chasing my own wife about her chambers?"

"Only if you move, sir," was her breathless quip.

Slowly, he shook his head. "What's your game, my lady? Not an hour ago you were sighing with pleasure in my arms, yet now you play the nervous maiden. Hot one minute, cold the next." His smile faded. "Tell me whom I married, Lady Neville...friend or foe?"

* * *

Thorne's heart sank as Gwynneth pressed her mouth into a thin line. He had asked rhetorically, never dreaming she harbored some grudge. It appeared he would have to risk her ire, perhaps even another scene, to discover its nature.

But she beat him to the draw. "First, you tell *me*," she said, a tremor in her voice even as she narrowed her eyes, "how long you have been in love with *Caroline Sutherland*."

SEVENTEEN

If Thorne had caught Gwynneth off-guard at Beck's Hollow, she had just paid him back in full. And then some.

"Sit down," he said.

"I'd rather not."

"Please."

Elevating her chin, Gwynneth perched stiffly on the edge of a chair.

Thorne took the other seat. "Forgive me if I seem stunned, but I'm having difficulty digesting the bizarre notion that I could be 'in love' with...your friend." He'd hoped the name would roll off his tongue.

"I used to think," Gwynneth said in a brittle voice, "that you disliked Caroline immensely, that you could scarcely bear to be in the same room. I never knew the reason, yet somehow I couldn't bring myself to ask. But then, on our wedding night-"

Thorne started to speak, but she held up a hand.

"To find you *sitting on the edge of her bed*, bent over her so solicitously, with your *hand in her hair*--oh yes, I saw that! I had pulled the curtain aside to see her face. I only wanted to know what was the matter, no one had bothered to inform me. Why was I not summoned? And lest you protest your chivalry was mere pity, I am quite aware that you also brought Caroline home from the *public alehouse* the night before--or rather early that morn!"

"Aye, and 'twas pity on that occasion as well."

"Then why say nothing of it? Did you also carry her to her chambers?"

"'Twas either that or drag her. She was in no condition to walk, I assure you. The maid let us in, and I promptly took my leave. As for our wedding night--if one can term it such," Thorne added wryly, "I can only plead a long-standing state of affairs, that being a household with no mistress. I'm accustomed to taking charge, my lady, to doing what must be done. I apologize for my negligence. Rest assured in future I shall use better sense."

Gwynneth folded her arms. "And why did you not mention escorting Caroline home?"

"Damnation, Gwynneth, 'twas our wedding day. Why spoil it?"

She gasped. "And now you utter a curse to mark the occasion?"

Biting off another curse, Thorne shot out of his seat. Gwynneth's surfacing tears failed to move him, because in all of this recrimination, one glaring detail had been overlooked.

She shrank back as he bent over and caged her in the chair with his sinewy arms.

"If you thought I was 'in love' with your friend, why the deuce did you then beg me, badger me, indeed leave me *bloody little choice* but to accompany her to London and *stay in her house*? And worse yet, commission me to *assuage her grief*? Did you not fear that under the guise of consolation I might seduce her? Were you testing my fidelity already?"

"Aye," Gwynneth cried, braving his fierce perusal, "but I had to know!" The tears spilled over. "I was tormented by the thought that you were secretly enamored of Caroline, that you married me only for convenience!"

"I put up a bloody good fight at the prospect of leaving you, did I not?"

"Aye, for the sake of appearances!"

Shaking his head, Thorne crouched down in front of Gwynneth and covered her clenched hands in one of his. "If you had only asked," he chided, "I would have told you."

She eyed him hopefully. "Told me..."

"That you were far off the mark to think I harbored any such sentiment for Caroline Sutherland." There, he'd said her name, and with a fair amount of ease. Gently brushing Gwynneth's tears away with a thumb, he was glad to see no flinching. "I'll admit to pitying the woman--until I saw her in action in London," he amended dryly.

"She will survive, then?"

Thorne smiled. "She will thrive, my lady. Mistress Sutherland is a force with which to be reckoned. Her agents and solicitors have their hands full."

"Then I can cease fretting. On *all* accounts."

"You can, indeed," Thorne said, rising to his feet. "Now, I'll send someone up to assist." He silenced Gwynneth's polite protest by playfully pressing a finger to her lips. Then, still feeling the warmth of those lips as he reached the door, he stopped to give her a long look. "After we've dined this eve, I shall attend you myself."

Did he only imagine the fleeting panic in her expression? Her reply sounded quite poised.

"As you wish, my lord."

* * *

"I'm going home." Radleigh tore a morsel of roast pheasant off the bone and chewed it with obvious relish. "I'd hardly be worth my salt as lord of the manor if I didn't oversee at least a portion of my harvest. After that, I've business in London."

Gwynneth cast an alarmed glance at Thorne. "Do stay on with us, Father. You've a capable steward to manage all your affairs at Radleigh Hall, and an agent in London."

"Radleigh," Thorne spoke up hastily, "I'd be glad to have you on harvest rounds."

Radleigh drained his tankard, then shook his head. "My thanks, Neville, but I'm a man who yearns to touch his mother-soil from time to time. Surely you understand."

Thorne nodded, ignoring Gwynneth's glare. "You'll depart soon, then?"

"In a day or two."

"I'll have your coach readied. But we'll expect you to return as soon as possible."

Nodding his thanks, Radleigh said gruffly, "So, Daughter, will you be sorry to see me go?"

"'Tis not your going that concerns me," Gwynneth snapped. "'Tis the doubtful prospect of your returning once you've indulged in London's night life again."

The bushy eyebrows collided. "Neville, this chit wants taking down a peg, don't you think?" Seeing Thorne's ill-concealed smile, Radleigh scowled at Gwynneth.

"You'll think twice before giving your *husband* such sauce! Take no nonsense from this sharp-tongued wench, Thorne. Exact all due respect and devotion."

Still looking at his father-in-law, but feeling Gwynneth's wary gaze upon his own countenance, Thorne smiled wryly. "Your advice is well-taken, sir. I've every intention of following it."

* * *

Leaving the men to their cigars and brandy in the library, Gwynneth fled to her chambers and found a filled tub awaiting her. Struggling yet again with the fastenings at her back, she heard a knock at the door and froze, until a woman's voice said that Combs was indisposed and Dame Carswell had sent her instead.

"Byrnes" proved eager to please, but clumsy. "Do hurry," Gwynneth fretted. "I must be out of the bath and into bed as soon as possible."

Rejecting Byrnes' awkward attempts to wield the sponge, she instructed her to turn back the bedcovers instead. Hence it was only the maid who saw the curtain move in the archway, and who stared wide-eyed at Thorne as he slipped through the velvet panels.

Putting a finger to his lips, he held the curtain aside. Byrnes shot a quick glance at her mistress, now immersed to the neck in her bath, before curtseying to the master and making a silent exit.

Lazy flames licked the applewood logs in the grate, their rosy light tinting Gwynneth's creamy skin and burnishing her upswept hair with copper. Thorne watched her in silence, reluctant to disturb the enchanting scene, but as she moved to rise from the sudsy water, he spoke up quietly. "Before you stand, my lady, be aware I stand behind you."

She gasped, gripping the tub's edge.

Thorne approached slowly. "Good evening, my lady."

He saw her glance downward, where her body was well hidden by the thick suds, before she met his eyes. "How do you do, my lord?"

The greeting was so breezy and unexpected it was all Thorne could do to keep a straight face. "I do quite well, thank you."

"And my father...inebriated as usual? I trust he's safely retired for the night?"

"He is indeed, and has left me quite at odds for a way to fill my leisure time this evening."

Gwynneth's gaze lowered to Thorne's lips. "'Tis a shame, my lord."

"Perhaps you could propose some task for me."

"I shall think on it."

Thorne drew off his waistcoat and laid it over a chair, then knelt beside the tub.

"You might hold my bath sheet up for me," Gwynneth said hastily.

"You're a fast thinker, my lady. Fast on your feet. I'd like to see how fast." Thorne dipped a hand into the water, and grinned at Gwynneth's alarmed expression. Still she didn't budge. "Very well then," he said, lazily swirling the suds. "We'll watch your metamorphosis instead."

"Into what?" she asked warily.

"A prune, if I know my physiology. It should be quite a sight."

"My lord!" she exclaimed indignantly, and lobbed the waterlogged sponge at his head. Laughing, Thorne dodged and then retrieved it. Gwynneth actually giggled as he sauntered toward her holding the dripping sponge away from his shirt and breeches.

"Carswell will have your hide, young lady, for water-spotting her floors."

"Her master will protect-" Gwynneth broke off with a gasp as Thorne fired the heavy sponge into the tub, spraying her squarely in the face. "Oh, you wretched man!" she sputtered. She shot up from the bath in an avalanche of suds and water, then shrieked as she remembered her nakedness.

"Ssshh." Thorne's eyes twinkled as Gwynneth plummeted into the water again. "You'll have the servants all a-twitter, my lady." Fetching the bath sheet, he gently blotted her face, then spread the snow-white cloth in wordless invitation for her to rise again.

She eyed him dubiously. "You won't look."

"Won't I?"

"My lord! Promise you won't look."

He grinned, shaking his head. "Sorry, but a white prune is a curiosity I cannot resist."

Gwynneth shot to her feet and grabbed the sheet, her body a blur.

No matter. Time and patience were Thorne's allies tonight. Chuckling, he steadied her as she stepped from the tub, then stayed her as she made to retreat. "I'll attend you," he said, his gaze holding hers. "We agreed, remember?"

She nodded, surprising him, then closed her eyes while he gently blotted her shoulders and back dry.

She stiffened when he untied the ribbon in her hair, and as he threaded his fingers through the silky length to smooth out any tangles, she clutched the corners of the bath sheet securely at her throat. Smiling behind her, Thorne knelt on the rug. Barely grazing her bottom, he resumed his blotting motions on her thighs, her knees, calves, ankles and feet.

Rising, he slowly ran his hands over the sheet, up the entire length of Gwynneth's body, his palms just skimming the fullness of her breasts. With deft but gentle fingers, he traced the curve of her shoulder and neck, then cupped the back of her head.

She opened her eyes.

Thorne had to swallow hard at sight of the sultry light in those green orbs, as they moved to his throat and then to his lips.

"You're dry, Milady," he said, his voice husky. "What would your maid do next?"

Blushing, Gwynneth gazed up at him through golden eyelashes. "She would fetch my shift. There, on the bed."

Without taking his eyes off his wife, Thorne picked up the length of embroidered lawn and held it over her head. The bath sheet dropped to her ankles just as the shift billowed downward, briefly exposing her thighs and calves. She started to tie the satin ribbons at the yoke, but stopped as Thorne shook his head. He took his time tying them for her, letting his fingers brush often against her skin. He noted the erratic pulse in her throat, the spreading stain in her cheeks. The seemingly innocent brush of his knuckles over one thinly covered nipple elicited a gasp, and through the diaphanous material he watched the tiny bud harden to an unmistakable point. Gwynneth's eyes swept downward.

The moment Thorne let go the ribbon, she turned to the sideboard, her shift fluttering about her bare ankles, and proceeded to pour a brandy. Accepting the glass, Thorne cocked an eyebrow. "'Tis a fortunate maid I am, to receive such service from my mistress."

Gwynneth smiled, apparently more comfortable at play, and settled herself regally in a chair at the hearth. Bowing, Thorne did the same. "Forgive me for neglecting your bath water, Milady, but I should like to drink my brandy first." He raised his glass in salute.

Gwynneth shook her head. "Beware, Maid," she deadpanned. "You risk your situation for such impertinence, and for your lack of ambition. I'd better see a curtsey in place of that bow you just gave me."

Thorne quaffed the fiery liquid, thumped the glass down and sprang from his chair to kneel at her feet. "Please, Milady, don't give me the sack!"

Gwynneth giggled, then resumed a prim expression, her eyes twinkling. "If you truly desire to keep your situation, you must prove your worth."

"Whatever Milady asks shall be done."

"Then I should like to be kissed."

Ignoring the quickening in his loins, Thorne frowned and sat back on his heels. "Strange behavior for the mistress--requesting a kiss from the maid? Milady, I am shocked indeed!"

Gwynneth laughed softly in spite of her blush. "Thorne, for shame! You mustn't tease about such perversity."

Smiling, he came to his feet. "I'm quite ready and willing to follow Milady's orders, but if it worries you to kiss this maid, I hereby resign my situation and *reassign* myself to the office of your husband--in hopes that you'll give him similar orders."

Gwynneth tilted her head, her smile turning coy. "Aye, I should much rather be kissed by my husband."

"Then kissed you shall be." He leaned over her.

"Wait," she whispered, her breath warm and promisingly moist on his face.

He nuzzled the tender skin beneath her jaw. "Aye, love, what is it?"

"First you must tell me something."

"Anything." He drew back, only to see her eyes narrow ominously upon his.

"I want to know," she said in a cutting tone, "why the Combs slut has yet to leave this house."

EIGHTEEN

Stunned, Thorne stared at his wife--this woman who had in an instant transformed from Eve to malevolent serpent. "*Jesu*," he whispered, then swore aloud in a choked voice, "*Jesu Christi!*"

He shoved himself away by the arms of the chair and strode to the window, where he threw the sashes wide and filled his lungs with soggy air. The baying of a hound and the chirping of late-summer insects filled the silence until he trusted himself to speak again. "You've a way of broad-siding a man, my lady. Hereafter, I shall beware your playful moods."

"My moods aside," Gwynneth retorted, "I've a right to know why that woman is still here. And I've a right to hear it without your blasphemy."

Thorne turned to face her. "I'm not in the habit of explaining myself, my language, or my actions," he said with a scowl, "but I'll make a partial exception this time. I've reassigned Combs topstairs. Essentially banned her, if you will, to the servants' quarters. Even her meals will be taken there." His gaze turned withering. "She'll not be available to cause embarrassment. For anyone."

Gwynneth shot up from her seat and squared her shoulders. "Just a few days ago, you accused me of undermining your authority over the servants. Now you've done the same. I dismissed the girl, and you revoked that dismissal with no warning."

"There is a phrase used in the practice of law, known as 'pre-existent condition'--an apt enough term in Combs' case," Thorne said sharply. "Meaning to say, my lady, that Combs' dilemma was brought to my attention *before* you joined this household, and that I'd arranged acceptable circumstances for all involved."

"Why keep her?" Gwynneth's lip curled. "She's of no use in her condition."

"I beg to differ. Our seamstress is losing her eyesight. She's taken Combs on, and as all the sewing is done topstairs, neither you nor anyone else will be burdened with the growing evidence of her pregnancy."

"Thorne!"

"What, I've shocked you again? No more than you've shocked me, my lady, by your lack of pity."

"Pity?" Gwynneth planted her hands on her hips and leaned forward. "*Pity* is what I feel when I see a child foraging for scraps of food in the back alleys of London. *Pity* is what I feel when I see Arthur coming from the forest with a slain buck over his shoulders. Pity is *not*," she said with a toss of her head, "what I feel for a woman who raises her skirts at the first sign of attention from a man!"

She stepped back quickly as Thorne advanced on her. "And is pity what you feel," he said in a voice cold with fury, "when you consider the future of the innocent child she carries? Must that child be starving in the streets before your *pity* is 'roused?"

Gwynneth's eyes filled with tears, whether for the child or herself, Thorne had no inkling. Nor did he care.

"Do you," he pressed, "foresee any quality of life for the child, with no father to claim it, if its mother is thrown out on the streets to make a living in whatever way she can?"

"She's already proven herself a whore...let her make her *living* as such!"

No sooner were the words out than Gwynneth seemed to realize she'd gone too far. Scooting behind the nearest chair, she raised an arm to shield herself from what she saw in Thorne's eyes, and in doing so was transformed again, this time from shrew to little girl.

The effect disoriented Thorne; he was a gun on the verge of firing and suddenly emptied of powder. Never had he felt such anger, especially at a woman; its venom made his stomach roil. He backed up a few steps, then turned and strode away--from her, from the very air she breathed. In a haze of conflicting emotions, he heard the chamber door, and vaguely wondered whether it was he or or his wife who'd slammed it behind him.

* * *

Elaine Combs froze, book in hand, and held her breath as she listened for something to follow the crash overhead. Fairly certain it had come from Lady Neville's chambers, she wondered if the new bride was ill. *No business of mine*, she reminded herself grimly. *Marginally ailing or at death's door, she will tolerate my presence no more.*

No sense in fretting, Elaine told herself. She had a roof over her head, a full belly and a bed in which to sleep--and all because of *him*. She'd known that immediately from the snide expression on Dame Carswell's face when the woman came to interrupt her packing. Elaine's heart had soared for one joyful moment before she realized that a situation topstairs would provide only an occasional glimpse of Wycliffe Hall's master.

She returned the book to its shelf and took another down, then paused again as she heard a heavy tread in the hall. It neared the library. Elaine's heart began to race.

The candle! She flew across the room to a chair near the dying fire, licked her fingers and snuffed the wick, then looked desperately for a place to hide. She had no time. She threw herself into the chair, gathered her garments up, and tucked her feet beneath her so that nothing of her would be visible from the hall. Heart thumping wildly, she clutched the book to her chest like a shield.

The latch clicked. A hinge squeaked as one of the double doors opened, then closed again.

She waited for a footfall. None came. Perhaps the intruder hadn't entered. Perhaps he or she had gone on after all. Yet no steps sounded in the hall. She was about to peer around the high-backed chair when, somewhere in the darkness behind her, a man quietly cleared his throat.

Elaine's heart pounded in her ears. Squeezing her eyes shut, she fought off a hysterical giggle at the notion she was better hidden if unable to see.

Footsteps commenced. Measured, unhurried, they approached and passed her chair. The stir of air wafted a familiar scent her way. Fear and excitement surged through her veins; still she kept her eyes shut tight. She heard the fire iron scrape the hearth, wood fall heavily onto the grate. Unless the intruder was blind, he would see her as soon as he turned around.

The fire iron dropped into its stand. Silk whispered on silk, no doubt a sleeve brushing against a garment. And then--utter silence. She had been discovered. She held her breath, sure she would either faint or explode.

"Are you sleeping?"

She'd have known that low, rich tone anywhere. She peeped through the slits of her eyes at the voice's owner. Little more than a silhouette against the reviving flames, his face was all but concealed, whereas she knew hers was clearly visible.

"I...I hope I didn't frighten you, M'lord," was all she could think to say, blinking rapidly as she opened her eyes.

"'Twould appear quite the reverse, Combs."

He moved away. Seizing the opportunity to rouse her paralyzed limbs and reclaim some dignity, Elaine untwisted herself and stood, then hastily smoothed her woolen cloak over her shift and wrapper.

He'd gone to a corner of the room. He stood in the dimness with his back to her, perhaps having forgotten her presence already. She set the book silently on the table and made ready to leave.

"Stay where you are." He hadn't so much as cocked his head.

Lacing her fingers in front of her and waiting with outward calm, she heard glass clink from the corner. He obviously knew his way in the dark.

He strolled nearer the fire, a bottle glinting dark-red in one hand and an empty glass in the other. He filled it before glancing her way.

Painfully aware of the strange sight she presented--nightcap askew, hair tumbling to her waist, and a width of worn muslin sagging below the hem of her gray cloak--she nonetheless stood quietly poised while he tossed back the contents of his glass in one greedy swallow. He appeared still dressed for the evening meal, long past, his waitcoast however missing and his sleeves rolled to the elbows of his waterspotted shirt.

She had no time to ponder that oddity, instead giving a violent start as he banged his glass down on the table and turned brooding eyes upon her.

"I...I am sorry for trespassing, M'lord."

"Is that what you call it."

She hoped he didn't hear her gulp. "It won't happen again, M'lord."

His gaze swept her from head to toe. "So, what have you been up to? Why the nightclothes under your cloak?" His eyes narrowed. "You've been outdoors at this hour?"

Elaine stiffened. "You're suggesting I've been to see Hobbs, M'lord?"

His silence was answer enough.

"I have not seen the man since the day he spurned me," she said firmly. "I only dressed so because..." Her words faded into embarrassed silence.

"You knew the room would be cold," Lord Neville ventured, "that the fire would soon be out." Eyeing her intently, he awaited her nod, then spoke again. "You've come here before?"

"Yes, M'lord."

"Once, twice?"

She steeled herself. "Many times, M'lord."

He filled his glass again. "And what do you read here?"

Elaine searched his face for some sign of disapproval, but found none. "All manner of things, M'lord. There are so many wonderful volumes...but of course you know precisely what is on these shelves. How stupid of me."

Thorne's mouth turned up at one corner. "I'm surprised I haven't discovered you here before."

Elaine almost smiled. "You very nearly have, sir, more than once."

"Do you come every night?"

She shook her head. "I used to, before you returned from university."

"I see. Then I spoiled it for you."

"Oh, no, M'lord!" Mortified, she pressed a hand to her chest. "I meant no such thing...I only meant it was easier..."

"Go on."

"'Twas easier to steal away here then, knowing no one would be about because no one used the room then, not even during the day, though I cleaned it regularly, which is how I came to be so interested in its contents, as I've always loved to read." She drew a breath. Good heavens, he must think her absolutely giddy. At least his brooding frown had disappeared, indeed his eyes seemed to twinkle in the firelight.

"So," he said, amusement in his voice, "my return forced you to play a game of cat and mouse to do your reading."

"Yes," Elaine admitted ruefully. "But I am less clever than I supposed, since tonight I thought..." Encouraged by Lord Neville's amiable expression, she went on. "I thought that you and her ladyship had retired for the night, that I was quite safe in coming."

He smiled briefly, but the light had gone out of his eyes. "Aye, well, I hadn't planned to be in this room at all tonight." Abruptly he quaffed the contents of his glass, then glanced at the mantel clock. "You'd better get some rest, Combs, and not only for yourself." He glanced at her midsection.

Elaine struggled to keep tears at bay; sometimes she wished he were less kind. "If you please, M'lord, I must say something before I go."

"Can it wait?" He was filling his glass again.

"No, M'lord, it cannot. Nor should it," she added firmly, seeing his cocked eyebrow.

"Say it, then, quickly."

"I should like to express my gratitude for the situation you've given me, M'lord. Your kindness is unique among the nobility. I am indebted to you." She dropped a curtsey at his inquiring look.

"You've definite opinions, then, Combs, in regard to nobility."

"M'lord?"

"You say my kindness is unique. You've been treated less kindly by someone of my circumstance?"

Elaine hesitated. "I would rather not say, M'lord."

He studied her face. "Well, you needn't feel indebted to me. Your new situation wasn't especially created, nor am I particularly kind. The seamstress was in need. However, if the work in some way lessens your burdens just now, I'm glad for it."

She nodded, grasping the diplomacy behind his denial. "Thank you, M'lord. May I pose one question?" At his silence, she boldly continued. "How does her ladyship feel about my staying on?"

Was there a flicker of ire in that inscrutable expression? If so, it fled as quickly as it appeared.

"I've explained it to Lady Neville," he said, "as I did to you just now. She sees the wisdom of my decision and will abide by it."

Elaine curtsied again. "Good night, M'lord." Approaching the library doors, she halted, arrested by his voice--and its studied indifference.

"Combs, a good seamstress should value her fingers, and not be chilling them to the bone over a book every night."

Her heart sank. "Yes, M'lord." She reached for the door handle.

"Henceforward," he said brusquely, "regardless of my whereabouts, a fire shall burn here throughout the evening."

* * *

"To what do I owe the pleasure, Milady?"

Gwynneth shaded her eyes. "Have you seen his lordship this morning?"

"Aye, Milady. He rode early this morning to meet Pennington for rounds. Shall I fetch him for you?"

"No! No, never mind. Thank you, Hobbs."

He bowed as she turned to go.

"Will you be riding today, Milady?"

"Perhaps," Gwynneth called back, already preoccupied keeping her skirts above the muck as she wended her way back through the stable yard.

Hobbs watched her until it occurred to him that someone at the Hall could be watching him, then turned back to his chores. He couldn't imagine why Neville would abandon his wife's bed so early without a word.

Sickening jealousy stabbed Hobbs through as he recalled their rendezvous yesterday at the Hollow. Bloody exhibitionists, the both of them, and her as much a whore as any other wench, for all her convent upbringing.

Swearing softly, he kicked a tabby mouser out of his path, then spat in the direction of Raven's stall.

* * *

"Lady Neville awaits your lordship in the library with a caller," Jennings announced, looking unusually tight-lipped. "Lord Whittingham, M'lord."

Stunned, Thorne stared at his head-footman. He hadn't heard seen the earl, whose birth surname he'd yet to recall, for nearly a decade.

He found Gwynneth looking repulsed but fascinated as she listened to their caller regale her with God-knew-what sort of tale. Hargrove, that was it--Lionel Stanford Hargrove, eleventh Earl of Whittingham. Leaning forward in his seat, the man all but devoured Gwynneth with his beady black eyes. At least fifty years old, he had the same thick mustache and head of hair as always, apparently scorning wigs as Thorne did, but vain enough to dye his hair. A scar Thorne didn't remember marred the swarthy brow.

"Young Neville," Lord Whittingham chortled, rising to greet Thorne. "To think, you're lord and master of the Hall now! Do you remember me?"

"Aye, my lord." Thorne bowed. "But you'll forgive me for remembering your daughter more clearly."

He felt, rather than saw, Gwynneth's sudden alertness.

The earl sobered. "Aye, you and my Maddie were good friends indeed."

The two men waited to sit while Gwynneth rang for an early tea. "So, my lord, what brings you our way after all this time?" Thorne wanted to know.

Lord Whittingham looked Gwynneth over as they all sat down. "In truth, I had hoped to see Radleigh."

"My father? You are acquainted?"

"Indeed we are." The earl's voice sounded smooth as silk.

"What a shame, he left Wycliffe Hall just this morn-" she began, but Thorne interrupted.

"What business, if I might inquire, have you with Radleigh, sir?"

Lord Whittingham's eyes sidled to Gwynneth and back to Thorne. "No doubt Lady Neville has better things to do. My business would bore her insufferably. Shall we speak in your father's...in your study?"

Gwynneth pursed her lips and abruptly stood up from her chair. "You are quite right, my lord," she said, far too sweetly in Thorne's estimation, as the earl scrambled to his feet and Thorne rose as well. "I've business of my own to attend, therefore you gentlemen please remain where you are."

Thorne suppressed a smile, but Lord Whittingham was all teeth, flourishes, and bows. "I am most pleased, dear lady, to have made your acquaintance."

"Lovely young woman," he said to Thorne when the doors had shut, smiling after Gwynneth like a sleek, fat cat contemplating a delectable mouse. He seemed oblivious of Thorne's frown as they reclaimed their seats. "Now then. When you learn the nature of my business with Radleigh, you'll appreciate my wish to exclude your wife."

Thorne waited in silence.

Lord Whittingham harrumphed. "Well, in short, Radleigh is heavily indebted to me. Over the last two years, I've carried his gaming losses in London, with little reimbursement. Then there was the recent matter of his daughter's dow-"

"What does he owe?"

Lord Whittingham's brow rose at Thorne's interruption. "He owes much. The debt has compounded, especially since his dau-"

"*How* much?"

The earl looked taken aback. "I say, sir, you are quite as direct as your father was. Perhaps more so."

Getting only Thorne's steady gaze for a response, he gave up his rhetoric. "Radleigh's debt is nearly ten thousand pounds, including what he borrowed to refinance his daughter's dowry."

Thorne bit off an exclamation. "At what rate of interest?"

"One quarter per annum."

"You've notes for these debts?"

"Of course. They're in a strongbox in my coach, at your front door. With your indulgence, I'll fetch them."

"Please do." Thorne kept his expression bland, realizing that even as a child he had instinctively disliked Lord Whittingham. No wonder Robert Neville had broken contact with the man. "Jennings will show you into my study."

Lord Whittingham returned in no time and presented the notes. Thorne's heart sank as he recognized Radleigh's bold signature.

Signing his own bank note for the full amount, Thorne sensed Lord Whittingham's glee behind the man's half-closed eyelids.

"You are a dutiful son-in-law," the earl fawned in an oily voice. "Your father, God rest his soul, would be quite proud of the way in which you handle-"

"If I may presume to offer advice to an elder and superior, my lord."

Lord Whittingham's mouth went slack at yet a second interruption.

"Think twice," Thorne said curtly, "before backing Radleigh's wagers again. Whiskey often blurs his mental faculties, so I ask you, in honor of the friendship you and my father once shared, to use your own good judgment where my father-in-law's may be lacking. I'd consider it a personal favor to myself and my family," he added, tasting gall with the statement.

Lord Whittingham only smiled, his eyes smug. He was making no promises.

"Jennings," Thorne said flatly, "will show you out."

* * *

Gwynneth poked her head inside the study door. "He's gone?"

"Aye," Thorne replied without a glance. "And good riddance."

"Amen to that." She closed the door and sat down. "What is this business concerning my father?"

"Venture a guess." Thorne opened the drawer where the cigars were kept.

"My lord, please," Gwynneth said, with a pained look at the cheroot in his hand.

Slowly, deliberately, Thorne replaced it in the box, and watched Gwynneth's gaze sidle to the fire.

"Father owes this man money, doesn't he?" She braved her husband's eyes. "How much?"

"The amount matters little. Then you knew he was indebted?"

Gwynneth's hands fidgeted in her lap. "He mentioned he owed money to a certain earl."

"Did your father reveal this before you and I were betrothed?"

Her eyes fell. "My lord, I-"

"Enough said. The matter is finished."

"You paid him off, didn't you?" Her pained gaze met her husband's. "You reimbursed him for Father's debts."

"I want no one in this family beholden to a man such as Lord Whittingham," Thorne said shortly, closing the ledger. "I consider it money well spent."

"Thank you," Gwynneth murmured.

He gave her a brief nod.

"Would you ride with me?" she surprised him by asking. "There's some time before your tea." She scowled. "'Twas wicked of me, but I sent it back to the kitchen! That man vexed me sorely."

Thorne laughed, the first time that day. His wife was a little spitfire when it suited her. All well and good for people like the earl, but not for those such as Elaine Combs-- or himself, for that matter. "No, but thank you." He hoped he sounded regretful. "I've business delayed by our visitor."

"Never mind," Gwynneth said lightly. "I am learning the paths in the forest."

"Have Hobbs send a groom with you. I won't have you riding alone."

She nodded, looking anxious to please. "As you wish, my lord."

* * *

Just past the hour of eight that evening, feminine laughter trilled from the direction of the great hall. Less than a minute later, a maid burst into the library.

"She's here, M'lord."

"None the worse for her disappearance, I hope?" Thorne kept his eyes on his reading.

"A bit mussed is all, sir. She says she'll join you in the dining room."

"Thank you, O'Connor."

He finished the periodical and glanced at the clock, then went unhurriedly to the dining room.

Already seated, Gwynneth seemed to accept his perfunctory nod as sufficient greeting. No one spoke while the meal was served, but when Susan returned to the kitchen, Gwynneth broke the silence.

"My lord, I must apologize for being away much longer than I'd realized."

Thorne tore some meat from the leg of mutton.

"Hobbs took me over some of your lands," Gwynneth went on after a hasty sip of spring water. "This is an impressive estate, to be sure."

Thorne swallowed, his eyes piercing hers. "I am gratified, my lady, to know you are so pleased with my assets."

Looking stung, she opened her mouth to protest, but her husband held up a hand.

He drank his wine to the last drop before setting the goblet down with quiet deliberation. His eyes probed hers. "For four hours, my stableman showed you about my lands?"

Gwynneth's bow-shaped mouth pouted. "You know how I love to ride. I simply lost track of the time, with the sun hidden behind the clouds and all. But you mustn't blame Hobbs. 'Twas I who insisted we keep on."

She flinched as Thorne, still eyeing her, grimly speared a roasted onion and held it on the tip of his knife. "Just yesterday," he reminded her in a low voice, "I expressed my displeasure at the notion of Hobbs showing you about."

"You didn't expressly forbid it. And none of your stable grooms is acquainted with the property. Not one could have shown me the old cottage ruins to the west, or that odd circle of stones in the clearing. Hobbs even told me some of the manor's history! You never mentioned his mother had served here."

Thorne frowned. "Hobbs' mother...a servant here?"

"Some twenty years ago, he says. You didn't know?"

"I don't recall. I was quite young, of course. Arthur would know."

How neatly Gwynneth had sidestepped the issue at hand--one of her father's traits. Thorne let it pass. At least she would never ride with Hobbs again.

* * *

- 113 -

Shortly before ten of the clock, Thorne closed his book and left the library after watching a maid stoke the fire according to the instructions he'd given Carswell.

He told himself he was restless, that his leaving the room had nothing to with Elaine Combs' imminent arrival.

He saw no sign of Gwynneth. Skulked off to her chambers, no doubt, thinking early-to-bed would ensure her safety from him. Thorne smiled grimly to himself, aware that some husbands would quickly rid a wife of that notion.

He paced the length of the great hall, debating whether to venture out or stay in. Duncan's wouldn't do, at least not by himself, and if he only wanted spirits, there were plenty here. Arthur was likely at home and abed.

It galled Thorne to realize how friendless he was in his own home. At Oxford he'd had no shortage of peers, and amusements to share with them. He'd forgotten what a solitary existence he'd led before university, even in this house full of people. Arthur seemed his only companion. Thorne had imagined Gwynneth his new bosom friend and ally, had dreamt of the two of them closing themselves off from the rest of the world each evening in their big, soft bed.

It has only been a week, he chided himself. But far more than a week's worth of his patience had been tested, and the prospect of more such trials discouraged him.

London, said a voice in his head.

But he'd just been there. Still, he hadn't visited any friends, Townsend in particular.

Aye, and Townsend lives not far from another place of which you are fond. Thorne could almost hear softspoken Gaelic at his ear, feel the silkly auburn tresses trailing over his body.

Best not pursue that avenue. But a certain appendage was pursuing it relentlessly. He glanced around the hall to make certain he was alone. A wife should ensure against such embarrassment and all temptation.

It has only been a week!

With a sigh of disgust, he decided on a long, brisk walk in the night air. Only later did he ask himself why he'd gone out of his way to pass the library doors.

* * *

Elaine glanced at the clock on the library mantel. Nearly eleven. A hearty fire burned in the grate, as promised. No longer needing a cloak and doubtful she'd have company, she wore only her muslin wrapper over her shift.

Still, she'd yet to lose herself in her book, listening instead for any noise outside the doors. She told herself she simply wanted to avoid detection, but her unpretentious nature was ready with the truth. *You await the sound of his step.*

She gave a start as footsteps approached in the hall. Pulse racing, she glued her eyes to the text in front of her, seeing none of it.

The footsteps reached the library doors--and then faded away in the opposite direction.

She let out her breath.

Perhaps it was Dame Carswell, making last rounds. But no, the housekeeper always retired before ten of the clock; otherwise, late-night visits to the library would be impossible. And that was not the tread of a petite woman.

But what difference did it make who it was?

Elaine knew full well what difference it made--and her fluttering heart proved it.

* * *

Wide awake in her curtained bed, Gwynneth lay listening for any sound that might announce Thorne's entrance.

Minutes passed, stretching into a half-hour. Only nature's noise intruded, and against those Gwynneth closed the sashes. Back in bed, her eyes shut at last, she prayed for the night to pass in peace. When next she opened them, dawn had arrived--time to say her Rosary.

NINETEEN

"Shall we go?" Gwynneth asked, as Thorne handed back the embossed invitation.

He smiled at the spark in her eyes. Was she thinking, as he was, that a weeklong house party in the Townsend household might work some magic to breach the impasse they'd reached? "Will you send the Townsends our acceptance?"

"I'll do it this minute." And she was out the door, almost running to her day room.

For the next few days, Thorne saw little of Gwynneth as she stayed in her chambers with Byrnes, choosing and packing a wardrobe for the journey to London. He spent his time making rounds to the manor farms and orchards and working in his study. On free afternoons, he hunted or fished, sometimes with Arthur. In the evenings, he walked outdoors or practiced billiards--and for increasingly longer periods of time, read in the library, where he found Combs' quiet presence both agitating and soothing.

* * *

With departure arranged for the following Friday morning, Thorne met Arthur at Duncan's Thursday evening for a pint of ale. "What is it?" he asked, seeing the steward's long face.

"A rumor." Arthur's face turned ruddy. "Though I don't think it's gone beyond the stables."

"Out with it, then."

Arthur took a deep breath and began. "'Tis said you and Lady Neville have yet...to share a bed." He flushed crimson but kept his gaze steady. "True or not, this drivel must stop before it reaches the village. I spoke to Hobbs this morning, warned him to keep his grooms' tongues in their heads and to guard his own."

Thorne nodded grimly. "You'll excuse me, then. I've a chambermaid to send packing with little more than a hard lesson on gossip. All the better for her next employer."

* * *

Drifting off to sleep, Gwynneth jolted awake.

Byrnes had opened her draperies and sashes earlier, hoping a breeze might stir the muggy chamber air. For some reason the night sounds seemed suddenly menacing. Wide-eyed, Gwynneth wondered if someone had just walked on her grave.

Talking herself out of the odd sensation, she turned over--and to her horror made out a dark shape on her bed not more than a foot away.

A scream tore loose from her throat, then died as a hand clapped gently but firmly over her mouth.

"Be still."

The low voice sent chills down her spine. The shape rose slightly, silhouetting a head and broad shoulders. Gwynneth caught a whiff of sandalwood; her heart went from racing to thudding. *Time to pay the piper.*

The hand lifted from her mouth.

"Sorry, I didn't mean to frighten you." Thorne's nearly invisible features made it difficult to gauge his mood or his intentions. "I thought you to be asleep."

"Why-" Gwynneth began.

"I've come to share the marriage bed," he replied, answering the question she couldn't ask.

"I...I see." But she didn't see, nor did she want to see. She lay on her side, facing him, her heart pounding now because without seeing or touching him, she knew he was naked.

"Goodnight," he murmured. Gwynneth jumped as if shot.

Bewildered, she lay still at least a half-hour before turning over. In another hour or so, she drifted off to sleep, reassured for the moment by the deep, regular breathing from the other side of her bed.

* * *

Hearing the lark's song, Thorne opened his eyes to what appeared a wide ribbon of spun-gold on the pillow. He lowered his gaze. The eastern light stealing through the open casements outlined the dips and swells of his wife's body and rendered her gauzy shift all but invisible. His manhood, already at half-mast upon awakening, took a startling leap.

Moving his head closer to hers on the pillow, he traced a fingertip around the rim of her ear before gently suckling its velvety lobe.

Gwynneth arched her back, and as Thorne slid his hand slowly but surely around her and over one breast, her gasp ended any pretense of slumber. Her heart raced beneath his hand, her nipple blooming into his palm like a flower under the sun's warmth.

Testing the supple heaviness of that firm, round globe with a slow, kneading motion, Thorne heard Gwynneth's breathing quicken. The gentle roll of her stiffened peak between his finger and thumb produced an all-out moan.

Gritting his teeth, he arched his throbbing erection away from her, wanting nothing more than to nestle it up against the cleft in her bottom-cheeks. He found some relief in rolling onto his stomach and pressing himself into the down-filled mattress. Easing his wife's shoulder toward him, he looked at her face, and smiled to see how tightly she had shut her eyes.

He slipped the shift off her shoulder and bared a breast, then proceeded to lave the milky-white mound and its flushed aureole with his tongue. He avoided the pebble-hard peak at the center until Gwynneth arched her back in wanton invitation.

He gladly obliged.

She cried out softly as Thorne began suckling, her body soon undulating in the ancient, instinctive rhythm of coupling. Her hands came to life, burrowing into his black locks and pressing him harder to her breast.

A fierce joy washed over him, drowning his misgivings. His wife did want his touch, the touch that only he could give her. Through the thin layer of her shift, he caressed her bottom. Her increased gyration encouraged him to ease her over onto her back. He slid the hem of her shift up to her thighs.

Gwynneth gasped, her eyes flying open.

Thorne knew what she saw--the passion and purpose burning in his eyes, the sensuality lifting his smile at one corner. He concealed none of it now that she'd responded to him with the zeal of a Pagan priestess enrapt in Spring rites.

"Let me make love to you, Gwynneth," he murmured, the words thick with desire.

She closed her eyes again, this time in surrender, breathing fast and hard as he stroked her quivering thighs. Thorne groaned his appreciation as she opened them, and grazed the silky curls there with his fingertips. The slick dew he encountered sent a wave of triumphant lust surging through his blood and into through his loins. His wife, his lady, was ready for him. With gentle but eager fingers, he parted her damp curls and stroked the velvety lips at her slit.

Gwynneth let go a moan so earthy that Thorne could hardly believe it came from her. He moaned in turn, descending on her as she lifted her head and parting her lips with gratifying ease. He delved deep into the honeypot of her mouth, his fingers smoothing her juices around her swelling feminine folds, his thumb stroking the jutting little bud there with a rhythm that soon had her whimpering into his mouth.

In return, Gwynneth suckled his tongue with a fervor that nearly unmanned him. God only knew what that sweet mouth might do to other parts of his body! She gripped his upper arms and then buried her hands in his hair again, all the while panting for air, yet unwilling to give up his kiss.

But as her mouth began to relax under his, Thorne knew her mind was turning inward, focusing on the building inferno at her core. Maintaining his seductive rhythm against her weeping flesh, he shifted his mouth to a nipple and suckled with gentle greed. Watching her fetching face contort, he knew that she was deaf to her own sharp cries, aware only of the explosion of heat between her thighs. As Gwynneth's body bathed his fingers in her hot lava, it was all he could do not to move down between her satin limbs and lap the warm flow into his mouth.

But he knew he must enter her now, while she was in the throes of climax and slick with her own juices, to minimize her pain.

He slipped a finger inside her. Feeling the incredible pull and pulse of hot, virginal walls, he nearly lost control. He grasped his rampant rigidity firmly beneath its head until the danger passed. Slowly, steadily, and with the aid of Gwynneth's profuse nectar, he entered her deliciously tight passage, pausing only when he reached the thin barrier of her maidenhead. Taking a deep breath, he prepared to breach that barrier and bury his fleshy sword to the hilt in his wife's slippery, simmering sheath.

But his pause made Gwynneth, initially lost in the shattering aftermath of her first climax, aware of the alien thickness penetrating her body. Suddenly she was pushing Thorne's chest and pounding his shoulders, her eyes wide with panic.

Quickly he retracted from the euphoric promise of her taut, wet grip, and held himself immobile above her, gazing tenderly at her despite his driving need. "Don't be afraid, sweeting," he said huskily. "'Twill pain only for a moment, then never again. Henceforward you'll feeling only pleasure in our coupling, I promise...pleasure beyond reckoning."

Her alarmed expression told him she'd heard nothing after the word "pain." He'd no way of knowing the word "pleasure" would alarm her more.

"No...*no*, I will *not*!" Heaving her hands against his chest, she pushed him aside, then untangled herself and her shift from the sheets, kicking Thorne in the process, and catapulted herself from the bed. "Th-this is wrong!" she sputtered. "I won't let you *do* this to me!"

"Do what?" he countered, stung and bewildered. "What in God's name have I done but drive you to the heights of pleasure?"

A desperate, almost hunted look entered her eyes. She flung her wrapper around her shoulders and clutched the edges tightly together. "Aye...and now you propose to tear me apart with that...that...*weapon* you carry between your legs!"

"No, my lady...God, no." Thorne rolled off the bed, slung on his dressing gown and wrapped it around him. "Listen to me," he said, reaching for her.

She jumped away. "Don't! Do not touch me!"

Thorne stopped short, dismayed.

"You should go now," Gwynneth whispered, her expression filled with anguish. "*Please* go!"

"No, my lady. We cannot leave it like this." Unspent passion and strained patience made his voice hoarse. "Tell me what I've done wrong."

"Everything!" she cried. "You cannot handle a woman so, 'tis a *sin*!"

Thorne dared a step forward; Gwynneth stepped back. "Who told you that?" he demanded in quiet fury.

"I simply know it, I needn't be told." Gwynneth wrung her hands. "My lord, do you not understand? I should burn in hell for such wicked pleasure!"

"Oh, my lady." Thorne shook his head, desperation rising. "Someone has trifled with your mind, misled you. There is nothing wrong or sinful about what we have done-"

Gwynneth shrieked, covering her face with her hands.

"What we have done," Thorne said, conviction strengthening his voice, "is *sanctified*, my lady--by the very Sacrament of Marriage."

"It *cannot* be!" She dragged her hands down her face and gazed at him with haunted eyes. "Oh dear *God*, you surely cannot expect this of me!" she wailed, and turned her back to Thorne.

She was actually addressing the Deity, he realized. In two strides he had her by the arm and turned her about. "Someone has *told* you 'tis wrong--who? Tell me who it was."

"Let go of me!" she screeched. "Oh, I *knew* I should have taken the vows! A pox on my father! I shall hate you, Thorne Neville, *hate you always* if you force me to do your will!"

Thorne released her like a shot and stepped back, feeling the blood drain from his face. "I have never forced a woman, nor shall I now. And as for 'the vows', my lady-- you took the vows of marriage. You promised yourself to me before of God and all present. You heard the words of the Gospel. 'They two shall be in one flesh.' How long am I to wait to claim my marital rights, Lady Neville? Even your priest will tell you 'tis your duty to beget an heir!"

Thorne advanced, but stopped short of touching her. "Counfound it all, Gwynneth, you *enjoyed* my making love to you, and you *lie* if you deny it!"

"Do *not*," she shrilled, backing away, "make me feel any more despicable than I already feel...aye, I was weak, as weak as Eve. I *did* feel pleasure at your hands, and it was *wicked* of me!" Her eyes took on a fanatic gleam. "'Tis one thing to submit to a man to beget an heir, 'tis quite another to take *pleasure* from such depravity! And *you*, Thorne Neville, are a practiced Epicurean, else you would not be so adept at coaxing forth the demon of lust in my body--one I hardly knew was there 'til your skill exposed it!" She swiped at the tears spilling from her eyes. "I shall ask forgiveness in confession, and double my penance, for 'tis my belief that God intended me for a higher purpose than groveling and thrashing about like a *bitch in heat*!"

Thorne stared at her in stunned silence, pain and despair vying with impotent anger. He found his voice. "We're to depart for London in less than two hours, my lady. However, I imagine your 'higher purpose' will not allow you to be trapped in a coach with a libertine such as myself for a day's journey. You may go alone, then, and relay my regrets."

"*You* go! They are *your* friends!"

Belting his dressing gown, Thorne gave her a curt nod. "Very well, I shall. I leave you to your Rosary, my lady. Good day."

* * *

Thorne slipped into his wife's deserted chambers and crossed to the unmade bed, where he took a small bone-handled dagger from his waistcoat pocket. First pricking a finger with quick precision, he bled several drops onto the bottom sheet, wiped his finger clean, and flipped the counterpane over the stain.

Below stairs, he told the housekeeper to dismiss the chambermaid. "Tomorrow," he cautioned. "Not a word to the wench until then." *Time enough to spread word that the master and mistress have shared a bed,* he thought with savage bitterness.

He bade farewell only to Jennings, helped the coachman with his bags, and was soon on his way down the Northampton road. He was determined not to look back, certain he'd find no one watching at any rate. But as the coach rounded the last bend, just before the forest obstructed his view, he could no longer resist.

She was there. Alone at a third-floor window, her mobcap and apron bright white in the sunshine, she stood watching the coach, one hand on her growing belly.

TWENTY

"What, he's business in London again?"

Hidden behind the half-open larder door, Elaine Combs stopped chewing a mouthful of cheese and perked up her ears.

"Aye, so I hear," Hillary answered Susan. "Sudden-like. Her ladyship stayed behind. Doesn't want to attend the house party alone."

"She's a timid one, all right."

"Not *that* timid," Hillary countered, a sly note entering her voice.

Susan gasped. "Do ye mean to say...?"

"Aye!"

Elaine stood stock-still, the empty cheese-crock forgotten in her hand.

"The chambermaid says the master's bed was untouched," Hillary went on in a lower voice, "and the mistress' mussed *quite* more than usual--with color on the sheets!"

Susan's reply was lost, drowned out by the crash of crockery on the larder floor.

* * *

Arriving at the Townsend estate near Chigwell outside London, the welcome Thorne received from Richard Townsend and his parents, Sir Dennis and Lady Townsend, nearly restored his good spirits. Gwynneth's Aunt Evelyn was ill and needed her, he lied with all the regret he could muster. Richard Townsend escorted him to his appointed guestroom.

"You can rest before tea, nothing doing 'til then at any rate," Townsend assured him. "Only half the guests have arrived. Better to take cover at any rate, my little sister has been to and fro on the lookout for you all morning. I think she was just as anxious for a look at her competition. Now she'll have you all to herself, God help you."

Thorne laughed. It felt wonderful to laugh; how long had it been? The thought of tall, reedy, sixteen-year-old Bernice, with her violet-blue eyes and fiery curls and the spattering of freckles across her impertinent nose, flying about the house as she waited for him to appear, was enough to rid him of any bad humor. "Bernie" had insisted since the age of twelve that she would marry him.

Escorted to a room he'd never seen, Thorne inwardly winced at the overtly feminine boudoir apparently chosen with his new bride in mind, though the view from the windows drew him as always. Eyeing the wide, silver ribbon of river wending through the valley, he heard a knock at the door.

"Sorry to disturb," Townsend said when Thorne opened the door, "but tea's delayed an hour to accommodate late arrivals. Can you spare a moment?" At Thorne's nod, he ducked in with a quick backward glance. "Bernie," he said with a comical grimace.

Smiling, Thorne closed the door, and the two men sat down.

"Neville, old chap, you look dreadful."

"Tact was never your strong suit."

"Sorry. You don't look well. What's the matter? Is it Lady Neville? Has she had another, ah, spell?"

Thorne knew he'd paused too long when he saw the purposeful gleam in Townsend's eyes; now there was no escape.

"Shall I pour a dram?" Townsend rose without waiting for a reply and went to the sideboard.

Thorne took the bottle he handed over and poured for them both. "Gwynneth is well. I must plead exhaustion for my pallor, what with the harvest and a new wife as well."

Townsend smiled. "Ah, so your bride *is* at fault. We should all be so fortunate to suffer such exhaustion."

Both men jumped at a loud rapping on the door.

"Richard? I know you're in there! Mama says to come at once, she needs you to move the settee in the Grindall's room. Come, now!"

Footsteps sped from the door and faded away.

Townsend stood up and drained his glass, then made a mocking bow in the direction of the door. "I'm off," he said wryly, "at little Miss Hooligan's command." He looked heartened by Thorne's smile. "'Til tea, then."

At the door he turned a cryptic look on Thorne. Sounding oddly apologetic, he said, "Get some rest, man. You're going to need it."

* * *

Tea, the eastern ritual Thorne had borrowed from the Townsend family, was served in the parlor for the women, while in the gaming room the men discovered heartier fare of meat pies and honey cakes with a token pot of tea and several pitchers of ale.

"I say 'tis time the Drakes handed over the reins in Amersham to new blood," Sir Dennis grumbled to Sir Kenneth Clifton. "What say you, Neville?"

Thorne eyed his ill-placed ball on the billiards table. "There will be a movement for it in Parliament, sir, but I doubt it will come to much. Not this session, at any rate." He angled his stick and shot off the bank, missing the leather pocket by a hare.

"Egad, Neville." Townsend approached the table with a look of relish. "If you'd only wagered your horse on this game."

Thorne eyed him skeptically. "I can't imagine why you'd want that devil of a beast back in your stables. We've yet to explain his attack on the groom."

"Yet you ride him still," Townsend countered. "What say we have him on the table before the week is out?

"I'll consider it." As his friend blasted a ball into a pocket, Thorne added with a wry grin, "But it won't be a billiards table."

* * *

"And tell the ladies, Bernice, what you are learning," Lady Townsend coaxed.

"The piano-forte," her daughter grumbled, frowning over her tangled embroidery.

"Perhaps you could play us a piece from your lessons?"

"I'd rather not, Mama." Bernice looked up with an angelic smile, only to see an expression that would have plastered most young ladies to the wall.

With a sigh and a roll of her eyes, she walked to the stool, spread her skirts and sat down, then straightened her back and poised her hands over the keys.

* * *

"What in bloody hell is that?" Sir Dennis barked, in the gaming room.

"Need you ask?" Townsend quipped. Thorne grinned.

"My cousin, no doubt," guessed a young man named Granville. "Poor Mistress Dearbourne shall have a heart attack straightaway, though how she can be shocked at anything Bernie does..." He shook his head.

"Rather unorthodox," agreed Mister Dearbourne, "A lively tune, though."

Sir Dennis chortled.

To no one's apparent surprise, the piece ended as abruptly as it had begun.

* * *

Entering the dining room early, Thorne found most of the male guests standing around with apéritifs in hand. At a table set to the side of the main table, Bernice Townsend sat laughing and arguing with three male cousins.

Thorne winked at Townsend, then approached the table and bowed as the gangly redhead looked up to see him for the first time since his arrival.

"Thorne!" Springing up so fast that Granville and the other boys nearly fell over themselves getting to their feet, Bernice embraced Thorne, something she'd never dare do if her mother were watching. "Oh, you look lovely!" she cried, stepping back to admire him at arm's length.

Returning the compliment with a laugh, Thorne saw Townsend shake his head and smile.

"But what is this I hear," Thorne murmured near Bernice's ear, "of your expulsion from not one, but *two,* young ladies' schools?"

Bernice glared at her brother, then gazed sweetly back at Thorne. "I should much rather be at home, where a 'young lady' can climb trees and ride and fish. Stitching and weaving are impossible, I shall have a seamstress when I am married. Besides, Papa insists Richard's old tutor is sufficient for my education."

"Nothing to do with keeping an eye on you," Thorne teased.

Behind Bernice, one of the cousins yanked on her skirt, and without batting an eye she swung her heel backward into his shin. "Papa," she allowed over the groans and titters behind her, "is a sly old fox."

The sound of feminine voices and laughter swelled from the hallway, and everyone turned as a bevy of women led by Lady Townsend poured through the doorway in a billowing sea of silks and laces.

One head rose above the others, its stunning face framed in coils of in raven-black hair. As Thorne froze, struggling to make sense of what he was seeing, the head turned, and his gaze locked on the dark, sultry eyes of Caroline Sutherland.

* * *

As his fog cleared, Thorne found himself seated for supper next to Caroline.

"No doubt you're thinking," she said below the hubbub of conversation, "that I should be at home. Mourning."

He glanced down at her gray silk frock, an apparent compromise with the customary black, its modest fichu a hopeless strategy to hide her voluptuousness.

"If I'm thinking at all," he said, eyes darting away around the table, "'tis merely that I'm surprised to see you."

"Particularly as you thought I'd be home, mourning," she countered. "I rest my case."

"Practicing law now, are you? Well, put this in your pipe and smoke it, Madam Barrister--you are no mind reader. Townsend never said he'd invited you, is all."

"I see. And does he generally submit his guest list for your approval?" She turned away to pass some gravy.

"You know bloody well what I mean," Thorne muttered. "I'd no idea he'd even consider-"

"Inviting me," she supplied, taking up her fork. "Particularly as I should be at home, mourning."

Thorne felt a tic in his jaw; it seemed she had the advantage in every situation.

"Where is Gwynneth?" she asked, far too casually.

"In Seagrave. Evelyn is ill."

As dessert arrived, conversation rose to a dull roar punctuated by a debate between Sir Kenneth and Sir Dennis over contested elections.

"But Papa," Bernice called out from her table, "just the other day, you said it would be a bloody good-"

"Quiet, child!" Sir Dennis barked. "Women have no say in this matter."

An immediate argument ensued at Bernice's table, her voice as strident as the boys' voices until one of them made an unsociable noise and sent the rest into gales of mirth. At the main table, flatware danced as Sir Kenneth made his point with a hammering fist.

"Oh, indeed!" Mistress Dearborne clutched her throat and plucked her fan from a sleeve with the finesse of an illusionist, then waved energetic blasts of air onto herself and Thorne in the process. "I shall *faint* from all this dissent!" she declared, the relish in her voice belying any cause for concern.

"You've known this family for some time," Caroline said from his other side. "Are they always this colorful?"

Thorne chuckled. "*There's* a tactful epitaph. They're downright barbaric at times," he admitted, "excepting Lady Townsend. I find them all delightful, and if I thought they could be convinced to live at Wycliffe Hall, I'd have asked them long ago."

"Spoken by a man in need of a family," Caroline said softly, then touched his sleeve. "Forgive me, I spoke without thinking."

Thorne smiled crookedly. "'Twas your due. I've spoken out of turn a time or two myself."

"We're only human, my lord," she said, a suggestive note in her chuckle before she sobered. "You and Gwynneth shall soon have your own family at any rate."

"Will we?" Biting his tongue, Thorne tasted blood.

Townsend came innocently to the rescue, dragging Caroline into a conversation with Miss Victoria Clifton, daughter of Sir Kenneth and Lady Clifton. Caroline drew the girl out, encouraging her obvious attraction to Townsend, whose face soon turned red as his hair.

Crystal rang out as Sir Dennis tapped a spoon on his goblet. "Gentlemen, join me in the library for a glass and a cheroot. Ladies, we'll meet with you presently in the drawing room for some music. Only those with talent," he said with a sidelong glance at Bernice, "will be asked to play."

Townsend coughed to cover a chuckle while Granville gleefully nudged Bernice. Not to be outdone, she neatly tripped him as they left the dining room.

Lady Townsend played music and recited poetry in the drawing room; then Bernice and her cousins performed an outrageously funny skit. While the audience applauded, Thorne slipped out the door, hoping to escape unseen to his room for a brandy before turning in early.

And found the very person he wanted to escape in the hall.

"I'm glad to catch you alone," Caroline said, drawing near. "I've something to ask."

He tried not to stare at her mouth. "Ask away, then."

"I'm wondering why Gwynneth hasn't answered my letters."

Dragging his eyes off her full, carmine lips, Thorne met Caroline's searching gaze.

"Something isn't right," she said, her voice softly urgent. "And you, Thorne. You look...haunted."

He managed a crooked smile. "Haunted?"

"Yes. I'd expected to find you fat and jolly. Married life generally suits men like you."

He grimaced. "Men like me?"

"Yes. You're not unlike Horace, and he found great contentment in matrimony. I thought you'd settle quite comfortably."

"Did you." Thorne couldn't keep the steel out of his voice. "And how did you suppose my wife would take to wedded bliss?"

Caroline shrugged. "She is more likely to chafe at the change, but..." She lowered her gaze, then looked coyly at Thorne through her long lashes. "Under the tutelage of an affectionate husband, she might soon bend and mold to his will."

Thorne suppressed a harsh laugh at her faulty theory. But knowing she spoke from experience, he felt his groin tighten. He could all too clearly imagine Caroline "bending and molding."

Fearing his eyes would betray him, he shifted his gaze to a portrait on the wall. "I shan't presume to know the workings of my wife's mind," he said brusquely. "Her reasons for failing to respond are known only to her." He met Caroline's eyes again. "May I escort you back to the drawing room?"

"Thank you, but I believe I've troubled you enough for one evening," she said coolly, and walked away before he could say another word.

* * *

Watching the sun rise to a chorus from the meadowlarks and orioles in the pine-scented hangers bordering the valley, Thorne eyed a stand of weeping willow at the river's edge. The mists would be lifting by the time he grabbed a trout pole from the potting shed. Perhaps he could hook one or two for breakfast.

He stopped short in the gallery. Beside a closed door sat two small trunks he recognized. As he wondered what their owner was up to, she opened the door and stepped out, barely glancing his way.

"Where are you going?"

She bent down and locked the trunks. "Home, if you must know."

"Why, may I ask?"

"Because I shouldn't have come." Pocketing the key, she smoothed the tiered black lace at her elbow and turned to face him. "I am in mourning, after all."

"Bollocks. You're leaving because of me."

"I've left a note," she said as if he hadn't spoken, her expression aloof. "I wouldn't think of insulting the Townsends by leaving without word." She went back inside her room.

She returned with a folded parchment, only to find Thorne blocking her doorway.

"Don't go," he said. "Especially not on my account."

Caroline narrowed her eyes. "I can see you've passed a bad night. I might have sympathized before our talk in the parlor, but I'll be damned if I try drawing you out again. Stay inside your miserable shell and rot, I'm going home."

She gasped as Thorne grabbed her hand. Apparently too stunned to protest, she watched him take the note she'd written and wad it up in his fist. "Why, of all the arrogance!" Her eyes snapped. "What bloody difference does it make to you if I stay or go?"

"Stay. Please."

His unveiled entreaty seemed to stun her. She blinked, found her voice. "Perhaps *you* should go home."

"I'd rather not."

"Then I shall stay." She looked surprised at her own words, then vexed; she'd obviously meant to be harder on him.

Thorne headed downstairs for the potting shed, but only after he had set Caroline's trunks back inside her room--and only then because she drew the line at letting him watch her unpack.

* * *

"I do not understand how he can desert you again so soon, my lady. First London, and now Chigwell."

Lady Neville elevated her head and fixed her eyes on the road ahead. "His lordship did not desert me, Hobbs. But your concern is well marked."

Hobbs' gaze fell upon his greased boots and coarse woolen cloak. Leaving Saint Michael's after Sunday Mass, where he'd stared the whole service long at Lady Neville from the rear of the church, he was prolonging their time together by keeping their horses at a trot.

But only until lightning ripped the sky. As Lady Neville shrieked like a banshee at the earsplitting crackle that followed, Abigail bolted.

Cursing, Hobbs dug his heels into Bartholomew. In a torrent of rain, he bore down on Lady Neville, who had lost the reins and clung to Abigail's mane instead. Hobbs grabbed the mare's harness, hauled her rider onto his own mount, then shouted a command and smacked Abigail's haunch to send her galloping home.

Shivering and soaked, Lady Neville huddled against him. Hobbs managed with some difficulty to open his lanolin-rich cloak and wrap it snug around both of them. Clasping the mistress in one burly arm, he kicked Bartholomew into a canter.

Steam poured from the gelding's nostrils while the air grew pungent with the smells of wet leather and horsehair. Hobbs felt his shirt turn damp against Lady Neville's soaked frock, but knew he was beyond any danger of taking a chill, what with those ripe curves molded against him and only two or three layers of fabric between. She, on the other hand, was drenched to the bone and terrified, risking illness or worse. It was that which prompted his hoarse shout for help as he carried her into the Hall.

While Bridey hurried to brew fresh tea and scolded Hobbs as if he'd caused the thunderstorm, Byrnes rushed in to fetch her mistress away to dry blankets and a roaring fire.

"Let me carry her to her chambers, or at least up the stairs," Hobbs insisted. Bridey refused, saying he'd done quite enough as it was.

Back in the stables, he went about his chores mechanically, not daring to stop and dwell on what he'd realized in the last hour.

He was falling in love with his master's wife.

* * *

Midday found the entire Townsend party at the river, a feast in tow. Wearing shawls in the early September air, several ladies paddled rowboats about under the huge willows, while Bernice and the men dropped lines further upriver.

"They love the crickets," she enthused to Thorne. "But you must hook them through their bodies. Their little heads will come off faster than Ann Boleyn's."

"Bernice," her father growled.

"Oh, Papa, you're just cross because I've hooked two to your one. Try my crickets!"

"I've fished these waters since long before you were born, young lady, so 'tisn't likely you've anything to teach me," he retorted over the other men's chuckles.

Down the bank, Lady Townsend, abandoning the boats for her tatting, shook her head. "They're at it again."

Tying the rowboat to a stake, Caroline squinted upriver at Bernice and her father. "They seem quite fond of one another, for all their spats."

"One wouldn't know what to do without the other," Lady Townsend admitted.

Caroline gasped. "Why, she's just slapped Mister Dearbourne upside the head with a fish!"

Lady Townsend clicked her tongue. "She does haul them in rather vigorously. Well, Mister Dearbourne will take it in stride and have a good laugh. He is quite charmed by her, as so many gentlemen seem to be." She kept her eyes on her tatting. "Lord Neville, for instance, is extraordinarily fond of her. The sister he never had, I suppose. Just between us, I think she reminds him of a girl he once knew."

"Lena," Caroline said without thinking.

"Yes, Lena." Pausing, Lady Townsend looked up from her work. "He's mentioned her?"

"Only in passing."

"Oh, I doubt that. You must know him better than I'd supposed."

Caroline only smiled.

"Well," Lady Townsend went on as she resumed her tatting, "then I don't mind telling you that we thought this Lena had spoiled Thorne for other prospects, and hence were quite surprised when he decided to marry. If he dotes on his bride even half as much as on our Bernice, she'll be a happy wife, indeed."

Caroline held her tongue; was the woman blind? How could she begin to think that there was any 'doting' being done by either of the Nevilles? One look at Thorne should tell her otherwise.

As Lady Townsend turned to compare stitches with Mistress Grindall, Caroline wandered up the bank toward the fishing party.

* * *

Bernice snorted. "Look at Richard. Does he really think he's teaching her to fish? Mistress Sutherland is no dolt, I can tell you."

Thorne smiled to himself at the girl's perception.

"I'll wager she could put him to shame," Bernice went on, "yet she looks at the bait like she's never seen such a disgusting thing in all her life. Ha! Now I see why Miss Victoria Clifton can't get so much as a nod from my brother. Oh Richard, you are dreaming!" she said with a laugh.

"Hush, Bernie, he'll hear you," chided her father, and something in his tone seemed to sober her.

Thorne slid his gaze downriver, all the while silently denying his interest in the little fishing lesson. He continued to deny it even as he sauntered down the bank in that direction as if he hadn't a care in the world.

* * *

"I've come to inquire as to Lady Neville's condition."

"What?" Bridey stared at Hobbs as if he'd grown horns. "Her ladyship's condition is no concern of yours, Toby."

"I'm at fault. I saw the storm coming. I should have insisted she stay with the priest, then fetched Dobson with the coach."

The old cook nodded curtly. "Aye, so ye should've. But she fares well enough, and for that ye can thank your lucky stars, 'cause if the master was home, ye'd never have took her to church today."

"I accompanied Lady Neville at her request." Defiance crept into Hobbs' voice. "I'm obliged to obey her wishes in the master's absence, just as you are."

Sighing, Bridey shuffled to the hearth. "Aye. Enough said, then, and no real harm done." She turned the spit. "Go on now, off with ye," she scolded, as if he were a boy again, loitering about the kitchen in hopes of an extra meat pie. Watching the proud way he carried himself as he left, she felt uneasy.

A body heard things in a great house like this, things that over the years might be left alone but weren't necessarily forgotten. And something was brewing, she could feel it--something that had lain dormant, like unleavened dough, until someone had come along and added yeast to the mix.

And that someone, she feared, was Lady Neville.

* * *

"*Now* what shall I do?" Caroline said breathlessly, having hooked a fair-sized trout on her line.

Thorne moved behind her and reached around to grip the bamboo pole between her hands. "Steady. It won't jump into the corf on its own. You must leave it a bit of slack and let it play some, then give it a tug and haul it in a tad more."

She leaned back for leverage; Thorne felt her shiver as his breath touched her bare neck. "Are you cold?" he murmured.

"No, just...excited."

Was her voice a shade huskier than usual? Thorne's pulse accelerated. Suddenly Caroline cried out, her ill-timed yank bringing the fish flying out of the water. Thorne chuckled as the poor creature swung into her skirts and she shrieked again.

"Bloody Hades," Bernie groused further up the bank. "Would someone toss that woman in a boat without oars and give it a good shove?"

"Bernice Margaret Townsend, keep your tongue in your head or go sit beside your mother. Mistress Sutherland is our guest. You will treat her with respect."

"Humph!" Bernice watched from a distance, hands on hips, as her brother and Thorne showed Caroline how to remove the hook and place the fish in the wicker corf. When Caroline scrubbed her hands in the water and looked around for something to dry them, Bernice doubled over with laughter.

"Actress or not, I was wrong about her," she gasped, wiping tears from her eyes. "The only thing that woman ever fished for is a man!"

* * *

"Thank Providence you're not ill, Milady. But perhaps we should wait until tomorrow. Darkness falls within the hour."

"Then we must start now. I want to reach the hollow before dark."

"Wait here." Excitement thickened Hobbs' voice. He'd no idea why it was so important to ride to Beck's Hollow before nightfall, but he would manage it or die in the attempt.

The sun hovered just above the horizon as they reached the south bank. Lady Neville dismounted before an old ash tree. While Hobbs looked on from his horse, she touched some scarring in the scaly bark.

"T and L," she murmured.

Hobbs drew Bartholomew closer. "What is it, my lady?"

"A heart. 'T' is my husband, no doubt." She turned to Hobbs. "Who might 'L' be?" You knew his lordship as a boy."

"He was fourteen when I came to the stables, no mere boy, my lady."

"Then you've no notion?" Her face fell like that of a disappointed child.

"No, my lady."

She went back to studying the crude carvings.

"The moon is on the rise, my lady. Shall we climb the ridge and ride to the clearing? The circle of stones I showed you is even more intriguing by moonlight."

After a long moment, she turned to look at him, her eyes aglitter, her smile strangely fierce. "Aye, Tobias, do let's ride to the clearing, indeed I shall ride all the night long if I choose...no one can stop me!"

His heart skipped a beat and then began to pound. It was the first time she had used his Christian name since the day they had met and Neville had quickly set her straight. "Very well, my lady," he said, struggling to sound calm. "But the forest is already dark and we must beware low branches. Stay just behind me."

* * *

Hearing Caroline's laughter peal for the third time, Thorne couldn't resist a glance toward the fire, where Townsend seemed to have her spellbound. Meanwhile, Miss Victoria Clifton cast doe-eyes their way and looked miserable as her mama encouraged her with urgent whispers to join them.

Feeling sorry for the girl, but at the same time finding his compassion highly suspect, Thorne sauntered up behind the high-backed brocade chairs and folded his arms nonchalantly atop the one in which Caroline sat. She immediately acknowledged him, to Townsend's obvious irritation.

"Thorne." Such a velvet voice she had, at the moment matched by her eyes. "Townsend has been telling tales on you." Smiling, she eyed Thorne through her thick lashes. "I'd never have guessed you were such a tearaway at Oxford. I'd pictured you poring endlessly over your books and papers, scarcely taking time to eat and sleep."

"He'd have done precisely that, if we had let him," Townsend broke in, staring coolly at Thorne. "But under that quiet, studious exterior, there proved something of the devil in him after all."

Thorne returned his stare. "Mark me, whatever Townsend lays at my door can be turned on himself thrice over."

Caroline glanced from one man to the other.

"Despite the ashes just heaped on my head," Townsend said with distinct diction, "I'm not quite the rake Neville would have you believe."

"I propose," Thorne said every bit as distinctly, "that neither of us further incriminates the other in the presence of the lady."

"Agreed."

Seconds ticked by in silence in their little group while other conversation carried on.

"Well, gentlemen!" Caroline stood, her eyes dancing. "I must beg your leave, I've promised Sir Kenneth a game of billiards."

Townsend rose and both men bowed, then watched Caroline's hourglass form float across the room. Miss Victoria Clifton followed her progress as well, a pout on her plump little mouth.

Thorne dropped into Caroline's vacated seat. Townsend stayed standing, his steady regard anything but cordial.

"Shall I fetch the pistols?" Thorne deadpanned. "Or might we share a smoke and conduct a mature conversation?"

With no change in his expression, Townsend took his seat again.

What in the deuce," Thorne asked coolly, taking two cigars from a slender case in his waistcoat and tossing one to his silent friend, "possessed you to invite her here?"

Townsend savagely bit off the cigar tip. "Rather a strong word, Neville...'possessed'? I ran across her at the Exchange."

"The Exchange?"

"Yes." He lit up with a piece of kindling, then held the crude match out for Thorne. "Don't you know? She's become quite involved in her late husband's business affairs."

"*There's* a shock."

"You should have seen them--clarks, merchants, tradesmen--all agog at the sight of her! Damned funny, quite a scene. At any rate, she looked so..." Townsend shook his head.

"Stunning? Ravishing?"

"I was about to say 'overjoyed to see me'...yes, *me*! And yes, I'll admit to being flattered, damned flattered, in fact. You needn't look so amused, Neville, I came to my senses soon enough, and realized she'd likely be glad to see *any* acquaintance from a happier time. But I could tell she was lonely--though 'tis hard to imagine a woman like her being anything but plagued by men--and I found myself asking before it even occurred to me that, being in mourning, she'd properly decline my invitation. But as you see, she accepted! At any rate," he added before Thorne could tease him further, "I thought your wife would be here, and that the two of them could have a pleasant visit together."

Thorne looked into the flames, then met his friend's intent gaze again. "Bear up, Townsend. I'm about to be blunt, if not downright rude."

"Fire away."

"Have you some romantic interest in Caroline?"

"Pardon?" Townsend's face flushed scarlet.

"You heard me."

Townsend flipped his cigar butt into the fire. "What, protecting the lady's honor? Or me from certain heartbreak?"

Thorne shook his head, irony twisting his mouth. "You have it all wrong, Townsend. I'm hoping you'll spare *me*."

"How so?"

"By telling me you've serious intention of courting Caroline. Tell me that, and you'll be the instrument of my salvation."

Townsend stared at him in consternation. "Salvation from what?"

Thorne closed his eyes and rubbed his eyes and rubbed them. "From my own little hell, is what."

"Christ, Neville." Townsend lowered his voice. "What's eating you?"

"Do you believe in sorcery?" Thorne looked up, and if Townsend had been about to laugh or ridicule, the torment on his friend's face must have stopped him.

"Come on, steady now." Townsend shifted to the edge of his seat, elbows resting on his knees. "God knows she looks at you as if you're her next meal," he muttered, "but has she gone so far as...has she tried to..."

"Seduce me?" Thorne shook his head. "I'm not sure. But we're repeatedly thrown in one another's path."

"Then 'tis nothing she does or says."

"No," Thorne said hesitantly, "and yes. She has a way of speaking..." He saw Townsend nod. "And a way of looking at a man, of searching him out in a crowded room. I sense that you empathize, but I think her effect on me is more profound...though the why is beyond me. And worst of all, she bloody well knows it."

"Are you in love with her?" Townsend asked quietly.

"No. God, no. Heaven help any man who is."

"And Gwynneth?"

Thorne only looked at him.

"She's at Wycliffe Hall, isn't she? Not with her aunt."

Eyes on the fire again, Thorne nodded.

Townsend sounded pained. "Is the marriage in jeopardy so soon?"

"I wish I could say 'no'...but I fear it is. My wife, you see, took the wrong vows."

His friend's blank stare begged explanation.

"You see, Radleigh forced her to leave the convent without telling her our plans. I've since realized she was gently coerced into capturing my fancy, my hand, and my purse--though not necessarily in that order. Radleigh is heavily in debt."

"Christ."

"Coincidentally, that name looms large in this farce as well," Thorne said wryly. "Someone has impressed upon my wife that any pleasure derived from marital conjugation is a 'mortal sin'. Hence she struggles against her otherwise passionate nature, and defends her position by saying she was meant for 'a higher purpose.' Aye, her very words," he said, seeing Townsend's dumbfounded expression. "My wife is convinced she should have taken the vows of the Sisters of Saint Mary."

Townsend groaned.

"So you see why your serious intentions toward Caroline would be my redemption. She has me under some spell, Townsend. I don't know what it is, but it cuts me off at the knees, and I don't know how much longer I can resist. I'm human, for God's sake."

Townsend shook his head, looking both regretful and vexed. "I'll confess I'm attracted to Caroline, what man wouldn't be? But I'd never ask her to marry me. She's far too headstrong, and frankly, I wouldn't trust her as far as the door. You yourself said, 'heaven help any man who is in love with her'...would you wish that on me? Besides which, let's call a spade a spade--she'd very likely laugh in my face at the mere suggestion."

"I doubt that," Thorne mumbled, his hopes disintegrating.

"Oh, all right, she wouldn't laugh, she'd just look at me with those incredible eyes and smile at me with that extraordinary mouth and tell me how sweet I was for asking, but...! So, no, my friend." Townsend snorted. "I suffer no delusions that she's drawn to me. I've quite entertained her this evening, not with tales of my escapades, but of yours, since there were many in which I took part. And by God, she hung on my every word, our cool Widow Sutherland...and not because of my voice."

Thorne felt his heartbeat quicken in spite of his dismay. He'd never imagined Caroline's interest in him was more than a game of wits and wiles for her own amusement. What Townsend had just told him only worsened the situation.

"So you see," his friend was saying, "I can't possibly pull you out of this pit into which you've fallen...and I'll lay ten to one she's good and ready to jump into it with you. She only awaits your beckoning."

"Christ, don't say that."

"It's the truth, and I think you know it. In the meantime, what of your marriage? Can you live with Gwynneth and have any true peace of mind? Are you willing to let her use your home as a nunnery?"

"She'd still manage the household well, I think."

"Oh, *there's* consolation. What of children, Neville--an heir? What of your marital rights, damn it?"

Raking a hand through his hair, Thorne gave his friend a withering look. "Do you think those things haven't occurred to me?

"Appeal for an annulment!"

"I don't want to shame her family--or mine, for that matter. Damn my stubbornness! Arthur warned me time and time again."

Townsend sat back in his seat with a sigh. "So, what will you do?"

"Beyond pouring a stiff dram of your whiskey?" Thorne managed a smile. "Deuced if I know, Townsend. Ask me again at the end of my stay."

* * *

Tiptoeing up the west hall at Wycliffe Hall, Gwynneth reminded herself she'd simply ridden later than usual, and it was no one's business but hers. Changing her pace, she glided up the thick carpet runner with her head held high, then paused before the great staircase and frowned, seeing a patch of light shining from under the library doors.

She approached stealthily and pressed an ear to one door, then slowly opened it.

A startled gasp came from the vicinity of the hearth. Gwynneth spotted the hem of a muslin wrapper between the legs of a high-backed chair.

"Who is there?"

Slippered feet touched the floor. Silhouetted in the firelight, a tall slender form arose from the chair. "'Tis I, Milady...Combs," came the soft, hesitant reply.

Indignation heated Gwynneth's blood. "What business have you in this room?"

"I beg your pardon, Milady, I was only curious to see one of its volumes. I shall go now." Combs hesitated, seeming unsure whether to replace the book on the shelf or lay it on the table nearby.

"Bring the book to me," Gwynneth said through her teeth.

"Aye, Milady." Approaching, Elaine held out the volume. Eyes blazing, Gwynneth snatched it from her.

"Keep your filthy hands off what doesn't belong to you...do you hear me, slut?"

The blood drained from Elaine's face. She swayed on her feet.

"Return to your own quarters, and do not let me see your whoring face again!"

"Aye, Milady," Elaine whispered...then fainted and fell to the floor.

TWENTY-ONE

On Monday the Townsend's house party took coaches into London for lunch in a popular tavern and a comedic matinee. Afterward, Thorne apologized to his hosts, saying he had pressing business in Westminster and not to expect his return before nightfall.

In Fleet Street he hired a hackney coach, which drove him through Hyde Park to the stately residence of Madame Claire.

By the time they reached the gate, Thorne was questioning his motives. Awaiting the madam in her luxurious parlor, he reminded himself he had quit this place for good and for all.

"Monsieur Adams," cooed Madame Claire's syrupy voice as she swept into the room. "Welcome. Whom are we visiting today?"

"Need you ask?" Thorne murmured. "Katy, please, if she is at leisure."

The madam shook her head, her smile at once sad and patronizing. "Katy is *malade*...ill, I am sorry to say. You must meet Jeanette, come recently from Paris. Beautiful breasts, and lips made for pleasuring a man." Her rouged mouth formed the pathetic pout of a coquette past her season. "Shall I send for her, monsieur?"

"May I inquire as the the nature of Katy's illness?"

Madame Claire elevated her chin. "She has contracted *la fievre*...an ague, monsieur. But she is receiving excellent care. You need not be concerned."

"Perhaps I could visit for a moment or two."

The proprietress shook her head. "Impossible, monsieur. *La fievre* is quite contagious, and I dare not risk the lives of my clients. Katy is *sous la quarantaine*."

Nor, Thorne realized, could he afford to bring illness into the Townsend home. Resigned, he reached into his waistcoat pocket and dug into his purse.

"Here then." He held out his closed fist to the baffled woman--who was quick enough to open her own hand.

"*Monsieur Adams,*" she said with a gasp, agog at the fifty-pound note. "*C'est trop d'argent!*"

"For Katy's care, I insist. And tell her..." Thorne paused, considering his words. "Tell her naught of the money. Say only that Mister Adams wishes her well and awaits her recovery. Say also that I might see her in November."

"Monsieur, I cannot thank you enough for your *générosité*!"

Thorne waved her fawning gratitude away. "Just relay my message, please."

Madame Claire nodded, her smile entirely genuine. "I shall, Monsieur Adams, *sans faute*."

"Until November, then."

* * *

Madame Claire watched her visitor exit the front gate and disappear from view, then climbed the stairs and rapped on Katy's door.

"Come in," came a glum voice.

"You might like to know," the madam said, slinking around the door and closing it behind her, "there was a *visiteur* for you. I sent him away."

"And why need he be sent away?" Katy groused, tugging the covers up to her chin. "There are women enough in this house to accommodate one little man."

"*Non, cheri.* Not *this* man." Madame Claire's smile was grim. "*Monsieur Adams* would see none but you." She dangled the fifty-pound note in front of Katy. "He kindly contributes to your keep. Quite *chanceux*, as you have refused all clients since you took 'ill.' He will visit again in November. Perhaps when he learns your '*fièvre*' is not cured, he will open his purse again."

"You mustn't take advantage of the poor man!"

"He is anything but *pauvres*...and how else am I to support you in your idleness until the babe is born?"

Katy threw the covers back and sat up, hand on her belly. "The babe's own father has given you means to do so! In little more than a month he's handed a hundred pounds over to us, and most of it from the kindness of his heart!"

"*Oui,* but another such contribution two months hence will line the nest nicely. And when the babe is born, 'twill fetch more than enough to make up for all my trouble...especially if 'tis a boy."

"You'd be selling my own babe?" Katy whispered, horror in her wide eyes. "Why, you're no better than my mum, selling me into service here."

"But *you* were a big girl of four-and-ten, quite ready for work. This is no place to raise *un petit enfant*! Or would you have me turn the two of you out into the street? 'Twas careless of you to forget your vinegar sponge and your douche on that long day with Monsieur Adams in July," the madam said crossly, "and as you won't abide getting rid of the wee thing, you must *payez le piper*!"

Despite the nausea and weakness that plagued her nowadays, Katy snarled a reply. "Like as not, I'm God's own fool for telling you this, but 'forgetting' had naught to do with the making of this babe!"

Madame Claire's powdered eyelids folded upon themselves as her painted eyebrows arched. "What are you saying, Katherine Devlin--that you conceived this child *intentionellement*, with purpose? Is that what you are telling me?"

"Aye," Katy snapped, "and I'll not foul myself *or* my babe with another man's seed whilst I'm carrying!" Tears glazed her glare. "I cannot lay claim to Mister Adams' heart, but he has mine, and for that innocent thievery I *do* lay claim to his bairn! And no one, not you or the midwife or anyone else shall take it away from me, I swear it before the Almighty!"

Madame Claire sidled closer to the bed. "And what of Monsieur Adams? Has he no right to his child?"

"He...he'll never know," Katy stammered, her gaze falling to the counterpane. "Not from *these* lips, at any rate. Saints above, why should he want to be saddled with my babe? For all we know he's...he might be..."

- 136 -

"Married?" The madam arched her brow again. "*Oui, just* married, little more than a fortnight ago. Hence childless."

Katy's eyes flew to hers. "And how is it you're knowing such things?"

"One of my more prominent clients keeps me informed, in exchange for services more perverted than the usual."

"And did he tell you Mister Adams' true name?"

Madame Claire shook a finger at her. "Tsk, tsk, *cheri*, you needn't know that. But when the time comes, I think Monsieur 'Adams' will quite willingly claim the *enfant* in return for his continued anonymity...for a considerable sum of cash, of course. No hardship to him, I assure you."

"You've no proof 'tis his," Katy argued, but she looked hopeful. "Not even a halfwit would take your word alone."

"*Oui, cherie*, but your Monsieur Adams has a conscience, unlike most of our clients. Even so, chances are greater he will claim the child than spurn it."

"How so?" Katy demanded. "By God's own grace, what could truly convince the man that this babe is his?"

Madame Claire smiled smugly. "By God's own grace and the ways of nature, *the babe will have its father's eyes.*"

* * *

"What the devil?" Thorne muttered.

Returning to the Townsend's at twilight, he found every window of the Palladian house lit from within. Was there a ball in progress? No one had mentioned any such event.

Stepping down from the coach, Thorne saw a figure in skirts streak past the colonnade. "See if I don't!" it yelled defiantly, and then called back, "Thorne, hurry! You're on my team!" before disappearing behind the hedgerow. A larger figure in breeches dashed across the lawn to where Bernie had vanished. "Give it up, you little heathen!" shouted Townsend's voice.

"Good evening, M'lord," said the Townsend's straight-faced butler. "I have been instructed to relieve you of your waistcoat and bid you join Miss Bernice, whom I believe you shall find running for dear life in the gardens."

Thorne's mouth twitched. "Surely Miss Bernice wouldn't be overly upset if I took some refreshment first?"

The butler didn't bat an eye. "Suit yourself, M'lord, but I cannot guarantee the young lady's leniency."

Chuckling, Thorne gamely relinquished his waistcoat and tricorne. "God forbid I should spark her temper."

Thorne headed toward the next shout he heard, in the rear gardens. Light spilled from the windows to his right. At his left, the tall hedgerow blocked his view.

One minute he was walking, the next he was sprawled face-down in dewy grass. Picking himself up, he heard smothered laughter behind the hedgerow.

He sprinted to the far end of the thick growth and rounded the last shrub, then paused as he spotted a tall shadowy form in skirts creeping back toward the other end.

He closed the distance on silent, winged feet. "Think twice before knocking *me* down again, you redheaded rabble-rouser!" Grabbing the skirted figure by the waist, he swept her up under his arm.

Even before she cried out in protest, he realized his mistake.

"What the deuce did you trip me for?" he demanded, setting his captive down hastily. "I thought you were Bernie, I expect such shenanigans from her."

Caroline burst out laughing. "I'm sorry!" she gasped out, clutching her midsection. "But to see such a prig as you, lying flat on the ground and not knowing how the deuce you got there...oh, I am sorry!" Her words slid into another peal of mirth.

"Give it up Caroline, you don't sound the least bit sorry."

She sobered. "I thought you were Townsend. Bernice left me here to waylay him. I'd no idea 'twas you."

"What game is this, who's playing?"

"*Everyone* is playing, at least 'til the fog comes in off the river. 'Tis a scavenger hunt! A bird's egg is on the list. Apparently both Townsend and Bernice knew the location of a nest, but she beat him to it, shimmied right up the tree. When I saw her last, her brother was in hot pursuit."

"Indeed he was. So, now I'm a prig, am I?"

"Not only now, but most of the time," Caroline said with a wicked little smile. "Come find Bernice, she's depending on us to help finish the list."

"Very well. For Bernie I'll make an exception."

"To what?" Caroline tucked her arm comfortably into his.

"To your otherwise immediate trial."

She slowed their pace. "I'm being tried? For what?"

"Slander. You accused me of being a prig," Thorne reminded her, an edge to his otherwise pleasant tone. "You may present your supporting evidence. But I shall prove you wrong."

"Evidence?" Caroline stopped to face him. "I rely on observation, 'tis all the evidence I need."

"And what do you observe, Mistress Sutherland?"

Squinting through the dimness, Caroline saw a wry twist to his sensual mouth and a gleam in his eyes. Her pulse began to race. "Only that you always do what is proper, Lord Neville."

"Always?"

"Always."

Standing nearly toe-to-toe with him, she felt his warm breath on her face.

"Tho-orne!" called a singsong voice from somewhere beyond the house.

"Bernie," Caroline murmured.

"I should answer," Thorne muttered, his gleaming eyes on her lips. "Since I *always* do what is proper."

"Thorne!" The insistent summons was fading in the other direction.

Without warning, Thorne's head swooped down on Caroline's like a hawk on its prey, his mouth slanting over hers. Demanding entry, he gained it with a single thrust of his tongue, simultaneously drowning Caroline's protest and evoking a moan as she closed her eyes in surrender to a thorough ravishment of her mouth. Their breaths mingled, faster, harsher by the moment, until Caroline's head reeled and the ground beneath her seemed to fall away.

As abruptly as Thorne had taken hold of her, he let her go.

She swayed, then steadied herself, eyes opening wide. With one searching look, she slapped him roundly.

Thorne's smile was brief and brittle. "I rest my case, Mistress Sutherland."

* * *

"What do you mean, she left?"

Townsend sloshed some cream into his morning tea. "Took her leave. Departed. Said she'd some business in town, but she might return tomorrow. Very apologetic, very charming with her excuses." He looked hard at Thorne. "And very anxious to know *your* whereabouts before she left."

"Probably looking to bid me farewell."

Townsend barely swallowed his mouthful of tea. "Not bloody likely. What the deuce did you say to her?" He set his cup askew in the saucer. "She kept her distance after the scavenger hunt. Didn't look your way again all evening."

"You watch her closely."

"As if you don't!"

Thorne dropped into a chair. "Damnation, Townsend, are we to come to blows over the woman before the week is out? Bugger it all, get to the point."

"Very well. She called you a cad."

Thorne snorted. "Is that all?"

Townsend's eyes narrowed. "I've known you to deck a man for less than that. She slandered your reputation, Neville. You, who are ever the protector and defender of the gentler sex."

"Did she say what I'd done to deserve such an epithet?" Thorne flicked imaginary lint from his sleeve.

"No, she didn't."

"Well, the woman has a right to her opinion. What say we take Bernie riding this morn?"

"Oh, so I'm to be left in the dark. Very well then, I'll see if I can abduct the little hellion from her cousins. You're a glutton for punishment, Neville, an absolute glutton."

* * *

Standing in the foyer of the Sutherland mansion, tricorne in hand, Thorne felt like a schoolboy come to beg forgiveness of his governess.

Old Marsh came trudging down the steps alone. "She'll not see ye, sir," she said, looking sheepish.

"Why not?"

Marsh shrugged. "She only says, sir, to tell ye she's not at home to callers today."

Coolly studying the gallery, Thorne considered scaling the elegant stairway and barging into Caroline's boudoir. "Tell your mistress," he said casually, "that I look for her to return to Chigwell as soon as she's able." He donned his hat and left the house, Caroline's butler, Gilbert, dejectedly holding the door for him.

"'Tis a rotten shame," Marsh muttered, eyeing Lord Neville through the window as he climbed jauntily into the coach. "After all he's done for her."

Gilbert shook his head. "Criminal, if you ask me." He winced as Caroline's voice chimed in from above.

"No one asked you, you old coot, so keep your bloody tongue in your head!"

* * *

"Too early for tea?" asked Arthur, tossing a corf on the worktable. "Four good-sized trout, caught this morning. Nigh forgot to collect them."

"Hilly, draw a breath!" Bridey called out, dropping an armful of winesaps on the worktable. The butter churn's rhythmic thump ceased, and Hillary came scurrying from the creamery.

"Come clean these fish, lass." Bridey eyed Arthur silently for a moment, then asked in an undertone, "Did ye perchance see Toby on your way in?"

"He's out," Arthur said, buttering a fresh scone.

"Aye, he's out all right," the cook grumbled. "Out with her ladyship. As usual, here of late."

Arthur paused, the butter knife in mid air. "What are you saying, Bridey?" he murmured, glancing Hillary's way.

The cook took a knife to the winesaps on her chopping board. "'Tis not my place to say anything," she replied flatly.

"'Twill go no further than my ears."

She eyed him grimly. "The pair o' them ride daily now...and of an evening as well, Monday past." She pursed her lips.

"Evening, eh." Arthur poured steaming orange-pekoe tea into his cup.

"Aye," Bridey chopped furiously. "Come in late, too. Found Combs in the reading room and raked her over the coals. Made her faint dead away, then turned her back on her." She gave an apple a vicious whack.

Arthur said nothing.

"Master'll be home soon," Bridey muttered. "There'll be no more midnight rides then, I'll vow."

"Midnight, Bridey?"

"Near enough. 'Tweren't more than two hours away when she sashayed in by the side door."

Arthur downed most of his tea, then pushed the trestle back from the table. "Well, as you say, Bridey, the master will be home soon. And *that*," he added firmly, "will be the end of that."

TWENTY-TWO

By Wednesday evening Thorne suspected Caroline wouldn't return to the house party. By Thursday morning he was all but certain.

He told himself he was merely restless when he took up a favorite book but couldn't concentrate, or began a game of cards only to lose and curse his luck aloud. He even found Bernie's impulsiveness more of a trial than an amusement, and it was Townsend who finally demanded an end to it.

"She has you by the bollocks, man, admit it!"

Thorne knew he wasn't referring to Bernie.

"You're like a brother to me, Neville, so I say this with sincere affection--get the devil home and get your house in order before you see her again. You're a lit powder keg at any rate, and damned if I want you around when you explode."

Thorne studied Townsend noncommittally. "Truly, I'm that much of a mess?"

"Every bit of it." Townsend softened his tone. "Not to say you're at fault, just that your situation isn't improving with time...although, who can tell? You might find Gwynneth's attitude changed, now that she's had some time away from you, and if that's the case, your...obsession, shall we call it?...with Mistress Sutherland will be a thing of your more tawdry past." He eyed his friend with fond annoyance. "Go home."

Thorne smiled crookedly. "I suppose there are worse ways of being put out of someone's house. I wonder, though, what Lady Townsend would do if she knew you were giving me the boot."

Townsend winced. "I may be twenty-six years old, but she'd box my ears soundly, and you bloody well know it. And that would be a picnic next to what Bernie'd do when *she* got hold of me."

Thorne chuckled. "Bless her, she's my champion all right." His smile faded. "All jesting aside, Townsend, you've probably done me a favor. You're right, there's little I can do from here. I'll collect my bag and find my hosts."

* * *

"Stop your dallying and fetch Bartholomew to the smithy's," groused Hobbs. When there was no answer he looked up to see Gwynneth silhouetted in the doorway. "Milady. Forgive me, I thought you were Nate."

"He's already gone," she said softly, "or I wouldn't have come."

Unable to read her expression in the dim light, Hobbs pulled a three-legged stool from under the worktable and set it out for her. 'Tis all I can offer," he said ruefully.

Gwynneth glanced about the room as she sat down. "I shouldn't be here."

"Why not?" Hobbs laid aside the harness he was repairing. "Are these not your husband's stables?"

"Aye, but I believe I'm being watched. From the Hall." She sighed. "Did you miss our ride yesterday?"

Hobbs debated a reply.

"I'd errands in town," she explained, then smiled at his expression. "If you don't believe me, Tobias, ask at the coach house. All my riding was done in comfort yesterday."

He picked up a narrow strip of hide and began weaving it into the damaged harness. "Aye, riding horseback is a poor second," he said evenly, keeping his eyes on his work. "But some of us have little choice. I'm thus reminded, Milady, that I'm naught but a simple stableman, hence far too lowly to accompany you on your rides. I was mad to think otherwise. You needn't say any more, 'tis done. Henceforth, I'll stay right here in the stables, where I belong, and leave the escorting to your husband."

Met with silence, he looked down to see reproach in Gwynneth's gaze.

"I came here," she said, a tremor in her voice, "to tell you I hoped to ride with you today. I wanted to arrange the time around your schedule so that no one could accuse you of neglecting your duties. But never mind, now. I shan't bother you again." Tears in her eyes, she shot up off the stool, gathered her skirts, and fled.

She was scarcely out the door when Hobbs seized her by the shoulder, but he let her go without a word as he spotted Arthur coming through the gate. Gwynneth never broke stride, giving the steward a nod and a terse "good morning" as she passed him.

One look at Arthur's face sent Hobbs back to his workbench.

"You've some business with her ladyship this morn?" Arthur pulled out the stool and sat down. Hobbs resumed his harness repair with a vengeance.

"Aye. What of it?"

"I'll not mince words, Toby. There's talk at the Hall, and I want it stopped before his lordship returns."

"Talk?"

"Aye, of you and her ladyship. Stay where you are and listen," he said as Hobbs made to rise. "This is for your own good. 'Tis up to *you* to prevent slander against the girl...and 'girl' she is, Toby, make no mistake. She's led a secluded life, hence is ignorant regarding certain matters, such as daily rides with her husband's stableman in her husband's absence. Steady, keep your tongue and your temper," he warned, seeing Hobbs bristle. "Hear me out.

"From this day hence, you'll refuse to ride with her ladyship, no matter how much she coaxes you. Be gentle but firm. Send one of the lads with her."

"Who started this 'talk'?"

"It matters not. What matters is her ladyship's reputation. Give an old man peace of mind, Toby, and keep your situation in the bargain. Lord Neville values you highly enough, but *by God*," Arthur said with quiet vehemence, "he'd kill you in a trice for cuckolding him."

Hobbs clenched his jaw. "Very well. For her sake, and hers alone, I shan't ride with her again. But I won't bar her from the stables. She likes to visit Abigail on the days she doesn't ride. Should I abandon my work and barricade myself in my quarters until she leaves?"

"Don't be insolent," Arthur groused, rising slowly to stretch the tension from of his limbs. "A polite greeting will suffice. Then leave her to her own amusement and go on about your business. Understood?"

"Aye, Mister Pennington." Hobbs muttered through his teeth. "Bloody well understood."

* * *

As Thorne's coach rolled out of the Townsend's drive and into the lane, all but one person waved farewell. Looking deceptively angelic in blue eyelet and white lace, Bernie simply watched him go.

He blew a kiss out the window, prompting a halfhearted wave from Bernie, and saw Townsend put his arm around her shoulders.

Another year or so and she might have been his wife. The kind of wife he'd envisioned in Gwynneth.

Enough. He'd made his bed--with considerable help from his father and Radleigh--and now he would have to lie down in it. He chuckled cynically at the old adage, since he seemed destined to lie only in his bachelor bed.

But, who could tell? Townsend might be right. Perhaps Gwynneth had experienced a change of heart. By the time the coach reached London proper, Thorne felt cautiously optimistic, and settled in for the ten-hour journey home.

* * *

Hobbs sucked in a breath. Gwynneth was leaning against the doorframe. Behind her, wisps of fog drifted in the light of a waning moon.

He looked back at his ledger, dipped his quill into the inkwell, and resumed tallying the grooms' hours and wages for the week. But all he could think of was how brown his arm looked against the pale parchment, and how it would look just that way against Gwynneth's bare skin.

His heart pounded. He made a nasty blot on the page, then gave up, laying the quill aside and sprinkling sand on what he'd managed to finish.

"I shall stand here until you acknowledge me."

Hobbs stared at his clasped hands, half hoping she'd turn and walk away. Hearing the dry whisper of silk approaching, he spoke without turning his head. "You should not be here."

Her pace slowed, though her fragrance advanced, assaulting his senses. He closed his eyes, then opened them to stare at the wooden wall.

"I've come to fetch Abigail. Will you ride with me?"

He gritted his teeth at the caress in her voice. "I cannot."

"I beg your pardon?"

"I'm to refuse you, Milady."

"By whose instruction?"

"That of my master's steward."

"Your master's...Pennington?" She came closer. "Then I *am* being spied upon, I knew it. No doubt he's following orders. Ride with me."

"I *cannot*. Ride if you must, but at your own risk. I've no one to send, the grooms have all gone home." Hobbs swallowed hard. "I answer to both Pennington and your husband, Milady, and I've no choice but to follow orders or risk losing my situation."

"This is outrageous!" She blinked back tears. "I am Lady Neville, Baroness Neville of Wycliffe!"

"You are," he agreed, rising, unable to bear the distress in her voice. She was so close her skirts brushed his breeches. Hobbs made fists at his sides, resisting the urge to caress her cheek, stroke her hair.

"Then I say that the stable master *shall* accompany me when I ride!" A sob choked her voice. "All my life I've been ruled by men! First my father, then the priest...and now that I am a baroness and mistress of the manor, what do I find? Only that I'm bound as ever by a man's rules and expectations--a man who doesn't love me, who only wants to possess me." Her green eyes blazed through her tears. "Well I am no longer a child, and I shan't be treated as one! Did Pennington also tell you to put me out of the stables?"

"No, Milady." Hobbs struggled to keep his voice calm, his heart racing at her revelation that Neville didn't love her. "Only that you're to ride with one of the grooms."

Gwynneth stared into his troubled eyes, and shook her head. "You're no happier about this than I, are you? Speak truth."

Emotion tightened his throat. "My happiness is of no consequence, Milady. You are your husband's chattel."

Bowing her head, Gwynneth began to sob.

Before Hobbs knew what he was doing, his arms were around her. She did not balk. Pressing his lips to the top of her head, he rocked her gently in his embrace while she wept, until the sound of something outdoors permeated his consciousness.

"What is it?" Gwynneth murmured, stiffening in his embrace as raised his head to listen.

"Wait here. Hide in that empty stall." Furious at the interruption, he strode to the doorway.

A coach was turning in from the Northampton road. Hobbs swore under his breath.

"Who is it?" Gwynneth hissed.

"Your husband."

"What?" She hurried out of the stall as Hobbs approached, her eyes wide. "But he isn't to return for two days!"

Hobbs twisted his mouth in irony. "Shall we march outside and tell him so?" He drew her cloak up over her shoulders, then jerked a kerchief from his pocket and blotted her face with it. "Pinch your cheeks."

"Pardon?"

"Pinch your cheeks. 'Tis a trick of my sister's when she's too pale."

Gwynneth eyed him dubiously. "Your sister."

"Yes," he said with a fleeting smile, then gave Gwynneth's face a quick inspection. "Now go. Use the west entrance and take the service stairs. You had better fly, he has a long stride. Go!"

* * *

"Quick, Byrnes, fetch me another frock, I don't care which. The master has arrived, and will likely be hungry." *For food, pray God, and naught else*, Gwynneth added silently.

"You answer it," she said as a knock sounded at the door. While the maid hurried to obey, Gwynneth tried to look casual in a chair near the fire, but craned her neck at the sudden clatter from the sitting room.

In came her husband, pushing a teakwood serving-cart bearing a cold supper and a dusty bottle of wine. "Good evening, my lady. I'm told you've had naught to eat since midday, so perhaps you'll share a small repast with me."

"Yes, of course!" Her tone was too bright; she could see it in his sharp glance, and her tension heightened. But while eating the Cornish hen, soda bread, Camembert, and poached pears in sweet cream and nutmeg, Thorne said little, and gradually Gwynneth relaxed. "You've returned early. Was the house party tiresome?"

"Not particularly. You were missed, by the by, and inquired after with much concern. You might want to remember that your Aunt Evelyn has been very ill."

Gwynneth's face grew warm.

"So, how have you occupied yourself?" Thorne asked pleasantly.

Expecting the question, Gwynneth had rehearsed a reply. "Needlepoint. Tending my roses, perhaps overmuch." She ruefully showed him her scratched hands. "I've helped in the kitchen, too, drying herbs and preserving apple butter." She ate a bit of pear before adding casually, "I've ridden, too, almost every day."

"Not alone, I hope?"

"Oh, no, I was quite safe."

Thorne lifted an eyebrow. "Hobbs was daily able to spare a groom?"

Pulse racing, Gwynneth managed an airy sniff. "Hobbs doesn't trust any of those simpletons. He thinks too much of you to leave your wife's safety to a mere boy."

Thorne eyed her intently. "Hobbs thinks very little of me, my lady, so you may as well save your breath on that score."

Speechless, she felt her cheeks burning.

Thorne downed the last of his wine, then leaned back in his chair, his eyes barely visible through slit lids. "So, again you've defied convention--and my wishes--by bullying my stable master into acting as your personal escort."

"No bullying was necessary!" Gwynneth cried, then regretted her outburst as Thorne gave her a crooked smile.

"No," he said quietly. "I thought not."

* * *

Gwynneth had long gone to bed when Thorne entered the east hall. Passing the library, he fixed frowning eyes on the darkness beneath the doors.

Despite the late hour, he found the housekeeper in her office. "Why is there no fire in the library?" he demanded.

First curtseying, Dame Carswell clasped her hands behind her rigid back. "Lady Neville's orders, M'lord."

"What the deuce?" Thorne's frown turned to a scowl. "Explain."

"Her ladyship discovered Combs there late one evening. She forbade her any further use of the room, and made it quite clear to me that no fire is to burn there at such an hour."

"Did she." Fury snaked through Thorne's veins and seeped into his low voice. "Is that why you are up and about so late? Guarding my library against intruders?"

Dame Carswell swallowed hard. "Her ladyship threatened me with dismissal, M'lord, should it happen again-"

"Do my orders not supersede hers? Is your dismissal not up to me?"

The housekeeper lifted her chin defensively. "Begging your pardon, M'lord, but 'tis customary for the lady of the house to handle such matters. She was quite lenient by most standards. Combs had no business trespassing or being about at that hour."

Something about Thorne's face must have betrayed his helpless anger--or perhaps he only imagined the tiny gleam in the housekeeper's eye, the slight curl in her lip.

"Will that be all, M'lord?"

"No, Carswell, there is one thing more."

"Yes, M'lord?"

"Get to bed."

* * *

It was nearly noon Friday before estate business was out of the way and Gwynneth's whereabouts could be confirmed. With Jennings' assurance she was gone to the draper's in Northampton, an immediate summons was sent topstairs.

One look at Elaine Combs, as she entered his study, told Thorne that she would gloss over the incident. Impatience prevented the usual polite greeting, but did nothing to slow his quickening pulse.

"Close the door and take a seat." As she did so without looking at him, Thorne stole a glance to see her skirts still hiding her growing belly.

Serene gray eyes rose to meet quizzical blue. "Welcome home, M'lord."

"Thank you," he said, and the ice in his marrow began to thaw for the first time in days. "I shan't keep you long away from your duties, but I *will* have an account of the incident in the library."

He saw it again--the guarded look in her eyes, the subtle straightening of her already erect back.

"Do not even consider telling me less than the whole story," he warned her. "Should I later hear of something you've omitted, you'll find yourself back in this room in a trice. You'll also find my mood far less gracious."

She nodded.

He went to stand at the window and turned his back to her, hoping she'd speak more frankly if spared his penetrating scrutiny.

In a voice so low that he sometimes had to cock an ear or ask her to repeat something, Combs recounted the event. Two long pauses interrupted her, one before she told him what Gwynneth had said to her and the other just before telling how she'd fainted dead away at Gwynneth's feet.

Thorne felt his wrath building beyond reason. Reminding himself he wanted Combs to suffer no repercussions, he took deep, quiet breaths. By the time she'd finished and he turned to look at her, the heat had almost left his face.

"No real harm was done, then, to you or the child?" His gaze pierced the maid through; no amount of deep breathing could help that. Oddly enough, it never seemed to rattle her as it did other people.

"Only to my foolish pride, M'lord."

"I suppose reinstating your library privileges is of no use. The experience is spoiled for you...you'd never come again."

She said nothing, but he saw confirmation in her eyes.

"Return to your duties, then. I thank you for your candor." He made his tone brusque, all business. "Consider the matter closed."

"Aye, M'lord." Lowering her eyes, she curtseyed and took her leave--for once without being delayed.

TWENTY-THREE

"How do you think it looks to my servants when you come barging into my house in your stableman's rags?"

"I don't give a rat's arse how it looks to that old hag you call a maid. As for Ashby and your cook, I can charm the garters right off them, rags *or* riches. And it's stable *master* now."

Caroline plopped into a velvet chair, her skirts flouncing.

"Might I sit as well?" Hobbs said with a mocking air.

"No, you may not! Say what you've come for. More money to keep your tongue in your head?"

"Not nearly that simple, dear sister." He smiled.

"What, then?"

"I've come to strike a bargain." Sitting down to spite her, he saw her eyes snap with anger. "When might you visit Wycliffe Hall again?" he said quickly.

She looked taken aback. "I...I haven't been invited."

"And why should that stop you?"

Her eyes fell. She fussed with the lace tiers on her sleeve. "His lordship and I," she said with obvious reluctance, "had words."

"All the more reason to visit. To apologize."

"Apologize?" She looked up at him grimly. "On a cold day in Hades, perhaps. 'Tis I who deserves the apology."

"Lady Neville is your friend. Mightn't she issue an invitation despite the rift?"

Caroline's eyes narrowed. "Perhaps. Why this sudden interest in my itinerary?"

"Lady Neville needs a friend just now." Hobbs put on a somber face. "Her marriage is not a happy one."

"How could you know that?"

"She told me so."

Caroline's bark of laughter ended in a sneer. "She confided in you? That prissy little saint? Tell the truth, Toby."

"Watch how you speak of her, Caroline. She's been kind to you, she deserves better than your peculiar brand of friendship. Sadly, I fear you're the only friend she has."

"My, my, such devotion. Coveting the master's wife, are we?" Caroline's taunting smile turned to a throaty laugh. "My dear boy, Gwynneth herself can tell you--and probably will--that there is a commandment against such 'wickedness'!"

"You're treading quicksand, Caroline," he warned, his face flushing.

Her jaw dropped. "Oh my God...I don't believe it...you're in *love* with the girl! Oh, this is too bloody rich for words!" Scathing laughter doubled her over.

Hobbs leapt from his chair to close the doors, then turned on his sister. "Shut up," he snarled, grasping her chin in one hand and jerking her face up to his, "before I break your precious neck!"

Caroline glared at him.

"I'll convince her to invite you," he said curtly. "Once there, I want you to do and say everything within your power to divide her and Neville--artfully, mind you." He let go her chin with a contemptuous little shove. "You can do it, artifice is one of your greatest talents."

Caroline furiously wiped her chin with a lace-trimmed handkerchief. "I don't see how."

"Don't play the ingenue with me. I can tell Neville fancies you. With your powers" --he leered at her bosom before meeting her eyes again-- "of feminine persuasion, you'll have him off Lady Neville's trail in no time. There are worse things," he reminded her with a cunning look, "than being a nobleman's mistress. Besides, landed gentry often marry daughters of *rich merchants* nowadays." He winked slyly.

"And how would this little sabotage serve *you*?" Caroline snapped.

"That is more than you need know. Suffice it to say that in return for your efforts, be they sincere and successful, I shall refrain from any future extortion of your considerable funds and will continue to keep your humble origins--and mine--to myself."

"Listen to you! Such eloquence, now that you aspire to seduce your master's wife! One would think you were educated with gentry..." Her words trailed off.

"That I *am* gentry." Hobbs smiled at her sulky expression. "You'll forgive my efforts then, sweet sister, to at least *speak* as though I was tutored in my father's house. You see, we've each our aspirations, haven't we?...though mine aren't entirely counterfeit."

Glowering at him, she replied crossly, "Very well. Should I receive an invitation to visit Wycliffe Hall, I'll accept." She narrowed her eyes. "Then let the games begin."

Hobbs smile took a malicious twist. "And may the best man win."

TWENTY-FOUR

"Caroline's arriving Wednesday for a visit," Gwynneth announced over supper Friday evening.

Thorne ignored the trip in his heartbeat. "I'm surprised she could make the journey on such short notice."

"She seemed glad at the prospect," Gwynneth said, adding peevishly, "and though you had to suffer her presence an additional three days, I have not seen her since the wedding."

"You should have gone to the Townsends' house party," Thorne said evenly. "The two of you could have visited to your heart's content."

The look on Gwynneth's face was priceless. "You never said she was a guest!"

He shrugged. "Out of sight, out of mind."

"You knew she was invited?"

"No. It seems Townsend met up with her days beforehand and invited her. By social standards she should have refused, but Caroline doesn't seem particularly bound by convention."

Gwynneth bristled. "You are so quick to criticize her."

"'Twas simply an observation, my lady."

"Did you pass some time with her?"

Eyes on his food, Thorne shook his head. "No," he lied. "Though I did manage to be civil." Another lie. Inwardly he winced at the thought of his last exchange with Caroline.

Her visit could only be trouble.

And Thorne knew he had asked for it.

* * *

Sunday morning dawned rainy and cold. As Parson Carey closed the worship service, Elaine sighed to think of the walk back to the manor. The ruts had been filled before the wedding, but the road had been gouged again during harvest and was pocked with puddles. There would be much dried mud to brush from her skirts and wash from her stockings, and even those small tasks seemed tiresome these days.

She closed her Anglican prayer book and turned to exit the front pew--then froze.

At the rear of the church, his impenetrable gaze fixed straight ahead, sat Lord Neville.

Elaine walked down the central nave, looking down as she passed him, but paused as he murmured her name.

"Wait in the vestibule," he said.

The other servants were nearly out the door, none of them hanging back for Elaine. She stepped behind a wooden column while Parson Carey exchanged a few words with their employer. As Carey exited through the vestry, she heard her master's familiar tread approach the rear of the church.

"Good morning," he said as their eyes met in the shadows.

"Good morning, M'lord." She curtsied, then sat on the bench he indicated just inside the door.He sat down at a discreet distance.Heart racing, she managed to endure his close scrutiny with outward calm.

"How fare you?"

"Well, M'lord, thank you."

He looked relieved. "Markham treats you kindly, then?"

"Yes, very kindly. She is a patient teacher and a pleasant companion."

"Your *only* companion, it seems," he said wryly.

Looking down, she nodded.

"Eyes up, Combs."

Surprised, she met his stern gaze.

"Keep your head up and your eyes to the fore," he said more gently. "You've nothing to be ashamed of. You need be humble before none but your Maker, and show due respect only to those you serve. The rest of the world can go to the devil. Is that clear, Combs?"

She could only nod, her throat tight and her eyes full of tears.

"Here," he said hastily, fumbling in his coat pocket and pulling out a handkerchief. "I didn't mean to distress you."

To Elaine's astonishment, he blotted her tears himself, with startling tenderness. The linen smelled of sandalwood. She breathed deeply as if to calm herself, while inhaling his fragrance. "You mistake my tears, M'lord," she assured him as he refolded the handkerchief and tucked it into his pocket. "I am merely grateful, as always, for your kindness and concern."

"Your gratitude is unnecessary. Is all well with the babe?"

Elaine nodded, a radiant warmth that was more than a blush infusing her cheeks as she carefully averted her eyes. "Aye, M'lord, as best I can tell."

"Let's be certain. We'll have Hodges out to examine you." He held up a hand as she started to protest. "'Tis useless to argue, Combs. I am your master and I will have my way."

Detecting a mischievous glint in his eye, she smiled. "Very well, M'lord."

He stood up and extended a hand. "Come then. My coach awaits. I'm taking you home."

Elaine knew that Thorne Neville was not in the habit of taking a coach to the manor church; rain or shine, he would come walking or on horseback, if he came at all. Speechless, she took the hand he offered.

As his warm fingers enclosed her own, something leapt within her.

"What is it?" he said quickly at her little gasp.

"I--I think the babe just moved." Wide-eyed, she saw something akin to pain cross Lord Neville's face before the heat of embarrassment flushed her own.

"Let's get you into the coach," he said shortly, and helped her up off the bench.

Once ushered into the shining black conveyance, whose interior already felt warm and toasty from the brazier of glowing coals on the floor, Elaine settled into the plush velvet seat with a sigh of pleasure. Lord Neville climbed in after her, and in the relatively small enclosure, she realized for the first time what a presence he commanded by his very height and breadth.

"This is no day," he said as the coach jerked into motion, "for you to be traipsing through the muck and mire." He smiled. "Hence I shall convey you in style to the west entrance, where you can slip up the service stairs unobserved." He sobered. "However, this will be the last Sunday you venture to matins."

"Why?" Elaine cried, forgetting protocol in her dismay.

He studied her face. "Does it mean so much to you?"

Considering it, she sighed. "Not so much in a religious sense, as I believe worship can be expressed in hundreds of little ways throughout the day, on the Sabbath or any other. 'Tis just...would I sound utterly mad if I said I'd miss the social aspect? Though no one has much to do with me these days, I somehow feel more a part of the human race when I join them in church."

He nodded, still studying her face, then glanced out the window. "We're nearing the Hall, so I must finish my say. Though it gives me no pleasure after what you've just told me, I ask that you confine yourself to the house 'til after the babe is born. This road is not safe for a woman in your condition, especially with winter approaching. And though I personally wouldn't object," he said with a wry grimace, "others might see it as nothing less than scandalous for you to be driven to and fro in my coach." He smiled as Elaine smothered a laugh. "'Tis only a matter of time before your confinement at any rate, as Doctor Hodges will no doubt declare."

She nodded, blushing along with him.

"You'll abide by my wishes, then?" If he was trying to sound brusque, he failed miserably.

"M'lord," she said impulsively, "you are without a doubt the most compassionate master God ever gave breath, just as I knew you would be-" She broke off with an audible swallow, her heart racing; she'd said far more than was wise. "Thank you, M'lord, I shall gladly do as you wish."

Seeing him gaze at her hands, she stopped clasping and unclasping them in her lap.

"You've aroused my curiosity, Combs. How could you have known anything of my temperament before you came to work here?"

"Your reputation is well known, M'lord," she replied hastily. She looked out the window, unable to endure his thoughtful perusal any longer, and breathed a silent sigh of relief as they turned into the drive of the Hall's west wing.

"Quickly," Lord Neville said, helping her down from the coach. With a slap on the roof, he signaled the driver to be off, then opened the heavy door to the Hall. Inside and away from prying eyes, he drew Elaine into the alcove of the service stairs.

"As you'll have no society but Markham's during your confinement," he said in a low voice, "I'm offering you the use of the library again. Hear me out before you refuse. You know I often sit there late into the evening, and I'd welcome...that is to say, I've never minded your company. You could read to your heart's content without any fear of discovery. Now that I'm home again, no one intrudes there of an evening."

Elaine's pulse quickened as she absorbed the full import of his words. That she, an unwed servant, expecting a child, should be invited to inhabit the master's favorite retreat, in his company and under his protection--this was madness! No, she amended:

this was Thorneton Neville. This was her lord and master, and if she had only ever thought she loved him, she knew it now beyond a doubt.

She willed away tears. "I should be glad to, M'lord...more than glad, I should be in your debt." She nearly took his hand in her fervor; catching herself, she dropped into a prolonged curtsey.

She stifled a gasp as his hand touched her face--a touch so light and so brief it shouldn't have burned her as it did, and she knew she would feel that warmth on her cheek for hours.

"You are more than welcome. But I must ask you to forego another convention," he said, supporting one of her elbows as she stood.

"Yes, M'lord?" She sounded breathless--too breathless from mere physical strain.

"Henceforth," he said firmly, "do not curtsey to me. Nod if you must, but do not bend your knee. You risk a fall."

She swallowed the lump in her throat. If he showed her any further kindness, she would weep. Or worse yet, kiss him. "As you wish, M'lord," she murmured, and slipped through the service stair door before he could say another word.

* * *

Atop Raven's back, on high ground in one of his orchards Wednesday morning, Thorne spotted the Sutherland coach on the Northhampton Road.

With a grim expression, he plucked a Macintosh from a branch overhead and tossed it into his saddlebag, where it joined a loaf of oat bread and a flask of Arthur's homemade blackberry wine. After lunch he would oversee the cider pressing for Arthur, who'd been called on family business to Kettering. But first he would borrow a pole from Carmody, who farmed the apple orchard, and slip away for some fishing when the pickers stopped for their midday meal.

He had just dropped his line on the north fork, where cold underground springs fed into the beck, when he realized he had company a few yards down the bank. The boy eyed him curiously but said nothing, and eventually Thorne all but forgot he was there. A quarter of an hour passed before Thorne hauled in his first catch. He was separating hook and trout when a pair of bare feet appeared on the mossy ground beside him.

"Not very big, is it, sir."

"No," Thorne agreed, squinting up at the boy, who appeared all of twelve. "Who might you be?"

"Clayton Carmody, sir. And ye're Lord Neville hisself," the boy announced solemnly. "I seen ye at ye're wedding."

Thorne chuckled. "Then I shan't bother introducing myself. Join me, Clayton, if you like. Perhaps between us we'll manage to catch something worth eating. Why aren't you in the orchard today?"

"Promised me mum I'd catch supper, sir." Clayton replaced his lost bait with a fat grubworm. "She give me two hours, then back to the press." He glanced toward the sun. "Reckon I've an hour to go."

After sharing his lunch, Thorne was about to leave when Clayton broke the silence. "Did ye know Henry, M'lord...the stable groom at the Hall?"

Startled, Thorne took a moment to reply. "Aye, I knew Henry. Was he a friend of yours?"

"Aye," Clayton acknowledged, swinging his line in and grabbing hold of the trout on his hook. "One of me best mates, he was. Talked to him on his last day." Biting his lip, Clayton baited his hook again and cast the line. "A mite upset, Henry was, with the master--oh, not ye, sir. The stable master. Seems Henry'd asked him a thing or two about the lady what was in the stables some nights before and had got into a row with the master."

"A lady in the stables," Thorne echoed with a frown. "And she quarreled with the stable master?"

"Aye, sir. She was a guest at the Hall, Henry said. Said the stable master nigh pulled her hair out."

"And what else did Henry say?" Thorne asked, as casually as if he were inquiring the time of day.

Clayton kept his eyes on his line. "Said the stable master called the lady his sister. Said he called her some wicked names, too. Didn't want her in his stables. The lady said he'd best treat her like a lady, and not tell anybody she was his sister. Then she give him notes and coin."

"Money," Thorne murmured, his mind racing. "Did Henry happen to tell you the lady's name?"

The boy screwed up his nose as he thought about it. "Might have, sir. I don't recollect."

"Never mind, your memory is remarkable. And you say Henry asked the stable master about the quarrel?"

"Aye, sir. The stable master was hopping mad at him, too, for knowing about it. Told Henry if he wanted to keep his situation, he'd best keep mum about the lady *and* the quarrel!"

Thorne stood up and wrapped his line, tucking the hook safely away. "Here. Take my catch. 'Tisn't much, but with yours it might be worth keeping."

"Much obliged, sir." The boy tipped his cap.

"Good fishing," Thorne said with a nod. "See you at the press."

The rest of the afternoon was a blur. Thorne could think of little but what the boy had told him, Caroline's arrival shoved to the back of his mind. Which of his wedding guests could be Hobbs' sister, and how was it possible? He recalled every female guest who'd stayed at Wycliffe Hall. None seemed a likely candidate. Could the boy be mistaken? It was hearsay, after all; he might have confused the facts. But only Henry or Hobbs could verify them.

And Henry was dead.

* * *

Stunning as ever, Caroline was warmer toward Thorne than he expected, though entirely proper.

The perfect actress.

Supper proved pleasant enough, but as an hour passed afterward in the drawing room, Thorne caught himself glancing at the adjoining library door. For the last three evenings, Elaine Combs had slipped into that room shortly after ten of the clock. As quiet as she was, he'd been keenly aware of her presence.

At half past nine, Gwynneth excused herself for the night. Thorne assumed Caroline would do the same, but she lingered on the velvet settee. Her posture seemed somehow languorous, catlike, and the moment the door had closed, she pounced--at least, verbally.

"You needn't feel obligated to stay with me."

Thorne's mouth quirked. "You're dismissing me?"

"'Tis of no consequence to me what you do with your time, or where you do it. This is your house. Stay or go as you please."

"Then I shall go," Thorne said pleasantly. "I've work waiting in the library."

Caroline shot up from the settee and, skirts awhirl, planted herself in front of the library doors. "You're not going anywhere, Thorne Neville."

"I'd have sworn you bade me stay or go as I pleased."

"You owe me."

"Owe you what?"

Her eyes narrowed, her bosom rising and falling more rapidly. "You know *bloody well* what. Your behavior to me at the Townsend's was inexcusable. You'd no right to maul me-"

"Maul you?" Thorne scoffed, coming closer. "I only gave you what you wanted...what you've wanted since you first set eyes on me."

She gasped. "What a *cad* you are!"

"So I've been told. Quite recently, in fact."

"How *dare* you suggest I asked for such abominable treatment!" Her low voice trembled with indignation. She beat a fist on her bosom. "That *I*, who have just lost a dear husband, would even *think* to invite such attention from you...from *any* man!"

It was too much. Thorne's laughter rumbled up from deep within his chest.

Caroline flew at him, one arm thrown back to strike; he whipped out a hand and grabbed her by the wrist. She raised her other arm, but it too was caught with lightning speed.

She glowered at Thorne, her helpless fury finding no outlet but the tears that brimmed in the seething blackness of her eyes. "*I hate you*," she hissed, twisting and pulling in his relentless grip.

"Of course you do," he mocked, tightening his hold.

"You're hurting me!" Her voice caught on an angry sob. "Let me go!"

"Admit it, Caroline. *Admit* it, damn you."

"What?" she cried softly, still struggling. "Admit what?"

Thorne yanked her to him, his face so close to hers he could feel his own breath; he ground his words through his teeth. "That you've deliberately teased and tormented me, time after time, hour after hour, day after day for weeks on end. That you've done everything short of throwing yourself at me. That you want me," he said with a growl, giving her a little shake to squelch her indignant protest. "*Have* wanted me, in your bed and in your grasp from the start...admit it, Caroline. *Say* it."

"*No!*" She shut her eyes against his burning glare and shook her head. "You're wrong, I never did."

"Look at me and tell me that," he rasped.

"No," she murmured. But as he kept his unforgiving hold on her trembling arms, she opened her eyes...and whimpered at what she saw in his.

The sound deepened to a vanquished moan as Thorne's open mouth struck hers with such force that he tasted blood. Neither knowing nor caring whose it was, he crushed her against him, still holding her arms behind her bent back as he plundered and pillaged her lush mouth with a rapier-like tongue.

His fingers loosened on her wrists, then released them, one hand going to the small of Caroline's back and the other cupping her skull to press her into the onslaught of his kiss. Immediately he realized he'd underestimated her.

He sensed her arms upraising, her fingers hooking to claw at his face--and chose that moment to glide his hands up and cup the the full curves of her bodice.

She gasped, her knees buckling. All at once she was clinging instead of pushing, clawing not his face but his back and shoulders, as she met the demands of his mouth in full measure, her heart beating wildly beneath the breast overflowing his right hand.

He had just caught her to him by her waist, when his eyes caught something else entirely--the soft glow of firelight beneath the library doors. He went stock-still.

Caroline opened her eyes, the naked hunger in them turning to hurt pride as she saw Thorne's transformed expression.

His hands slid down her arms. He turned his back on her and, pacing to a window, drew the back of his hand across his mouth--a futile effort to erase his folly. He turned swiftly at the sound of her brief, mocking laughter.

"And you wonder I should call you a cad," she taunted, her voice husky with unspent passion. She touched trembling fingers to her bleeding lip.

"No," he said hoarsely, and shook his head. "I don't wonder in the least."

He turned back to the window and waited, then heard the door latch release and catch. Leaning his forehead against the cool glass, he released a long breath and stared hollowly at his reflection.

He hardly recognized it.

* * *

Elaine looked up at the library mantel clock again. Apparently she was to have no company this evening.

And as quiet and respectfully distant as her companion would have been, she felt his absence with a depth and an ache that left her nearly ill.

TWENTY-FIVE

"What a greasy, despicable man," Gwynneth muttered as the coach lurched forward on the road to Northhampton.

"Who?" Caroline demanded, halting her fan mid-stroke.

"The Earl of Whittingham. He and my father have come calling, after a fortnight in London doing heaven knows what. Which is why, when Thorne suggested I take you into Northhampton and shop for the day, I leapt at the chance to escape." Gwynneth shivered. "How that man looks at me with those beady black eyes, as if I were a prize thoroughbred on the block and he about to bid! Thank Providence they are leaving tomorrow."

"Did you say...Whittingham?"

"Yes, I--why Caroline, you are white as a sheet. What ails you?"

"Turn the coach 'round."

"Pardon?"

"Turn it 'round or I shall be sick on the spot."

Once inside the Hall, Gwynneth ordered an herbal concoction and some broth and took her friend up the service stairs. "Stop fussing," Caroline said. "'Tis nothing, I'll be fine in a day or so. Give your husband my regrets at supper."

Seeming delighted to learn Caroline was visiting and disappointed to be deprived of her company, Radleigh praised "the Widow Sutherland's" attributes to the earl. Lord Whittingham expressed polite regret at missing an introduction to the legendary society maven.

Radleigh retired early, and as Gwynneth followed soon after, Thorne found himself alone with the earl--all according to plan, he suspected. His suspicions were shortly confirmed. With little prodding, Lord Whittingham admitted that he had, "only because of a long acquaintance with Radleigh," recently provided additional capital for the viscount's gaming pursuits.

Thorne's expression turned stony. "I thought I'd made myself quite clear, my lord. I asked you, in the interest of your old friendship with my father, not to loan money to Radleigh again."

The earl shrugged. "I tried to discourage him, but he was certain luck would be with him at the tables. I had accompanied him"--he leaned forward and lowered his voice--"to a certain establishment the evening before...perhaps you know of it, the lovely home of Madame Claire DuFoire? All Radleigh's idea, of course." Lord Whittingham settled back in his chair and smiled crookedly. "One of Madame Claire's young protégés read his fortune in a teacup. Puffed him up a bit, you might say, in more ways than one." The earl chuckled, then sobered. "Alas, after a couple of wins, Lady Luck departed."

"Just how much damage did she leave behind?"

"Four-thousand seven-hundred sixty-three pounds."

Thorne arched his brow. "In one evening?"

"Over several evenings. Very persuasive Radleigh is, as you know. I happen to have the receipts with me."

"I thought you might. In my study, sir, if you please."

Thorne's study stayed ominously quiet but for the crackling fire and the scratching of his quill. Keeping the note in hand, he withdrew another document from the drawer. "You'll take no offense, I trust," he said as he handed the latter over to Lord Whittingham, "to my requiring your signature on this agreement I've prepared. Read it at your leisure. I've the entire evening if necessary."

"What's this?" The earl eyed it with obvious suspicion.

"Only your pledge that you will no longer serve as my father-in-law's moneylender."

Lord Whittingham reluctantly traded his signature for Thorne's note of payment.

"This is the second and last of these," Thorne warned. "Be advised that if Radleigh persuades you again, you'll find a suit on your hands."

"Beg pardon?"

"A lawsuit, my lord. I would bring you before the magistrate on charges of pandering, as well as for breach of contract."

"You would do no such thing!"

"Try me."

"Pandering?" Lord Whittingham's chin folded on itself as he drew back incredulously. "You'd be obliged to expose your father-in-law as a drunkard and a gambler, incapable of holding his own estate. Would you bring such infamy on your wife's family?"

"If it keeps you from bleeding me dry."

For a long moment the two men stared at one another, then Lord Whittingham blew out a sigh. "Well." He slapped the arms of his chair. "You are your father's son, I've no doubt of that."

"I shall take that as a compliment."

Lord Whittingham snorted, rising from his seat. "You'll excuse me, then. The hour grows late, and we must leave tomorrow."

"'Tis unfortunate you can stay no longer," Thorne said pleasantly, and rose to bow.

"Indeed," was Lord Whittingham's surly reply as he strode from the study.

* * *

Jerking awake, Thorne heard it again--a scream he recognized all too well.

He sprang from the study settee and ran into the great hall, then bounded up the stairs three at a time. Gwynneth met him in the gallery. She stood back as he pounded on Caroline's door.

"*Damnation*, Ashby, let me *in*!"

Again the scream sounded from within. Thorne rammed the door repeatedly with his shoulder. The old oak splintered under the stress. With two more teeth-gritting shoves, the latch and bolt hung useless.

Cowering in a corner, hair in wild disarray, Caroline clutched pieces of her ripped shift together at a shoulder. "Thank God you've come!" she cried, then pointed a quaking finger at the drapery folds between the bedchamber and the sitting room.

Thorne froze. Lord Whittingham had just stepped out from behind a velvet panel.

"What on earth...?" Gwynneth began, and then cried out, "Thorne, no!"

But his fist had already smashed into Lord Whittingham's face.

Blood sprayed from the earl's nose, while his lips split against his teeth. With surprising strength, he lunged at Thorne with a well-placed body punch, then found himself pinned to the floor.

"What," Thorne growled into his guest's florid face, "in bloody, blazing <u>hell</u> are you doing in these chambers?"

Lord Whittingham only wheezed and groaned, helpless beneath a knee-lock and the iron hand at his throat.

"*Answer me,* damn you!" Eyes blazing, Thorne tightened his grip on the earl.

"My lord." Gwynneth sounded shaken. "The man cannot speak while you're strangling him-"

"He's lucky I haven't slit his worthless throat," Thorne snarled, nevertheless relaxing his hold a bit. Lord Whittingham coughed, one hand under his dripping nose.

"Wet this." Thorne glanced about the room as he whipped a linen handkerchief from the earl's breast pocket and gave it to Caroline, whose wrapper now concealed her torn nightclothes. "Where the devil is that maid of yours?"

"I...I don't know...she was to spend the night on the chaise. She was here when I fell asleep-" Caroline broke off, but Thorne heard her whispered curse.

"I'll see if she's gone topstairs," Gwynneth said hastily, and fled the chamber.

Caroline wet the handkerchief at the washstand and held it out gingerly to Thorne, then withdrew a safe distance.

"Your visitor seems reluctant to talk," he told her grimly. "Suppose *you* tell me what the illustrious gentleman had on his mind. Did you let him in?"

"Of course not! I was sleeping, though not very soundly, and I heard a noise. I opened my eyes, only to see *him* standing over me...God's teeth, what a fright!"

Thorne stood up without bothering to extend a hand to Lord Whittingham, who was still nursing his bleeding nose. "Did he hurt you?" he asked Caroline in a tight voice.

"No, but if I hadn't wakened when I did..." Eyes wide and brimming with tears, Caroline bit down on her swollen lip.

Thorne dragged his gaze off that ripe, forbidden fruit that he himself had bruised just hours ago. He turned on the earl, who was lurching to his feet. "I'll have the rest of this bizarre story from *you*, sir. How did you enter these chambers?"

"The door was unbolted," Lord Whittingham grumbled. "The missing maid, I suppose."

"And what the devil were you thinking when you let yourself in?" Thorne demanded, more incredulous by the second. "Were you sleepwalking? Did you somehow confuse my home with the brothel?"

"*Thorne!*" Gwynneth stood slack-jawed in the doorway. "*Please*, mind what you're saying! I couldn't find the maid," she told them. "Caroline, haven't you some notion where she's gone?"

Caroline's eyes narrowed. "Oh, I've a notion, all right. You might try the stables. Her head has been turned more than once by your stable master."

Gwynneth's face drained of what color it had, but Caroline had no time to wonder as Thorne broke in impatiently. "My lady, have Byrnes wake William, and then send him to the stables to inquire...no, on second thought I'll go myself--*after* our guest accounts for his actions."

If the Nevilles had been incredulous over the earl's behavior up to now, they were utterly stunned when he turned his beady eyes on Caroline and said with a sneer, "Well, *Mistress Sutherland*, shall we tell our host of our past acquaintance?"

Caroline drew herself up to her considerable height and gave Lord Whittingham a scathing look before meeting Thorne's stare. "This blackguard," she said with a shudder, "was once my husband."

Gwynneth gasped and made the Sign of the Cross. Thorne nearly did the same. "This," he said hoarsely, "is the perverse tyrant of whom you told me in London?" At Caroline's reluctant nod, he fixed Lord Whittingham with a glare of fast-building fury. "I suppose that, in your twisted mind, prior claim on the lady gives you the right to enter her chambers uninvited?"

"Lady!" Lord Whittingham seized on the word, then cackled like a crone. "She's *anything* but a lady, Neville, mark me."

More than his words were marked, as Thorne's fist undercut his jaw and sent him sprawling and sliding across the polished wood floor, where Lord Whittingham's skull met the plaster wall with a satisfying "thunk." Thorne turned to Gwynneth, who stared at him with hollow eyes. "Take Caroline to your chambers for the night."

"Very well...but then I shall accompany you to the stables."

He scowled. "What for?"

"Ashby is a woman," Gwynneth said, looking pale but resolute. "If you must confront her, I think it best I be there."

"Very well," Thorne muttered, "but be sure Caroline fastens the bolt on your chamber door. And put on some proper clothing." When the women had gone, he turned a jaundiced look on Lord Whittingham, who had struggled to his feet and was gingerly feeling his jaw.

"You needn't worry, I'll take my leave now," the earl said nervously. "I'll just wake Radleigh-"

"You will not go near my father-in-law. Not now, and in the interest of your good health, never again. Do I make myself clear?"

"Quite." Lord Whittingham indicated the door with a jerk of his head. "By your leave."

"Mine and everyone else's," Thorne said sharply. "I'll see you off myself."

* * *

"Hobbs, open the door."

Nothing sounded from within. Thorne glanced over his shoulder. "I think it best you wait here, my lady."

"I am a grown woman, my lord."

"A frightened one, I'd say, from the tremor in your voice. Get behind me, then."

He knocked sharply and listened again. This time he heard feet shuffling on the plank flooring. Someone drew the bolt, and the door slowly opened a crack.

Blinking in the light of the tallow candle he held, Tobias Hobbs ran a hand through his tousled hair. "Aye, M'lord?"

"Send the girl out."

"The girl, my lord?"

Thorne knew Gwynneth had moved out from behind him when he saw Hobbs' eyes shift and widen. "Ashby," Thorne said curtly. "Send her out, she's needed by her mistress." He was amazed to see Hobbs' cheeks turn ruddy. Perhaps bringing Gwynneth had been wise. Her presence seemed to embarrass the stable master.

The door shut again, practically in Thorne's face. Loud whispering ensued from the other side. Gwynneth looked about to faint. No doubt her morals were highly insulted. Thorne had no time to muse further as the door opened again and Ashby appeared with a sheepish expresion on her pretty face, her employer's shawl clutched tightly about her shoulders.

After leaving his ashen-faced wife in care of Byrnes, Thorne sent Caroline's maid topstairs to face her mistress' wrath. Back in bed, Thorne tried to sleep, but found it impossible after something struck him like a thunderbolt. When he had told Caroline about Lena, he had mentioned that Lena's father's pet name for her was Maddie. If indeed Caroline and Lord Whittingham were once married, why had Caroline failed to react? She was too bright not to have made the connection.

Then she must have known all along. The perfect actress, indeed. Thorne felt his anger rising. To think that he'd felt like such a cur for his behavior in the drawing room! He'd even planned to apologize at the first opportunity.

His visit to the kitchen at the crack of dawn garnered fresh-baked scones, potatoes fried in bacon fat, and a fresh pitcher of milk. After bussing a flustered Bridey on the cheek, he headed across the great hall, then heard the officious tones of Dame Carswell hail him from her office under the stairs. He waited as she approached, her mouth pinched in obvious disapproval.

"What is it, Carswell?"

She curtsied. Only then did Thorne see the odd glow in her eyes, a glow one could only call triumphant.

"I have just spoken with Markham and thought you should be informed, M'lord. Elaine Combs has disappeared."

TWENTY-SIX

"Where the deuce could she have gone?" Thorne heard his voice--taut, demanding, the second time he'd asked in less than a minute. Carswell's expression had turned bland, but he had little doubt she was enjoying herself.

"As I said, I've no notion, M'lord."

He tried to look nonchalant. "References, then. Surely she had them. Who were they? Where is her family?"

"There was but one reference, M'lord, that of her last employer, in Sturbridge. Combs is an orphan. She has no known living relative."

"Friends, then?" Thorne tried to ignore a hollow feeling in the pit of his stomach. "Perhaps she went to visit someone who's sick, or dying."

"I doubt it, M'lord. There has been no courier, and Combs retired quite as usual for the night. However, this morn she is nowhere to be found, and what few possessions she had are missing."

Thorne nodded, his mind racing. "We would be remiss if we made no effort to locate her, particularly considering her delicate condition."

The housekeeper said nothing.

"I'd planned to make rounds today," he said, more to himself than her, and ran a hand distractedly through his hair. "Very well, I'll make inquiries along the way. Tell Pennington he'll have to catch up, that since I was up early I saw no point in wasting time." He forced a chuckle. "Tell him to keep an eye peeled for wandering maids."

"Aye, M'lord." Carswell's expression told Thorne she wasn't the least bit fooled by his casual tone.

He hurried to the stables to inform Hobbs of Combs' disappearance. "You will help me search for her," Thorne added flatly. "Father of her child or not, you must realize the difficulty she might encounter away from home and on her own."

Surprisingly, the stable master looked uneasy. "Regarding last night, M'lord..."

Ah, you first look after your own ass! "I've no interest in your peccadilloes, Hobbs."

"Please, M'lord, let me say this. The girl came to *me*, you see. I was quite shocked to find her here."

"No doubt she overpowered you, rendering you helpless to resist," Thorne said dryly. "But why defend yourself to me?"

"If I had known that Lady Neville would come seeking the girl, I would never...what I mean to say is I'm sorry to cause her ladyship such embarrassment. Perhaps you'll tell her so for me."

"Surely you'll have the opportunity to tell her so yourself, Hobbs, since she's in these stables as much as she is anywhere. In the meantime, I expect a sincere effort in this search. And should you find Combs, you had best treat her with the gentleness due a woman in her condition...because if you think to take revenge on her for having 'slandered' you, you might as well put yourself in the sights of my flintlock here and now."

* * *

Radleigh listened in apparent disbelief as his daughter recounted the events of the past night, his face flushing with indignation as she told him of Lord Whittingham's connection to Caroline.

"So, Father, you may remain here as our guest as long as it suits you, or you may go as you please. No doubt Thorne will lend you a coach and team."

Gwynneth sailed past her speechless sire and slammed the door behind her. She strode up the long gallery and stomped up the stairs to the servants' quarters, where she encountered a slug-a-bed parlor maid on her way downstairs.

"Milady," the woman gasped in obvious alarm, then curtsied. "Might I fetch someone for you?"

"You might indeed," Gwynneth said, lifting her head to look down her nose at the taller woman. "The Ashby girl was sent up here by her mistress to finish the night. Tell her to come at once to my day room." Gwynneth's eyes narrowed. "Then report to Dame Carswell. I would have her know of your tardiness."

"Aye, Milady."

In the day room, Gwynneth watched the clock while she paced the floor and, by the time Ashby arrived, was several degrees nearer her boiling point. "Shut the door and sit down," she snapped.

The maid did so hastily, hands fidgeting in her lap.

"Now," Gwynneth began. "You will tell me how you came to be in the stable master's bed last night. Spare me no detail, however sordid. The truth only. Time is of no matter, we shall sit here all the day long if need be."

Ashby made a gulping sound, then said faintly, "Aye, Milady."

"Speak up, there will be no cowering. Did Hobbs in any way suggest your visit, or otherwise lead you to feel you would be welcome in his quarters?"

"No, Milady."

"So, you played trollop on the sly! Were you even acquainted with him beforehand?" Gwynneth leaned forward like a cat eyeing her next meal.

"Aye, Milady. Toby--er, Master Hobbs calls upon my mistress in London now and again."

Gwynneth nearly dropped her jaw. "He...he calls upon Mistress Sutherland?"

"Aye, Milady. He comes to the house by the back door, and Marsh shows him up to the drawing room to see the mistress."

"I see." Gwynneth mentally filed the maid's stunning news away for later consideration. "And did Master Hobbs speak to you earlier yesterday? Perhaps wave at you from the stable yard?"

"No, Milady. I only wandered outdoors last eve' to see the horses-"

"The truth, you little witch! I said I wanted *the truth*!"

Ashby paled. "Aye, Milady, begging your pardon, I wanted to see Toby--I mean to say, Master Hobbs--but he was surprised," she admitted lamely.

Gwynneth sat stiffly back in her chair. "I thought as much. What happened then?"

"I told him I should like to see the horses, Milady."

"And then?"

"Well, he showed me the horses..."

"And?"

"And then he...he sort of sniffed me, like...you know, like-"

"Like a cur sniffs a bitch in heat?" Gwynneth offered, fury underlying her bright smile. "Aye, I've seen the ritual amongst the hounds here. Do go on."

Ashby faltered. "No, Milady, I meant he was smelling my hair, and my neck...that tickled a bit, so it made me breathe faster. And then he asked me how old I am. His voice sounded different, rough-like, and it gave me a funny chill. Seventeen, I told him."

"What then?" Gwynneth prodded in a brittle voice.

"I looked at his lips, and I..."

"Say it."

"I wondered how it'd be to kiss him."

"No doubt you'd wondered for some time." Gwynneth watched the girl with burning eyes.

"Aye." Ashby ducked her head. "But then a funny thing happened. His eyes got all hard and stared at me strange, like he'd just thought of something..."

"And what do you suppose that something was?"

"Well, I didn't know, Milady, not then. We kept staring at each other, and then he leaned over and-"

"Yes?"

"He kissed me, Milady." Ashby's face pinkened again, this time with a dreamy expression. "He kissed me in a lovely way, just as I thought he might...but then he started kissing me harder. I've been kissed before, my lady-" Ashby shook her head, her sultry eyes rounding. "But not like this, not ever! It made me breathless, and gave me such a feeling in the pit of my stomach! And all at once, he picked me up in his arms and *carried* me--still kissing me, mind you!" Fanning herself with one hand, she blotted her forehead on her sleeve, missing Gwynneth's wince.

I can bear no more of this. Gwynneth nearly spoke the words aloud. "So he took you into his bed," she said with outward coolness. "I assume the two of you then fornicated?"

"We...we did what, Milady?"

"*Fornicated*, young woman. Have you never heard the word?"

"No, Milady." Ashby frowned in obvious consternation. "But it sounds...bad."

"'Tis *wicked*!" Gwynneth shot up from her chair as Ashby shrank back in her own. "A *mortal sin*! And you committed it...*the sin of fornication*! Gwynneth's skirts whipped outward as she came around the desk. "What is worse," she hissed, bending over the cringing maid, "is that you caused *Hobbs* to sin! You tempted him, then took your pleasure-"

"And gave him his!" Ashby whined in protest.

Gwynneth raised a trembling hand high in the air. "Aye, and for that offense you shall burn in *hell* at the end of your worthless life, you little whore!"

Down came the hand, delivering a stinging slap to the maid's left cheek. Tears filled Ashby's wide eyes, her mouth trembling as she visibly steeled herself for a vicious backhanded blow to her right cheek.

It came with a loud crack.

"Get your despicable form out of my sight, whore," Gwynneth snarled through her teeth. "Keep away from me while you are in my house. And if you value that pretty skin, you'll stay away from my stableman as well, or so help me, I shall *flay you alive!* Now go! And wash your face before you attend your mistress. Not a word to her of our meeting, or I will have you beaten straightaway!"

Ashby fled as best one could on limbs stiff with terror, not daring to stop and close the door behind her.

Gwynneth heaved it shut and leaned back against it, fingernails digging into her palms, eyes darting wildly about the room until they lit upon the silver filigree-framed miniature of the former Lady Neville. How serene she looked. A woman content with living out her short life as her husband's partner and lover, bearing his child, and overseeing his household.

"Hurrah for you!" Gwynneth whispered furiously. "Perhaps you were more to your husband than a piece of property and a breeding mare!" Face contorting, she ran to pick up the miniature, then dashed it to the floor.

"Milady?"

"What is it?" Gwynneth shrilled, turning a livid stare on Dame Carswell. "How dare you open my door without admittance!"

"Begging your pardon, Milady." The housekeeper curtsied humbly, looking straight at Gwynneth instead of the shattered glass on the floor. "I knocked, but you did not answer, and I knew you'd want to be informed."

"Informed of what?"

"Combs's disappearance, Milady."

"What? When...?"

"Sometime during the night, Milady."

Gwynneth blinked rapidly. "Indeed. And no one knows where she has gone?" "No, Milady."

"Well then, good riddance, I say."

"Aye, Milady." A sly look surfaced in the housekeeper's eyes. "But I fear the news was not so well taken by his lordship."

"No," Gwynneth said tersely, "it wouldn't be. My husband is uncommonly concerned for common people. How he came by such an odd fault, I cannot imagine."

Dame Carswell's lip curled slightly. "His father had the same weakness, Milady."

"I suppose he has ordered a search?"

"Aye, Milady."

"In which he's taking part, no doubt."

"Of which he is the leader," the housekeeper countered, then snapped her mouth shut.

Gwynneth smiled thinly. "I see that you and I are of a mind in this matter, Dame Carswell. Well, God willing, the search shall prove futile."

"Amen, Milady."

* * *

"Yes," Caroline said matter-of-factly. "Mister Hobbs calls to see Horace. They'd some sort of business between them, though my husband never confided its nature to me."

"But she expressly said that Hobbs called upon *you*." Sulking, Gwynneth pushed food around her plate with a fork.

Caroline blotted her lips with a napkin. "He did insist upon seeing me in Horace's absence. He fancied I'd my husband's confidence in matters of trade."

"But you never said a word!"

Caroline sighed. "I rather disliked the man, but I thought it impolite to say. Hence, I said nothing. He doesn't seem to recognize me, either."

Gwynneth eyed her guest dubiously, her thoughts turning again to Hobbs' escapade last evening. Her fists tightened. He would regret his betrayal. She would see to it personally.

* * *

Radleigh waylaid Thorne in the great hall. "My daughter says you'll provide me with a coach, since I've lost my means of transport." He shook his head sadly. "Bad business, that. She told me the upshot of it. Never did I dream-"

"What's your destination?" Thorne cut in, in no mood for dithering after a five-hour search for Elaine Combs.

"Why, I want to return to my house in Covent Gar-"

"I'll be more than glad to lend you a coach, but only to Radleigh Hall."

Radleigh eyed him in silence, then said gruffly, "I imagine his lordship's purse was somewhat fatter when he left."

Thorne barely nodded.

"Order the coach then, with my thanks. I shall reimburse you in full, I promise. With interest."

Again Thorne nodded. "Safe journey, Radleigh. God speed."

He had no delusions he'd ever see that money again.

* * *

Mid-afternoon, thick clouds hung over Wycliffe Hall and unleashed a cold, torrential rain. Watching it run down the study windows, Thorne grimly contemplated Elaine Combs' whereabouts. Hobbs had taken the Wycliffe road, while Thorne had searched high and low off the road to Northampton, even forcing Raven halfway up the side of a wooded ravine where he knew of a small, hidden cave. Inside he'd found only small bones, long dried out, with some droppings.

Why was he so concerned for a servant--a lone, unwed, pregnant castoff of his stableman, at that?

Because she has no one, he answered himself crossly. *And because the man who should be standing beside her in all this has just bedded Caroline's maid.*

But there was more, and Thorne knew it. Combs' quiet, unassuming air, and the way her poise and grace went hand in hand with such steely determination, fascinated him. Her voice, by turns as soothing as the flow of the beck or as clear and musical as the ring of silver on crystal, seemed tuned for his ear in particular. The innate honesty and clarity in her dove-gray eyes riveted him, and the joy and appreciation he saw there for the smallest of pleasures made his heart swell. And not once during all these weeks of ostracism by her peers had she ever bemoaned the new life she carried within her. Indeed, Thorne knew beyond a doubt that from the day of her child's birth, Elaine Combs would lavish upon it all the love and tender care of which a mother was capable.

How he had enjoyed her presence here on recent evenings. He loved the room by day, when sunrays streamed through the solar and sought out the aged, mellow hues of furnishings and books, but there was something more compelling in those quiet hours when the shadows lengthened and receded in the rich warmth of the fire's glow. He'd sensed an expectant air, a palpable quickening in the atmosphere. It seemed the room anticipated Combs' arrival as eagerly as he did.

Each evening she had bowed her head in greeting, mindful of his request to omit the curtsey, and had kept a decorous silence until he spoke. At first she'd sat far across the room to do her reading; later she'd hesitantly agreed to leave only one fireside chair between them. In the meantime, Thorne's covert glances had committed her classic profile to memory. He'd also stolen glances at her thickening waist. Though guilt tweaked his conscience, he'd savored a keen sense of patriarchal protectiveness.

He'd noticed something else those evenings. The library, always his father's domain, now seemed his own. In making it Combs' sanctuary as well as his, Thorne had taken true possession of it.

But the last two evenings had kept him away. He could hardly blame Caroline for Wednesday night, when he'd deliberately and perversely spurred a confrontation. Yestereve was another matter. Thanks to Lord Whittingham and his own brand of perversion, Thorne had missed his library sojourn again.

Something else must have occurred in those forty-eight hours--something significant enough to provoke Combs to flee without regard to her condition and her lack of means. Thorne had initially pinned his hopes on Markham, but the old seamstress, though bewildered and sad, knew of no reason for Combs' departure or of any change in her circumstances.

Nothing. It was all anyone knew. It was all Thorne felt.

Finishing some of the work he'd neglected that morning, and thinking Gwynneth secluded in her chamber with no prospect of riding today, he returned the wedding record book to her day room. He'd hoped to deduce from it which guest might be Hobbs' sister, but the book had offered no more than a bittersweet look at Elaine Combs' genteel handwriting, leaving Thorne to conclude either Henry Pitts or Clayton Carmody had heard wrongly.

A trace of lemon verbena hung in the air of the deserted day room, spurring him to open the drawer hastily, but as he replaced the wedding book he noticed a framed miniature. He picked it up and turned it over.

Between small shards of glass stuck in the frame, his mother looked back at him with an enigmatic smile. Thorne frowned. With a bit more petulance in her expression and smoldering fire in her eyes, Catherine Neville could almost be mistaken for Caroline Sutherland.

Staring at the tiny painting, he walked slowly back to his study. He carefully pried the bits of glass out the frame and, without quite knowing why, propped the portrait on the desk where he could view it at will.

Perhaps the next best thing to a likeness of Caroline? mocked his inner voice. He turned grimly away from the miniature and strode from the room.

He was taken aback to find the very subject of his thoughts in the library. Silhouetted against the gray light of the solar windows, Caroline watched his hesitant approach with no rancor in her expression, and quietly thanked him for his rescue during the night. "If you had not come when you did," she said, "you might well have had to send for the undertaker this morn." She nodded solemnly at Thorne's stare of disbelief.

"Surely you don't mean to say he'd have murdered you."

"Quite likely, but only after forcing himself upon me. Surprise, bondage, and cruel force are just a few of his trademarks. 'Tis a wonder I survived our marriage with all my limbs and features intact."

Thorne averted his gaze. "Then I wish I'd killed him."

"Because of me?"

Jaws clenched, he fought to keep his voice level. "Because he has imposed himself upon my family time and time again, even before my father's death. Now the bloody bastard nearly rapes and kills a guest in my house, and how do I repay him? After little more than bloodying his nose and blacking an eye, I send him away with a full purse!"

"You acted with righteous anger. And whether or not you admit it, you defended my honor, as is your way."

"My way," Thorne scoffed, his eyes pinning hers. "And was it my way, Caroline, when I nearly crushed the life out of you in this room two evenings ago? Was I so righteous then?" His voice tightened as Caroline touched her swollen lip. "You speak of 'cruel force' at his hands--did I not use the same against you?"

"There is no comparison. And you more than made up for that aberration by flying to my rescue last night."

"Aberration." He gave her a grim look. "Have you forgotten our exchange behind Townsend's hedgerow? I suppose that was an aberration as well."

Caroline pursed her lips, then turned away. "I shall take my leave, you're unreasonable this morning."

She turned as Thorne grabbed her hand, and the irony in her eyes acknowledged the familiarity of the gesture.

"Caroline, please." He gave her a mirthless smile. "What I'm trying to say, with piss-poor results, is that I'm heartily sorry for my behavior yesterday and that night at Townsend's house. There was no excuse for it. You'd every reason to call me a cad, for no matter what effect you have upon me, I haven't the right to impose my...impulses...upon your person, or to accuse *you* of impropriety...not then, not now, not ever. Intellectually, morally, I know this. But..."

"But what?" Caroline prodded.

Abruptly he let go her hand and went to the hearth, where he stared into the fire. "But," he said with soft deliberation, "I cannot promise it won't happen again."

Caroline watched closely as he turned to face her. Even with his back to the light, there was no mistaking the cynical gleam in his eyes.

"Shall I send for your coach?" he asked.

"No," she whispered.

Each regarded the other in silence. A challenge had just been flung--and met without hesitation.

The stroke of four of the clock broke the tension. It seemed to startle Thorne onto a different tack.

"Something has perplexed the devil out of me since your revelation last night."

Caroline merely arched her brow.

"When I first told you of Lena, I mentioned her father's pet name for her, which was Maddie...do you recall?"

"Yes."

"Didn't you make the connection? Surely you knew Lord Whittingham had lost a daughter. Was your fear of revealing his identity all that overpowering?"

Caroline stared at him in horror. "Heavens, no--oh, you must have thought me a monster since last night! No, Thorne, no, a thousand times no. He never mentioned a daughter to me, nor was there any trace of her existence. I assumed he was childless. I *swear* to you, Thorne, I hadn't the least notion Lena's father was my first husband! You must believe me."

"I do." He smiled weakly, but not before Caroline saw the terrible disappointment in his eyes. "Well, no matter. I was only curious." He settled into a chair and glanced at the clock. "Tea's on the way. Wait with me, Gwynneth should be along presently."

Caroline took a seat, still hearing the poignancy in his voice as he'd spoken of Lena.

No matter, he'd said.

But it does matter, Caroline thought glumly. *It matters more than he will ever say. You were right, Toby, there is much wrong with this marriage. But there are only three people who can hasten its end.*

And I am not one of them.

TWENTY-SEVEN

Lying on his cot in pitch-blackness, Hobbs heard the nickering of the horses--and then another noise.

Footsteps. Slow and stealthy, they entered the passageway and approached his door, which he never bolted when alone.

The Sutherland maid again? He doubted it. Caroline had probably clipped her wings for good.

He slipped a hand beneath the mattress. Fingers curling around cold steel, he waited until the door began to move. In one fluid motion, he sat up and drew the pistol, cocking it and aiming it squarely at the dark doorway.

And then smelled lemon verbena.

"Shite!" He kicked the covers once before remembering he was naked. "Pardon my language, my lady, but I nearly shot you." He laid the flintlock down and rolled off the cot, winding himself in the blanket. He knotted it at his waist, then lit the stub of tallow on a table. His heart sank at the look on Gwynneth's face. This was no friendly visit.

"Milady," he said as if he were gentling a horse, "wait in the stables while I put on my breeches. I'll join you in a trice."

"I shall stay where I am, thank you all the same."

Uncertain, he took a gamble and held his arms out away from his naked upper torso, knowing his muscles would ripple and his skin gleam bronze in the candlelight. "Very well then, have at me. I deserve it."

Before he could even register her quicksilver advance, she slapped him full across the face.

Her voice shook. "Why? When only days ago you embraced me in these very stables--" She blinked away tears, fury in her eyes. "How could you even *think* of taking that little trollop into your bed?"

Hobbs resisted touching his stinging cheek. "She meant naught to me," he muttered. "A penny-arsed harlot would have mattered no less. And forgive me, my lady, but you are not entirely without blame."

"What? How dare you!"

Already he felt his arousal hardening under the wrapped sheet. "How dare I? You know bloody well 'tis you I want. Am I to live like a monk while your husband takes his pleasure with you at will?"

Gwynneth recoiled. "You are saying I drove you to...oh, *spare* me, Tobias Hobbs, I am not one of your stupid, simpering whores, and I shan't listen to any more of this!"

He sprang for her as she rounded on her heel, but stopped short at the venomous glare she turned on him.

- 170 -

"If you lay so much as a finger on my person, I shall scream!"

Hobbs' heart began to pound. "Then save your breath, Milady." His voice lowered, turning husky. "But I vow I can make you want more than my finger on your person, and in short order."

Gwynneth's face flushed scarlet.

"Night after accursed night I lie on this cot, thinking of naught but you, my lady. I see you next to me in the darkness. I reach for you, only to find mocking emptiness. Thin air, my lady. And thin air does little to comfort a man suffering the agony of a denied love."

He edged toward her. She did not retreat.

"To know that you are just behind those walls," he murmured, his throat constricting, "and that *he* lies beside you in that big, soft bed and runs his hands over your milky-white skin and tastes that rosebud of a mouth--" Hobbs clenched his teeth. "And that he sheathes his sword where I would give everything I own to trespass but *once*--"

"Stop it!" Gwynneth said in a choked voice. She made no move to flee, only clutching her cloak tight around her neck.

"I was in *torment* by the time that giddy little wench offered herself to me," Hobbs muttered, "but in my mind's eye they were *your* lips I kissed, and 'twas your body I pleasured..." With one more step, he took hold of Gwynneth's shoulders, his face contorting with arousal. "God's blood, my lady, don't you know that you drive me mad?"

The green eyes narrowed on his. "Thou shalt not take the name of the Lord thy God in vain," Gwynneth said coldly.

Hobbs made a sound that was half chuckle, half moan. "Mark me, my lady, God knows the hell I've endured of late. He has already forgiven me."

Gwynneth made no protest as he began to unfasten her cloak, indeed she surprised him by shrugging the heavy velvet off her shoulders and letting it fall to the floor.

He gathered her to him with a groan. All that came between them was her shift, and as Gwynneth's breasts pressed against him, his manhood surged triumphantly beneath the blanket, his quest for Lady Neville nearly at end.

His mouth covered hers. He let out a roar as passion turned to searing pain and disbelief--Gwynneth had bitten bit his lip and then his tongue.

He wrenched free of her, tasting blood, and stumbled backward, grimacing in pain.

"*God* may have forgiven you," Gwynneth snarled, then wiped her sleeve across her mouth. "But I haven't! How *dare* you think of me whilst you paw and rut with that ignorant little slut!"

Hobbs jerked his head aside and spat, then raked blazing eyes over Gwynneth's scantily clad body. "Easy enough, with all your teasing and come-hithering. You've deliberately primed my pump on more than one occasion, my lady baroness!"

"You *lie*, you spawn of Satan!" Gwynneth's face turned livid. "So help me *God*, if ever you lay a hand on me again or speak to me unbidden, I shall see to it you're relieved of your situation immediately!" Her lip curled. "I've only to lie and tell my husband you've admitted fathering the bastard in Combs's womb--trust me, you'll be out on your ear then. And now that I know you for the filthy vermin you are, I suspect 'tis true! Lie with dogs," she said in a vinegar-syrup voice, "rise with fleas."

Blood thrummed in Hobbs' veins and pounded in his ears, drowning out all such niceties as title, station and pedigree, and leaving him with but a single thought. This woman--the only one he had ever loved--might just as well have plucked out his heart and stomped it into the ground while he watched.

He lunged for her.

* * *

Gwynneth's scream died as Hobbs clapped a hand over her mouth. Again she used her teeth, sinking them viciously into the web of skin between the stable master's thumb and forefinger.

Hobbs growled like a cornered beast as he tore flesh to yank his hand free. Grabbing Gwynneth's wrists in his good hand, he pinned them against the rough wall above her head.

Gwynneth jerked her knee upward, but managed only a glancing blow to his groin--just enough to enough to fuel his anger.

She cried out as Hobbs ripped the embroidered yoke of her shift from neck to waist with his bleeding hand.

Her cry faded as she took in the shocking sight of her bare, heaving breasts. She couldn't afford to be rescued. Her very presence here, in these clothes and at this hour, would condemn her. Defense--survival--was entirely up to her.

Still holding her wrists, Hobbs pushed his thighs against hers, immobilizing her knees. Outraged, Gwynneth squirmed within his grasp. Her anger turned to fear as she saw the animal lust in his eyes. She froze.

The smell of man-sweat invaded her nose. As Hobbs's golden head swooped down to capture a nipple in his mouth, his free hand smearing blood on her alabaster skin, Gwynneth found her voice. Her frantic threats turned to pleas as he yanked the flimsy shift upward and bunched it between her chest and his midsection. She struggled with renewed vigor, which only seemed to inflame his lust. In vain she strove to cross her thighs while his long, nimble fingers wriggled between them and slipped easily through her silky thatch of curls. Tears of fury and humiliation squeezed from under her closed eyelids, as he found her hidden folds of flesh with unerring deftness and grunted his satisfaction.

Gwynneth prayed she would faint. Then maybe Hobbs would unhand her and leave her limp body lying in the straw. She only wanted to be left alone--by him, by Thorne, by everyone. When Hobbs suddenly withdrew his probing fingers, hope burgeoned--and died almost immediately as he jerked the blanket from around his waist and flung it to the floor.

Gwynneth's instinctive glance and horrified gasp prompted a proud, throaty chuckle from the stable master.

"Puts his bloody lordship to shame, doesn't it?" he rasped. "Aye, Milady, 'tis not for naught I'm in demand from here to London."

Gwynneth could barely stifle her scream as Hobbs wedged the fleshy club between her trembling legs. Slowly, her limbs gave way under his brute strength. She moaned in desperation.

"Aye, sweeting, you'll have it soon enough," he assured her, his voice trembling with obvious anticipation. Bending his knees and bracing his stance with her wrists still in hand, he spit into his hand, took his proud manhood in hand and guided it up to its goal, his eyes meeting Gwynneth's with proud excitement. His entry was slow, constricted. "Tight as a drum," he said with relish.

Pinpoints of light exploded behind Gwynneth's eyelids; a keening moan of pain burst from her lips. The stableman seemed to take it for surrender as he tightened his grip on her wrists, pawed a breast, and thrust deeper into her, nearly ripping her apart.

Something warm and dribbled down her thighs. Hobbs grunted his pleasure and drove himself in and out of her body with increasing speed and violence. She wanted to scream, to sob hysterically, but the risk of discovery terrified her even more. Nor would she give Hobbs the satisfaction. She would bear the consequences of this rash visit the way martyred saints had endured torture before their deaths. It was the only grace she could salvage from this abomination. Her pain receded into blessed numbness as she imagined various ways Hobbs would be tormented in hell for his unforgivable crime.

His guttural gasp jolted her to awareness, and her body stiffened as his rutting motions accelerated to a frenzy. Sensing the end of her ordeal was at hand, she held her breath, then uttered a muffled cry as she felt the explosion and heat of his spewing seed deep within her.

With each spasm of Hobbs's release, Gwynneth was bitterly reminded why she had come to the stables tonight, as over and over through clenched teeth her ravisher chanted the words like a mantra--

"I love you...I love you, Gwynneth...I love you..."

* * *

Hobbs looked away as Gwynneth pulled the two useless halves of her shift together. Knotting the blanket at his waist again, he glanced at the bite wound on his hand, where the blood had long dried. He picked up her cloak and handed it to her.

"You'd best be getting back. He might come looking for you in your chambers. God knows I would." His eyes roved Gwynneth's pallid face. "I'm sorry for the damage to your shift. Burn it, no doubt you've another. Next time we'll remove it properly." He guided her as far as the outer doorway. "I dare not walk you to the Hall," he said, growing unnerved at her silence. "The moon is still high. If worse comes to worst and you're seen, you can say you were unable to sleep and visited Abigail as I slept. Are you all right?"

"Yes." Her voice sounded far away.

"Good. Come to me again as soon as you can." He pressed his lips to the back of one limp hand. "Goodnight, Gwynneth...my love."

Her eyes met his for the first time since he'd ravished her. They may as well have belonged to a stranger. "I gave you no leave to call me by my Christian name," she said tonelessly. "Nor shall I acknowledge your term of endearment. You have presumed far too much this night, Tobias Hobbs, infinitely more than my own husband has, and you shall pay for it."

"My lady," he protested, but broke off at the sudden hardness in her expression. Watching her go, he shook his head. One never knew with gentlewomen. One minute ice, fire the next, and then ice again.

Back in his cramped quarters, he lit the lamp and poured fresh water into a basin. Cleaning away the sticky evidence of his tryst, he rinsed the cloth, then stared with growing wonder at the water's odd tint. He glanced down at his nakedness.

He knew immediately the blood wasn't his. Nor had he felt a trace of moisture when he'd entered Gwynneth.

Smeared from tip to base and onto his thighs, it mocked him--thin but abundant, and garishly bright.

TWENTY-EIGHT

"I've no desire to be presented at Court." Gwynneth turned her back on her husband so Byrnes could lace her stays.

Thorne watched from the doorway. "My lady, I did not invade the sanctity of your chambers for my own amusement. There stands a messenger in the anteroom awaiting a reply, which I would have given but for deference to you."

"And must I reply in the affirmative?" she sulked.

"When the king requests your presence at one of his 'Drawing-rooms', particularly for his birthday reception, there is no reply but 'yes.' And no excuse but death."

Gwynneth ignored his dry humor. "And if I refuse?" She held up her arms as Byrnes slipped an azure underskirt over her head.

"A sure way to gain immediate notoriety."

"Meaning?" Gwynneth demanded, her head emerging from the overskirt as it rippled down swaying panniers.

"Meaning that your name would instantly be anathema at Court."

"And yours as well," she ventured sourly.

Thorne kept a bland face. "Once Parliament has opened and we are in residence at your father's townhouse, you'll change your mind. I'll convey our acceptance. I daresay the messenger has never waited so long for a reply to a royal summons. Good morning, my lady."

As Thorne turned to go, Gwynneth fixed a baleful eye on the maid, who could not conceal her excitement. "Well, Byrnes, it seems you shall see the palace after all."

* * *

Relegated to a cramped apartment with other visiting ladies' maids at Saint James, Byrnes seemed thrilled enough just to be in the vicinity of royalty.

Gwynneth found the palace daunting, despite its run-down condition, and forgot her vow not to be impressed by the pomp and finery of the king's forty-fifth birthday celebration. The Drawing-room on that tenth of November was such a noisy, scented blur of silks, velvets, jewels, swords and fans that it was hard to be jaded, especially with King George II and Caroline of Ansbach presiding from their ornate thrones.

She felt all eyes upon her as she walked the aisle to the dais, curtsied, and murmured a few words to the Royal Couple. She noted the king's ocular dip into her cleavage with mixed feelings. The queeen's own remarkable and renowned bosom, a source of pride to the king, was stunningly displayed in a jewel-encrusted gown of embroidered silk and velvet.

The presentation was over in seconds--an interminable time by Gwynneth's reckoning. She clung to Thorne's arm as they wended their way through the crowd of powdered and perfumed guests, and between introductions confided a longing, not for the house in Covent Garden where they were in residence for the opening of Parliament, but for her quiet existence at Wycliffe Hall.

Aye, back to your chambers and prayer retreats, thought Thorne, fighting yet another wave of hopelessness. Gwynneth had been fretful and cross for weeks now, but the one time he'd mentioned it, she had burst into tears and fled the room. From then on he'd taken silent note of her mood swings. He suspected they had to do with ending her rides now that Hobbs had been caught in *flagrante dilecto* with Caroline's maid. Gwynneth loved Abigail, but not enough to tolerate the presence of such a "sinner" as the stable master. This suited Thorne fine. In his estimation Gwynneth had already spent entirely too much time in Hobbs's company.

Caroline had left for London just a week after her early-October arrival. Oddly, Gwynneth had seemed relieved at her departure.

Meanwhile, Thorne's vision of a house full of guests and laughing children had grown dimmer by the day. He'd spent late evenings alone in the library, where he often imagined hearing a light step outside the door or the quiet turning of a page somewhere in the room. He would grit his teeth at those imaginings, fearing that if there was a lingering spirit in the room, it might not his father's, but Combs' instead. He could not bear the notion she might be dead.

He could turn to no one, not even Arthur, and had felt unusually glad when the time came for Parliament's opening. Though this year's session had little import for the Lords and Commons, the familiar order of procedure and protocol reassured him. Even more comforting were visits to old haunts, namely the taverns of Fleet Street, with his peers.

Gwynneth had found her own diversion in the abbeys, priories, cathedrals, and churches. Saint Paul's, Westminster Abbey, Saint Bartholomew-the-Great, Saint Martin's, Saint Clement Danes, Saint Mary-le-bow; the list went on, as did the days, with poor Byrnes wearily in tow. The mists rolling off the Thames and the frequent cold drizzle were no deterent. "At least 'tis dry sanctuary," Thorne had heard Byrnes quip of yet another church on the agenda.

He was jerked back to the present as two royal armsmen appeared to escort Gwynneth to the king himself for the next dance. In seconds the floor was cleared, all eyes turned their way. When the minuet ended, the monarch escorted Gwynneth directly to Thorne's side.

"*Bezaubern*, Lord Neville. *Und schon.*"

Thorne bowed. *"Danke, Ihre Majestat."*

"*Bitte schon.*" The king kissed Gwynneth's hand, lingering over it before turning away with his attendants.

"Oh Thorne," she breathed, once they were out of hearing range. "I think I shall faint. I'm so glad that is over."

The king had stopped to converse with a plump, attractive woman well-known at Court, and as Thorne watched, the two of them turned and looked his way. "Your social life has just advanced," he murmured to Gwynneth.

"Whatever do you mean?"

"I predict you'll soon receive at least two invitations, one to the Queen's salon. She's fond of cribbage."

"So I've heard. And the other invitation?"

"Will likely come from Marble Hill House." Thorne lifted a pint of ale from a passing tray.

"I've heard of the place. Is it one of the king's residences?"

"One might say that." He discreetly indicated the smiling woman at the monarch's side. "'Tis the newly-built home of Lady Suffolk."

"But you just said-" Gwynneth broke off, looking suddenly suspicious. "Thorne, are you telling me that the king...?"

Her eyes widened at her husband's nod.

"You're saying the Queen's own Mistress of the Robes is the king's *paramour*?" she cried.

"Hush." Assuming a wooden smile, Thorne drew Gwynneth toward a table nearly dripping platters of meats, cheeses, pastries, exotic fruits, and confections.

"Does the queen know?" she hissed at his shoulder.

"Aye, Gwynneth, the queen and several hundred courtiers."

She frowned. "Including yourself. Obviously *I* am ill-informed."

"'Tis not the sort of information you relish, my lady. Be grateful you were spared it for a while." He lowered his head as they strolled, his unbound hair falling forward and blocking his face from Gwynneth's view.

"You're laughing, Thorne Neville, I can tell." She shook his arm. "But I see nothing amusing about it. Do you for one moment think I would lower myself to accept an invitation to the home of such a woman?"

Pretending to nuzzle her neck, he said into her ear, "You should at least humble yourself, Gwynneth. 'Tis no passing matter to refuse an invitation prompted by the king himself. Swallow your pride for one afternoon, and for God's sake, do not be rude to Lady Suffolk."

"I might have known you'd involve God in such a charade." Gwynneth snatched her hand from his sleeve. "I wish to leave now."

"So soon after your conquest at Court? There are several young swains casting moonstruck glances your way...won't you let one or two spin you around the room?"

"The hour is grown late," Gwynneth said through her teeth, smiling and nodding at the Marchioness of Kent, a friend of her father's and a guest at her wedding. "On the morrow is Martinmas, the Feast of Saint Martin. I had hoped to attend early Mass in Saint Martin's Church."

"I see. Let's be off, then, by all means," Thorne said wryly. "I would not stand in the way of devotion."

* * *

The Feast of Saint Martin came and went without any observance from Gwynneth. The only thing she could observe that morning was her empty basin, which soon contained the meager contents of her stomach.

"Bless ye, Milady...perhaps ye took a little ale or wine last eve, seeing as how you're at Court and all?"

Gwynneth shook her head miserably. "I'd no spirits, Byrnes. It must have been the excitement of meeting His Royal Highness."

"Likely so," Byrnes said, keeping her voice light. She'd noticed something, but dared not broach the subject.

Nearly three fortnights had passed since she'd last disposed of her mistress' bloody flux. If tomorrow dawned with the same ill effects as this morning had, she would feel certain that Lady Neville was with child.

TWENTY-NINE

"Ah, Monsieur Adams, *bienvenue*." The sultry voice accompanied rustling silk as Madame Claire made her signature sweep into the anteroom. "What may we do for you today?" she asked, a gleam in her eye despite her demure manner.

Thorne removed his tricorne. "I've come to inquire after Katy's health. I hope the illness has passed?"

The madam sobered. "*Non*, Monsieur Adams. Indeed it has worsened."

"She remains in quarantine?"

"Insofar as *quotidiennes affaires, oui*, monsieur."

Thorne frowned. "And what is the doctor's diagnosis?"

Madame Claire's eyelashes fluttered downward. "*Une infection des poumons*," she said with a sigh.

Thorne's heart skipped a beat. His father had died of diseased lungs. That someone as young and vital as Katy might waste away in such a manner seemed beyond reckoning. "I understand that she is under quarantine insofar as daily business, but might I visit her at bedside a few moments?"

"Monsieur Adams, *la fièvre*, though 'tis low-grade, is yet contagious. A *femme d'affaires* such as I must take extreme care that none of her clients is infected. But I shall tell Katy of your visit and your *souci*, your concern. 'Twill do her good to know that one of her clients has inquired after her welfare."

Thorne winced, and the madam saw it. "If it pains you to think of Katy as a *prostituée*," she said in a solicitous tone, "it might comfort you to know that she thinks quite highly of you. So much so, that she wept after your last meeting."

She nodded at Thorne's surprised expression.

His surprise suddenly hardened to suspicion. "No doubt Katy is one of your more profitable commodities?"

Madame Claire looked taken aback, then defensive. "Your point, monsieur?"

"In your business, personal involvement is best avoided. It could prove detrimental to your profits, if one of your more lucrative ladies grew attached to a particular client and showed less attention to others. No doubt you would dissociate her from that client." He eyed Madame Claire intently.

Her back stiffened. "Only on one occasion did I *dissociez* a client from one of my girls, and only then because he was too *enthousiaste* and injured her. So you think I have fabricated this *fièvre* and infection as a *pénalité* for Katy's affection for you, Monsieur Adams?"

"It had occurred to me. Have I your word she is truly in need of a doctor's care?"

"Indeed, monsieur."

Lips pressing together, Thorne slipped a hand into his waistcoat, then said tersely, "I shall at least contribute to Katy's medical care." He held out two fifty-pound notes.

"*Merci*," the madam whispered, taking the currency from him. "Your *générosité* is astounding, Monsieur Adams. With such care as this will purchase, Katy's health can only improve!"

Thorne nodded grimly. "That is my hope, Madame. Do convey my sincere wishes for her recovery. I shall return come spring. Hopefully you will have better news then."

Her smile turned coy. "*Oui*, monsieur. Spring will surely bring long-awaited news."

* * *

The madam sailed through the door into her private salon. "M'lord!" she trilled softly. "Our cash cow--or should I say bull?--has just paid a visit, and left yet another generous sum." Waving the fifty-pound notes, she smiled triumphantly into the beady, black eyes of the Earl of Whittingham.

He shrugged. "Hardly enough to stiffen *my* cock."

"Not all of us possess an earldom, M'lord," she chided, brushing her fingers under his whisker-stubbled chin as she passed to pour a drink at the sideboard. "In this business, one hundred pounds is *not* trifling change. And as generous as Lord Neville has been so far, will he not be utterly foolish when it comes to buying his bastard babe away from here? Especially if that babe is a boy." She smiled dreamily at her reflection in the huge wall-mirror. "*Des milliers, je devrais dire.* Thousands upon thousands of pounds, all yours and mine."

"What of the mother?" Lord Whittingham said with a grunt.

"*La me're*? *She* is lucky to have her keep, and a doctor's care to boot!" Madame Claire handed him a full glass, then bit her lip and frowned. "In truth, *she* is my cash cow--or was, and will be yet, if she recovers her figure after the birth. But she will soon see what a trial it is to have a wee babe bawling for the teat night and day."

The earl's squint turned lewd. "You talk too much, woman--at least in English. I'd rather be frenched." He wagged his tongue at her.

She sashayed toward him with a sly smile. "Is there anything else you would like, *cherie*?" she cooed, stroking his greasy black hair.

"I'd like you," he said in a wheedling voice, "to pretend *I* am a babe bawling for the teat."

She bent over, her ample décolletage confronting his salacious gaze, her rouged lips pouting. "I thought you had eyes only for Jeanette."

"You won't let me see her," he groused, looking hopeful in spite of it.

"You were a *bad boy* with Jeanette. She still has the whip marks on her buttocks."

"Well, she got cheeky with me," he said, and laughed uproariously at his own jest. He reached for Madame Claire's bodice; she slapped his hand.

"You are beyond reformation, M'lord, a very bad boy." She leaned in closer. "Come to *Mama*, *cherie*," she purred.

Lord Whittingham stared intently at her bosom. "I've one other request, Claire," he muttered, breathing harder. "'Tis in regard to the Neville matter."

She inhaled deeply. "Oui, M'lord?"

He licked his lips, his pudgy hands pushing the madam's breasts together inside her straining bodice. He looked up to meet her sultry gaze. "Only that you let *me* inform the holier-than-thou Lord Neville that his whore has borne his bastard babe."

She shivered as the earl slid the tip of his tongue into her cleavage. "*Oui, mon cherie*," she said in a throaty voice, then lifted her skirts to straddle the bulge in his lap.

Grasping her silk frock at one shoulder, he worked it down roughly with her shift. He shoved her breasts together again and, covering both nipples with his mouth, suckled like a starveling.

Madame Claire's laugh was soft and husky. "You are a̲vide un garcon, a greedy boy, as well," she murmured, reaching between her thighs to unbutton his breeches. She gave him a conspiratorial wink. "Though perhaps no greedier than I."

* * *

"Do come up," Caroline said to Thorne, her face beautifully flushed. "I'm sorry for your wait, Marsh is confoundedly slow today."

"'Tis I who should apologize. You weren't expecting me."

Her laugh seemed strained. "No, but you're welcome, nonetheless...come!" She halted outside the open drawing-room door. "Let's visit in the library today, shall we?" She pulled Thorne back toward the stairs, but not before an odor from the drawing room had reached his nose.

His eye lit on a dark-brown smear on the otherwise spotless carpet runner. Mud? Dung? Caroline was moving too swiftly for him to decide.

A meager fire burned in the library. Caroline called for Marsh.

"Never mind, I'll see to it." Over her protests, Thorne stirred the embers and added more coals, buying time as he stared into the reviving fire, his mind racing.

She is anything but a lady, Neville. Lord Whittingham's insult after invading Caroline's chambers suddenly took on a whole new meaning.

Henry said the lady was a guest in your very house, sir. Clayton Carmody's voice rang clear in his head. *The stable master called her his sister.*

He thought of the night in Duncan's tavern, when Caroline had referred to Hobbs as Toby--and then denied any previous acquaintance with him.

By her own account she'd worked in a tavern on Fleet Street while on the run from Lord Whittingham. It had sounded reasonable at the time she explained it. It seemed reasonable even now, knowing the earl for what he was...still, a wealthy merchant's daughter should be ill-suited for such employment.

Thorne slowly stood up from the hearth. Reluctant to turn and face her yet, he feigned interest in bric-a-brac on the mantel, eyeing a polished ivory tusk drilled with holes and stuck with little ivory pegs.

"I see my cribbage recorder has caught your eye," Caroline said in a bright voice. "Horace bought it in Morocco, I think. But come sit down, and tell me what brings you here. Is Gwynneth well?"

"Not entirely." He took a seat. "Some chronic stomach ailment."

Caroline's polite smile faltered. "Perhaps she's with child."

"Not likely," Thorne muttered, and then stiffened. Would Caroline let it pass?

Of course she wouldn't. Her voice was very soft. "Thorne?"

He rose abruptly and strolled to a window, then frowned resentfully at the garden, which looked as lush and exotic as its owner. "What I tell you goes no further than this room," he heard himself say, even as his inner voice warned against it.

Behind him, Caroline gave soft agreement.

"Gwynneth," he said, "will never bear a child."

"Oh, Thorne...she is barren?"

"She is unbroken. And will remain so."

He heard Caroline's stifled little gasp. He paced about the room, pausing to examine *art de objects* and moving on after each cursory perusal.

"Perhaps she needs more time," Caroline said cautiously. "Surely she will change her mind."

"There is no changing her mind--do you think I haven't tried?" Thorne stopped pacing, then held up a hand. "Sorry. Her father," he said more evenly, "removed her from the convent against her wishes. She wanted only to take their vows."

"Then why..."

"...did she agree to marry me? For her father, of course. Radleigh has a terrible weakness for wagering. His estate was dwindling away, and Gwynneth knew it."

"And you didn't?"

He stared out the window again. "Someone tried to tell me, but I refused to listen...mostly out of loyalty to my father." His tone turned wry. "And once I saw that Gwynneth seemed enamored of me, I was all the more determined."

"And now?"

"Now?" He turned an expression of irony to Caroline. "Now she lives the life of a nun. Wycliffe Hall is her convent. She has a shrine to the Virgin in her chambers, says her Rosary daily at dawn. Attends Mass at every opportunity, studies the lives of the saints, tends her roses, and stitches her tapestry. Eats, though lately not much. Rises and retires early.

"The servants avoid her at all cost, and tiptoe about when I am home, which is as little as possible. Arthur looks solemn as a judge but holds his tongue." Thorne scowled. "My cook has the audacity to eye me as if I were one of the pitiful stray cats she's always feeding, even offered me warm milk one evening to help me sleep! I shouldn't be surprised if she takes up patting my head and scratching behind my ears."

Caroline's eyes twinkled, but her tone was sober. "Are you resigned, then, to a life without a true wife, and without children? Tell me if I misspeak, Thorne, but I am concerned."

"You needn't be." He sat down again, settling back and crossing his ankles on a needlepoint stool. "I'd no intention of making confession today. There is just something about you..." He smiled crookedly. "Shall we close the book on my sorry tale for the moment? I've just had a revelation, and I'd sooner share it with you than anyone."

"Indeed." Caroline tilted her head, looking pleased. "So *that* was the reason for your visit."

"Initially, no." Thorne watched her grow restless under his scrutiny--fiddling with a curl at her temple, touching the fan folded in her sleeve but resisting the urge to pull it out. "You once told me you'd a half-brother, but that you seldom hear from him."

Her eyes narrowed. "Yes. What of it?"

"I think you said that the two of you aren't the best of friends, or something to that effect."

"I might have said that, yes." She sat up straighter by the moment.

"Did you not think," Thorne said casually, "I'd care to know that your brother and my stable master are one and the same?"

It was a shot in the dark, but there was no mistaking its accuracy. Caroline's eyes turned to flint, her cheeks to bright copper. "Were you *born* rude, Thorne, or is it something you've cultivated? I seem often to be the whetstone for your razor-sharp repartee."

"Bollocks, Caroline. You give as good as you get. Does Gwynneth know of this kinship?"

She sprang from her chair, and for a moment he thought banishment was in the offing. Instead she used his favorite ploy, crossing swiftly to the window to escape his perusal. "*No one* knows of it," she said in a stony voice. "At least, no one did. I've taken great pains to see to it."

"Why?" He took his feet off the stool, rose from the chair.

"Do you really think," Caroline scoffed, her back to him, "that I could possibly have made the two marriages I have, were it known to Whittingham and Horace that I was sibling to a *stableman*?"

"You might have been spared some suffering, had Lord Whittingham known," Thorne observed, slowly approaching her. "And Horace eventually learned the truth. Still, I doubt it would have mattered." He stopped just behind Caroline.

She moved to the next casement. "Indeed. And what makes you so certain they'd have married me despite my humble beginnings?"

Thorne stared at the silky tendrils grazing her nape. "I cannot be certain," he said quietly. "I only know it would not have stopped me."

* * *

Caroline drew a long breath to slow her rapid pulse. "How did you find me out?"

"There were clues all along. I just today put them together."

She turned to face him. "Why today?"

Thorne smiled. "I've spent a fair amount of time in the stables. The odor is unmistakable--and it lingers. I'd wager my stableman was let out the back entrance as I was let in the front."

Caroline tossed her head. "I should boot *you* out the back, this very minute, right on your bum."

"You wouldn't."

"Wouldn't I, though?"

"And what would the servants say, seeing their mistress cast a nobleman out into the alley?"

"They would say 'good riddance' if they knew how you torment and abuse me!"

Thorne chuckled. "There are two sides to *that* coin, Mistress Sutherland." He sobered. "I'm told you and Hobbs had a heated discussion in the stables just before my wedding...that he struck you."

"I struck him first. Who told you?"

"Why did you strike him?"

"He insulted me."

"I see. And for that you paid him cash?"

She scowled. "Who the deuce was spying on me? Never mind, you won't tell. I paid him to pretend he and I were strangers."

"Yet today he was in your drawing-room."

"He was here to plead his case for my maid," she lied, her thoughts racing. How would Thorne react if she told him Toby had come to beg her help making peace with Gwynneth? For what reason, Caroline hadn't a clue.

"So, he's truly interested in Ashby! I'm pleasantly surprised."

"Nothing will come of it. Toby isn't a man to settle for one woman."

"Aye, he's proven that," Thorne agreed with an edge to his voice, but before Caroline could take issue with him went on to ask, "Your maiden name is Hobbs?"

Sighing, she tapped her foot. "Yes."

"You and Hobbs are paternal siblings, then."

"No, we shared only a mother. She gave my father's name to Tobias to avoid gossip. My father had been dead for some time before Toby was conceived. Mother made the mistake of confiding that to the vicar's wife, and thereafter in Birmingham, Toby was tormented for being a bastard."

"Ah. Perhaps that explains his combative attitude."

Hardly, Caroline wanted to say. She shrugged.

"Gwynneth once mentioned that Hobbs' mother--your mother--was employed at Wycliffe Hall, some two decades ago."

"Yes." It was nearly a whisper. Caroline stopped tapping her foot.

"In what situation?"

She elevated her head slightly. "She was a chambermaid."

"And where were you?"

"I lived in Kettering at the time, with my mother's sister."

"Pennington's birthplace," Thorne murmured before going on to ask, "When did your mother leave my father's employ?"

"I was seven, perhaps eight years of age."

"Where did she go?"

Damnation, would his curiosity never be appeased? "First she came to collect me," Caroline said shortly. "Then 'twas off to Birmingham. Toby was born a few months later."

"So your mother was with child when she left Wycliffe Hall."

Caroline nodded, her heart beating so hard she feared Thorne would hear it. "Mother worked several years for a seamstress while I tended Toby. When he was old enough, we trotted off to school. I was probably seventeen, Toby nine or thereabouts, when Mother took him to Wycliffe Hall. There your father's steward kindly put him to work in the stables."

Thorne smiled. "How like Arthur. And you and your mother, where did you go then?"

"Mother returned to Birmingham. By that time I had done with school and was helping her with the piecework she brought home at night. With Toby gone, she and I opened a shop not far from our home. But I tired of the place, and Birmingham in general. I advertised for a situation." Caroline smiled without humor. "Which is why Lionel Stanford Hargrove, eleventh Earl of Whittingham, took me on as seamstress at Hargrove Hall--and two years later convinced me to marry him. Soon after we wed, he discovered my father was *not* a prosperous shipping merchant in Plymouth, that he was actually a deceased miner from Newcastle--and that there would be no inheritance. 'Twas then the perversion and the beatings commenced."

Caroline saw Thorne's mouth tighten in profile.

"Mother stayed on in Birmingham. I sent her money when I could. She died of consumption just two years ago."

"I'm sorry."

"You needn't be. Her death was a relief, she could barely draw breath toward the end." Caroline cocked her head. "Enough about me. You've yet to tell me why you've come today."

Turning to see her curious gaze, Thorne shrugged. "Perhaps I wanted the company of a woman who doesn't shut herself up like a hermit," he said quietly. "One who can talk *to* me, instead of *at* me, and who isn't so much inclined to speak of saints and feast days, Rosaries, the Mass, and sin...particularly sin." He chuckled, but without humor, his expression hardening before he looked away. "Especially as I seem, these days, to be at the brink of hell. I only wonder if I'll be pushed into it...or leap of my own will."

From the garden, a mockingbird pealed off several shrill, discordant notes.

"If the very pit of hell can tempt a man to leap," Caroline ventured softly, "chances are his present existence is already a sort of hell."

Thorne turned to look at her intently. "But what if that man, despairing of the hell behind him, takes the leap and finds he's entered an even worse hell?"

Caroline's gaze did not falter. "If he has already leapt from one hell, he can leap yet again from another."

"And into a third," Thorne murmured.

She shook her head. "Not necessarily. He generally has a choice. There is right...and there is left."

He smiled briefly. "I thought you were going to say 'wrong'. So, you don't believe a man can back himself into a corner."

"No. Nor can a woman." Caroline's own fleeting smile went unanswered as Thorne stared at her lips.

"My good friend Townsend," he said slowly, "believes I am already in the pit. And that if I but beckoned...you would follow."

His eyes met hers.

For a moment she forgot to breathe. Only a stupid woman could fail to comprehend his words, and only a silly one would pretend otherwise. She was neither.

"Thorne...are you asking me to be your paramour?"

She waited, barely hearing the mockingbird's song over the sound of her pounding heart...and then, from two blocks away, the bells of Saint James Church ringing the Angelus on the clear November air.

She read her own thoughts on Thorne's face, and silently cursed those tolling bells.

"I must go," he said.

She felt her head jerk in what passed for a nod. "Gilbert will show you out."

Flinching, she listened to Thorne's steps pound across the room and fade away down the hall.

The mockingbird, perched on the garden gate, tilted its head and looked at her with knowing eyes. "Yes, he is angry," she said softly, as if to the bird. "But not with me...though I think it will be some time before we see him again."

She knew Thorne was on the run again from his demons, knew that today they had almost caught up with him, indeed had very nearly shoved him into the pit he sensed yawning at his feet. She also knew that Townsend was right.

She would have followed.

THIRTY

Gwynneth glanced up from her embroidery. "I thought you'd gone out for the evening."

"I'm flattered you noticed. Yes, I was out. I've just had word from the palace. The invitation to Christmas at White Lodge has been rescinded."

"What?" Gwynneth dropped her work in her lap.

"Not to worry, you haven't fallen from the queen's favor. All invitations have been withdrawn. She won't be in residence at Richmond Park this Christmas, nor will any of her family."

"Her family." Gwynneth looked blank. "The king, and who else?"

"The prince. Young Frederick has been summoned to Court by His Majesty. It seems our future king has been up to some political maneuvering of his own, but his scheme was discovered before it came to fruition."

"What scheme?"

"Marriage to Princess Wilhelmina of Prussia."

"Good heavens!"

"The king had a similar reaction," Thorne said with a dry chuckle. "Frederick was landed without ceremony at Whitechapel quay and driven by hack, no less, to the palace--where he was received instead by the queen."

"No doubt she hoped to prepare him for the king's wrath," Gwynneth ventured, then glanced warily at Thorne. "So, you and I are to spend Christmas here? Perhaps Caroline would join us."

That startling thought made Thorne's tone firmer than he'd intended. "I'd like to be home for Christmas."

"But Christmas in London could be fun!"

"We'll make it fun at Wycliffe Hall, I promise. I've stayed away the last four Yuletides, but this year I feel less haunted by old ghosts. And since you've refused to see a doctor here in London, I want you to see Hodges as soon as we arrive home."

"For my stomach? 'Tis nothing, Thorne, I told you! Merely a case of nerves over life at Court."

"All the more reason to leave. I'd like to go in two or three days."

"Very well." Gwynneth took up her needlework with a long-suffering sigh. "You shall have your Christmas at Wycliffe Hall."

* * *

"Allow me to be the first to offer congratulations, Milady," John Hodges said. "Your husband will be a happy man today, happier still in six months or so."

Gwynneth's face slowly drained of color. "You...you cannot mean...?"

The doctor's smile faltered. "Aye, you and his lordship are to be parents-" He broke off at her strangled sound and snatched up a small basin. "Where is Lord Neville? Awaiting you in the coach?" He leaned over her, holding the basin under her chin.

"He's with his steward today."

"I should think he'd want to be with you for this visit."

Gwynneth stared at him. "I--I did not tell him I was coming today, and I only thought it was an upset stomach! My maid is in the coach."

Frowning, Hodges gave her hand a reassuring pat. "Hold the basin and take deep breaths while I fetch her."

Gwynneth's head spun. How could that single, brutal, selfish encounter with Hobbs turn into something as sacred as conception? *Do not panic*, she cried silently as she retched into the basin. *The child must be Thorne's, if only in his mind. Think!*

She blotted her tears and then her mouth on her handkerchief. By the time Hodges produced her ecstatic maid, the solution had dawned. Gwynneth managed a trembling smile for them both.

"Oh, Milady, what blessed news! We must get ye into the coach and find his lordship."

"No!"

Gwynneth blushed hotly at the bewildered stares of her doctor and her maid. "No," she said more calmly. "I shall tell his lordship in due time. He must be prepared for such an announcement."

Hodges shook his head. "But Milady, he is more than prepared, he is-"

"I shall tell him in my own time," Gwynneth cut in sharply, "and in my own way." Fear brought anger; anger brought strength and resolve. "Give me your vow, each of you, that you will say nothing to *anyone*."

"Very well, my lady, I'll keep word of your good fortune under my hat until I hear it from your husband or until you tell me the secret is out." Hodges, accustomed to the whimsy and changing moods of expectant females, assumed the bland manner of professionalism. The maid looked dubious.

"Byrnes?" Gwynneth arched her brow.

"Aye, Milady," the woman agreed with obvious reluctance. "I'll keep mum 'til ye give the word."

"You had better, your situation depends upon it," Gwynneth snapped, then gazed into the doctor's eyes with all the warmth she could muster.

"For the present, John, let us say I have a nervous stomach, for which you have prescribed such things as soda bread and peppermint tea--which are all I can tolerate these days at any rate." She made her smile rueful and charming, and saw by the doctor's suddenly ruddy cheeks that she'd successfully drawn him into collusion.

He gently cleared his throat. "Aye, Milady, you do indeed have a nervous stomach. Soda bread and peppermint tea are my very recommendations."

Her smile turned radiant, the doctor's cheeks more rosy.

"Come Byrnes, I've much to do."

Throughout the coach ride back to Wycliffe Hall, Gwynneth mentally steeled herself to use a talent she had never cultivated. And though she despised the very notion, it would mean survival and security for herself and her unborn--and would after all involve only her husband. Her mate in the eyes of God.

You will do it, she told herself firmly. As repugnant and humiliating as it would be, she must seduce Thorne.

The sooner, the better.

* * *

"What the deuce...?" Thorne squinted into the shadows. What he saw there made him spring out of bed, forgetting his own nakedness. His eyes pierced the gloom.

The diaphanous form moved slowly toward him. It had nearly reached the open curtains of the dividing arch when the firelight struck its face.

"Gwynneth!" He halted, baffled.

"Oh, Thorne." Her voice broke as she ran to him like some nude nymph from the wood. "You *are* here! I dreamt...oh, 'twas horrid!" She threw herself against him and shuddered.

He clasped her to him out of mere reflex, nor did his body respond as he would have feared, despite Gwynneth's near-nakedness and his own lack of clothing.

He relaxed then, and held her as she wept. She clung to him as her tears abated, only tightening her hold when he tried to set her away.

"Sshhh," he soothed her, then lifted her and carried her to the bed, where the warmth of his body still lingered. He covered her, then donned his dressing gown and secured it, all the while discreetly perusing his wife's body through a transparent rose-colored shift and wrapper he'd never seen. She might have been carved from marble if not for the patch of coppery curls amid all that milk-white flesh. He could swear her coral-tipped breasts had grown larger. A hollow sadness overcame him as he realized that despite her ripening femininity, the sight of Gwynneth's body no longer stirred his own.

He sat on the edge of the bed and smoothed Gwynneth's fevered brow. "You dreamt I wasn't here?"

"Yes." She sniffled piteously. "You'd gone away. You can't imagine how frightened and how alone I felt...because that hideous man Lord *Whittingham* had come to stay!" Shivering, she hugged herself, her breasts pressing together in wanton fullness.

Thorne chuckled, albeit grimly. "That was no dream, my lady, 'twas a nightmare. But Lord Whittingham is at least a half-day's ride away, and I am very much here."

"Yes, you are." Her eyes fluttered downward; he heard her swallow. "I dare not go back to my chambers, I have foolishly risked a chill already in coming here so...so little dressed. But come, husband." Her eyes met his briefly, shyly, before closing again. 'Tis your bed and I am your wife, you needn't sleep elsewhere."

He waited for her to pull the covers to her chin, but she only lay still with her eyes shut tight.

He slipped the belt of his dressing gown, shed the garment at the other side of the bed, and slid in beside her.

* * *

As the mattress moved beneath Thorne's weight, Gwynneth's skin fairly tingled. She told herself it must be fear. She recalled Thorne's caress as sinfully pleasant, but fresher in her mind was the brutal touch of his stable master.

She prayed for strength, for endurance. Finishing, she heard her husband's breathing--deep, slow, and regular, it came from where he remained, on the far side of his wide bed.

He was asleep.

She brushed away sudden tears. She'd no notion what to do now. No doubt Thorne was tired, she'd awakened him in the middle of the night. Come morning, he'd see her lying in his bed with her feminine charms all but laid bare--for even if she had to freeze all night with those accursed windows open, she would not cover herself.

* * *

Drowsing at the blush of dawn, Gwynneth became aware of a warmth and comfort she had lacked throughout the night. Her eyes fluttered open to see woolen blankets piled atop her. The draperies were parted, the shutters open, but the sashes were closed and latched. Fragrant applewood burned steadily in the grate.

Thorne was nowhere in sight.

* * *

Bridey entered the kitchen, where Hillary was already pumping the bellows at the huge hearth. The old cook lumbered into the larder, humming to herself, then stood still, frowning, and shook her head. Twice she backtracked to the kitchen and looked about, then headed to the larder again.

"By the saints," she said, pique in her voice, "I left fried chitterlings in a bowl here, covered in cheesecloth...so where's it gotten to?"

"What's going on, missus?" Hillary called out.

"More like what's going *out...food* is what's going out 'round here, right out of the kitchen...what's going *on* is *thieving*!"

"The deuce ye say!" Hillary gasped, then clapped her hand over her mouth.

"Aye, ye *should* be covering such a foul hole," the cook scolded, wagging a finger.

Hillary ignored the lecture. "But thieving, missus? Who'd be a-thieving in a God-fearing house such as this?"

"Nobody," Susan contended, coming from the creamery. "Not a soul within would steal from this larder."

Bridey's old eyes flashed. "Then, 'tis a soul without."

"What? Who'd come creeping in the night for our scraps?" Susan demanded with a chuckle.

"Scraps my arse!" Now the cook covered her own mouth. "Well, pardon an old lady for getting her dander up," she sputtered at the giggling maids, "but there's more than scraps disappearing from 'neath our noses! A thigh here, a wing there. A keg of cider a week past, two jars of preserves and a Cornish hen since. And speaking of hens, the laying hens have been a mite stingy of late--could be there's more than one person gathering eggs! This morn 'tis chitterlings...and the bloomin' crock besides! And what of my cayenne pepper? That's the first thing turned up missing."

Susan hooted with laughter. "That box of cayenne was missing long before all this food started to disappear! If our thief made meals off *that*, then I say he deserves whatever he can find!"

"Well, lass, why don't ye just make up a basket for the little villain?" the cook huffed, hands on her ample hips. "Whilst ye're at it, tie a pretty ribbon on it and meet him at the back door to save him a step or two!"

"Now, missus, I was only having a little fun. But how can we bag the scoundrel without laying low all night on watch?"

"I've held off saying anything to Her Royal Prissiness in there," Bridey mumbled, nodding toward Priscilla Carswell's office. "But I suppose there's no help for it now, I reckon we'll be bolting the doors this day hence." She shuffled off toward the great hall, shaking her head.

"Who do ye think it is?" Hillary stage-whispered to Susan.

"Deuced if I know," Susan replied in kind. Hand over yon' butter mold."

Hillary passed it to her, then attacked the stone basin with coarse ashes and a brush. "Well I don't envy the pitiful wretch if her ladyship gets a hold of him. She'll have him wearing a hair shirt and saying Hail Marys for a year!"

"Hush now, we've work to be about." But Susan's twitching mouth and twinkling eyes gave her away.

* * *

Arthur brought a tray of tea and cross buns to the worktable in his kitchen. "Cook's ailing," he explained.

"Ah," Thorne said in a wry voice. "I thought perhaps you were priming my pump."

"No sense pumping a dry well." Arthur pretended not to notice Thorne's glare. "How fares her ladyship?"

"Generally, or particularly?...now that you're pumping."

Arthur took a cross bun from the plate. "She was seen entering Hodges' place. Good news, I hope?"

"Aye, if that's what you call a nervous stomach." Thorne took a huge bite out of his cross bun and chewed it slowly.

Sighing, Arthur did the same, resigned to waiting out the silence. It was a surprisingly short wait.

"Have you any word from Sturbridge yet?" Thorne asked, having barely swallowed.

"The Etheridge family, aye. I'd an answer to our inquiry just before you arrived home. They've neither seen nor heard from Combs."

"What else had they to say? Word of her background, her family?"

"They said that for three years she was governess to their children."

"Governess!" There was relish in Thorne's slow smile. "I should have suspected as much."

"Why's that?"

"I once discovered she'd a penchant for devouring books, is all. Reading, I mean. What else did they have to say?"

"Mistress Etheridge had only good to say of Combs' tenure--diligent, bright, well-mannered and so forth. They were sorry to let her go, but their son was of an age to enter his father's business, their daughter betrothed."

"They know nothing of Combs's past? Had she no references?"

"Aye, but..." Arthur frowned. "Let me fetch the letter, my memory isn't what it once was."

When he returned, he was struck by the restlessness he detected in Thorne. There was a hunger in the burning blue gaze, and when Arthur offered the folded parchment, it was all but seized from his bony fingers.

He watched Thorne peruse the page.

"They say she came to them bearing a 'confidential however most excellent reference from a titled gentleman in the east midlands'." Thorne scanned it further. "Claimed *and* confirmed to have no living relative. Damnation!"

"M'lord?"

"That is the strangest part of this mystery." Thorne laid the letter down with a scowl. "That a woman as educated and genteel as she could come from nowhere and have no family, no friends...then just as mysteriously disappear without a trace, or a word to anyone."

He means himself, Arthur realized, trying not to look startled. "Perhaps, being with child, she felt it wise to take refuge in a convent."

"Refuge from what?" Thorne countered sharply. "From whom?"

As Arthur shrugged, Thorne slammed a fist down on the letter and shot up from the trestle, stalked off, and then turned abruptly about. "By God," he said, his face flushing, "I *will* have it from you before I leave this house, Pennington--did my wife do something, say something, to offend or harm the Combs woman? You've your ear to the ground, what's the rumor?"

Arthur refrained from raising his eyebrows. "M'lord, if her ladyship gave Combs cause to leave, I've heard nothing of it."

"She had *better* not have given cause, or by God I'll throw her over the back of my horse and deliver her without further ado to the front door of Saint Mary's--the shame of annulment be damned! In any case," he muttered, seeming oblivious to Arthur's stunned expression, "I'd give my eyeteeth to know the identity of this 'titled gentleman' from the midlands. For all I know, he could be an acquaintance of mine. If she's fled to her home, her roots, he might know the locale."

Mind still reeling at the word 'annulment,' Arthur said, "You'll likely bite my head off for this, but why are this woman's whereabouts so important to you? Is it only because she's without family and expecting a child?"

"Is that not enough to stir compassion in you? Would you not feel the same, were you her master?"

Aye, but not to the point of obsession, Arthur nearly protested, but said only, "Perhaps."

Thorne leaned against the kitchen basin and stared out at the bleak December sky. "Yuletide approaches. A time when Christians celebrate the birth of a child." His mouth took a grim set. "Meanwhile, for expectation of that same joyous event, a good woman is made to feel an outcast in her own home." He shook his head. "At least the Virgin had a stable," he muttered.

"And a husband," Arthur reminded him. "There is hardly a comparison."

- 192 -

"And I say there *is*."

Arthur silently endured the glare of this man who lately seemed a mere impostor of someone he'd known since infancy and loved like a son.

Thorne finally looked away, picking up his cloak and tricorne. "Forgive me, this has nothing to do with you. I'd no intention of making you my whipping boy."

Arthur nodded and watched him go, an ache in his old heart. Thorne's pride would obviously not allow him to confide in the same man who'd warned him against the folly of a union without love. Hence Arthur could only stand by and observe the ravages of that silent suffering. He hoped fervently that Thorne, who forgave others easily, would eventually find the grace to forgive himself.

* * *

The frigid wind whistled around the corners of the staid old Hall. Casements rattled like oversized, chattering teeth, while the drafts on the north and east sides made the windows squeak in their fastenings. Gwynneth paced up and down her chambers and cast nervous glances at the wooden panels, fearing one or more would fly off its hinges under a barrage of wind and broken glass and come hurtling toward her.

The clock chimed three quarters past eight. She stared into the pivoting looking glass, seeing herself arrayed for bed in a fetching ensemble that set her skin and her eyes off to perfection. *Con*fection, she amended in silent disdain. *I might have come from a box of petit fours.*

She despised the calculation of this seduction, and hated Thorne for not having neatly fallen in with her plans already. Most of all she hated Hobbs for making it necessary. He, the one person she'd thought loved her and respected her as a person with individual rights, had instead taught her more than she ever wanted to know of a man's potential power over a woman.

And with that lesson had come the bittersweet realization of what a prize she'd once had in Thorne--who had consistently shown her that a man could be tender, patient and protective of a woman--even if he did not love her.

She shot one more grudging glance at the mirror. Good-hearted, simple-minded Byrnes had assumed all this preparation was just to inform Thorne of impending fatherhood. She would have been shocked to realize that a woman nearly two months pregnant was in full carnal pursuit of her own husband.

But I am no wanton, Gwynneth reminded herself, fighting tears as she so often did these days. *I was taken by force. And even if I had strutted stark-naked into Hobbs' room and performed the Dance of the Seven Veils, he'd no right to take advantage of me--his master's wife!*

But the deed itself was a *fait accompli.* Her mission was the important thing now, and it must not fail. Once she'd played her part with Thorne, she need only tell him, lie though it was, that Hobbs had admitted fathering Elaine Combs' babe--and the filthy cur of a stableman would be out of their lives forever.

* * *

Thorne left his study for the library, where the fire he still commissioned--in hopes of finding a lone occupant there some evening--was already reduced to glowing chunks of applewood. From the sound of the black fury outdoors, tomorrow's routine would be replaced by damage assessment. He preferred, as his father had, calling upon the herders and farmers himself rather than holding court in the great hall. His tenants appreciated it, preoccupied as they were with wind-stripped thatch and flattened shearing sheds and cow byres, not to mention dead animals and ravaged crops. His only concern was for Arthur, who would insist on going as always, despite his aching joints and Bridey's efforts to treat them with burnet-leaf wraps.

Thorne looked at the lone chair in the corner. There, before he'd convinced Combs to move nearer the fire--and his own chair--she used to sit with her book.

On a whim, he lit a taper and pulled out the last volume he'd seen her take from the shelves. He leafed through the book of poetry, wondering which rhymes had caught her fancy. He froze at sight of his own signature in a page margin.

Not so, he realized; it was his name but not his signature. His pulse quickened. He'd seen that handwriting before, in Gwynneth's wedding-record book. He would know Elaine Combs's refined script anywhere.

Thorneton Thomas Wycliffe Neville. Twice she had written it--his entire name. She must have gone to some trouble to learn the second. Hardly anyone knew it and no one ever used it.

He brought the taper closer to the book.

> *Thou art blind tho' thou doth see--*
> *Search thy mem'ry--discover me*
> *Met long ago--yet twained by fate--*
> *Thou know'st me not--here at thy gate*
>
> *Tho' oft-times now thou speak'st to me--*
> *Thine eye hath yet to know*
> *The face that came'st to love thee*
> *So many years ago*

He read them again. Did they mean something to Combs, touch some chord of nostalgia in her, remind her of someone? If so, whom? She'd no family, no friends. But surely she had a past. He smiled at the thought. Of course she had a past, she was flesh and blood, not some meadow fairy.

He closed the book and put it back, his fingers lingering on its spine. Resting his forehead against a row of volumes, he closed his eyes and surrendered to an unexpected wave of grief. He would give a small fortune just to know Combs was safe and comfortable, never mind her whereabouts. His dreams would be far less troubled if he knew that alone.

He considered rebuilding the fire in the grate, but as he looked at the empty chairs at the hearth, the impulse died. This room, indeed this very house, had lost much of its charm for him, his marriage as cold and lifeless as the ashes would soon be in the fireplace, and the one kindred soul under his roof gone without a trace.

He decided to retire early, to seek solace in sleep. On the threshold of the library he paused, then crossed to the shelves and took down the book of poetry again. Somehow the notion of having it in his chambers was comforting.

He caught wind of her scent as soon as he closed the door behind him. *Of course--the storm.* He smiled wryly. That Gwynneth would again brave the dangers of his bed said much about her fear of inclement weather. Well, she could sleep there undisturbed. He would spend the night on the upholstered chaise.

He carefully laid the book of poetry on a shelf of the sideboard, then tossed a spare blanket from a chest onto the chaise. He reached for a pillow, then heard Gwynneth's muffled voice.

"You need not sleep there, husband. This is your bed, and I take up little space."

He almost smiled. She seemed so vulnerable just now. He saw no sign of the cold, unreasonable nature lurking beneath that fetching face and form--the latter of which was again quite visible through the rose-colored shift and wrapper, now that she'd rearranged the covers.

"It will be hard enough for you to rest, Gwynneth, with this infernal wind howling throughout the night. My tossing and turning won't help. I'll be nearby. You need only call and I shall come."

"Then pretend you've heard me call, for I need you now, to comfort me."

Was there a hint of promise in those honeyed tones? He came to the bedside and bent over her, his hands pressing into the mattress on either side of her. She smiled tentatively.

"'Tis only the wind," he assured her in a soothing voice. "You needn't fear, and as I said, I'm near enough." He brushed a wayward strand of hair from her cheek and kissed her lightly on the forehead. "Goodnight, my lady. Sleep well."

Feeling her eyes on him, he blew out the tapers in the candelabra and undressed in the firelight. He'd just settled himself on the chaise when he heard her voice over the racket of the storm.

"Thorne," she said plaintively, "I want to have a child."

* * *

Gwynneth listened to the shrill wind and the crackle of the fire. Looking no lower than Thorne's naked back, she watched him pad to the sideboard and pour a glass of brandy. He tossed it and poured another, then turned suddenly around--to shock her, it seemed--and held his glass up in salute.

"You do have a way of blindsiding a man, my lady."

Heart pounding, Gwynneth sat up and lit the tapers, then lay back against the pillows and tried to smile seductively. "But husband, are there not worse ways to be blindsided? Is it not an appealing prospect, the two of us making a babe?"

Thorne set his glass down and leaned his naked hips against the sideboard, folding his arms across a broad expanse of dark-furred chest. "You've called me 'husband' twice in the last few minutes, yet I can hardly believe this is my wife speaking."

"Why not?"

"Because my wife has made it quite clear that physical union is beneath her, altogether unpleasant. And I, being a gentleman for the most part, have vowed never to visit such gross indecency upon her person again."

Gwynneth felt her smile fade. A quick downward glance at Thorne confirmed that this was not going as it should. And shouldn't he have sounded bitter? Instead he seemed polite and matter-of-fact.

Apparently considering their discussion at an end, Thorne strode casually to the chaise, rolled himself onto it and flipped the blanket up over his hips.

Gwynneth grasped at the only weapon left in her limited arsenal: she began to weep.

"God's blood and bones," Thorne muttered. Rising, he yanked on his dressing gown, then came to sit on the edge of the bed beside Gwynneth.

She pouted, her lashes beaded with tears. "You only want to punish me for wounding your pride. But you cannot deny me a child. Indeed you once said to me that even my priest would tell me that begetting children was my duty...do you remember?"

He met her gaze levelly. "What I remember most, my lady, is that you informed me that the disgusting act of physical union was perhaps for others, but not for you...that you believed you were intended for 'a higher purpose'."

"I was <u>afraid</u>, can't you understand? For a woman, the 'act of love' is a degrading ritual, a trial to be borne all her married life. And I shall do so! But you, sir, must not try to pleasure me in any way, because 'tis pleasure that turns a mere trial of necessity into a sin of wicked depravity--a *mortal* sin, Thorne, and I do not want to go to hell when I die!" She closed her eyes, shuddering, and murmured, "And the pain...such dreadful pain, I wasn't prepared for that..."

He frowned intently at her. "What pain, Gwynneth? I caused you no pain. I warned you of it, damn my idiocy, but I never followed through."

Gwynneth's cheeks began to burn. "It sounded as if it would be dreadful," she said lamely.

"I tried to tell you the pain would soon be over, never to be endured again, but your fear had already made you deaf." He rose, but she grabbed hold of his hand and gave him a pleading look.

"I was yet a girl, Thorne, in many ways. I've since confided my feelings to Father Chandler, and-"

"But you couldn't tell them to me," he cut in. "I, who struggled to understand your reticence and did my damnedest to be gentle with you."

"You needn't curse!" She hurled the covers back. "Why must you resort to that whenever we disagree?"

"I apologize. 'Tis late and I'm tired...no doubt you are, as well. We'll discuss your maternal inclinations tomorrow. Whatever we say now will only alienate us further. Good night, my lady." Belting his dressing gown with a jerk, he strode through the arch.

"Where are you going?" she demanded, scrambling from the bed and trailing him into the sitting room, her stomach knotting.

"Where I can be assured of some rest," he said without turning around.

"But the storm!" she cried. "I shan't be able to sleep for terror!"

Already in the gallery, hand on the door, Thorne sounded wearily patient. "Then I'll send for Byrnes."

* * *

On the library settee, Thorne lay staring at the wavering shadows on the walls. The wind and rain had finally subsided, but sleep eluded him for the fact that in this room he could think of little else but Elaine.

Elaine? When had he ceased thinking of her as "Combs," he wondered, startled.

A good name, Elaine--sturdy and brave like the women warriors of legend, yet feminine and refined. "Elaine."

Good God, had he just said it aloud?

He forced himself to consider Gwynneth's unexpected proposal. Even if he could somehow manage to perform--and performance it would be, no two ways about it-- there wasn't any guarantee Gwynneth's womb would quicken at once. Few things made him queasy, but the thought of repeated attempts at coupling with a frigid shrew brought a bitter taste to his mouth--and of course the minute she knew she was *enceinte*, she would bring all physical relations to a halt, he was certain of that.

Until she wanted another child.

Hearing the clock strike one, he threw the blanket back impatiently, his stomach joining in the protest with a growl. And no wonder. Supper had been a strange affair for the second consecutive night, Gwynneth playing ingenue instead of nun and he wondering at the charade--though the objective was clear enough now--so he had eaten little and left the table early.

He padded on bare feet to the great hall, past the glowing coals in the huge hearth and through the kitchen door. As the only light in that room came from the banked fire, he reached for the nearest candle. He'd no sooner struck tinder than there came a commotion from the direction of the larder, and then a muffled grunt.

A male grunt.

Thorne quickly lit the candle and, with his hand cupped around the flame, charged toward the disturbance. But just before he reached the larder, he heard the bolt being drawn on the door to the garden. "Ho there, halt where you stand!" he shouted, and ran for the heavy portal--which was slammed in his face.

"Bloody buggerer!" He kicked the door wide and ran out into the cold dampness. The mist was thick, and the intruder was well outside the weak light of Thorne's candle. There was no telling which direction he had taken.

Back inside, Thorne bolted the door and held the candle high; a close inspection revealed no evidence other than some spilled wheat flour, and none of it had hit the floor, where it might have exposed some footprints.

So the thief came from within, Thorne realized grimly. Tomorrow he'd tell Carswell, and God help the poor beggar after that.

Actually it had been rather a lark going after the fellow--more excitement than he'd had in a long while. He grinned ruefully, thinking it was surely a sad state of affairs when the master of the house had to resort to wee-hour cloak-and-dagger shenanigans for entertainment.

But the leftover roast hen he found had never tasted better.

THIRTY-ONE

At Arthur's insistence, he and Thorne were on the Wycliffe road heading east before seven of the clock next morning, tricornes pulled low and steaming scones inside their pockets. Three hours later they'd covered five farms and logged only minimal amounts of damage. On their way to the sixth, Thorne glanced southward and sharply reined in his mount. Arthur did the same.

"Who the devil would find that fit to live in?" he wondered aloud. They were staring down a dray path in a field of wheat stubble, where stood a run-down wooden shack, which had been uninhabited for years. But this morning the chimney was exhaling a slim plume of smoke.

"Likely some Gypsy." Thorne lightly flicked the reins. "Whoever he is, he's welcome to it. He'll wander along come spring."

"Perhaps he's your thief," Arthur ventured, urging his mount to a trot alongside Raven.

Thorne chuckled. "A far piece for a man to walk for his daily bread."

"Oh, I think he makes off with at least two or three days' rations in one heist," Arthur said with a droll expression. "Keeps it down to a couple of raids per week that way. I can always tell when he's come calling, he does get Bridey's dander up."

"Well, 'tis not the Gypsy," Thorne said, still smiling, "but apparently a member of my household, though none of the servants goes to bed hungry--that I'll warrant, or know the reason why. And at any rate," he added, suddenly sobering, "Carswell and Lady Neville will get to the bottom of the matter today."

* * *

"I have assembled all the servants in the great hall, Milady."

Gwynneth jabbed her quill into its stand on the desk in her day room. With militant stride and head held high, she followed the housekeeper as far as the foot of the central stairs, and there stopped to scan the line of men and women, young and old, that ranged along the walls of the great hall.

She began with an austere nod. "Good morning ladies, gentlemen...though one of you does not deserve that distinction...in particular, the individual who has been helping himself to the foodstuffs in the larder. I shall now address that person directly.

"Have no doubt that before the year is out, I will have determined your identity. From that time on," she declared coldly, "your wages will be withheld while you work until complete restitution is made...at which point you shall find yourself without situation or reference." She smiled with grim satisfaction. "You were nearly discovered yestereve by his lordship. 'Tis only a matter of time until you are exposed. However"

- 198 -

--she looked at each servant in turn-- "if you, the thief, can find it in your meager conscience to report yourself to Dame Carswell this very day, you will be required to make only partial restitution, and shall be given a passable reference upon dismissal." She paused expectantly, but the Hall was silent. "Very well then," she snapped. "Back to work. There is much to be done toward the joyous celebration of Christmas!"

* * *

"Come in," Thorne said shortly.

Gwynneth closed the study door behind her. "Pardon me for interrupting, my lord, but I thought now might be as good a time as any to discuss...that is, to decide-"

"Sit down, my lady, please. The floor is yours."

She gave him her most engaging smile. "We needn't conduct this discussion under Parliamentary procedure, husband. I'm simply your wife, come to consult with you."

"Gwynneth, in your case, 'simply' and 'wife' do not belong in the same sentence."

"Which is what I want to remedy. I've come to beg your forgiveness, my lord. I have not been a complete wife to you. You are a man who deserves...attention."

Her face was slowly reddening, but her eyes remained on his, and in them Thorne saw the determination she was trying to conceal with her smile and sweetly rueful tone.

"Henceforward I shall be an attentive wife...if you will allow me, dear husband."

Thorne leaned back in his chair. "If nothing else, I'm curious to know what prompted your sudden largess. Is this a self-imposed penance for some wrong you imagine you've done me?"

Her pale lashes fluttered. "I denied you what is yours. My confessor has helped me see the error of my ways."

"The good Father Chandler."

"Yes."

"How benevolent of him to be concerned with my marital rights."

Gwynneth's smile was wearing thin. "He is more concerned with your right to have an heir than your right to have...me."

"Ah, yes, procreation versus recreation."

"Thorne, must you make a case out of everything? I am asking you, once and for all, to forgive my past behavior."

"And to join you in the marriage bed."

"Aye." She blushed scarlet.

"And once it is confirmed you're to be a mother, how stands the marriage bed then, my lady?" He paused. "Empty, I'd venture, from the look on your face."

"Thorne, please." The requisite tears surfaced. "I've always thought you a fair man, a kind one. Was I so errant in my judgment?"

"I wouldn't know, Gwynneth. Judgment is your forte, not mine." Seeing her lower lip quiver, he casually gave her his handkerchief and went to stand before the fire. He looked into the flames for a while, before saying quietly, "Gwynneth, I won't lie to you."

He turned to see her clutching his handkerchief and watching him expectantly.

"'Tis a biological fact that a man must feel desire in order to bring on...the necessary physical condition for child-getting. But desire is diminished by strife, Gwynneth, and there has been so much of the latter between us that the former is, I fear, entirely obliterated." He paused, but saw no sign of comprehension. "I mean to say," he pressed gently, "that I cannot force my anatomy into the state that is necessary to...sow my seed. I'm sorry, but I must be honest."

Her tears were starting again; she finally understood.

"Do what you must," he said with sincere regret. "Stay or leave as you please, continue as you have, or demand annulment of our marriage...but I can't give you a child."

Gwynneth was shaking her head. "'Tis not true, Thorne. You *can*, indeed you *must*...I don't know what I shall do if you don't..." She was starting to look wild-eyed. "I deserve another chance...*we* deserve it! You may do whatever you wish with me, I shan't give you any resistance...please!" Her voice was breaking. She stood, holding her arms out to him. "Please, Thorne, say you'll at least try...you *must try*!"

He was struggling for words when she suddenly flew toward him, yanking the fichu out of her bodice. "Here, you see?" She crushed her ripe décolletage against his shirtfront, her small hands gripping his shoulders. "I am yours to do with as you please!" Frantically she tried to pull his head down and press his mouth to hers, at which point he gently extricated himself from her clutches and held her at arms' length.

"Gwynneth, please...don't make this any more difficult than it is..."

She threw off his hands, blinking furiously. "Keep off then! If *you* won't give me a child, perhaps another man *will*!" As Thorne stared at her, shocked into silence, she laughed through her tears, ending on a bitter sob. "You think no other man would want me? Well, you are wrong, husband!"

Thorne felt a slow burn in his gut. "I've no doubt Hobbs would take you riding in a trice, my lady...without a horse."

The Hall seemed to hold its breath and the walls to suck inward, as all color drained from Gwynneth's face. With the flat of her hand, she struck Thorne hard on the cheek.

He took the blow without flinching. "Forgive me, Gwynneth, but you do make it hard for a man to pity you."

"*Pity*?" Her wet eyes blazed. "I've no need of your pity, *you* are the one to be pitied...a man who cannot please his wife, who cannot give her a child! You might as well be a eunuch!"

"Hush, Gwynneth. You're making a fool of no one but yourself, and the servants are bound-"

"I don't care if they hear, I hope *every single one of them* hears! They should know their master for the pitiful, impotent wretch he really is!" Her laugh verged on hysteria.

Accosting her so swiftly she'd no chance to back away, Thorne wrapped his arms around her, pressing her face to his waistcoat.

Slowly she pounded a fist on his chest. "You have broken my heart," she said through her muffled sobs. "For shame I shan't be able to hold up my head."

Still he held her, and after a moment said quietly, "Gwynneth, I'll do everything possible to ensure your comfort and your happiness in any other way, but I cannot be your bedmate." He gently kissed her brow. "I wish to God I could."

She wrenched free of his hold. "As if you ever wished anything of God!" she said vehemently through her tears. "Take heed, Thorne Neville. In denying me my God-given right to be a mother, you might well have reserved your place in hell this day." Her lip curled. "And I hope you rot there."

She flung the door open and fled up the hall.

Feeling cold all over but for his numb cheek, Thorne sat back down at his desk. The framed miniature stood just inside his peripheral vision, and his focus was suddenly drawn to it. The beautiful, enigmatic face of Catherine Neville looked back at him.

"Caroline," he murmured, startling himself. *Caroline.* This time it was in his head, whispering...beckoning, teasing, promising...and he was both amazed and dismayed as his body responded to the mere thought of her, in the very way it no longer responded to the flesh-and-blood presence of his wife.

Caroline. Again, the soft whisper. He felt light-headed, almost drunk.

Suddenly, Christmas in London seemed a very desirable prospect.

* * *

Gwynneth shot the bolt on her chamber door and threw herself on her knees before the small creche her father had sent as a Christmas gift.

"What shall I do?" she cried softly. She snatched up her rosary beads and threaded them through shaking hands, then pressed them to her lips to quell a rising scream.

"I *hate* you, Thorne Neville," she whispered when the impulse had passed, her nose stinging with fresh tears. "You've ruined my life, you and Hobbs...may God rot his soul with yours! Oh God," she moaned, "why didn't you leave me in peace at Saint Mary's? I hate this accursed place, and I hate my *father* for bringing me here!"

With one mighty jerk of her hands the rosary snapped. Jet beads scattered and danced madly all around her. As the last bounce dwindled to stillness, she looked down at her tight fist, and loosened her fingers, one by one. In her sweating palm was all that remained of her beloved rosary: the worn sterling Crucifix inlaid with mother-of-pearl, on it the likeness of the Christ in pure gold.

Her eyes darted, widening, to the porcelain figurine of Mary kneeling in the straw next to her babe. A startled sound escaped her lips.

"You're telling me then, Mother, that this is my cross to bear?" Her breathing slowed; her trembling eased. She took in the peaceful sight of the creche as a whole-- mother, father and child in a lowly stable, the animals and shepherds, angels and wise men looking on with vacant stares.

The stable! Of course. She almost smiled. *The family, together in the stable.* It was a humble scene, but beautifully appropriate. The Christ was born in a stable; *her* child was conceived in one. And if it was good enough for Him, it was certainly good enough for her babe...whose father, after all, was a stableman.

* * *

"Master'll not be here to dine this eve," Bridey announced, up to her elbows in a bowl of dough.

Susan glanced up from the silver she was polishing. "He'll come later, then?"

"Not likely," the cook grumbled. "He's gone to London town."

"What?" Hillary was indignant. "With Yuletide nearly upon us?"

"Aye." Bridey gave the dough a hard punch. "The master gone off, and the mistress shut away in her chambers, no guests invited--leastways none that Her Prissiness bothered to tell me about, after all, I'm only the cook and have to feed them. By the saints, I'd reckoned on a merry Yule', what with his lordship home and wed in the bargain...ha! 'Twill be no different from the *last* four, more's the pity."

"Oh, Mister Pennington'll see to the gold for the tenants, and our wassail bowl as well, like he has since the old baron passed on," Susan said placidly. "At any rate his lordship could return ere the day's upon us, and who knows, he might fetch some company along with him...now wouldn't that be grand!"

* * *

The coach rolled to a stop, its crystalline-dew-covered windows giving no indication of their whereabouts. Thorne only knew that not enough road had been put between him and the Hall. His coachman was soon at the door, his breath puffing in steamy clouds.

"We're at Wolverton, sir--mightn't you want to stop? The fog's got thick and the horses a mite skittish." He rubbed his hands together. "A bit chill up there, as well," he added sheepishly, nodding toward his perch.

"Have we passed the inn?"

"No, M'lord, I wouldn't ask to go back. 'Tis directly ahead."

"I don't know how you can tell in this stew. Hie to it, then. Just one buttered rum, Dobson, you'll need your wits about you." He peered over the coachman's shoulder. "The moon will be up in a while."

Dobson nodded. "You coming in, sir?"

Thorne shook his head. "I especially need my wits about me. And I'd like to be in London before daylight."

Dobson tipped his hat. "We will be, M'lord. Thank you, sir." He shut the door firmly against the cold, creeping dampness.

Thorne leaned down and shook the copper brazier to stir up some heat and, drawing out his pocket watch, settled back to await the coachman's return.

* * *

Hobbs' heart leapt into his throat as he glanced up to see Gwynneth. She hadn't set foot in the stables since the night he'd stolen her virginity, and he hadn't dared inquire after her. He stood, searching in vain for any sign of emotion on her face. "Milady," he said hoarsely. "May I be of some service-"

"You've serviced me quite enough, thank you. Like the braying jackass that confuses a thoroughbred filly with his own kind. And now there is a mule on the way."

He stared at her, his breath suspended, his head suddenly light. "You're carrying my child?"

"I am. No other has ever planted seed in me...not even my husband, as you must surely know by now."

He tried to speak, but she wouldn't let him.

"The babe shall be born nigh summer solstice, by John Hodges' estimation. Not," she said caustically, "that I had any doubt as to the eve of its conception."

Dumbfounded, Hobbs could only stare. That he had fathered the first offspring of Lady Neville, Baroness Neville of Wycliffe, was a miracle of profound justice-- recompense for the land he would never own, for the power and respect he would never enjoy without benefit of an estate. Add to that the years he'd labored from sunrise to sunset for a living, when all along he should have been waited upon by others for even his simplest needs, amidst all the luxury of the manor house up on the hill.

He wanted to shout his triumph from atop the tower.

"I never guessed you were a virgin." A tremor in his voice betrayed his effort to match her reserve. "Otherwise, I'd have exercised more restraint." *But I would bloody well have taken you nonetheless.* "Have you told him?"

She gave him a withering look. "Do you think I'd be standing here on his land if I had? I should be in the nunnery whence I came, Tobias Hobbs, or deposited at my father's rotting shell of a Hall. And *you'd* be cold in your grave."

"Oh, I doubt that, Milady. Your husband is far too lily-livered for violence. Consider the strange brand of justice he administered when the Combs slut found her belly swelling and laid the blame at my door...he kept both of us on, and invented a new situation for the lying tramp!"

"Aye," Gwynneth said grimly, and pulled her cloak tight around her. "He'd have kept that woman in his house even were she a murderess, I think. But his benevolence has limits. And I'm not his serving wench, I'm his wife--his chattel, as you've said before--and you've taken me right under his nose. Thorne Neville may appear mild- mannered under most circumstances, but I have seen murder in his eyes...as will you."

"Then you will tell him."

"I must tell him something. He doesn't believe in virgin births."

Hobbs almost smiled. "Nor will he believe the babe is his nephew. Or niece."

Gwynneth frowned. "Pardon?"

"The babe will have Wycliffe blood running through its veins," he said softly.

She slowly shook her head. "There is no Wycliffe blood in my line. My father would have told me long ago."

Hobbs laughed--briefly, bitterly, hands clenching at his sides. "I should have known you'd misunderstand."

She stamped her foot. "Then *what* are you saying to me?"

"I am saying," he rapped out with sudden cold fury, his fist striking the post, "that *I am Thorne Neville's brother.*"

* * *

"You," Gwynneth said when she found her voice, "are a raving lunatic."

She turned on her heel and beat a staccato path to the doorway, her hood flying back onto her shoulders. "I'll not stay to hear more, indeed I must tell your master of your lapse into utter madness!" she cried, her heart pounding.

"Hearken, Milady!" Hobbs was smiling when she whirled to face him, but his eyes were like flint. "I am not mad. I should be, knowing what I've known all this time, and helpless to do anything about it. I told you once that my mother was in service on this manor--a score of years ago."

Gwynneth blinked, remembering immediately.

"Her name was Cornelia Hobbs, a chambermaid...and some time after Catherine Neville's death, she swept herself right into the amorous clutches of the grieving widower."

"You lie."

"Do I? I wasn't given the sordid details. Suffice it to say that their dalliance resulted in 'the bearing of fruit.' More poetic than your mule analogy."

"And I suppose *you* were the fruit."

His silence and bitter expression were more convincing than anything he might have said. Slowly, grudgingly, Gwynneth moved to the rough-hewn bench and sat down, pulling a watch locket out over her cloak and snapping it open. "Five minutes. Then I shall take my leave...and God help you if you dare try to stop me."

Hobbs seemed unfazed by her threat, almost as if he hadn't heard it. "She was ashamed and afraid to tell Robert Neville her secret, despite his affection for her, and rather than risk rejection or humiliation, she fled the manor, collected her daughter of seven years from a nearby relative and high-tailed it to Birmingham. She reared us there, working her fingers to the bone for a seamstress in the town, although my half-sister had as much to do with my raising. We were both schooled for a time, until my mother saw fit to take me to Wycliffe Hall, where Pennington took me on as a groom. My mother returned to Birmingham with an easier mind. By that time she and my half-sister had a little dressmaker's shop there."

"And Robert Neville never knew you were his son?"

"Never."

"Your name didn't 'rouse his curiosity? And your age?"

Hobbs shook his head. "No doubt my mother was long forgotten," he said bitterly.

"Then Thorne has no notion you're his half-brother."

"None."

"Why haven't you told him?"

Hobbs gave a snort. "Ah, indeed...why haven't I simply trotted up to the south gardens entrance of his ancestral home, traipsing mud and dung through his spotless kitchen and down his carpeted hall and into his holy sanctuary--pardon me, *study*, with my hat in hand--only to inform him that I, his stable master, am in fact his *blood brother* by half?" His expression mocked her. "Because, Milady, he should think me quite mad, as you did moments ago."

"No, you're wrong!" Gwynneth cried softly, her face suddenly alight. "He would listen. Thorne always listens, and you will convince him as you have me."

Hobbs smiled slyly. "You're thinking that then he'd be more likely to forgive me for cuckolding him? I think *not*, Milady." He sobered. "The reason I've kept it to myself is that I haven't a shred of proof to back my story. And were I Neville, and my stableman approached me after several years of relatively quiet service and claimed to be my brother, I'd laugh him out of my house straightaway--after I'd sacked him, that is."

"Yes, but you're *not* Thorne, and you don't know him as I do. He would at least listen, and give your claim some consideration. He might even make confirming inquiries."

"Of whom?" Hobbs scoffed. "My dead mother? There is no one to validate my claim, Milady. Certainly no one in Birmingham knew my father's identity. They only knew I was a bastard."

Gwynneth paled. "As this child of ours shall be, if you shirk your responsibility."

Hobbs gave a snort. "What, should I take you off to live in some hovel and seek another situation, with no references to give? I cannot leave this place, Milady. It has been my home for many years...and my goal, my quest, for the last two, ever since my dying mother told me of my birthright."

"'Tis *not* your birthright. You're the second son, you've no claim to the estate."

"I'm not stupid," he groused. "I'm well aware that Neville is the elder. But if he were to die, who should inherit?"

"I should, at present," Gwynneth said, her voice faltering. "But when he learns of this child, *neither* of us shall be his heir--you'll be in a pine box underground, and I'll be resident at Saint Mary's, a solitary outcast, never to take the veil. As for our child, who knows? Thorne might see fit to make it his heir. 'Twould be quite like him."

Hobbs sat down at his worktable, forehead in hand. "Proof," he muttered, rubbing his brow. "If I'd but proof of my siring, I should already have been declared next-in-line to the heir-apparent. You would be my dependent upon Neville's death...and free to marry me."

Gwynneth shivered. "There is no point in such ramblings. He is quite alive. You are simply the stable master by his reckoning, while I am fertile with seed that does not belong to him. 'Twill not take him long to see a connection--he has several times chastised me for treating you as a familiar."

Hobbs' voice was ominously quiet. "He won't live forever."

"He will outlive you. He'll see to it." Gwynneth rose from the bench, staring down at Hobbs until he met her eyes. "You are a coward," she said quietly, and in some deep recess of her mind saw a fleeting vision of herself standing on the battlements. "Better our child should die, than to know its father is less than a man."

"See here now-"

"Your crude notion of love, and your consuming greed," she went on as if he hadn't interrupted, "have been my undoing." Having spoken without rancor, she felt a quiet strength steal over her, a peaceful acceptance of her situation. "Remember that, Hobbs. Remember it whenever you remember me."

She turned away, her head held high, and walked over the threshold--out into the night, and out of Tobias Hobbs' life.

* * *

"I am sorry, M'lord, but the household has long retired for the night," said the politely surprised voice from below. "Might you call again tomorrow?"

Caroline came out onto the gallery and leaned over the balustrade. "Who is it, Gilbert?" She peered just beyond the small aura cast by the footman's candle. "Thorne? Is that you?" She drew her scarlet China-silk wrapper snugly over her breasts and descended the stairs, her hair a luxurious mantle over her shoulders. "Lord Neville," she said graciously, having gathered her wits. Reaching the foot of the stairs, she ignored Gilbert's scandalized expression and held a hand out in greeting. It was promptly grasped in long, strong fingers.

"Mistress Sutherland. Please forgive my intrusion at this strange hour, but I must speak with you." The piercing blue eyes all but demanded admittance.

"Come to the drawing room, then. Gilbert will take your hat and cloak." Turning to lead the way, she scowled at her disapproving footman. "You may retire, Gilbert. Lord Neville knows his way out."

Inside the drawing room, Caroline stepped around Thorne to shut the doors behind them. She hadn't so much as taken her fingers off the brass handles when she sensed him behind her, and froze. Somehow she knew he was standing as close to her as he could without touching.

Seconds ticked by; still he made no contact.

"I should go and change into something more appropriate," she said faintly. Her fingers tightened on the handles.

The scent of sandalwood floated beneath her nose and mingled with her fragrance. She closed her eyes, struggling to calm herself, and whispered tautly, "Why have you come?"

Chills raced from her scalp to her toes and back again as his warm breath caressed her ear.

"Upon my last visit," he said huskily, "I confessed I stood hovering at the edge of a certain pit."

Caroline bowed her head against the paneled door; her breath caught as she felt the subtle press of Thorne's powerful body against her barely clad curves.

"I have just this day," he murmured, his lips grazing her ear, "been pushed into it headlong."

THIRTY-TWO

Caroline opened her eyes to the gray light of impending dawn. The fire had died in the grate, but she felt warmth aplenty under the blankets. There the fire had died less than an hour ago. She smiled to herself, then heard a soft rustling across the room.

Thorne was at the window, holding the long velvet draperies aside to peer into the chill morning gloom. Caroline knew there was nothing to see on the street or the green; residents of this wealthy suburb of London would never dream of being about so early, and the servants took the alleys. But Thorne, with his rural roots planted deep, had seldom been able to out-sleep the dawn.

She turned over, gathering the covers cozily around her. "Come back to bed," she purred, yawning and stretching like a sleek, sated feline.

She heard the smile in his voice as he let the drapery fall and approached the bed. "Have you slept at all, vixen?" He leaned over her. "Seek your dreams," he murmured, and touched his lips to her eyelids. "I'll not take my leave before breaking fast with you."

She frowned slightly. "Leave?"

"'Tis Christmas Eve," he reminded her. "I must leave for Wycliffe this morn."

"Must you?" she asked, then mentally kicked herself. Of course he must. Thorne wouldn't spend Christmas away from his home and his wife. Too, there were the servants to consider, and perhaps even some guilt to assuage, as he'd spent the last two days in Caroline's home...and the last three nights in her bed.

As she pressed two long-nailed fingers against his lips to signify her acceptance, he caught them gently between his teeth and flicked them with his tongue. Caroline's hips bucked with the sudden lightning in her loins, prompting a low chuckle from her agitator.

Pride pricked, she nonetheless reached for him, and in one fluid movement he lifted the covers to slip beneath them and slide willingly into the silken trap of her long limbs. Their mouths merged hungrily for a time before she suddenly threw the bedcovers back--only to straddle her lover's brawny thighs.

"Whoa, what's this?" The huskiness of his voice sent delicious shivers up her spine, but she resisted when he took her by the hips and tried to sit her astride his rigid member. He ceased his efforts then, and waited, the gleam in his eyes momentarily eclipsed by curiosity.

She held herself above him, warning him with a slow shake of her head against any sudden movement, then took the middle finger of his hand and slid it into the warm wetness of her mouth.

He grunted and tried again to pull her down onto his straining shaft, but she'd been prepared for that, and gripped his wrist; holding him at arm's length, she resumed her oral assault on yet another long, brown digit.

He lay there, glaring as best he could through the lust in his eyes. "Am I to endure this teasing indefinitely?"

Caroline filtered a smoky look through her lashes. "You've little choice, my lord...you are entirely at my mercy." She bared her teeth in a wicked smile before clamping them gently on the pad of his thumb.

Thorne lunged into a sitting position. Holding Caroline at the small of her back, he reached down to cup the thick-thatched mound between her legs, making her gasp as he slid his long fingers through her moist folds and deep inside her, where he stroked her with a relentless rotating rhythm that sent liquid fire through her veins and turned her knees to water. Meanwhile his tongue thrummed a taut nipple, and as Caroline groaned in delicious agony, he closed his mouth over it and suckled hungrily.

Her climax was sudden and convulsive. In a half-daze she lay atop him, where she'd collapsed at the first onslaught of pulsing contractions, and was nonplused to hear a low rumble of laughter in his chest.

"So, I'm entirely at your mercy."

She raised her head to see his goading smile. "Do not be so quick to mock, my lord," she warned, and before he could say another word had straddled him again. "Now," she said softly, digging her knees into the down mattress, "you must promise to behave, and not to interfere."

He said nothing, made no move. Watching his face, Caroline sensually rolled and massaged her colossal breasts until their dark peaks projected in bold invitation.

The predatory flame in Thorne's eyes flared like a fresh-fueled torch. Caroline felt his hardness leap and throb against her inner thigh, where it left a moist, pearly precursor of his seed; still he kept his hands down on the bed, if only by clutching desperately at the counterpane.

"Well...do you promise?" Lifting one breast, she slowly circled its aureole with her tongue, watching Thorne hunger after every move. When with a soft moan she closed her lips over her taut nipple to suckle, she heard him groan long and deep from within his chest. His every muscle was rigid, and his manhood--thick, heavily veined and lengthened beyond Caroline's expectation--waved and lunged wildly in the air, searching frantically for some warm, wet softness in which to bury itself.

"I promise," he said thickly. "I promise...God's blood, wench, but you're a merciless tease!"

With altogether a different sort of promise in her black-velvet eyes, Caroline released her shiny, jutting peak with a flick of her tongue. "Very good," she whispered, and felt Thorne's skin break into gooseflesh as she ran her nails lightly up his rib cage and into the thick mat of black curls on his chest.

Settling back on her haunches, she stroked his thighs, all the while gazing at his magnificent member. Knowing he was watching raptly, she ran her tongue slowly and deliberately over her lips; scooting backward a bit for better leverage, she deliberately wriggled her curvaceous bottom in the air.

"I cannot endure much more of this," he said through his teeth.

Her hair tumbled forward then, wave after black silk wave assaulting his hard belly, making him flinch and suck in his breath as she bent over him with a throaty chuckle. "Not to worry, my lord," she purred. "Deliverance is at hand...this hand, in particular." She wrapped her slender fingers as best she could around his engorged manhood, and gently retracted the cowl of velvety foreskin to bare his glistening glans; then, giving him a sultry look, she parted her moistened lips and slowly lowered her head.

* * *

The oriel windows of the great hall were unusually bright, as Thorne had expected. As the coach drew near, he noticed a dim glow from Gwynneth's chambers. His own chamber windows were more luminous; apparently he was expected home tonight despite his neglect to send word. He steeled himself to act the cheerful and contented master for the evening, though he hadn't felt the peace and quiet joy of Christmas since before his father's illness and death. This year would be no exception.

But Jennings' enthusiastic greeting was heartening, and rounding the wood screen into the festooned great hall with its roaring fire, Thorne sensed his own mood elevating, and the savory aroma of succulent roast goose stuffed with sage and onion only heightened it.

From the dais, Arthur and Dame Carswell were keeping watch on the festivities. Byrnes, Markham, Bridey and numerous scullery, parlor and chambermaids were gathered up and down the length of the U-shaped table, which bore a wassail bowl and several platters of food. Some of the footmen and grooms, all young men with roving eyes, were swaggering about with cups in hand for the benefit of the many unattached females, while others, having braved the risk of rejection, were now dancing to the tune of a sprightly fiddle.

Thorne spotted William milling about the outer edges of the throng, then saw him exit alone through the larder--a rendezvous to keep? He wouldn't have expected such from the shy, gangly youth. Just then Dobson entered from the kitchen with his men, having unhitched the horses and returned them to the stables in short order, and William was forgotten in the merry mayhem that ensued.

Conspicuously absent was Hobbs. Thorne cynically supposed he'd found more entertaining means of celebration.

One other glaring absence startled him. Gwynneth seemed to be missing from the revelers. As mistress of the manor she should have hosted graciously in his stead until he arrived. But then again... He experienced a wave of guilt as he considered his own deliberate absence the last three days.

Arthur, having waited to distribute the manor's monetary brand of Christmas cheer, seemed greatly mollified by Thorne's arrival. He knew nothing of Gwynneth's whereabouts, but refrained from looking too sympathetic at Thorne's obvious embarrassment.

"She took tea in her chambers this afternoon, M'lord," Byrnes replied to Thorne's terse inquiry. "She give me leave 'til the morrow and said she'd be praying in her chambers this eve, as 'twas only fitting, and said she hoped I'd do the same in mine." The maid glanced guiltily at her half-empty cup.

Thorne's smile was grim. "Aye, well, saints have no need of Christmas. 'Tis we sinners who have cause to celebrate. Carry on, Byrnes."

The huge pewter wassail bowl was refilled, and mugs of the steaming beverage were lifted for any and every possible excuse. If Gwynneth's retreat was resented, there was no sign, and Thorne reflected, again cynically, that the night's revels were all the merrier for her absence. High-spirited conversation punctuated by peals of raucous laughter echoed through the rafters of the great hall. Manners slipped a notch or two; cheekiness was more than usually tolerated, kisses and embraces stolen under the great cluster of mistletoe that had been cut from an apple tree in Carmody's orchard. The traditional Yule log was burning--an entire beech tree, fed trunk-end first into the roaring fire throughout the twelve days of Yuletide--and with music that seldom gave pause, since when one fiddler tired another took his place, the dancers were soon working themselves into a lather.

Thorne sat at the head of the table, Arthur to his immediate left and Gwynneth's empty seat to his right, and tried to enjoy the merriment. But no matter how many mugs of wassail he consumed, he could not dull his painful awareness of one woman's absence.

Where was she this night, Combs and her unborn? Though not a praying man by habit, he sent a fervent hope heavenward that she was alive and well and sheltered by more than a mere stable.

The celebration dwindled to an end long after midnight, the Yule log carefully dowsed and the clutter abandoned for morning. After seeing that no drunken bodies littered the great hall, Thorne retired to his chambers, pausing outside the door as he considered visiting Gwynneth--a moment of madness he let pass.

And so it was that the master and his household settled down for the short remainder of the night, not in the least suspecting that Christmas festivities at Wycliffe Hall would be over almost as soon as they had begun.

* * *

"M'lord!" Byrnes hastily curtsied to Thorne, who had just stepped out into the gallery. "A happy Christmas Day to ye, sir. Does her ladyship await in your chambers?"

One eyebrow took wing. "No, Byrnes, I haven't seen your mistress this morn. Perhaps she's gone to the church."

"But M'lord, her bed hasn't been slept in, and her fire burnt out last eve from the looks of it. I...I thought she was with ye, sir." She blushed to the roots of her mouse-brown hair.

"You thought wrongly," Thorne said, though not unkindly, and turned toward the great stairs. "She very likely went to early Nativity Mass," he said over his shoulder. "Have William inquire at the coach house."

* * *

"M'lord."

Thorne looked up from his ledger, surprised to see Arthur. "Shouldn't you be on your way to Kettering?"

"That can wait. I've just come from the coach house, where I heard William asking after her ladyship." The furrows in Arthur's brow deepened. "Dobson says no coach was ordered this morn. Her ladyship has not gone to the church."

- 210 -

Thorne went back to his work, his jaw tightening almost imperceptibly as he said, "Perhaps Hobbs escorted her there on horseback."

Arthur shook his head. "He's in the stables. And though he reeks of spirits and gawks at me cross-eyed, he swears he hasn't seen her ladyship in two or three days."

Feeling a bit cross-eyed himself, Thorne sighed and said tersely, "Very well. 'Twill embarrass her no end when she's found, but call for a search. Get Carswell to organize it. Only the house, mind you. I doubt she's ventured out into the cold and damp."

"Mightn't you want to join in, M'lord? The servants might otherwise think-"

"Let them think what they may." Thorne slammed the ledger shut. "As they will at any rate." Looking up, he saw Arthur's discomfiture and softened his expression. "I'm the last person she wants to see. Nevertheless, when she's found, have her sent to me."

* * *

A half-hour passed, and as reluctant as Thorne was to admit anxiety over Gwynneth, he found himself glancing frequently at the mantel clock. His door was ajar, and the sound of muted voices and hurried steps told him the search was still on. After another quarter-hour, Arthur poked his head in the doorway.

"Where is she?" Thorne asked sharply.

"I wish I knew, M'lord. I do know she's not in this house."

He stepped back as Thorne sprang from his chair and rounded the desk.

Thorne took the east hall with long pounding strides, stopping at the great hall so abruptly that Arthur nearly ran over him. There most of the servants were gathered, Dame Carswell at center, and all eyes were suddenly upon the master.

"You've searched every chamber and hallway? Every wardrobe, every privy closet?" he barked at the housekeeper.

Never had she looked so flustered, and ordinarily he might have enjoyed it. "Aye, M'lord. There is no place left to search." She curtsied.

"No place. You're certain."

"Quite, M'lord. Except for the tower...shall we search there as well?" If her tone was overly ingratiating, Thorne's was downright scathing.

"And why search the tower, Carswell? It requires at least two strong men to budge the door--how should Lady Neville manage such a feat?"

"But...M'lord." She advanced warily, and murmured for his ears alone. "Milady knows of the secret entrance above stairs."

Thorne felt the blood drain from his face. "How? How does she know?"

"She inquired, M'lord, one day not long ago, if there was another entrance to the tower, one which wouldn't require assistance to access...and I told her yes, I knew of such a doorway, that it was above stairs in the chambers directly opposite hers...whereupon she asked that I show it to her, and naturally I did her bidding-"

"You fool, do you know what you've done?"

There was a collective gasp from the servants, but Thorne paid them no heed, instead wheeling about to find Arthur behind him. "Come with me!" he rasped, and turned for the east hall, then murmured to himself, "No, 'twill be faster from the stairs," and, reaching them on a run, bounded up three at a time.

He could not even feel his legs moving, so numb was he to everything but the panic that threatened to engulf him, and he found himself in the northeast corner chambers without any memory of having traversed the long east gallery. Dimly he heard raised voices below, and was faintly aware of pounding footsteps on the great stairs. His hands shook; his fingers were stiff with fear as he ran them along the hidden seam in the carved wood panel, frantically searching for the tiny niche that would indicate the door's triggering mechanism. Almost unaware, he let go a hoarse stream of words that might have embarrassed the most seasoned of sailors. And then the panel gave way.

He was through it at once. The dank, sour odor of the tower assaulted him with nauseating strength. But his panic quickly asserted itself, becoming a driving force that sent him racing up the winding steps like a madman until he reached the door that opened onto the battlements. The thought that Gwynneth might be below, secure inside the keep itself, had barely formed before being replaced by a more hideous certainty.

He crashed through the door and sprinted toward the parapet, a silent scream already roaring in his head. His lungs sucked cold mist in deep, harsh spasms as he sprawled across a crenel and stared at the flagstone terrace far below.

For decades to come, until the last of those in the Neville household that day went to his eternal rest, there would be whispered accounts of the tortured, bloodcurdling, almost inhuman howl that went up from the battlements of the tower at Wycliffe Hall on Christmas Day, the year of our Lord 1728.

THIRTY-THREE

"That you give him sanctuary," Hobbs said hoarsely, "and make him welcome in your bed, for naught in return...it kills my soul."

"You haven't a soul, Toby, you sold it to the devil long ago." Caroline smoothed the lace tiers on her sleeve. "So, you'd have me charge him as if I were a common whore?"

He snorted. "Nothing common about you."

"Apologize, this minute," she said sharply.

"Why should I? You're only common by birth--and you pay me to forget that."

"I'm no one's whore, Toby. And Thorne Neville wouldn't stoop that low."

"Maybe he should have, instead of bullying his wife." His shoulders sagged. "She carried *my child*, Caroline. And she wanted me to take her away, far away from his tyranny...but I refused." Feeling the rare sting of tears, he flung himself into a chair, a hand shielding his face.

"Thorne is no tyrant, Toby. Nor was he a cold husband. He may not have loved her, but he was once very fond of her. You don't know the hell she put him through! Her constant complaining, preaching, refusing him her bed, her body-" Her lip curled. "Of course, Thorne never tried it your way. He has a strange propensity for *asking* a woman-"

"Enough!" Hobbs slammed fists down on the arms of his chair, then sprang up from the seat, his face flushed. "She deliberately goaded me into a rage that night, and I bloody lost control...God knows I'd kept my hands off her as long as I could." Caroline flinched slightly as he leaned over her and shook a finger in her face. "So say no more of what *his bloody lordship* would or would not have done," he snarled. "I hate the man. I hate his fortune, his rank and his holier-than-thou ethics, and by God, I'd sooner slit his bloody throat than set eyes on him for the hell he's put me through!"

"'Twas *Gwynneth* who put you through hell, Toby," Caroline chided softly, as he stood over her, his chest heaving with each harsh breath. "Just as she did him. Yet he's grieved for her these two months since, and he will always grieve for the waste of her life, and for what might have been. So mark my words, Toby, and mark them well-- Thorne Neville will hie you to hell if he ever learns his wife was carrying your child. I've seen a dark side of your brother, and I think he's quite capable of killing under certain circumstances."

I have seen murder in his eyes...as will you. The words, like the woman who'd spoken them, were fresh in Hobbs' memory. He pushed away from Caroline's chair, turning his back to her.

"Thorne is not a man who advertises his feelings," Caroline said somewhat defensively. "It took him a long time to admit his marriage was less than perfect."

Hobbs spun around with a sneer. "And how long was it before he 'advertised his feelings' for *you*?"

"There now, Mister Hobbs, that will be *quite* enough." Caroline shot up from her chair, her dark eyes snapping. "You will leave my house now." She swept across the room and threw open the double doors. "Good day and good riddance!"

"Well and good, Mistress Sutherland. Do convey my greetings to your lover and my brother when he returns." Jamming his hat upon his head, he secretly counted himself fortunate to escape without bodily injury--all too soon. She delivered a well-placed kick to his shin as he stalked past her.

Swearing, he bent over to rub the throbbing limb: too late, he heard her ominous little snicker behind him. The drawing room doors were slammed directly into his buttocks, then bolted from the inside as he pitched to the floor.

* * *

"Good afternoon, M'lord." Gilbert held the door open as Thorne tossed the rain out of his tricorne into the hedges, then took the hat and laid the water-beaded cloak precisely over one arm while Thorne extracted a posted letter from its pocket.

The sender, he'd already noted with curiosity, was Doctor John Hodges.

"Mistress will be with you presently in the drawing room, M'lord. Do make yourself at home."

"Thank you, Gilbert." Thorne broke the letter's seal on his way up the wide staircase and disappeared into the drawing room.

"Was that the door, Marsh?" Caroline asked, poking her perfectly coifed head into the hallway.

"Aye, ma'am." She nodded toward the upper gallery. "His lordship awaits."

"Excellent! Order up a brandy for us, and tell him I'll be with him presently."

With another "aye, ma'am," Marsh trudged off to the kitchen.

When the brandies were delivered, Thorne was sitting in a chair and holding a sheet of parchment, his face like chiseled stone as he stared blindly into the crackling fire, all but oblivious to the maid's presence. The sound of the closing door brought him to awareness again. Willing his hands to loosen their death grip on the paper, he perused its seemingly innocuous and well-intentioned missive for the second time.

Dear Lord Neville, it began,

> *I have refrained from writing until now, as I feared you would not have the heart to read it. In truth, I scarce had the heart to write it.*
>
> *It has been two months now, time enough for me to collect my thoughts, hence I make no more excuses. If this proves painful for you to read, I apologize with all my heart, but it must be said.*
>
> *I am heartily sorry for your tragic loss, as much as for the world's loss of such an innocent, endearing and admirable lady. She surely was the light of your life, and a blessing to you and your household. I pray that someday I shall find someone, if not as sweet and*

good as Lady Neville, then at least with many of her fine qualities.

Now to that portion of my message over which I truly labored, not being a very superstitious man.

It is widely known that your wife was found at the base of the tower. You might recall your conversation with me on the day of your wedding, when you took me to task for minding a patient's account of some malicious force atop Wycliffe Hall's tower. Please do not lose patience with me now, but what I have to say is in some measure relative to that subject.

It is my sincere belief that Lady Neville did not take her own life, for by that time she was guardian for a life far newer and more vulnerable than her own. Though according to her maid she had not found a suitable occasion to tell you of it, Lady Neville would soon have given you the news that she was approximately eight to ten weeks with child. I tell you of this only after considerable deliberation, the crux of which was my determination that were I in your place, I should indeed want to know of it.

There was more, but Thorne had no use for Hodges' posthumous thesis on why Gwynneth would never have considered leaping from the tower. In fact, for the first time, he began to see just why she had.

* * *

"Well!" Caroline exclaimed aloud, to no one but herself. She'd entered the drawing room only to find two poured glasses on a serving tray. Neither had been touched.

"Thorne?" Her frown evolved into a quirky smile; at times the man could be quite playful. Then she noticed the folded sheets of parchment, lying on a fireside table as if carelessly tossed aside. Swooping down on them like a hawk in a swirl of cinnamon-colored silk, she snatched them up and quickly scanned their fastidious script; with each paragraph, her jaw dropped a little more.

"God's blood and bones, he's taken to horse, if I know him at all! Oh, Toby, I pray you're riding hard...oh, God help me!" She whirled in place, tears rising; she blinked them back with instinctive discipline. "Think. You must *think!*" With trembling fingers she folded the letter and shoved it inside her bodice.

Toby had at least a two-hour start on Thorne; but what if he'd stopped in some tavern, dallied with some maid or other, before setting out for Wycliffe Hall?

And what if he hadn't? One way or another Thorne would eventually overtake him--what then?

He will kill him, is what. Kill him without a second thought.

Caroline strode onto the gallery, heels pounding the floor. "Marsh!" she bellowed, and when at last the old servant showed her ruffled white cap below, ordered, "Send to the livery for my roan hunter, and hurry! Tell them I want a man's saddle." With that she flew up the stairs, calling for Ashby to assist, and was soon outfitted for riding. As she drew on leather gloves, Ashby pulled the hood of her red-wool cardinal over her firmly pinned tresses for her.

"If Mister Sutherland could see you, he'd turn in his grave," she fretted.

"Hush," Caroline said grimly. "Even he couldn't stop me. This is a matter of life and death."

"Then take the livery boy with you, there might be highwaymen lying in wait 'twixt hither and yon!"

"Not before dark. And if there are, I'll trample them."

"Not if they shoot you first...or shoot the horse and ravish you and steal your jewels and leave you for dead!"

"You know very well I'm not wearing jewels." Caroline bustled through the foyer and out the front door to where the livery groom awaited.

"Aye, but *they* don't know it!" Ashby had trailed her as far as the threshold, and watched from the doorway, arms akimbo. "Besides, they'll be happy enough with your money--I know you've some hid on you--and they'll leave you just as dead!"

"Hand me up, boy," Caroline urged, hiking her skirts up well above her booted ankles. As he obliged, she grasped the pommel and threw her right leg over the saddle. Settling into it easily, she wondered why women hadn't the sense to ride astride as a rule.

* * *

The sun was setting when Nate looked up to see a horse and rider approaching on the Northampton road at full gallop. At first he assumed it was Hobbs, but as they drew closer, silhouetted by the western sky, he noted the horseman's long black cloak, and the tricorne from which streamed a long tail of dark hair.

His heart beat faster. Wycliffe Hall's master hadn't come home since the mistress leapt--since nigh on two months, he amended the thought uneasily, and watched, openmouthed, as horse and rider cantered through the open gate into the stable yard, the former coming to a frothing halt just outside the doorway.

"Rub him down," he was ordered without so much as a nod of greeting. "My horse is at Wolverton, I've borrowed this one. Mind his left foreleg, 'tis strained and will need binding." Thorne jumped down. "Where is your master?"

"He's to London, M'lord. He'll be back soon."

Already striding to the stables, Thorne turned sharply about. "Tend the horse quickly then, and lead him 'round to the front of the house. Tether him there. I don't want him within sight of the Northampton road. Then be off, it's time you were home." He gave Nate a look that brooked no nonsense just before ducking through the stable doorway.

A few minutes later as Nate led the beast up the lane, he pondered what solitary business the baron might have in the stables. Reaching no conclusion, he shrugged his shoulders and began whistling a tune, tugging a little harder on the tired horse's halter. The sooner he tied it up, the sooner he'd be off to enjoy an unexpected evening of leisure, knowing Master Hobbs couldn't be cross with him for abandoning his duties by order of Lord Neville himself.

* * *

At the center of the tack room, Thorne stood looking about with a mixture of grim purpose and deliberate detachment, then shed his cloak and began a methodical search of every nook and cranny, shelf and cubbyhole. As gut wrenching as it might prove, he hoped to find some evidence that might associate his late wife with the stable master.

On the highest shelf on an interior wall, his long reach netted a small box that had the look of a spice container, and was in fact labeled "cayenne." He frowned slightly, wondering to what possible use it was being put in the stables, and slipped it impatiently into a pocket.

Finding nothing else of any consequence, he seized a lantern from its hook and hastened down the narrow passageway at the rear. The door to Hobbs' quarters opened with a grating whine.

Thorne observed his sparse surroundings. There seemed little to search until he used the toe of his boot to flip an edge of a worn rug. Stooping for a closer look, he noticed a misaligned seam in the floor, and a loose board, which he carefully pried up and laid aside.

Within the exposed cavity lay a worn leather pouch, containing money and some promissory notes signed by individuals unknown to Thorne. Apparently Hobbs was a small-scale moneylender. Thorne tossed the pouch aside, then realized he'd uncovered something else; he pulled out a small apothecary jar.

He pulled the stopper out, and for a long moment only stared at the yellowish-black crystalline powder inside, his eyes narrowing. He poured a few grains into his hand, wet a fingertip and placed it in the powder, then brought it to his tongue.

Grunting at the bitter metallic taste of the substance, he gathered a mouthful of saliva and spat. Twice more he purged thus, then firmly plugged the bottle.

He needed no chemist's analysis to know that it contained pure arsenic.

* * *

Darkness closed in rapidly on the forest and the rolling hills, mists forming in the dales. Behind Wycliffe Hall, the sprawling stone stables with their thick blanket of thatch stood as they did every evening, their dimly lit interior giving an impression both prohibitive and inviting.

Tobias Hobbs rounded the curve of the Northampton road and veered his mount into the rear lane, unaware that on this particular evening his humble abode harbored a creature far more malignant than those of the four-legged variety...one whose heart thudded with cold fury as it lay in wait for its quarry.

* * *

"'Tis a shame," Bridey mumbled, shaking her frizzled gray head. "He might just as well be back at university for all the life in this old Hall. Day in, day out, we all keep the place going--and for what, I ask ye?"

Arthur, eating a bowl of stewed beef and potatoes at the worktable, soaked up the broth with a hunk of day-old bread.

"Ye could have stopped him, if ye'd wanted," she grumbled. "Ye need only tell him the place is too much for a man of your years, and he'd high-tail it here directly, I vow."

The steward laid down his spoon with a sigh. "I'll not lie to him, Bridey. In your mind I might have one foot in the grave, but I can still manage this estate in the dead of winter. When lambing season is on us I'll ask him to come home."

"And worst of all," she lamented, as if he hadn't spoken, "he's to London where that black-eyed wench can get her hooks in him. Oh, don't look at me so, ye know full well I speak truth! She's had her eye on him since she first set foot in the Hall, even whilst he was betrothed to the mistress."

"Could be. But he's unattached now, and so's she. And she's damned fetching."

Bridey threw up her hands. "Men! Och, he'll tire of her though, they always do of women like that one--but will it be soon enough, I wonder."

Arthur slid off the stool, mouth twitching. "I'm off to the stables for a bit, then I'll be on my way home."

"Laugh if ye will," Bridey said grimly, "but ye'd best hope he don't make her the new baroness in a fit of fancy."

* * *

Having entered his quarters only to find his crude little hiding place gaping at him like an empty eye socket, Hobbs was momentarily immobilized; then, glancing quickly about, he knelt down, only to discover the pouch and its contents intact. He'd obviously surprised an intruder. But where was Nate?

He sucked in a breath as he noticed the vacant space beneath the pouch, and stared at it blankly.

"Something missing?"

The voice, directly behind him, chilled his blood. Instinctively he started to turn, but was immediately checked by the feel of cold hard steel just below his ear.

"Get up," came the deadly bidding. "Slowly, or I'll blow your buggering head off."

With the sinewy grace of a lion, Hobbs rose, muscles tensed and ready to spring as he prepared to undercut the outstretched arm behind him and knock the weapon away--until he heard the hammer cock, and recognized the sound of his own pistol.

"Don't!" he implored. "I'll not resist, but let me turn and see you."

He sensed his captor stepping slightly away; the icy metal was removed from his neck. "Now," he cautioned, "I'll come 'round, my hands up. I'm unarmed, by the by."

As there was no objection, he slowly turned...and looked into the face of hell.

"Were you on the battlements with her?" The voice trembled with pent-up fury. *"Did you push her over?"*

Horror replaced fear, and Hobbs felt the blood drain from his face. "Never," he rasped, when he finally managed a sound. "No...God, how could you even think...I would never-"

"*Sit.*" Thorne indicated the cot with a jerk of his head.

He did so, the old resentment bringing the blood rushing back into his cheeks, while the pistol followed his movements, maintaining its deadly line of trajectory.

"Make yourself comfortable," he was ordered in a tone now as stony as it had been savage a moment ago. "You've a fair bit of explaining to do in front of this one-man firing squad, and you'd best do it fully...aye, 'tis loaded," Thorne added grimly, seeing his wary glance at the weapon. "And I've no qualms about *un*loading it--right into your heart. But not before you've told me just how my wife happened to be carrying a child when she died."

"So, you've forgotten your biology after all."

A slight shudder betrayed Thorne's tremendous effort to control his temper. "Insolence is not your friend at the moment, Hobbs, mark me. Now, spare us both the time and trouble of defending yourself, for the child wasn't mine by any stretch of the imagination, and you're the only other man with whom my wife spent time. What I *will* have from you are the circumstances...apparently the sword stayed in the scabbard this time."

Hobbs looked hard at the pistol, then at its wielder. "Let's just say your wife needed a man. A real man."

"You? A man who refused to claim the *last* child he'd sired?"

"A man who loved her."

"*And* her station in life. Had it not been for that, you'd have abandoned her just as you did the Combs woman. So much for your brand of love."

"'Twas a bloody sight better than that she got from you," Hobbs said with a sneer, all but certain by now that Thorne hadn't the nerve to pull the trigger. "I've noticed, too, that the Combs woman is never far from your thoughts...was it she who warmed your bed at night? Did it so well, in fact, that you kept her on in spite of her swelling belly, and hence found your wife's bed quite unnecessary? Aye," he said cunningly, noting the sudden the flare of Thorne's nostrils and the set of his jaw, "an eager little piece, Combs. I should know. 'Tis not often a woman begs to be broken."

* * *

Thorne's finger twitched on the trigger as he fought a desperate impulse to rend Hobbs from limb to limb and pound his head to a pulp on the hard oak floorboards. It was only the thought of Caroline and her grudging familial fondness that kept him from acting on primal instinct--that, and the fact that such a quick end would be too merciful. He wanted Hobbs to suffer. But first he must have the whole gut-wrenching story. He raised the pistol just a hair, a gentle reminder of its potential. "My wife didn't beg to be broken," he said tightly, "for she'd no more have tolerated your lovemaking than mine or anyone else's."

His prisoner looked down, and at that instant the bloodlust nearly overcame Thorne as he realized he'd surmised correctly: Gwynneth had not willingly surrendered her virginity. Her consequent shame, the quickening of her womb, and the magnitude of her terrible secret were undoubtedly enough to send her pell-mell over the battlements. At least now, after two long months of soul-searching, he could begin to understand what propelled her downward through the fog-thickened darkness in the wee hours of that Christmas morn. He could even begin to see, knowing Gwynneth's obsession for the saints, how she might have viewed her desperate act as martyrdom, a noble sacrifice to her God.

But he could not--*would not*--comprehend how this cur of a stableman, for even a fraction of a second, could have thought himself worthy to possess his master's wife.

Eyes narrowing, Thorne lowered the gun and fired.

THIRTY-FOUR

The howl that came from Tobias Hobbs--one to put the hounds to shame--was quickly overlaid with Thorne's dry, guttural chuckle. He had deliberately sent the bullet whistling past the stable master's left ear. The newly chipped surface of the stone wall gleamed white in the light of the tallow.

"Now, you *God-damned cuckolder*. Tell me why you *ravished my wife*."

Hobbs had blanched. "She knew I loved her," he croaked, "yet she'd the gall to taunt me. Raked me over the bloody coals for bedding Caroline's...the Sutherland widow's maid, and threatened to have me sacked. She even bit me, and drew blood. But when she called me flea-infested vermin, and a liar, and said that I should never touch her again" --he shook his head-- "I couldn't abide that. Not after she had already let me embrace her, kiss her-"

"*Enough.*" Longing to give Hobbs the unforgettable experience of choking on his own teeth, Thorne instead drew a deep breath and, with a keen eye on his hostage, began reloading the pistol. "So, we've established that you're capable of loving. Tell me, did you feel any of that noble sentiment for Henry Pitts?"

Hobbs averted his eyes. "Aye...he was like a son."

Thorne nodded, then with utter nonchalance took the box of cayenne pepper from a pocket in the lining of his waistcoat, and turned it over in his hands as if to study the stenciled name of the East India Spice Company. "To think," he murmured, "that the dried, crushed seeds and pods of the *Capsicum annum longum*...perfectly edible, albeit rather spicy...could serve" --he lifted brooding eyes to meet those of the stable master-- "as an instrument of death."

Hobbs sprang from his cot. "'Horseshite!" he cried. "What possible-"

"*Sit down*," came the laconic order once again.

Hobbs obeyed, mouth snapping shut as he glanced uneasily at the pistol.

"You're well aware that Kendall found naught wrong with the stallion that night," Thorne said. "Not so much as a pebble in his hoof or a bur in his tail, let alone anything that might cause him to trample a boy to death." He pulled the lone chair away from its little table, flipped his waistcoat hem and took a seat, the pistol casually but nonetheless directly pointed at his captive. "But, you see, by the time the good veterinarian arrived, the heat of the capsicum in Raven's mouth and throat had run its course--helped along, no doubt, by a draught of cool water from his keeper."

The amber eyes were suddenly hooded. "Why the devil would anyone put pepper in a horse's mouth?"

"*To...drive...him...mad,*" Thorne said, each word lashing the air. "Mad as a March hare'--those were Pennington's very words. Mad enough to rear at the first person who dared confront him, namely poor Henry. And where were you at the time, Hobbs? Not in London, I'll wager my life! 'Tis my guess you'd left the stall gate conveniently unlatched, and were but a few yards away...so how did it feel to watch while a mere boy perished at your hands? A boy you'd rescued from the gutter and taken in as if he were your own...what kind of guardian from hell does that make you, Hobbs? By God, you shed tears enough at his burial to convince even *me* of your innocence, you bloody whoreson-"

He broke off, lunging so swiftly that the stable master hadn't a moment to react before he was yanked to his feet by the fist-twisted front of his shirt. Nose to nose, the two men panted like wolves, the one with seething, savage anger, the other with primordial fear.

* * *

I have seen murder in his eyes...as will you.

No longer was Hobbs skeptical of Gwynneth's prediction--there *was* murder in the molten blue orbs, and the fact that the barrel of his own pistol was pressed hard against his left temple only underscored the folly of any such doubt.

"You killed an innocent boy," Thorne snarled, hammering his shirt-clutching fist against Hobbs' sternum for emphasis. "Cut him down in cold blood...and why? Merely because he'd overheard a quarrel between you and your sister, the one and only Caroline Sutherland! Aye, and what of it? For her secret and your greed you deemed *murder* necessary?" The twisted knot of homespun shirt was jerked upward once more; as the stable master emitted a gag, he was given a vigorous shake. "The boy worshipped you, Hobbs! He'd have kept your counsel at all costs, had you but asked. So that won't do, you buggering cur...I'll need a better reason!"

With that, Hobbs was let go with a shove that sent him sprawling into the stone wall and rebounding flat out on the cot. For dizzying seconds he lay still but for his heaving diaphragm, his ragged breathing merging with Thorne's and creating a strange, harsh synchronization that struck him as ironically appropriate in light of their secret fraternal bond. He opened hot, dry eyes to find his world was no longer spinning...and that the pistol hanging loosely at Thorne's side seemed to have been forgotten.

"'Twas not the whole of it," he muttered. 'Twas not *all* the boy overheard."

"I'll wager it wasn't. 'Twas not all he saw, either!"

Hobbs cautiously levered himself upright on the cot. Disappointed to see Thorne's hand tighten on the pistol, he said sullenly, "He didn't see anything."

"He saw this."

The apothecary jar was tossed into the air; by reflex Hobbs caught it. He stared at the familiar glass vessel, his heart rising in his gullet. He'd nearly forgotten it was missing.

Oddly, Thorne was smiling. On second thought, it was more a grimace--the kind of look many a dead man must have seen just before the trigger was pulled. Hobbs tensed, ready to dive for the floor--or the door.

"Don't try telling me 'twas for rats. The mousers in these stables are just a meal or two away from starving."

Hobbs held his tongue.

"Henry discovered your little cache, did he not?"

Hobbs glanced at the cavity in the floor. "He'd seen me uncover it, and though I warned him, he couldn't resist a look. I caught him."

"Looking, not stealing."

"Aye."

"But, as his was a rather gregarious nature, you feared he might not keep the contents confidential."

"He was inclined to blab to Carmody's boy."

Thorne smiled grimly. "Yes, I've had the pleasure of talking with the lad myself." Once more the hammer was cocked, and any trace of a smile was gone. "You killed an innocent boy as if he were naught more than a rodent that had gotten into the feed...but a rodent would have died much more humanely." He narrowed his eyes. "So help me God, Hobbs, if I could force you under my horse's hooves, I'd do it...and I'd *revel* in watching the black blood spurt from your nose and mouth, just the way it did from poor Henry's."

"Stop it!" For a moment Hobbs feared he'd be sick, but decided he'd choke on his own vomit before giving Thorne the satisfaction. "You don't understand. I'd a true affection for the boy, but he'd heard things...things that compromised my situation, my very life, as it could be...things," he added, glowering at Thorne, "that I dared not allow beyond these walls."

He saw by the look on Thorne's face that it made no difference what the boy had overheard: he, Hobbs, was a condemned man. Hands in the air, he shifted toward the cot's edge and stood slowly and carefully on his wobbling legs, determined that if his life was to end here and now, he would at least be on his feet when that end came.

"*Nothing,*" Thorne said in a voice as deadly as his gaze, "that either you or she might have said could possibly justify that boy's *cold-blooded murder.*"

Hobbs swayed on his feet. He squeezed his eyes shut the instant he saw the flash.

The lead ball whizzed horribly close to his cheek and struck the wall behind him again, its ricochet blessedly missing him as well. His breath exploded from his lungs in a fearful moan as he struggled to control his bladder.

"There's but one grievance remaining to be settled," Thorne said coldly, already reloading with frightening efficiency. "I *will* have your reasons for poisoning my livestock, before I fire this weapon the third time--by the by, you'll not be spared *that* shot, though I might only maim you. Painfully," he added with obvious relish. "And although instinct bids me hie your black heart to hell, reason says I should see you hanged in public for your crimes against me and mine." His teeth gleamed in a malevolent grin. "The magistrate in Northampton is known to have a strange predilection for the rope. Speak, Hobbs." The grin disappeared. "I'm your lone tribunal, and you'll answer to me or suffer all the more. Tell me whence, how, and especially *why* you procured this arsenic. Don't trouble yourself to invent, for I'll know it as surely as I know you...and I'm in no mood for fantasy." As if to prove it, the hammer was cocked yet again.

"I got it from Horace Sutherland," Hobbs grumbled. "I chanced to see him entering an opium den in Whitechapel with some of Whittingham's bloody henchmen, and he was quick to pay me however I liked for my silence. He wanted to protect Caroline from scandal, and to preserve her respect for him. You see, he loved *her*, not only her sexual favors, as *some* men are wont to do."

"Don't preach to me," Thorne warned. "My dealings with your sister have naught to do with you. And you're a good one to talk about a man taking advantage of a woman. To the subject at hand, then. You're not one to do his own dirty work, so tell me who it was you bullied or bribed to skulk about my pastures in the dead of night."

Hobbs licked his lips nervously as Thorne tightened his grip on the haft of the pistol.

"Give it up, Hobbs, 'tis not worth a hole in your head."

Mumbling, the stable master averted his eyes.

"Louder."

"I said, 'Barker'. Tom Barker."

A weighty silence ensued; then Thorne said softly, "And old Tom is no longer among the living."

There was no reply.

"If the dead could only speak."

Hobbs pursed his lips.

"God knows Tom spoke often and loudly enough in *this* world," Thorne mused. "I imagine he and little Henry had some commiserating to do when they met in the next. Likely they'll have some business with you, Hobbs...before you're consigned to warmer regions."

Still Hobbs kept mute. As he saw it, he'd said more than enough.

"Very well, then, keep your counsel on that score. But you'd best loosen your tongue on the next, for it concerns me directly. Why did you poison those poor dumb animals, and why just as I was due home? What the devil was your quarrel with me?"

There was a faint swishing sound from the shadowy passageway. Thorne merely cocked an ear, but Hobbs whipped his head about to stare.

"Tell him, Toby." Breathless, disheveled, and ruddy-cheeked from the cold, Caroline stepped into the room behind Thorne. "If you don't, *I bloody well will.*"

* * *

"Stay where you are, Caroline," Thorne said without turning around, "or your brother's gray matter will be splattered over us and the four walls. You've no business here. Just how the devil are you so close upon my heels tonight, have you wings?" When there was no sound, he had second thoughts. "Move over here where I can see you, damn it."

Hastily Caroline took up a stance between the two men.

"Stand aside," Thorne said sharply. "He doesn't need your protection."

"Apparently he does," she countered, nevertheless following orders. "You, sir," she said as she passed him, her brow delicately arched, "are brandishing a pistol. *He* has no weapon."

Thorne spared her a mocking glance. "Aye. If he had, I'd be lying dead at your feet." He nodded toward Hobbs. "Your brother is not nearly as self-controlled as I. My late wife could have attested to that."

Caroline inclined her head. "Yes, he told me just today. I am mortified for him and heartily sorry for you. You are indeed benevolent, I venture some men would have drawn and quartered him by now. But Thorne, there is a tale yet untold, and before you decide Toby's fate, you must hear it. For me," she pleaded, as he dragged his eyes off Hobbs and looked reluctantly at her. "For me, and for what there is between us."

"Don't beg, Caroline!" Hobbs' lip curled. "And for God's sake, don't bargain your favors, not with him. He only amuses himself with you. Saves him the pocket change he'd be obliged to spend on his whore."

"Hush!" Caroline hissed, turning on him. "Do you not realize, Tobias Hobbs, how very close you are to the grave at this moment? For once in your ill-spent life, *keep your bloody mouth shut!*" She turned back to Thorne, her expression softening. "Please. For me. Listen to him, if only for a few minutes...for the tale concerns you as well, Thorne." She started toward him, her hand out in supplication, but he warned her off with a mere look.

"I'll listen," he said curtly, "for as long as it amuses me. But the instant your tale ceases to hold my interest, Hobbs, I'll pierce your sorry hide with lead. Sit down, Caroline."

This time she obeyed without comment, placing the lone chair into the small space between the washstand and doorjamb, and settling into it with a nearly imperceptible nod of encouragement at her brother.

With obvious reluctance and resentment, the narrative was begun, and presently an unnatural stillness seemed to settle in the low-lit room. Late evening merged unnoticed into the pre-dawn hours of a new day, as the voice of Wycliffe Hall's stable master droned on, occasionally faltering but never quite overcome by long-contained emotions.

For more than a quarter of an hour, that voice was the only sound in Thorne's world, and it was allowed to play out uninterrupted.

* * *

Questions were inevitable. Thorne demanded names, dates, places and circumstances, then demanded them again. To his credit, or perhaps his occasional good sense, Hobbs stayed calm, responding with compelling sincerity. Caroline refrained from speaking unless directly addressed, and for long periods of time her presence was all but forgotten.

Then came the more amorphous questions: why hadn't Hobbs presented his case when first informed? Had he made no inquiries on his own behalf?

"Inquiries of whom?" he scoffed. "Who the devil would know?"

"I would, lad." The hoarse declaration elicited at least two gasps, and three heads turned simultaneously toward the doorway.

There, face drawn and thin frame slightly bent, stood Arthur Pennington.

* * *

Arthur bowed--a dizzying gesture, what with his light head and racing heart. "Good evening, M'lord. Good to have you home again." Extending a hand, he politely but firmly gave his master an order for the first time in their long acquaintance. "If you would, please, M'lord...pass the pistol to me."

As Thorne looked first at his outstretched hand, then into his eyes, Arthur saw what pain Hobbs' revelation had wrought. "Please, M'lord," he appealed, and said a silent prayer of thanks as the gun was wordlessly put into his hand. He glanced at Hobbs, whose attention to him had not wavered since he'd made his stunning declaration in the doorway. "I trust you'll stay put, Toby. I've been known to use a pistol when the need arose. Mistress Sutherland," he said in acknowledgement, and bowed. She nodded.

"*What is it you know*, Pennington?" Hobbs demanded.

Arthur was dismayed to feel the sting of tears.

Caroline rose abruptly from her seat. "Please, Mister Pennington, sit down and be comfortable. You must excuse my brother's eagerness, 'tis just that this has been on his mind for some time."

Arthur settled himself into the chair, Caroline standing by solicitously.

"Now, Toby," Arthur began, giving his eyes a furtive wipe with a rolled sleeve. "You might well hate me when you hear what I have to say, but 'tis a risk I take gladly, nonetheless." He looked somberly at Thorne. "I've oft wished I could break my silence over the years."

Thorne regarded him without a word. Arthur turned again to Hobbs.

"Your mother, God rest her gentle soul, took only one person into her confidence after she found herself with child. I was that person."

At a glance he saw Thorne's eyes close, as if the words had pained him beyond bearing, but knew he must go on. What had been spared the father was now necessarily inflicted on the son.

Both sons.

"She was utterly insistent," he said with a tremulous sigh, "that *no one*--not even her sister in Kettering, whom I knew well--should know her reason for leaving the manor. She only told me because she knew I was in Robert Neville's confidence. Her instincts were right, I was indeed aware of the liaison between her and his lordship." He paused, sensing he now had Thorne's full, if grudging, attention.

"I realized Cornelia was more distraught over the upset her leaving might cause his lordship than for her own difficult circumstances, as he'd already suffered such a blow at Lady Neville's passing. 'Twas then that I knew what the master saw in her, aside from her physical appearance." Arthur glanced at Caroline. "Your beauty was no accident, ma'am.

"Cornelia hoped I would somehow be able to soften the blow of her departure. I understood her dilemma, she was in no position to marry Lord Neville, and her condition would not be long in manifesting itself, naturally causing speculation and perhaps scandal for the family. Time was of the essence, and she'd her young daughter to consider."

His eyes misted as he regarded Caroline. "You were a fetching lass, with your dark curls and your dancing black eyes, laughing and teasing and causing general mischief all about you. Your aunt was quite fond of you."

"Aye," Caroline whispered. "I remember you now. You brought your wife to visit sometimes."

Arthur nodded. "Anna. Aye, she and your Aunt Clarissa were of an age, and generally of the same mind. Their families had known one another for years." He touched a sleeve to his face again, and allowed himself a little smile. "You see, even after so many years, a man still grieves the loss of his wife."

"Some men," Hobbs retorted, looking at Thorne.

"That's enough, Toby." Caroline glared at him. "I believe I made things quite clear on that point just yesterday."

Arthur softly cleared his throat. "Cornelia left on a chilly gray morning before sunup," he went on. "I myself spirited her away to Kettering, and there hired an old friend of the family to convey her in his rattletrap cart...and you," he said with a nod at Caroline, "to Birmingham."

Caroline nodded. "I remember."

"And there, I believe, is where Toby's story took up a while ago," Arthur said, sighing deeply as he felt the weight of years being lifted from his bent shoulders. "I overheard most of it in the passageway. She was a wise and admirable woman, was Cornelia Hobbs. And when she turned up some eight or nine years later at my home, asking for some occupation for her bold bright boy, well...I was right quick to find a need for him in the stables."

He turned to Thorne, who stood staring at him dully. "Your father never knew, M'lord...and why should he have? I allowed myself a bit of deceit and told him that the boy had been orphaned in my village, that his name was mere coincidence. Lied a bit about his age, too...aye, Toby, he asked, did Robert Neville. Your father asked. And 'twas a hard thing I did looking into those eyes, as honest as they were blue, and telling that lie. But aside from that, Toby, I watched out for you more than you'll ever know. And many was the time," he confessed, his throat tightening on unshed tears, "that I bit down hard upon my tongue to keep from telling you that Master Thorne was your brother...but I'd made a solemn promise, lad. Your mother made me swear to keep her secret to my dying day. And now I've failed her. But God help me," he said, the tears rolling at last down his leathery cheeks, "it has been the hardest thing I was ever called upon to do in all my born days."

Caroline was first to move; she bent over Arthur, placing a gentle hand on his shoulder. "Come, Mister Pennington, you should be off now, and abed. 'Tis late, and grown colder by the hour." She shivered as if to make her point, and looked at Thorne. "Perhaps you should ride home with him."

Thorne suddenly seemed to awaken from his daze. "You've known this all along."

Caroline sighed. "I was at my mother's bedside when she told Toby. But it was not my place to tell you, anymore than 'twas Arthur's place. Toby alone reserved that right, and I respected it."

Thorne appeared to mull that over, then said to Hobbs, "So you've known of our kinship for some two years. All the more reason for me to ask why you would attempt to sabotage my herds, my finances, and my family's security."

Resentment shone from Hobbs' eyes. "There you have it, *my lord...your* herds, *your* finances, *your* family's security! It all bloody sickens me!"

"Hush, Toby, 'tis not Thorne's fault!" Caroline cried.

But Hobbs ignored her; in his eyes, there was no one in the room but Thorne. "Can't you see, I did it because you'd been given *everything*...whilst I could claim *naught* as mine," he ground through his teeth. "*Not even the father who sired me.*"

* * *

The two men stared at one another, hot hatred versus cold anger, until a quiet moan broke the unnatural stillness. Thorne moved to Arthur's side and helped him up from the chair, at which point the old brown eyes searched his.

"I can understand how you might find reason to hate *me*," Arthur told him sorrowfully, "but the fact remains that Toby is your blood brother by half, and I love the both of you as if you were my own sons. You're as fair-minded as your father was, M'lord...can you not find it in your heart to accept Toby as part of the family, and mend the rifts between you? You were friends at one time, in your youth...surely you recall?"

Thorne met that entreating gaze in silence, thinking things that couldn't easily be spoken, such as how he loved Arthur and considered him his dearest friend and ally, indeed more of a father than his own had ever been; and how he would do anything and everything within his power to please the faithful old steward, if only to make his remaining days on this earth all the easier.

But some things were simply not within his power.

"Fetch Dobson and his men to stand watch 'til morn," he ordered Arthur. "If Hobbs should attempt to run for it, they're to bind him."

He ignored Caroline's horrified gasp and Arthur's sudden pallor, turning instead to Hobbs, whose expression had gone from surprise to the wariness of a hunter's prey.

"Sleep if you can, Hobbs," he said coldly. "Early tomorrow you will be brought before the magistrate in Northampton as an accused felon, where you will be thrice charged...for the rape of my late wife, and for the cold-blooded murders of Henry Pitts and Tom Barker."

* * *

The old cook dabbed repeatedly at her eyes with a corner of her apron, but still the tears snuck into the creases of her chubby face. Lifting the copper kettle from the fire, she glanced furtively toward the table where Arthur sat with his hands curled around an empty cup, and exclaimed under her breath, "Saints preserve us!"--for it looked as if even *he* was weeping.

She sniffed, then tried to speak in a normal voice. "Tea'll be right up."

"Fog's bad this morn," Arthur remarked as if to himself, then said thickly, "The master'll not be able to take him straightaway."

Bridey stared sorrowfully out the small widow. "Aye, 'tis heavy all right, but 'tis early yet." She shook her head. "Seems fitting for such a day." A sob escaped her. "Dear heaven, I still cannot believe he did such a deed--our Toby, *killing* our little Henry! Tom now, he mighta been killed no matter, he riled so many folk. But Henry...oh, his was a dear, sweet soul." She ended on a long, sniveling sob as she crossed the room to fill Arthur's cup. Noting a sudden wariness on his face, she turned to see Lord Neville entering from the great hall.

No hearty "good morning" fell from his lips this dawn, no teasing words to make Bridey laugh or blush. His cheeks were pallid, his face drawn, his eyes hollow and bloodshot. When he sat down to pull on his boots, she set a cup of her strong-brewed orange pekoe in front of him. "Here, M'lord. 'Twon't hurt, and it might help."

"Thank you." He latched onto the handle of the cup as if grateful for something to hold. "We'll not be away as early as I'd hoped," he said tonelessly. "Nor am I certain the sun will burn this one off, 'tis heavier than most."

Arthur nodded. "No matter, Dobson's men will stay at their posts."

"Aye, but awake or asleep?" Thorne downed his tea, oblivious to its heat, and poured another cup, filling Arthur's as well. "You've given some thought to advancing Nate, I imagine."

"He's a bit young, rather clumsy at times." He regarded Thorne soberly. "Do you also imagine your brother has even the slightest chance of returning home, once gone before the magistrate?"

He winced as Thorne banged his cup down on the saucer, splattering tea. "I venture to say," was the latter's harsh reply, "that Hobbs will have his neck in a noose for all to see in the public square before the next month is out. Betwixt now and then, his home is more likely to be the gaol than the stables." Thorne threaded a hand through his disheveled hair, then struck the table with a fist; spoons and china clattered. "Damn it, Arthur, I understand your affection for the *man*, but not for the buggering *murderer*! Where in hell else *should* he be?"

Arthur nodded, somewhat chastened. "Aye, M'lord. Gaol is meet punishment for such deeds as he has done. But the noose?"

"*Two* pre-meditated murders, Arthur--one of them a child--and the rape of a married virgin," Thorne reminded him sharply. "The latter having very probably been the cause of her suicide."

"Search your soul, M'lord," Arthur said quietly. "Would you feel nearly so vengeful had she been broken by you?"

A dark flush obliterated Thorne's unhealthy pallor; in one fluid motion, he sprang from his seat and swept the teacups and saucers from the table with his open hand. Arthur flinched, then froze as the delicate china smashed into a hundred pieces on the flagstone floor.

From the larder came a muffled cry. "Oh, M'lord!" Bridey wailed, hurrying toward the mess in her most expeditious shuffle. "Your dear mother's-" Glimpsing her master's face, she broke off, pressing a finger tightly to her lips, and hastily withdrew to a safer proximity.

"I'm well aware you never approved of my choice of a wife," Thorne said, leaning on white-knuckled fists over the table in front of Arthur. "But by God, that does *not* give you the right to belittle my differences with her, or to speak lightly of what she suffered at the hands of my stable master--my *brother,* as *you* would have it--may God rot his soul in hell!"

Another startled cry sounded from the larder. Thorne stormed out of the kitchen, the door to the south gardens announcing his exit with a thundering slam. Bits of herbs and flowers drifted down from the rafters where William had hung them in bundles to dry.

"Jesu Christi," Arthur murmured with a despairing look at the wild-eyed cook, and put his head in his hands. "What have I done? What possessed me to speak so?"

Bridey's only reply was a keening moan as she sank into a chair and covered her face with her apron.

* * *

Thorne slowed his pace considerably when confronted by the blinding fog. Making his way down the sloping gardens, he used the vague silhouettes of the outbuildings as guides, but upon reaching the gate, it was as if the earth dropped off into a cloud.

"One of you men, bring a light!" he shouted in the direction of the stables. His voice sounded strangely muffled to his own ears in the soupy mist, but he was quickly hailed in reply. It seemed an eternity before one of Dobson's men approached, his lantern the first thing to bob within Thorne's vision.

The two men carefully crossed the lane and entered the stable yard. Finding the door, Thorne held a hand up to his escort. "I've business with Hobbs. If I need assistance I'll call for it."

He closed the door quickly behind him as he entered. The fog had slipped its tendrils past the shuttered windows; some heat was needed to burn it off. The brazier was cool to his touch.

"Hobbs?" He lifted a lantern from its hook, frowning to see it nearly burnt dry. He made his way cautiously toward the rear passageway. Several of the horses nickered softly in greeting, but he paid no heed, wondering if perhaps Hobbs had taken a foolish notion to ambush him.

He reached the closed door of the stable master's quarters, tasting gall to think that the man might actually be sleeping. *No conscience, no fear.* Rage, so recent and simmering near the surface, threatened to boil over, making his voice harsher than he had intended.

"Hobbs! Open up!"

When there was no answer, he hung the lantern up and proceeded to pound his fists a half-dozen times on the solid oak portal. "Open up at once, Hobbs!"

There was no reply. Pent-up fury was unleashed at last, as he drew back and gave the old door a powerful kick with the heel of his boot. The heavy iron bolt held, but another blow splintered the dry wood that surrounded it. He crashed through shoulder-first, leaving the door sagging on its loosened hinges.

The room lacked windows, and here too the lantern was nearly burnt dry. For the few seconds it took Thorne's eyes to adjust to the dimness, he almost feared Hobbs had slipped by the guards during the night and into the concealing fog.

And left a windowless room bolted from the inside? Not likely.

Spotting the chair turned over on its side, Thorne frowned. It was then that he became fully aware of the rhythmic creaking sound, the protest of stressed wood; then, too, that the significance of the malodorous air struck him. He had first associated it with unswept stalls.

His heart slowed, his blood chilling. Every muscle in his body tensed. Forcing his head to turn, he looked over his left shoulder.

His breath caught and held; bile rose in his throat.

Less than an arm's length away, the body of Tobias Hobbs hung by the neck from the soot-blackened rafters, its bulging eyes staring sightlessly at Thorne.

THIRTY-FIVE

I am cursed.

Perhaps from the cradle. The sins of the father...

Raising the glinting decanter of Scotch whiskey high, Thorne sucked its dregs as a babe would suck life from its mother's teat.

Cursed in life, cursed in love; cursed in every righteous endeavor. He swallowed the fiery liquid, then chuckled aloud.

Why do you laugh? he asked himself, and realized that one minuscule part of his brain still held its head above the churning sea of Scotch.

Then I'll fetch more Scotch and drown the little buggerer. But his limbs refused to budge from their comfortable position in the chair. As chilly as it was in the room, he cared not a whit. There was warmth enough in his veins at the moment, or perhaps no feeling at all, which was just as well.

He stared through the tall windows of the library solar, the room in total darkness behind him. Something told him the moonlit landscape was every bit as cold as it looked tonight. Across the lane the stables stood stark and stony, for all the world appearing uninhabited, but somewhere behind those shuttered windows was Nate--who had adamantly refused to take Hobbs' old quarters, in fact was loathe to stay anyplace under that roof overnight. It had required a sticky bit of negotiating for Arthur to convince him.

Thorne barked a laugh. Nate was undoubtedly the most highly paid stable groom in the shire, if not in the whole of Mother England.

By grace of dogged determination, he heaved himself out of the chair and lumbered toward the corner cabinet, where, he discovered with a mumbled curse, there was no more Scotch. Such a catastrophe demanded a dangerous trek up the great stairs to his own chambers, where, by God, there had *better* be another bottle in his sideboard, he wasn't paying the chambermaid for naught...but shouldn't stocking the spirits be a task for his manservant? *I must advertise soon...*

Once inside his chambers, he staggered toward the sideboard and groped blindly in its recesses until his fingers encountered hobnailed crystal. He nudged the heavy decanter forward, accidentally knocking something out onto the floor with a soft thwack--and stared, spellbound, at the volume of poetry he had confiscated from the library.

Elaine.

The thought hit him so squarely in the diaphragm it might have been a fist--and he went down that quickly.

He sat as he landed, legs splayed on the bare waxed floorboards, arms clutching the leather-bound book to his chest. He could think of nothing more appealing, more comforting, than to imagine she was in the library at this very moment...that he'd only to creep down the stairs to find her in that chair, a mere two maddening yards from his own, her shining chestnut plait cascading to her waist. She would be bent over her book, her long lashes poised just above her cheeks and lips slightly parted, entranced by the words on the page. Those generous lips...aye, his eyes had more than once lingered on them undetected, had often seen them spread into a heartbreaking smile at one of his abrupt inquiries or muttered asides. She would hold her book in those long, slender fingers as if it were fragile and priceless--this book he held now, the very one in which she'd written his name.

Twice.

But she left you, didn't she, taunted the cynic in him. *As did the rest of them...Catherine, Lena, Robert, and Gwynneth. Even Caroline.*

The book was tossed onto the shelf, the decanter of Scotch dragged out in its stead. Using the sideboard as a prop, Thorne pulled himself up, then wove his way across the room and fell heavily into a fireside chair. Knees apart and back slumped, he uncorked the bottle and resumed what had been his chief diversion since Caroline Sutherland departed four days ago, after Hobbs' burial.

She'd refused to meet his eyes upon her arrival, much less speak to him, and had turned up her nose at his offer of guest chambers. Her coach had stood ready in the churchyard to fetch her back to London immediately after the service.

As badly as Thorne felt about Hobbs' suicide, he'd yet to feel any softening toward the man himself--which only made him feel heartless, although he suspected few men could forgive such abomination as Hobbs had perpetrated on the Neville family and one of their servants. No true brother would have behaved so.

Hobbs had left a note, undiscovered until late the day he was found. The scrap of paper read simply, *As I am bound to hang, I shall at least choose the day.* Always contentious, was Hobbs. Ever ready to pick a fight or to argue a point.

And Arthur. For the last four days, as Thorne had wandered about the house or sequestered himself in his chambers, his steward, his friend and mentor, had stayed away. True, there was no pressing business, this being the time of year when there was little to be done other than keeping the herds, with the ground too wet to plow and the salmon still down-river. And Arthur had been quite civil, but Thorne knew he was grieving, and not just for Hobbs. *I love the both of you as if you were my own sons,* he'd told them, and Thorne knew that no matter what was to come or what had gone before, the old man's love for him would prevail.

But Arthur was not long for this world, a few years at most, and who would be left then? Not Gwynneth. Not Caroline, which was probably a blessing.

And not Elaine...even if society allowed.

He lifted the bottle high and drank, first to slake his thirst, however ineffectively; second and more importantly, to numb whatever remaining nerve or two was indulging in this damnable self-pity. He kept one eye on the decanter, uncertain of his coordination even at close range, and the other on the view from his windows. The moon had just reappeared from behind a cloud when he noticed something in the Northampton Road.

With what felt like a Herculean effort, he pushed up from the chair, and veered his way to a window.

Someone was there. Thorne held onto the casing for support as he squinted, trying to focus his Scotch-blurred eyes. The figure--slightly built, cloaked and hooded--moved again. It appeared to be examining the rose hedges. A strange pastime after dark, Thorne mused, and hadn't the roses had only barely begun to bud?

Curiosity held him there, along with the lead in his limbs, not to mention the fact that it was comforting to discover another human about the place, as even the servants were lately steering clear of him.

The cloaked figure reached to finger a tender branch; simultaneously its hood fell back.

A woman. Thorne frowned and started slightly, for even at this distance there was something familiar about her. Long hair, colorless in the stark moonlight, was loosely cradled in the folds of her fallen hood.

Who the deuce are you?

The thought was intensely curious, and as if she'd actually heard him speak, the woman turned suddenly to gaze at the Hall.

For breathtaking, blood-draining moments Thorne stood rooted to the spot, unwilling to believe what he was seeing, yet unable to tear himself away. At last, when it felt as if his chest was about to implode, he gasped for air; then with a hoarse, garbled cry, he pushed himself away from the casing with such force that he staggered, reeled, and fell hard to the floor. Vaguely aware of striking his head on the way down, he watched as the room and its contents began to spin with nauseating speed; then he shut his eyes.

Merciful velvet-black unconsciousness closed in upon him, his last thought fading away...

I'm dying. Thank God, I am dying.

* * *

"He's coming 'round." John Hodges brought the candle nearer his patient's face and lifted an eyelid. "Ah, his pupils are contracting a bit. 'Twon't be long." He turned to Arthur. "When he wakes, send up warm broth and strong black tea with sugar. Get someone to force it down him, for I'll wager he's had little but spirits in several days."

Arthur nodded, indicating the bandage on Thorne's temple. "Need we change that soon?"

Gathering the contents of his black leather bag, Hodges shook his head. "I'll see to it tomorrow." He eyed Arthur gravely. "He needs rest and light nourishment. Absolutely no spirits. And you," he added, "look as if you could use some rest yourself. Doctor's orders."

When Hodges had gone, Arthur plumped pillows and straightened bedcovers, at some point glancing up to find the patient's bleary, half-opened eyes upon him.

"Have I sacked the chambermaid again?" Thorne rasped.

Arthur almost smiled. "No, M'lord. Hodges has been and gone, and I thought I might as well make myself useful."

Thorne tried to sit, but was gently pushed back against the pillows. "How long have I been out?"

"Two days." Arthur moved the candle out of harm's way. "At first we thought you a goner, with that goose egg on your temple." He looked sternly at Thorne. "Hodges claims you and the bottle have been close friends these last few days. Friends such as that tend to turn on you sooner than later, and I'd say you were bloody-nigh killed by yours. Have you never heard of alcohol poisoning?"

Thorne grimaced. "Spare me the lecture, Arthur, 'tis one with which my bloody conscience badgered me the whole time I imbibed. But sometimes," he said through his teeth, trying again to sit upright, "a man must hit bottom before he can rise again."

This time Arthur aided him with an extra pillow. "Well, I can't say I agree with your philosophy, but what's done is done. Just thank Providence that the bump on your head is no worse. Seems you fell against the edge of the ottoman. Now, I'm on my way to the kitchen. Hodges says you're to eat, and if you refuse, I'm to force it down you."

Thorne snorted at the idea, though he felt surprisingly hungry. Arthur was soon out the door, moving with more energy than he'd displayed in a long while. It suddenly struck Thorne that as long as Arthur felt he'd a purpose in this life, he was more than likely to be around for a good while; hence, he quickly reversed the decision he'd made days ago that his old friend needed more rest and less work. He should have known better. The man had always thrived upon activity.

He glanced toward the windows. Dusk had fallen. Memory came flooding back, standing the hairs at his nape on end.

"You were drunk, Neville," he muttered, then glanced about to make certain he was alone. "Drunker than a bloody sailor on his first night in port..."

Of course...that would explain it. He was fortunate, he told himself, not to have seen far worse than he had.

* * *

By nine of the clock next evening Thorne was comfortably ensconced in his room, quite sober, and determined to prove to himself that his vision three nights past had been the product of drunken delirium.

He was perturbed to discover an hour later that the vision had been no hallucination. But in his sober state and perhaps because he was prepared, he felt no fear. In its place was anger as he watched what appeared to be the same person inspecting the pubescent rose hedges again.

He abandoned his chambers. Encountering William on the service stairs, he dispatched him to "inquire of the person lingering in the Northampton road," but was keenly disappointed when the bewildered youth returned only to say that the road was deserted.

Once more Thorne sought the solitude of his rooms. Ignoring the inclination to indulge in a glass of Scotch, he strode to the window.

She was there--still in the road, in practically the same stance as he'd left her. His heart began to race.

Turn 'round, he bade her silently, while he stood stock-still with dread that she might do just that. He told himself she was one of the villagers, or perhaps one of the maids out for a late-night stroll in spite of the risk of incurring Dame Carswell's wrath.

Wrong!!! she seemed to say, at that very moment turning directly toward the house. Her eyes were like tiny brilliant beacons, aimed directly at the southern windows of the old structure...and at the man who stood watching her in dumbfounded disbelief.

It wasn't until she smiled--a gesture so unmistakable and sweetly horrifying in the harsh moonlight--that Thorne's skin broke into gooseflesh. With his heart in his gullet, he scrambled backward, unable to assimilate a second more of the shattering reality that the woman's mere presence implied.

For the first time in his life, he drew the heavy draperies over every window of his bedchamber. Hampered by dread-stiffened limbs, he kept his hot dry eyes obstinately averted from what surely awaited him beyond the myriad panes of glass.

* * *

The night passed in dead silence, the room stuffy, dark and muffled with all the windows shuttered and draped. Shortly past two in the morning, Thorne rose to light a fire, then impulsively pulled a velvet panel just a hair away from the window and peered through the slit.

There was nothing...no one. The road was quite deserted.

As he let the air out of his lungs, he briefly considered opening the draperies--very briefly. When dawn finally broke, he jerked each panel impatiently aside and secured it. In the light of day it was easy to forget that that familiar and beloved landscape had turned so malevolently alien by the light of the moon.

Besides, if the chambermaid found his windows covered, she'd likely suspect some kind of subterfuge afoot. Thorne made a wry face. No one but himself had been in his bed since the night Gwynneth-

He left the thought unfinished, lest the night's horror overcome him again.

* * *

The next two evenings found Thorne's windows well shielded from any prying eyes in the countryside. Both nights he kept vigil, and on both nights the woman was at her post. Although he'd peered through a mere crack to see if she was there, she seemed to sense his presence each time, turning to look at him almost immediately. And then, the smile. Of anything she could possibly have done, that was the most terrifying, the most hideous.

By the next evening he was irritable, impatient, and haggard, having snatched only short, restless periods of sleep since the day he'd awakened to find himself under the doctor's care. He'd since eaten as well as he could, more out of need than hunger as he tried desperately to keep a clear head.

But on this night, well after the moon had risen, the woman in the road surprised him. No sooner than he moved the drapery aside to look, she turned toward the house again...but this time she pressed a white rosebud to her lips. Then, lowering the blossom, she smiled...and executed a flawless curtsey.

It was that final gesture which turned Thorne's blood from freezing to boiling. He bolted from his chamber, up the gallery and down the great stairway, with no thought for appearances, his crippling fear banished by a burning determination to confront the woman, to demand her reasons for tormenting him--and more than anything, to prove to himself that she was among the living.

For everything about her--size, stance, hair and smile--told him she was none other than Gwynneth Stowington Wycliffe, the late Baroness Neville of Wycliffe.

THIRTY-SIX

The smell was the first thing that struck him as he came up the back lane toward the Northampton road.

The roses.

A week since, they'd been but tiny buds. Now they were open, fresh and fragrant. *Odious. Nauseating.* He found it hard to believe he'd taken so much satisfaction in seeing the plants set into the ground. Even the scent of damp earth was mildly disturbing now, something to which his rural blood had always quickened before.

He began counting his steps to keep from thinking; even two minutes of mindlessness would be a welcome relief. But a dog's bark and the shout of a herder alerted him to falling dusk. Despite his recovered cynicism, this stretch of road was the last place he cared to be after dark. He turned about and headed for the Hall.

Yestereve he'd felt quite foolish, tearing up the lane at breakneck speed only to round the curve and find the Northampton road deserted. For a time he'd stood still, his chest heaving and his mind running rampant as he fought the urge to howl his frustration to the sky.

Obviously he was losing his mind. Something, perhaps some sense of guilt for Gwynneth's fate, was taking him over the edge and into an abyss quite apart from that into which he'd dreaded falling with Caroline. How long could a man survive without sleep, he wondered? In this state of mind he was likely to see more and worse apparitions, which would only hasten the inevitable conclusion: if he wasn't first driven to take his life, he would wind up in Bedlam for the rest of his life, chained to a wall and put on display as a curiosity, a freak, for anyone inclined to buy a ticket for such a dubious and depraved form of entertainment.

Insane, his mind had whispered last night as he stood there on the empty road. *Incurably insane.*

And then he had spotted the rose.

Tender and white, plucked before its prime, the shriveling blossom lay where it had been dropped, in the middle of the Northampton road.

* * *

Having relieved Nate for a couple of hours while the youth went into the village to sup with his family, Arthur rounded the stables just in time to see Thorne approaching, the sun low at his back. As he drew closer, the steward noted an ominous set to the square jaw.

"Saddle Raven," was the terse order.

"But M'lord-"

"Let me be." One hand up as if to ward off a blow, Thorne strode straight to the tack wall. "I'll do it myself."

Wordlessly, Arthur watched him bridle and saddle the Arabian and lead him from his stall. Feeling fairly certain of his destination, he made one last effort to dissuade him. "M'lord, you'll find no comfort there."

Thorne leapt astride Raven and threw his cloak over the pommel before lancing the steward with a look. "Then I'll find diversion. And perhaps sleep in the bargain." He turned the prancing stallion to heel and set him off on a trot toward the back lane. "Don't expect me until you see me," he called back hoarsely, and urged his mount into a gallop.

Watching them well into the distance, Arthur shook his head and murmured, "Let sleeping dogs lie, my boy...and you needn't lie with them."

* * *

"'Tis the middle of night! And Gilbert knows I've no intention of receiving that blackguard," Caroline snapped at a sleepy-eyed Marsh. "Tell the old booby to do his duty or I'll sack his ar--I'll give him the sack." She firmly shut her door.

Moments later, Marsh was back. "Mistress," she hissed, "his lordship refuses to leave!"

The boudoir door was readily yanked open. "Does he, now? Then I'll give his bloody lordship the boot myself." Ignoring Marsh's gasp, she swept past her onto the gallery, where she all but spilled her near-naked bosom onto the polished baluster as she leaned over it and clutched it with long-nailed fingers.

"You, sir, are without shame *or* scruples to set foot in my home uninvited," she said in a ringing voice, sparing only a warning glance for the mortified Gilbert, who was standing beside their caller with nightcap in hand. "I cannot receive you in good conscience, and I am shocked you would have the unmitigated gall to expect my hospitality!"

She tossed her head as Thorne swept off his tricorne and bowed low to her, then watched in haughty silence as he replaced it and turned to leave. Though he'd not said a word, there was something about the set of his shoulders that tugged at her meager maternal instinct.

"Wait."

Both men turned, Gilbert looking pathetically hopeful.

"Send Lord Neville up," she said coolly, then sailed toward her boudoir. "To the drawing room," she called over her shoulder. "I shall be with him presently."

She covered her scanty shift with a scarlet China silk wrapper, but thought crossly that she needn't have bothered, as her caller hardly glanced at her when she entered the drawing room. He did wait until she was seated before seating himself. Amazingly, Marsh had already lit a candelabrum and started a fire in the grate.

"Well?" Caroline folded her arms, making her breasts jut impressively. "What is so urgent you had to rouse me at such an hour?"

When there was no immediate reply, no retort, she slid the candelabra closer to Thorne's chair, then barely stifled a gasp.

The handsome, sun-bronzed face she knew so well was now pale and drawn across the prominent cheekbones, with dark hollows lurking beneath bloodshot eyes.

He seemed to have aged a decade. Caroline's resentment was all but forgotten as she sprang from her seat, her silk wrapper whispering as she knelt and clasped his cold hand in the warmth of both her own. "What is it, Thorne?" She massaged his stiff fingers, anxiously searching his haggard countenance. "Tell me, for God's sake."

"Godforsaken," he rasped. "There's a good word. 'Tis what I am. And perhaps I deserve to be." He gave her a hollow, haunted look. "Caroline, I think I'm losing my mind."

"Here now," she scoffed, struggling with her own sudden fear, and rose to tug him out of the chair. With almost childlike obeisance, he followed her onto the gallery. First scouting for lurkers below, Caroline drew him into her boudoir, then closed the door and turned the key. She crossed to another door and turned the key in that one as well. Ashby was now locked in the little room adjoining, and hopefully deaf to the world.

Nothing was said as Thorne let Caroline disrobe him and guide him toward the large bed. Upon shedding her wrapper and her shift, she slid into the bed beside him and pulled him close, enfolding him in her long, sleek limbs.

"Tomorrow," she said softly. "You can tell me all about it then."

"Aye, tomorrow," he murmured, closing his eyes. "God, I need some sleep."

She slid a hand beneath the bedcovers. Finding what she sought, she surrounded it with caressing fingers, and was rewarded with Thorne's sharp intake of breath. "You will sleep this night, my lord," she whispered. "I shall see to it."

* * *

Awakening briefly before dawn, Thorne felt Caroline's arm wrapped loosely about his back. He moved his head close to hers on the pillow, where her hair was a rippling sea of silk beneath his whisker-stubbed cheek. He inhaled its fragrance, deliberately keeping his mind empty, his cares at bay, and once more found deep, dreamless sleep.

Surfacing near mid-day, he discovered a steaming bath awaited him, with several pitchers of cool water nearby to temper it. While he was soaking in the gleaming copper tub, his hostess entered with a covered tray.

"You're looking much better." She set the hot food down.

He opened one eye and smiled wickedly. "Feeling better, too."

"Yes, so I see." Caroline settled into a chair and leaned sideways on an elbow, lending a coyness to the provocative lines of her hip and cleavage. "But are you feeling well enough to tell me what last night was all about?"

He closed the eye momentarily, then opened both. "Aye...but I warn you, 'twill not be an easy dose to swallow."

She shrugged. "Try me."

Thorne matter-of-factly related events surrounding the first sighting of the woman in the road, confessing his drunken state at the time. Harder to tell were the events of the previous four nights, and even more so, his discovery of the wilted white rosebud in the Northampton road.

Caroline shifted to the other hip, frowning. "You'd stopped drinking...might it have been a hallucination brought on by lack of sleep, perhaps even by your own expectation?"

Thorne stood up, water sluicing off his bronze skin, his muscles rippling under its shine. "Aye," he conceded with a crooked smile, noting the direction of Caroline's unabashed gaze, and reached for the bath sheet. "But how do you explain the rose?"

Looking thoughtful, she watched him dry his hair and wrap the damp sheet about his waist. "Coincidence," she concluded. "You and I are far too pragmatic to entertain the idea of ghosts. But if there are such," she added dryly, "Horace has had the good grace to refrain from haunting me."

Thorne burst out laughing, and sauntered over to plant a kiss on top of her sleekly coifed head. "You're good for me, Caroline Sutherland. Not long ago, I feared the worst that could happen to me would be to fall under your spell."

"I'm no witch, Thorne." But there was an alluring gleam in her eyes. "I do not cast spells."

"The devil you don't." He tipped her chin up and gazed into the black velvet orbs. "You're a sorceress. Worse yet, one who knows her power."

It was hard to say who moved first. He only knew that he was suddenly taking her mouth like a parched man who'd stumbled upon a well, and by the time they drew apart for air, he was as stunned as she looked.

Without a word, she yanked the bath sheet from his body. His eyes flamed as she stared first at his looming arousal, then up at him through her lashes.

"Come to bed," she said, her voice husky.

He needed no coaxing. He stretched out on the bed and waited, every muscle and one organ taut with expectation.

She turned her back to him, and, with a maddening lack of haste, began pushing the tiny jet buttons through the gold-corded loops of her frock. Thorne rolled to the bed's edge to assist, but once she'd withdrawn her sleek arms from the sleeves, she deliberately slipped out of reach.

As intrigued as he was aroused, Thorne lay back again to observe. He knew she'd lowered her panniers when she stepped gracefully to one side. After the silk frock had skimmed over her sumptuous curves and fallen to the floor, she removed the pins from her hair one at a time, letting the long black tresses tumble in sections onto her back. Still without hurrying, she removed her stays, then lifted her shift up over her head.

Thorne had only a glimpse of her strong, shapely back before the entire mass of her hair cascaded down over it. He looked down at her high, round bottom, just in time to view a heart-stopping display between her thighs as she bent over and slowly peeled off her silk stockings.

"If you don't get into this bed *now*," he said tautly, "I swear I'll take you like a wild beast."

He saw her shiver, heard her involuntary sound, half moan and half taunt. "Remember, my lord, I cast spells...I can tame any beast that dares set upon me."

Her words ended in a soft cry as Thorne's hard bulk and probing warmth pressed against her from behind. "Taming," he all but growled, "is out of the question."

* * *

Thorne's glance about at the room's lengthening shadows brought little surprise. Time spent with Caroline always flew by. He brushed his lips along the length of her jaw, then smoothed her hair away from her face.

"The coffers were quite full," she murmured, looking up at him with a sultry smile. "I would have thought after last night..."

"You see?" Thorne leaned down to nuzzle the soft hollow behind her ear. "You *are* a sorceress."

She kissed his razor-stubbled cheek. "Then you are a sorcerer," she said softly, "for your spell over me is every bit as powerful."

He drew back and looked at her soberly. "You've forgiven me, then."

"Oh, Thorne." Averting her eyes, she tried to rise.

"Stay, please." When she reluctantly sank down into the pillows again, he cupped her face in one hand. "I must know. Have you forgiven me?"

She said nothing.

Wounded pride made Thorne blunt. "He'd have hung at any rate. You must know that."

Her brow furrowed slightly.

"Say you've forgiven me, that you no longer blame me."

She sighed, shaking her head. "'Tis not that simple, Thorne."

"Then I've no business being here." She made no protest as he levered himself off the bed. He dressed with his back to her, and soon heard the sounds of her own toilette.

When she'd buttoned her frock as much as possible without help, she turned to find him fully clothed and waiting.

His bow had never been more courtly. As he straightened, his bold scrutiny took her in from hem to neckline, lingering on the latter. "I thank you, Mistress Sutherland, for your bouncing...I mean to say, boundless, hospitality." His gaze shifted to meet hers. "You were more than generous with such a cold-blooded ruffian as I. I wonder you didn't slit my throat when you had me trapped between those lissome thighs of yours. Your kindness will long be remembered." He smiled jauntily. "If ever I may return the favor, you've only to appear at my door--no doubt you can find my chambers without any help from Jennings. Feel free to come and tuck me in...though not necessarily in that order."

Turning to go, he glimpsed her arm swiftly raising, and ducked; a well-heeled shoe struck the door. His smile turned wry. "You needn't trouble yourself, I'll see myself out. Good day, ma'am."

Halfway down the wide stairs, he heard her door open, then the sound of her quick step on the gallery; continuing his casual descent, he steeled himself for whatever was to come.

"I'll have you know, Thorne Neville," rang out a strident voice he barely recognized as Caroline's, "that you couldn't bewitch me no matter *what* your powers! And 'tis not *mine* whose spell hangs over your proud head, you fool...'tis your *mother's*!"

He stopped in his tracks and turned to glare at the she-cat leaning over the balustrade.

She sneered. "Do you think I'm blind? Did you truly think I wouldn't notice her likeness hung on your walls, perched on your desk? Any *fool* could see the resemblance between us...can't *you*?"

"Stop it," he said, his voice deadly.

"Really, Thorne, haven't you noticed that whenever your life is out of kilter, you come running to me?"

"Cease this tripe."

"We shall cease it indeed, for I'll not be a party to incest, even by proxy! And when next you think to treat me so, talking of favors and seeking out your bed, think again, Thorne Neville--I am *not your whore!*"

"I could never mistake you for her," he said coldly. "She has far more heart."

He finished his descent under a cloud of colorful curses. A scarlet-cheeked Gilbert was handing him his tricorne when Caroline recovered sufficiently to take a parting shot.

"Go home, Thorne! Go home and face your ghosts, and what is left of your life! We *all* have our troubles, and whether or not you choose to admit it, the two of us have recently lost a brother--I, for one, am not *past* that loss."

She turned away without waiting for a response. It was just as well, for one never came, and as Thorne crossed the threshold of the Georgian mansion, he knew he had done so for the last time.

THIRTY-SEVEN

"I must speak to you."

Arthur gave a start, as Thorne had appeared in the stable with all the subtlety and suddenness of a ghost. In fact he looked only slightly better than one.

"Here, M'lord?"

Thorne shook his head, glancing grimly about the tack room. "In my study."

It wasn't difficult to gauge Thorne's state of mind, as they entered the room where the two of them had most often conducted business until recently. The fire was hearty, the furniture glowing with fresh beeswax, and the air redolent of tobacco smoke--the last of which warned Arthur that this meeting would delve deeper than manor business.

"I am taking stock," Thorne said flatly.

"Of what, M'lord?"

"My life." Thorne opened the gold humidor and pushed it across the desk. "My life, and my obligation to all those whose lives I've touched."

Arthur selected a cigar without comment, cutting and lighting it before taking a seat across from the desk.

"Yesterday," Thorne said, closing the humidor, "it was succinctly pointed out to me that each of us has his own problems. And though it pains me to admit it," he confessed on a stream of blue smoke, "I've gone about my life rather half-cocked since my Oxford days, and others have suffered into the bargain." He stared at the blotter. "I owe a debt to them, and I feel that until that debt is paid, my life shall continually veer off course--until at some point I'll either wreck or drown."

Arthur softly cleared his throat. "I've begun to think you're a man of the sea, M'lord, despite your love for the land. But might I inquire what, or who, prompted this revelation?"

Thorne pulled a wry face. "An acquaintance, one who looks like a goddess but rants like a fishwife. At any rate, I owe *you*, my friend, the greatest debt of all, for I've caused you to lose the closest person to a son you ever had."

Arthur regarded him soberly. "You, Thorne, are as near as I've come to having a son. I loved Toby, but he was belligerent, rebellious and conniving--traits of which I'd not have been so tolerant, had he been anyone but who he was."

"Nevertheless, he is dead because of my high-handedness," Thorne said glumly. "And my need for vengeance."

"'Tis hardly high-handed, M'lord, for a man to avenge his wife's honor, let alone her life. And as you reminded me, there are two other souls gone to their reward prematurely, hastened there by none other than Toby Hobbs. His death was recompense. Even I know that."

"Aye, well I'd sooner he'd hung from the hangman's rope than mine."

Arthur shrugged his bent shoulders. "What better way to avenge himself than borrow yours, and thus find a way to torment you even after he's gone? In no way do I blame you for his end, indeed had he lived I shudder to contemplate the brevity of your own life--for I suspect he'd an eye toward owning these lands someday."

A pained frown touched Thorne's brow. "Just as he laid claim to my wife. Very well then, we've eulogized the man sufficiently, I think. I appreciate your efforts to purge me of my guilt."

"On to other debts, then?"

Thorne nodded, tamping out the cigar. "Gwynneth. I owe her the greatest debt after you. God's blood, Arthur, if I'd only listened to you when you warned me that her religion would come between us...although 'twas I who came between Gwynneth and her religion...as did Radleigh. Who, by the by, fares poorly. His love for rich food and spirits is taking a toll, gout and jaundice. At least Lord Whittingham no longer backs his wagering, and no one else has taken the reins from the bloody bastard, thank Providence."

Arthur nodded, aware of past dealings with the unsavory earl.

"Radleigh grieves for his daughter," Thorne allowed, "but then he was well into his cups most of the time he was here, too, and Gwynneth was quite alive."

"A pleasant man, though, Lord Radleigh."

"Aye, and a good one as well. And he'll never go hungry, cold, or unkempt as long as I'm living. His estate will pass to me in lieu of his debt, but with no living heir, he claims he'd be inclined to leave it to me at any rate, as homage to my father. Still, I see no way to pay my debt to Gwynneth."

Silently puffing away, Arthur soon felt Thorne watching him through the blue haze between them.

"What is it?"

"What do you mean?"

"I can see you've something on your mind, Pennington. Say it, then."

"Very well, I shall. Do you not think that, with the hell your wife put you through, she owed you a debt as well?"

"Surely not her life!"

"No, God no. Lay that at Hobbs' door. I meant before that."

"Perhaps. But my debt is the larger by far. And at any rate, 'tis hard to compensate a ghost." Thorne's face suddenly and inexplicably paled.

"Not necessarily," Arthur countered, startled by his odd pallor but determined to pull him out of this quagmire. "I once heard her tell Lord Radleigh she would have liked to confer her dowry on the Sisters of Saint Mary in Leicester."

For a long moment Thorne only stared at him; then he grinned almost idiotically. "Capital! A splendid idea!"

"You catch my drift, then," Arthur said, pleased and relieved.

"I most certainly do, my friend, and an inspired drift it is! I hope Radleigh will see it as such...I think out of respect for Gwynneth, he'll agree. The prioress and the priest will be overjoyed, and the endowment will stand in Gwynneth's name...by God, Arthur, you are the very best of stewards! My father knew bloody well what he was about when he advanced you." Arthur's face had grown warm, and Thorne chuckled. "I don't mean to embarrass you," he said apologetically, "but I feel as if I've just been given a good dose of tonic. On, then, to other matters that weigh on my conscience, and perhaps you'll offer still more inspiration."

"I'll try." Arthur couldn't help but smile; it was gratifying to see his young master in good humor. But the mood changed swiftly.

"I know I said we'd spoken enough about Hobbs, but there is one matter unresolved. His babe--my nephew or niece--is in this world somewhere, whether inside or out of its mother. I want them found, Arthur."

"M'lord?"

"I want Elaine Combs and her child found. And whatever you or anyone else can accomplish toward that end will be rewarded."

"Rewarded," Arthur echoed dully.

"Aye, and generously so. I'll offer a thousand pounds to the person who can direct me to their whereabouts. In gold, if that increases the allure."

This time Arthur held his tongue, but he could hardly help looking shocked. "Very well, I'll put word out."

"Good." Thorne smiled wryly. "You needn't worry, I've no intention of hounding the mother. I only want to assure myself that she and the child are properly lodged and amply fed, and of course I'll see to it that the child is educated and its future provided for. After all, he or she is of my blood. No, don't go just yet, there is something else."

"M'lord?"

"I want both entrances to the tower sealed. Permanently." As Arthur only stared at him, Thorne lifted an eyebrow. "What, have I grown horns?"

Arthur shook his head in bewilderment. "May I ask why?"

"Only if you've no intention of arguing the point," was the somewhat impatient reply. "I might remind you that, for some ungodly reason, two inhabitants of the Hall have felt inclined to take flight from the battlements. As I can think of no good reason to keep the tower accessible, I shall here and now end all further temptation for any other misguided souls."

"What of the watch, if we need it?" asked Arthur.

Thorne snorted. "'Twas only needed while Tom Barker was dusting my fields at Hobbs' behest! I say we can do without the tower. Leave the damned thing to the bats, they make much better use of it."

"Very well," Arthur said slowly. "I'll see to it, though 'twill likely give some credence to the 'haunting' story."

Thorne looked at him sharply. "What 'haunting' story? What do you mean?"

"Why, the man on watch at the top of the tower, the one who claims he was pushed from behind...surely you remember?"

"Aye." Thorne looked oddly relieved. "Well, 'tis of no matter. If people are wont to talk, they'll talk. 'Twill all die down after a few days, and at any rate, most folk will credit my decision to my wife's death. Which is entirely correct."

"You're right, of course. Silly of me." Arthur tamped out the tiny stub of his cheroot. "If we've finished here, I'll get on with it."

"And Arthur..." Thorne looked mildly exasperated.

"Aye, M'lord?"

"If I am truly like a son to you, will you please dispense with formality when we're alone and call me by my name?"

"If you insist, Lord Neville." Arthur tried not to smile.

"My Christian name, Arthur."

"Ah, that one!" The steward grinned. "Aye, Thorne...I shall be honored to do so."

* * *

The clock struck ten. Thorne silently counted the strokes despite his acute awareness of the time. It being his first evening home since he'd fled to London, he was determined to avoid windows, particularly on the south and west sides of the Hall.

Let her stand there 'til the sun rises, he thought. *If her specter is inclined to haunt the road, it will do so unobserved by me.* He smiled grimly to himself.

Reading for a while, he was not even once drawn to the window, though the draperies were wide open. When at last he snuffed the candle and climbed into bed, he felt triumphant, untouchable. Nothing, he thought smugly, could haunt him in such a mood: not ghosts, not memories, not regrets.

He failed to consider dreams.

* * *

He thought he was alone in the dream, standing in the lower nave of the manor church; then he became aware of someone behind a wooden column. His first thought was that Elaine had come back, and his heart skipped a telltale beat.

And a woman *did* step out into the open, with the hood of her cloak pulled well up over her head, and her face in shadow. Thorne started forward, then stopped, his breath hitching as the hood fell back, just as it had on the Northampton road.

He stumbled backward, his heart racing, but slowed his retreat when Gwynneth tilted her head and looked perplexed at his reaction. Then came the gesture he'd learned to dread: she smiled.

To his surprise, the gesture wasn't the least bit terrifying, but sweet, open and gentle. It was then that he knew he was dreaming--for shouldn't she be blistering him with that sulfurous glow her eyes acquired when her rage was high? Punishing him for the hell she'd deemed his making in her last days on earth?

He tried to speak, but no sound passed his lips. He gestured impatiently, only to see her shake her head slowly and smile all the more, as if she were amused at such childish impetuosity.

So he waited; after all, *she* had appeared to *him*. The next move should be hers.

She turned suddenly toward the carved column, and nodded her head. Thorne clutched the side of the pew as yet another woman stepped from the shadows.

Katy.

Katy?

He was utterly confused. Even dreaming, he felt his mouth open and close as a question struggled to escape his throat. But then Katy smiled down at a bundle of cloth in her arms--something he hadn't noticed until now.

He felt as if he were floating down the nave instead of walking. His heart hammered, although his conscious mind had yet to accept what his subconscious already knew.

Katy stepped forward, holding her burden out to him; rather awkwardly, he took it. Inside the lightweight bundle, something moved, giving off a sweet-smelling warmth, and Thorne brushed the edge of the blanket aside.

The babe was a wee thing, born no more than a month ago, from the looks of it. As it gurgled--the only sound in the dream--it opened its eyes.

Thorne's heart lurched: he was looking into Robert Neville's eyes. Vivid, of an arresting blue, they could even be his own.

He gazed inquiringly at Katy, vaguely aware that Gwynneth was no longer in the church but that somehow it didn't matter. Katy reached to take the babe from him, and he was stunned by the bereft sensation he felt as it was lifted from his arms. He wanted to hold the wriggling creature a while longer, perhaps take it home with him.

As if reading his thoughts, Katy smiled, but stepped back and shook her head as if to say, "Not just now."

A tapping sound began to invade his consciousness--the first sound he'd heard other than the cooing of the child. It escalated in rhythm and volume, finally waking him altogether.

He lay staring through the windows into utter blackness, until a bright flash of lightning informed his now cognizant mind that a pre-season thunderstorm was in progress, and that hail was bouncing off the windowpanes. He sprang from the bed, as determined now to look as he'd been earlier to stay away.

When the next streak of lightning illumined the landscape, his eyes were fixed on that specter-plagued stretch of road. Except for a few battered roses the gusty wind had dashed into the mud, the road was empty. Relief flooded his veins, and with it came a sense of gratitude. He lay back down on the bed to ponder his strange dream while it was still fresh in memory.

Katy and Gwynneth? What irony! Two such juxtaposed lives; yet, had they ever met, their reactions would most likely have been directly adverse to their aspirations: Gwynneth's the least tolerant, Katy's the most charitable. Understandable enough, Thorne had to admit, considering it would have been a meeting between wife and former lover. Why was it, he wondered, that so often in dreams things were illogical?

And what of the babe, with eyes that mirrored his own...how could it be Gwynneth's unborn?

Of course! He felt a fierce sense of triumph at his intuitiveness. It wasn't her actual unborn, the child of Hobbs, the babe that died with her; it was her abstract unborn--the child that he, Thorne, had denied her by refusing her amorous but belated advances.

So, despite her sweet smile, she wants only to torment me with visions of what might have been! How typical of her, he mused; then he frowned. Why in his dream had Katy, of all people, presented him with the child he had denied Gwynneth? Again his mind was ready with an answer. No doubt it was Gwynneth's snide way of telling him that she was aware of his past relationship with the "harlot."

It was a dream, and dreams seldom parallel reality, he reminded himself tiredly. His true antagonist was not Gwynneth, but that bitter and unwelcome acquaintance known as "guilt," come calling in his sleep when he was most vulnerable and likely to receive it.

For the remainder of the pre-dawn hours he slept undisturbed, and for nearly a week more, nights at Wycliffe Hall passed without incident.

* * *

The second thunderstorm arrived in mid-March, at an hour when most residents of the Hall were preparing for bed. Still disenchanted with late evenings in the library, Thorne pored over accounts in his study while enjoying the disharmonic symphony outside. An hour later, after all within the Hall had settled for the night, an extended roll of thunder trailed off into a rather peculiar noise for a storm. Thorne decided it had come from inside, perhaps from the west wing. Peering up the east hall, he saw nothing, and had just turned back to his desk when the sound came again.

Swift and silent, he reached the great hall just as the noise commenced with a sudden flurry. He headed for the kitchen door and stood outside it to listen.

The larder! He might have suspected as much, though it had been some time since he'd heard any complaint of theft. Slowly he turned the handle and pushed the door inward, taking advantage of each clap of thunder to make bolder progress, then stood stock-still in the doorway.

In the corner on top of a wheat-flour barrel, a stub of candle had been stuck into a mound of its own wax. Scarcely a yard from its sputtering flame, a hand extending from a worn sleeve was hurriedly opening and closing one cupboard door after another.

For a few minutes Thorne only observed, curious to see what would finally catch the thief's interest. But after several swift and futile searches, the intruder swore under his breath and scratched his head.

"Perhaps I can assist, William."

The boy cried out in alarm as Thorne stepped into the room.

He went to the barrel and lifted the candle near William's face. "What is it you seek?" he asked gently.

The youth's fear waned to wariness; his mouth worked in mime as he tried to explain. "'Tis for a friend," he finally stammered, his pubescent voice cracking under tension.

"*What* is for a friend?"

"I've got to find the cam--chamo-" William broke off, worry creasing his young brow.

"Chamomile?"

"Aye!" The boy sighed in relief. "Some chamomile and some honey."

"For whom, and why?"

William stared down at his wet shoes and shifted from one foot to the other.

Thorne chucked him under the chin. "For whom?" he said more sternly.

"The miss, sir," came the grudging reply. "The miss what lives in the little shack off the Wycliffe road."

Thorne frowned. "You mean the Gypsy, the person who has sheltered in the shack all winter? I thought he--or she--would have moved along before now. Why should she be needing these things at such an odd hour, and why the devil bid *you* to confiscate them?"

"She ain't a Gypsy, M'lord." William shook his head earnestly. "'Tis the miss what once lived at the Hall and stitched. She's having her babe, and 'tis almost here!"

For a time Thorne forgot to breathe, and stared at William so intently that the boy retreated a step.

- 247 -

"Begging ye're pardon, M'lord, I ain't a thief, leastways not truly! I take only what she needs, and for a lady what's carrying a babe, she done without most all but what I fetched for her, and even most of that she didn't ask for-"

"'The miss,'" Thorne interrupted in a choked voice, for it seemed his heart had caught in his throat and would suffocate him at any moment. "Is 'the miss' *Elaine Combs*?"

"Aye, M'lord, and she's in sore need of this--this cam-"

"Chamomile," Thorne said tersely, already turning toward the other cupboards. "Get a lantern in here."

William ran to the kitchen, no longer concerned with stealth.

"Now," Thorne said, all but grabbing the light from him, "go and wake Mistress MacBride."

"But the miss says to wake no one, sir-"

"And I said wake Mistress MacBride, damn it!"

"Aye! Aye, M'lord!" William was already halfway across the kitchen.

"Where the deuce does she keep it?" Thorne railed, searching each shelf with frenetic energy and shoving tins, bottles and jars right and left in the process.

"Here now, M'lord!" Having come from the kitchen on a shuffling run, wrapper half closed and nightcap askew, Bridey practically shoved Thorne aside to open another cupboard door. "Here we are!" She grabbed a small crock and opened it to show him some dried yellow flowers. "Surely she has a kettle?" she asked breathlessly, turning to William.

"Aye, mistress. But she could do with more linens."

"Och, of course she could, poor soul. We must hurry. Run and fetch clean ones from the big chest topstairs, William, and wake Janie while ye're at it, but do it quiet-like, she's in the bed nearest the door. Let's see, I'll need my cayenne, and some shepherd's purse in case the bleeding don't slow as it should..." She took a deep breath. "M'lord, ye might's well send for Dobson to bring the coach 'round, I can't sit a horse, much less mount one."

"The devil take this bloody weather!" Thorne fumed, starting toward the cloakroom. "The road may be too muddy for the coach."

"Send for a cart, then," Bridey said soothingly. "A bit of rain never hurt nobody. We'll manage, ye needn't fret." Thorne gave her a grateful look.

William returned with the linens and was immediately dispatched for a cart. The dozen minutes it took for the horses to be harnessed and hitched and led through the gardens seemed a lifetime to Thorne, who had felt like running the whole considerable distance on foot from the moment William revealed his secret.

The cart, drawn by two horses to help prevent the wheels from sticking in the mire, made slow but steady progress. The devil must have seen fit to take the weather after all, for by the time everyone had boarded the cart, the downpour had abated to a fine mist.

According to Thorne's pocket watch, checked every few seconds by lantern light, five-and-twenty long minutes had passed when they finally reached the shack. Slivers of dim light sliced through rag-stuffed chinks in the squared logs, and he fought a tide of helpless anger as he wondered if Elaine Combs had known a minute's warmth over the winter.

William was first through the door. Thorne tried to be patient as he helped the women off the cart. With a low command to the horses and a few long strides, he was soon over the rotting threshold.

Immediately noticing that the room was too smoky, he forced himself to ignore the muffled moans of pain from the little cot, where Janie and Bridey were already busy. He rolled up his sleeves and poked a stick of kindling up the chimney, smelling the hair on his arms singeing as he cleared caked soot, rotted leaves and bird nest debris from the chimney. Satisfied once the fire was producing less smoke than heat, he wiped his hands on his breeches and went toward the cot.

"Now, now," Bridey chided, glancing over her shoulder at him. "Ye might as well wait by the fire, M'lord, or outdoors with William. Men have little stomach for these things."

"*This* man," Thorne retorted, "has birthed foals, lambs, calves and pups, and managed to keep both his stomach and his wits. Stand aside, woman, if only for a moment...for by God, I *will* see her."

Bridey squeezed her bulk past him without meeting his eyes. "I'll just see to the hot water," she mumbled.

Thorne's heart leapt with his first glimpse of the swollen-bellied woman lying on the straw-stuffed mattress.

"M'lord," she whispered, smiling through her pain. She held out her hand, a gesture which opened Janie's eyes wide with its impropriety, but Thorne took it without hesitation and held it firmly in both his. Riveted by her eyes, he drank in the quiet strength that radiated from them even in the midst of her labor.

"How do you do?" he asked urgently, feeling inane and inadequate as soon as the words were out of his mouth.

Her smile widened. "As well as can be expected, I imagine...oh!" she gasped, and suddenly Bridey was immediately behind Thorne.

"Come, M'lord, yield me quarter now. The babe is on its way."

Thorne gave Elaine's hand a gentle squeeze. "You'll be fine," he assured her, wanting desperately to say more but at a loss for words. She tried to smile at him, but winced dreadfully at the next onslaught of pain.

It was more than he could bear. Taking Bridey's earlier advice, he grabbed his damp cloak and stepped outside, silently cursing himself for not thinking to bring a flask of whiskey. Then he remembered the brandy Bridey had brought along for disinfecting. But no, he would feel humiliated asking for even a little of it, and the cook would be quite bemused.

The wait seemed an hour or more; in fact it was less than half that time. Bridey's chubby face fairly beamed when she opened the sagging door to tell Thorne it was over.

A pre-arranged consensus seemed to ensue as she and Janie went hastily to the other end of the shack. Scarcely aware of them at any rate, Thorne defied convention by sitting on the edge of the cot. Gently he stroked the downy head of the sleeping infant, though his attention was on the mother. "Bridey didn't say--'he' or 'she'?"

"I've a daughter," Elaine said with a tired but grateful smile. "And you've a niece."

He pressed his lips together, then said quietly, "I gather William has kept you informed."

"Aye." She gathered the swaddled child closer. "'Tis a shame Mister Hobbs would have none of her...though I'd like to think he sees her now, and knows she is his." She touched her lips to the baby's wrinkled little forehead.

Pierced through the heart by that simple maternal gesture, Thorne had to look away. "Hobbs was a fool for disowning the babe," he said huskily, "and I told him as much."

Elaine smiled, closing her eyes. "You were ever my champion, Thorne," she murmured. "I haven't forgotten." Her eyes flew open to find him staring at her intently. "I...I beg your pardon, M'lord, for speaking familiar...'tis just that..."

"Just that what?" he whispered harshly, every nerve of his body feeling inexplicably raw, as if he were about to be flayed.

He was dismayed to see tears trickle from her eyes. Unmindful of the servants, he gently wiped them away with the backs of his fingers. "Tell me," he entreated her, his voice choked with a tenderness the depth of which he'd never experienced. "I cannot bear to see you unhappy."

A small sob escaped her. "You never could."

Thorne heard the bustle of skirts behind him. "Leave us," he said tautly, and heard the skirts retreat. He stroked the infant's head again. "Why," he murmured, making no effort to mask the pain in his voice, "did you go?"

Elaine looked sadly touched. "'Twas necessary."

Cold anger slithered through Thorne's veins and hardened his features. "Lady Neville."

"No," Elaine whispered, and shook her head weakly. "I'd have gladly suffered her abuse to remain in your house."

"Then what?...who?" He squeezed her hand.

"Lord Whittingham," she answered, then seemed to hold her breath.

"That whoreson threatened you, made overtures? God's blood, he *was* in my house the night you disappeared, and he did the same to my guest!"

"No," Elaine whispered with a shudder. "He didn't threaten me. I made certain of it."

Thorne heard a stir in the room; the midwifery team was about to swoop down on him again. He held a staying hand out behind him, saying to Elaine with soft urgency, "I don't understand...had Lord Whittingham threatened you before?"

She managed one exhausted nod. "Aye...before."

"M'lord," Bridey broke in plaintively. "Ye must let her rest now." She approached the bed with a determination that defied all authority.

"Rest now," Thorne murmured close to Elaine's ear. "We'll talk again." It took all the self-discipline he possessed not to touch his lips to her cheek in plain view of the cook. "Can she be moved tonight?" he asked Bridey.

A glad light came into the old cook's eyes as she replied in the affirmative, but Thorne saw guarded speculation there as well. He supposed he'd broken several rules of class distinction as well as decorum this eventful evening, and Bridey wasn't stupid. Too, he realized that some self-examination and soul-searching were in the offing, but just now the welfare of the new mother and child were his only concern. "William, make a bed in the cart with some of these linens," he said kindly to the anxious youth. "The 'miss' is coming home."

"Aye, M'lord!" The smile on William's face was infectious, and Thorne felt a lump rise in his throat again, this time one of gratitude for the solicitous care given Elaine by this loyal young servant. A reward of some kind was certainly in order; he would enjoy deciding its nature.

For the first time in months, his heart began to lighten.

* * *

"The largest of the guest chambers on the south side," Thorne repeated to his stunned housekeeper.

"Will she require attendance?"

"She will indeed. Byrnes should do nicely."

"For how long, M'lord? I ask only because Byrnes is assisting Markham."

Thorne stared at her pointedly. "For as long as I deem appropriate. That is all for now."

"Aye, M'lord." Her curtsey was deep and exaggerated. She turned to go.

"One thing more, Dame Carswell."

As if moving through mud, she faced him. "M'lord?"

"I shall say this once and only once. Elaine Combs' child is my niece, a member of my family, and as such shall enjoy full rights and privileges in accordance with her station."

The housekeeper hesitated only a moment. "Certainly, M'lord, there was never any doubt. With your permission, I shall find her a proper nurse."

"She has a nurse. Her own mother. Leave it to you to call the propriety of nature into question. And until her mother is in the pink of health, she'll recuperate in the comfort of my home."

Though the housekeeper's narrow jaw had taken a set and the light of battle was in her eyes, her voice was admirably controlled. "Of course, M'lord, and when Combs is up to it, perhaps you'll reinstate her as Markham's assistant. 'Twould be a fine arrangement. She could easily visit the nursery for the child's feedings."

Thorne's mouth quirked at one corner. "Ah, I see your logic. Quite sensible, really. The woman can resume her duties, hence being no burden to my household, and, except for the occasional nuisance of wet-nursing, can forget she ever bore a child."

"Aye, M'lord." Carswell appeared somewhat mollified. "She'll have spent little time with it, a few days at most, and things would be much easier on her if 'tis given into the care of an experienced woman of higher rank. Two years hence, when it no longer requires a wet-nurse, Combs will be left to her principal duty, that of seamstress in your house--if, indeed, you should even wish to keep her on."

Thorne's smile was benign enough, but if the housekeeper had been less determined, she might have noticed the ice in his eyes. "I should remind you that this 'it' of whom you speak is a 'she,' Dame Carswell. Now then, let me clarify your proposal for my own understanding. When two years have passed, Combs should forfeit all claim to her natural-born daughter, that being the time when her mammary glands are no longer needed to serve. Have I got it right?"

"*Sir!*"

"Forgive me, ma'am, if I've insulted your fine sensibilities, but I tend to be blunt on those rare occasions when my authority is challenged by a servant, even one so erudite and highly ranked as yourself...you are my servant, are you not, Dame Carswell?" At her mumbled affirmation he said heartily, "Good! For a moment I thought perhaps I'd only dreamed it. Then kindly carry out my orders as I've given them. And send Byrnes to me directly."

Dame Carswell's silent indignation barely allowed her to execute a curtsey. Thorne made a mental note to put a word of inquiry about Northampton, perhaps London, for a new housekeeper. This time she'd come dangerously close to outright insubordination, and just as before, the bone of her dogged contention was Elaine Combs.

"By God, I suffered my wife to slander her, time and time again," he muttered to himself as she glided away, "but I'll be damned if I'll endure the same from you!"

* * *

"Good afternoon, M'lord," Elaine said softly.

Giving Byrnes a nod, Thorne approached the bed.

No longer in pain and in far more comfortable surroundings, Elaine fairly glowed. Her muslin wrapper was faded, but spotless, and Byrnes had brushed the tangles from her hair and woven it into a thick plait, leaving it to cascade over her bodice and onto the velvet counterpane. It was as much for that picture that Thorne smiled as for the sight of the sleeping infant in the crook of her arm.

"And how are the ladies today?"

"Quite well, thanks to your lordship." Elaine darted a glance at Byrnes, who waited by the open door. Thorne was quick to interpret the look, and asked the maid to leave them alone for awhile. When she'd gone, he leaned down to caress the baby's cheek.

"Like satin," he murmured. "She has your complexion."

"Thank you."

Thorne pretended not to notice her blush.

It was the fourth day of shelter for the two refugees. Each day he'd visited for a longer period, but today was the first time he'd been alone with his charges.

The baby stirred and whimpered, rosebud mouth puckering. Her eyes opened, squinted. The whimper quickly amplified, and she beat tiny fists irregularly against her chest.

Elaine smiled down into the reddening little face, glancing briefly at Thorne. "She's hungry. There, don't fret, sweeting, I shall feed you presently."

"May I..." Thorne began, feeling as awkward as an adolescent, then tried again. "I'd like to watch her nurse."

Elaine smiled, lowering her eyes, and nodded.

Thorne pretended to look away while she discreetly unlaced the bodice of her wrapper and shift, but his peripheral vision caught her gathering the babe close and touching a nipple to her cheek. Instantly the infant rooted for it, latching onto it and suckling as though she knew her very life depended upon it.

"You may look now."

He was taken aback to find himself physically aroused by the mere sight of a milk-swollen mammary. But he was emotionally stirred as well, by the intimacy between mother and daughter, and subsequently filled with self-loathing for envying

- 252 -

the babe that intimacy, not to mention her right to suckle from that breast. Amazed and shamed by his near-rampant erection, he made a quick check of his buttoned waistcoat and prepared to take his leave, murmuring something--later he would forget what, as it was a total fabrication--about a call from his solicitor.

"Good afternoon, ladies," he mumbled, and strode quickly from the chamber. Unable to resist a backward glance, he saw that neither mother or daughter paid any mind to his departure, each caught up in the other as they should be.

His questions had waited for months. They would wait another day.

* * *

The next afternoon Thorne arrived at the guest chamber armed with determination and a certain book of poetry. He was delighted to find that Byrnes was out for an hour or so: time enough to make his inquiries.

Elaine greeted him warmly, but Thorne wondered if she could be nearly as pleased to see him as he was to see her. It had occurred to him that she might be grateful for any company at all, lying in that big bed with little to do but rest, read, eat, and feed her daughter, who at present was asleep in the bedside crib.

"Please, draw up a chair," Elaine bade him. "You looked so uncomfortable standing there yesterday."

He complied without comment.

"You've come to read to me?" She looked surprised and intrigued.

"Aye. I thought you might like this book in particular." Willing the tremor in his hand to still, he leafed through the book until he reached the page he sought, and began reading in a low voice--although he could have recited the words from memory.

> *"Thou art blind tho' thou doth see--*
> *Search thy mem'ry--discover me*
> *Met long ago--yet twained by fate--*
> *Thou know'st me not--here at thy gate*

His quick glance at the luminous gray eyes revealed that Elaine was either mesmerized or in shock. He made himself go on, trying hard to keep his voice evenly modulated.

> *Tho' oft-times now thou speak'st to me--*
> *Thine eye hath yet to know*
> *The face that came'st to love thee*
> *So many years ago*

When he'd finished, it took him a moment to brave her inscrutable gaze.

"Why did you read that particular selection to me?"

"I think you know," he said quietly.

"I should like to hear the reason from you."

"Very well then. 'Twas the last book I saw in your hand before you...disappeared." He watched her intently. "And because I discovered my full name written in the margin, in a hand I suspect is yours." He held the book out for her to see, but she made no move to take it.

"Aye, 'tis my hand," she admitted.

"How is it you know my full christened name? I'm the only one who uses it, and rarely at that."

Elaine looked down.

Thorne leaned forward, closing the book. "Tell me," he said, trying hard to conceal his eagerness. "Is the verse on that page somehow significant to you?"

She bit her lip, then sighed. "Do you remember how on the first morning you saw me about my duties, you wondered if I had served here as a girl?"

"I do indeed. You seemed oddly familiar. But you quickly rid me of that notion with your ready reply."

"Yes, I did." She returned his gaze for a few moments, then indicated the volume of poetry. "Will you read it to me again? But this time," she added softly, "read it as if I were the poet, and you the person to whom I've written."

* * *

Thorne Neville's dubious gaze eventually fell to the page; he began to read again, but silently. When he'd finished, he glanced at Elaine, then perused it again, and afterward sat and stared blankly at the page.

All the while she said nothing, allowing him any time he might need to assimilate his thoughts.

"Having read it in that context," he said at last, an edge to his voice, "I must conclude that I should know you from another time, that your face was familiar to me for good reason."

Elaine made no denial, only waited hopefully.

"Rubbish." Rising abruptly, he tossed the book aside. "If we had been previously acquainted, I'd remember." His sun-browned visage seemed a shade paler than normal, and Elaine sensed that somewhere within his subconscious mind he'd guessed the truth, perhaps even before now. For some reason he wasn't ready to acknowledge it; indeed he seemed to be fighting it tooth and nail.

She was loathe to force him into confronting it, fearing irreparable damage to the strange and wonderful bond woven between them in the past year. She fought back tears of frustration--after all, *she* had dealt with her unique circumstances for years; how could she expect *him* to accept it all in one evening? She cautioned herself to be patient.

"I must go," he said tersely. "Arthur expects me for tea this afternoon."

It was a lie, she knew, but she also knew that he couldn't stay another moment in her presence, on the brink of what he obviously sensed was some terrible revelation.

"Good afternoon, my lord," she said faintly, as he strode from her bedchamber.

There was no reply.

* * *

By the stroke of five that evening, Thorne was ensconced alone in the library. By six he'd downed half a decanter of Scotch whiskey.

At half-past six, he was asleep in the overstuffed chair. An hour later, when Jennings woke him for supper, he requested that a tray be sent to his room.

By eight of the clock he was into the decanter on his sideboard, his food untouched. Until the hour of ten or thereabouts, he drank and slept intermittently, sleep being the only sure method by which he could stave off conscious thought. No amount of liquor seemed able to curtail it.

For the next hour he surrendered, giving free rein to his conscious mind, inebriated though it was, and letting the thoughts flow as they were bound. When the clock struck eleven, he rose with enough resolve to leave his bedchamber and tread the east gallery with surprising steadiness, until he reached the occupied guest chamber. There he hesitated, some part of him still struggling, still unwilling to face what he knew must be faced.

The door was unbolted, and he entered without any attempt at stealth. From the little room to his right came the deep, rhythmic breathing of the sleeping Byrnes. To the left, through the open-curtained archway and the parted bed hangings, he saw Elaine sitting quite still against the pillows, coverlets folded back neatly over her lap and hands clasped loosely in front of her.

How long, he wondered, had she been waiting for him?

* * *

How long I have waited for him...and for this moment.

She could see him standing in the shadowed sitting room, still clothed in his workaday chamois and linen, and knew he'd foregone the evening meal. His shirt was partway out of his breeches, and his hair had fallen down. How she wanted to smooth it back and press her lips to that furrowed brow.

His eyes pierced the gloom, impaling hers; her heart slowed to a dull thud.

"I've but one question." The words were just slightly slurred. "And then I shall leave you to sleep...if you can." With the painful dignity of a man trying not to appear drunk, he stood taller, and she knew he was bracing himself.

She managed little more than a whisper. "Ask away."

He clutched the archway drapery in a white-knuckled fist. "You are not who you claim to be. Your name," he avowed with a visible shudder, "is not Combs."

Slowly she shook her head, her breath suspended.

"You are, in fact," he said, his voice gone hoarse, "The Lady Madelena Harrison Hargrove, daughter of Lionel Stanford Hargrove, eleventh Earl of Whittingham...are you not?"

Her reply stuck in her throat, but she knew she must breach the awful silence--it was killing him, she could see it in his face.

"Yes," she cried, the breath bursting from her lungs with a sob. "Yes, Thorne, *yes*...I am Lena."

THIRTY-EIGHT

Through the solar windows, Thorne stared absently at the woolly sheep in the northwest pasture. Lambing season was well upon them, and then would come shearing, but this morning his thoughts were of more human matters--as Arthur had discerned in their brief meeting, judging by his wry looks. Instead of lingering, as he usually would have, over this year's strategy to net more of the salmon running up by the thousands from the Nene, Thorne had practically hustled him out the door.

He paced to and fro, glancing frequently at the library door he'd left ajar. Would she ever come, he wondered for the umpteenth time. Surely she hadn't fled again. He was relieved beyond measure to see her fingers slip around the jamb.

She closed the door softly and crossed the room with quiet grace, her eyes downcast.

Aye, and well they should be, after the farce she's played on me. On all of us! Yet his heart was in his throat. To see her again in this, their favorite room, was far more than his hopes had allowed for some time.

"Please, Lady Hargrove, do take a chair."

She complied, but not so quickly as to please, and perched on the edge of the seat as if awaiting dismissal.

"I trust you'll forgive me if I continue to pace. That sheepdog in yon pasture could keep still longer than I at the moment." His scowl was lost on her as she stared out at the dog. "I've much to say, but more to hear," he warned, and, as her eyes met his, nodded toward the table beside her. "There is water in the pitcher, brandy in the decanter. Help yourself. For myself I must decline, thank you, I've consumed more than my share of distilled spirits since yesterday." He saw her swallow hard. Good, she was nervous. Or perhaps consumed with guilt. She ought to be both. He stopped his pacing. "You look rather pale this morning, Lady Hargrove. Not bad, though, for a woman who is dead of jungle fever."

"What?" Her eyes widened.

"Lord Whittingham told us you had died in the tropics. Malaria."

"Oh dear God." She shook her head. "I am so sorry, Thorne...I thought he would say I'd eloped, or some such. No wonder you didn't know me!"

"I knew you," he groused, and took up his pacing again. "Or at least my heart did. My head, however, had no room for such foolishness. So you're not dead, we've established that. But you are--pardon me, *were*--living, working, in my house under an assumed name. Some trouble with the law, perhaps? You've killed someone?"

She met his glittering gaze gravely. "I'll let that pass. You're angry, and rightfully so."

"Ah, so you're not a fugitive, or a gaol escapee? You'll pardon my considering it, but you have been known to fly the coop, and quite successfully."

She bit her lip. Was she trying not to laugh? God, he hoped not. He was in anything but a laughing mood.

"You were employed as a governess to a family in Sturbridge," he said tersely. "The Etheridges."

"Yes, I was." She looked surprised and somewhat wary.

"You came to them with only one reference, compliments of a titled gentleman from the midlands."

"Yes," she said after a moment's hesitation.

Thorne halted in mid-step. "Well, who the devil was he?"

He saw her hands clench involuntarily. "Your father," she whispered.

"My...*my father*...?" He gaped at her for a moment, then swore under his breath. "My father." His eyes narrowed. "What in blue blazes would *my father* have known of your qualifications as a governess, Lady Hargrove?"

"He did it as a favor to me," she said calmly, though the knuckles of her clenched hands were white. "I had written of my...of some difficulty with my father...and Lord Robert, as I called him, was quick to act." She looked steadily at Thorne. "I shall save you the trouble of asking. My father was endeavoring to seduce me."

Thorne forgot to breathe. *I should have killed the bloody bastard the night he assaulted Caroline.* He closed his eyes, rubbed his forehead. "Did he...violate you?" The tremor in his voice conveyed only a little of the sickening fury in his gut.

"No, but not for lack of trying. My days were typically spent inside my chambers with the door bolted, except for those times he went to London for gaming and whoring...*then* I was able to breathe, eat and sleep normally.

"Eventually I reached my rope's end. I wrote to your father. I was nearly eight-and-ten," she said with a faraway look. "I'd no prospects for marriage. My father's possessiveness was too daunting an obstacle to any would-be suitors." Her cheeks grew rosy. "There was a time when you and I were promised to one another." She nodded as Thorne's face betrayed his surprise. "Aye, but that was nipped in the bud when your father saw mine forcing unseemly attention upon me. I was of a tender age, and Lord Robert was absolutely livid. Out of my sight, but within earshot, he ordered my father to leave and never to cross his threshold again."

Thorne's jaw sagged. No wonder Robert had been so vague about the cessation of Lord Whittingham's visits.

"My situation with the Etheridges was arranged with utmost secrecy. I took on a new name, and Sturbridge is far enough away from my home that I was able to maintain my new identity. My father hadn't the least notion where I'd gone, and for the first time in years, I began to *feel* again...to live, and to quietly enjoy life."

"Why did my father not arrange to bring you here?" Thorne demanded, though not unkindly, as he pulled a chair up to hers. For the first time that morning, he sat down.

Lena's smile chided him. "Wycliffe Hall was one of the first places my father inquired, just as Lord Robert predicted. Too, I think your father feared you mightn't attend University were I to come live here...and by that time," she said with a sigh, "you were promised to Radleigh's daughter."

Thorne felt the blood drain from his face.

Lena looked at him sadly. "Your father had to pretend ignorance, Thorne, for your sake and mine."

"Yours, aye, but for mine?" he croaked.

"He loved you, Thorne." Lena was firm. "He wanted Whittingham out of your life, and the only way to keep him out was to break all ties and betroth you to someone other than myself."

"Yet you sought employment here after my father died!"

She nodded, acknowledging the irony. "Three years after the Etheridges employed me, I was needed no longer. The girl was to marry and the boy to follow in his father's profession.

"I learned through an acquaintance that you had recently enrolled at Oxford, and I...oh Thorne, I couldn't resist applying for a situation in this house." Her voice faltered; tears filled her eyes. "I love this old place. My best days were spent in this house and on its lands. And I thought that when you returned, I'd be able to..."

"Deceive me," Thorne supplied bitterly.

"No. To make you believe I was but a simple servant, and an orphan."

"A simple servant? God's bones, Lena, there is naught simple about you! I give myself credit for at least knowing that."

"Well," she admitted, smiling through her tears, "the transition from governess to chambermaid was not as effortless as I'd hoped."

"Ha." It was all he could say at the moment.

Her expression turned grim. "Now you might imagine how I felt when, after seven years of anonymity, I discovered that Whittingham was a guest in this very house."

"Not by *my* choice, damn him!" Thorne raked a hand from hairline to crown. "But why leave? Why not simply stay topstairs 'til the brute was gone?"

"I panicked, Thorne. Completely and utterly flew apart. I'd no idea how long he would stay, especially as he'd arrived with your father-in-law. You might recall that my reputation was already in shreds. You were my sole champion, else I'd have been thrown to the wolves long since. And I knew--as you do, Thorne--that if my father happened to see me and recognize me, he would have every legal right to haul me home. Worse yet, I was quite obviously with child, and unmarried to boot. Oh, he would have reveled in teaching *me* a thing or two!"

"Say no more," Thorne said hoarsely, "or *I'll* be the fugitive from justice, because I'll have murdered the bloody cur. Let's move on." He leaned forward, resting his elbows on his knees, and tried not to look as eager as he felt. "Where did you take refuge when you left? Hobbs and I searched high and low for the better part of a day." A day, he was tempted to tell her, which had only been the start of a desperation and desolation he had never before experienced, even upon his father's death. And never mind the other days, the other odd moments that he'd kept his eyes peeled and ears open for any hint of her whereabouts, or the discreet inquiries he had put about in writing.

Lena looked wryly amused. "I don't think Hobbs was all that eager to find me, Thorne. He rode by the shack twice without stopping. You can't imagine how relieved I was for that! Two nights hence, I came to your kitchen and helped myself to an old kettle and some threadbare linens, and who should cross my path but young William." She smiled at the recollection. "He was in quite a dither, knowing you'd combed hill and dale to find me, but I convinced him of the need for silence. He is a rare gem, that boy, and he'll make a wonderful husband in time. He saw to all my needs. How he managed to do his chores and get any rest is beyond me."

Thorne was ashamed of the tightening knot in his gut; after all, William was a mere youth! But he knew that at the heart of his jealousy was a fervent wish that he himself had been the one to provide for Lena. The thought of her living in such crude surroundings still made him furious. He reminded himself to reward William for his kindness.

He frowned as a thought occurred to him. "But surely William told you Lord Whittingham was gone--I threw him out, you know! But that's another story, for another time. Why didn't you come back then?"

She smiled sadly. "Thorne, your influence is far-reaching, your opinion highly regarded, and your charity well-known, but despite all that, you couldn't have defended me any longer to your wife. I imagine she considered your household well-rid of me, and there would have been the devil to pay if I'd had the gall to reappear at your door...especially," she added wryly, "after absconding from a situation that had been so generously *created for me*--yes, Thorne, you'll never convince me otherwise. At any rate, I was loathe to cause further trouble between the two of you, having already been, shall we say, a catalyst...in your past disagreements."

He arched his brow.

"Surely you know how the servants talk, Thorne. Elaine Combs took a few arrows, both in the heart and the hindquarters."

Thorne sat back, falling silent. He'd now come to a point in his inquiry where the asking would take more courage than the answering. He got up from his chair and strolled back to the solar windows. Behind him, Lena was patiently silent.

"Why," he began after a moment, then swallowed hard and tried again. "Why did you let Hobbs..." Damned if he could say it.

"Take my maidenhead?"

He flinched, although he appreciated her unwillingness to sugarcoat the facts. However, it seemed she was not about to say more until he turned around and faced her.

"I can't excuse myself, Thorne," she admitted, her gray eyes soft on his. "My only defense is that I was starved for affection--*true* affection, not the tawdry impostor that my father had always tried to foist upon me. Hobbs' attentions seemed genuine. He had charmed me and tried to court me for months, and...well, God's teeth, Thorne, I was a maiden of four-and-twenty, with no prospects and no one to care for. Yet I'd a hopeful heart. And a weak moment...one in which my life was changed immeasurably."

"I came home only a fortnight or so later," Thorne grumbled.

"Meaning?" Her eyebrows took wing.

"Meaning..." He thought better of the truth, knowing how ridiculous it would sound, and settled for a lesser issue. "Meaning that you might have confided in me, and taken refuge under my roof with your *true* identity." He knew he was pouting, loathed it, and yet had to have it out.

"Thorne." Her look reproached him. "I couldn't risk *anyone's* discovering my identity, for rumors spread like wildfire from the Hall to the village. Whittingham would soon have been at your door with the constable to claim his 'chattel'."

His expression remained sullen. "You could have trusted *me*."

"And continued in my guise as a maid? Would you have been able to sustain the charade? A single lapse--a familiar word, a glance, the unintentional use of my name-- any number of things might well have been my undoing."

He sighed as he came back to his chair and sat down. Leaning forward again, he looked into those guileless eyes. "Very well. And now that the ruse is up, what do you intend to do?"

She didn't hesitate. "Byrnes says you want to keep my child, to raise her here."

"Aye, if you'll allow it."

"Because she is your sole blood relative at the moment?"

He hesitated, nodded. "She is that, but-"

"And what becomes of her when you decide to marry, and sire children of your own?"

The words had cost her, despite their gentleness--she'd blinked thrice rapidly. Thorne fought to keep a passive mien. "And whom would you have me marry, my lady?"

Lena's sudden smile was like bright sunshine on frosty ground; Thorne nearly lost his composure. "It has been years since anyone has addressed me as 'my lady'," she reminded him sheepishly.

"A wretched injustice to one so deserving of the title." Thorne studied her face, then let his gaze wander to her slender throat and linger on its slow, steady pulse. God, what he would give to press his lips there. "You were going to tell me whom you'd have me marry," he prodded. When Lena only bit her lip, his manner turned cool. "No doubt you're thinking that any woman in her right mind would be wary of me. That my one attempt at marriage was a miserable failure. A fatal one."

"It takes two persons to make a marriage, and two to destroy it," she said almost angrily. "You did not drive her to suicide, Thorne, regardless of how you see it."

He smiled briefly. "You and Arthur would have me utterly absolved from guilt, which is something only my Maker and I can accomplish. But again you dodge my question...whom shall I take to wife?"

"'Tis not my place to say, or even to speculate," she retorted. Her composure seemed to be crumbling, too. "Besides, neither did you answer *my* question. What shall be my daughter's fate, once your wife has borne you a child?"

"I'd like to think they would be siblings." He made his tone as even as possible, but his heart had started to pound.

Lena sighed, shook her head. "'Tis a noble sentiment, Thorne, but not at all practical. She would always be second-"

"*Listen* to me, Lena. I said siblings...not cousins." His pulse was hammering in his ears now.

Her eyes darted to his. "Siblings," she echoed, a tiny furrow forming between her delicately winged brows.

"Aye." His voice vibrated with emotion he could no longer conceal. "Both children of your loins...both of Wycliffe blood."

Her mouth opened, but before she could utter a word, he was on one knee before her.

"If you will have me, that is." He gathered her hands, nearly crushing them in his. "Say that you'll marry me, Lady Madelena Hargrove. Tell me you will be my wife."

She hesitated, looking down at the hands that gripped hers.

"Ah." Thorne's smile was grim. "You fear that I ask for the wrong reasons...obligation to my niece, protection from your father." His throat constricted. "By God in Heaven, I love you more than life, Lena Hargrove...have always, and shall always." He tipped her chin up to make her look at him, to show her the truth in his eyes.

"I've been a hollow shell of myself since you left me last autumn. I grieved in silence, night and day, hating this house, hating my life, and marking every accursed hour of each passing day as another wasted, lost, without you." His fingers caressed her jaw, his thumb spreading the warm wetness of a tear across her cheek. "I would have given up my fortune to know your whereabouts, even just to know that you were safe. You took," he told her in a ragged voice, "the very life out of me."

Lena briefly bowed her head, then sniffed her tears back and said low, "And now that Elaine is gone...forever...how do you feel?"

"She has brought my Lena back to me, that is all that matters," he said without even thinking, then added earnestly, "but if you need proof, I shall woo your h-"

She pressed a finger to his lips. "Not once," she said, smiling through her tears, "have you stumbled on my name, my true name, since you learned my secret...which tells me you have integrated the woman Elaine and the child Lena. That is better testimony than all the wooing you could do in a lifetime, because I knew even as a girl, Thorne, that you loved me with all your heart...and though the mind may be fickle, the heart is constant."

Thorne kissed the finger she held to his lips. "What irony it was," he said in a hollow voice, "to have my father warn me on his deathbed against entrusting my heart to a woman. I saw no point in telling him I *had* no heart...that it had died with you."

Lena leaned down and laid her cheek against his bent head. "But we did not die," she murmured near his ear. "Indeed it was your heart which sustained me through some lonely and unhappy years. And you," she whispered, "had mine. I have loved you since I was but a girl, Thorneton Thomas Wycliffe Neville. There has *never* been anyone but you--no, even Hobbs can't be counted. Forgive me, my lord," she pleaded, as he raised his head to look at her dubiously, "but this *must* be said. I thought never to have you, knowing you were on your way home to be wed, and I sought what brief happiness I could find with Hobbs. It proved a poor decision, and though I regret giving myself to him," --she shook her head, her eyes grave on his-- "I shall never regret the result of that union."

He cupped her face in both hands. "You doubt I can love Hobbs' child. But I tell you this Lena--I loved her from the moment I set eyes upon her. I shall always love her, certainly because my father's blood runs through her veins, but moreover because she was borne by you." He stared at Lena's lips, the first he'd ever kissed, some dozen years ago. "Don't you know, " he murmured, "that I was more than ready to take care of Elaine Combs and her babe?"

They were startled to their feet by a knock.

"Pardon, M'lord, but Combs is needed just now," Byrnes said primly upon opening the door at Thorne's bidding. She curtsied and quickly retreated.

"Feeding time," Thorne guessed, a sudden tightening in his loins accompanying the memory of Lena suckling the babe. She nodded, smiling. Seeing she was prepared to go, he caught her by the wrist. "You've not given me your answer."

She laid her other hand over his and regarded him candidly, her heart in her eyes. "Aye, I shall marry you...oh, Thorne, I have dreamt of it since we were children. 'Twas hard to give up that dream when you wed another, but I thought I had...until you showed me such kindness. Then I saw again the young man I had known, the one who was my champion, my confidante and companion." She smiled lovingly. "Aye, I believe you knew me in your heart. So many times, when you looked at me, I was certain the ruse was up! And how I wanted to tell you my secret, or to at least encourage you to guess it. But fear of my father always brought me to my senses, and 'twas that fear which gave me the strength to bear the cruel weight of my own deception, particularly when I realized there was a child in my belly."

Thorne's mouth twisted. "You need never fear that perverse vermin again. You'll not be his chattel much longer, we shall see to that." His fingers traced her delicate jaw, tilting her face up to his. "As for secrets," he said, gazing solemnly into her eyes, "there will be none between us ever again. Agreed, my lady?"

"Aye, my lord. With all my heart."

He looked down at her lips again and slid his hand behind her head, his fingers threading through her loosely bound hair to touch her scalp. He felt her shiver, watched her lips part slightly. "Do you remember," he asked huskily, "kissing me in the larder, all those years ago?"

"Aye," she replied, as he watched the fluttering pulse at the base of her tender throat. "And our tree in Beck's Hollow. How I've treasured those memories all these years."

Thorne inclined his head and grazed the corner of her mouth with his. "My feet," he murmured against her lips, "did not touch the ground for days hence." He pressed a kiss to her eyelids, then trailed his lips to her temples, and further down, nibbled at the satin shell of her ear.

"Oh God, Thorne, have mercy!" she whispered, shuddering. Her hand splayed against his chest for support.

"But then you were gone," he rasped, "and my feet hit the ground as if they were lead." His tongue darted into the whorls of her ear, making her gasp aloud.

"But I came back," she protested, shivering deliciously. Her lashes fluttered; her fingers clutched at him for balance. "I came back!"

"Aye, to my home. Not to me," he muttered, nibbling a tender earlobe.

"To you," she breathed, and drew back, catching his face in her hands. "To *you*. For I knew you'd return, as much as you loved this place...oh, Thorne, I counted the days and the hours when word arrived you were coming home."

His heart leapt within his chest; still he denied himself the joy within his grasp, as yet uncertain of its substantiality. "And then you left me once more."

The words held no rancor, carried no indictment, but realization must have dawned upon her, for suddenly she was uttering the words he wanted to hear.

"You can trust beyond a doubt, my lord...my love...that I never shall leave you again."

* * *

A fortnight later, in the manor church, Lady Madelena Hargrove happily moved down a few slots on the Table of Precedence, becoming Madelena Hargrove Wycliffe,

Lady Neville, Baroness Neville of Wycliffe. Only five witnesses other than Parson Carey attended the wedding. Arthur was all smiles, certain that this time Thorne's vows were based on a firm foundation of love. Bridey beamed away while dabbing at copious tears with a handkerchief. Behind her, William hung back slightly with his eyes riveted on the bride, winning Thorne's secret sympathy and even a bit of guilt--though Thorne consoled himself with the knowledge that Lena was not likely to be the center of William's emotional universe much longer. According to Arthur, the young comely Celeste, daughter of Lizzie the barmaid, had her mind set firmly on the youth.

Dame Carswell was not among the well-wishers. Thorne had given her notice on the day he and Lena agreed to wed, along with a stipend equal to six months' wages, and some excellent references. He'd taken a wicked satisfaction from seeing her reaction to one of those written recommendations--signed, as it was, by Lady Madelena Harrison Hargrove.

He'd tried to present Lena the emerald betrothal ring that had belonged to his mother, but she was understandably reluctant to wear it, having seen it on Gwynneth's finger too many times. She suggested passing it on to the next generation. Thorne agreed, and on the morning of their wedding, presented in its place a large Marquis diamond surrounded by sapphires.

Following the marriage ceremony, Parson Thomas Carey christened the babe "Catherine," naming the fourth and fifth witnesses, Richard and Bernice Townsend, as godparents.

As they left the church, Lena handed little Catherine over to Thorne. "Just a moment, please," she said softly. She retrieved her wedding posy from Bernice, who was holding it for her, and entered the churchyard. Curious, Thorne followed.

She went to Robert Neville's grave and gently set the flowers against his headstone, then turned to Thorne.

"You," he said, too overcome to say more.

Lena nodded, smiling through tears. "No secrets, remember? Besides, he is my father now, too...and protected me like a father while he lived."

Thorne swallowed hard, determined to squeeze a few more words past the heart that seemed to have stuck in his throat. "I love you, Madelena. You've no idea how much. But with God, my father's spirit and our daughter here to witness, I vow I shall spend the rest of my life showing you."

THIRTY-NINE

No secrets. It was a vow taken aside from those of the marriage, but a vow nonetheless. *No secrets.* The words echoed in Thorne's head as he perused the strange letter for the fourth time in a quarter-hour.

"Catherine is fast asleep," said Lena cheerfully as she entered the library. She sobered immediately as she noticed Thorne's expression. "What, Thorne, what is it?"

He handed the letter over to her. "No secrets," he said, looking her in the eye, but his heart was racing.

She read quietly and intently, while he tried in vain to gauge her reaction to the letter's stunning allegations.

25 May, Year of Our Lord 1729
The Right Honourable Lord Neville
Wycliffe Hall
Northamptonshire

Dear Neville,
As partner in business with one Madame Claire DuFoire, London, I am hereby called upon to bring a situation of some import to your attention.

Some ten months ago, you were purportedly a guest in Madame's residence and place of business, at which time you were known to be in the company of one Katherine Devlin, otherwise known as "Katy." Unbeknownst to you, Miss Devlin, being young and somewhat irresponsible and more of a "romantic" than is generally wise in her time-honored profession, determined that she was of a mind to conceive a child, and that the father of that child should be none other than yourself.

At this point, I give you pause to assimilate such startling news. But you more than anyone are in a position to lend credence to such a possibility; for the girl left no doubt in Madame's mind that she was besotted with you. No doubt you were aware of the fact.

At any rate, Miss Devlin knew her moon cycles well, and was successful in her endeavor to conceive.

Be assured that the young woman entertained no further callers following your last visit with her, in order to ascertain upon pending conception that you were indeed the babe's father. I hope you will understand Madame's refusal to allow you later visitations, for Miss Devlin had no intention of your ever knowing of her little scheme. The foolish woman wanted only to bear your child, and past that event gave no consideration to what manner of future was in store for it. What she did not expect was to expire in the process, and I regret to say that such was indeed her fate.

Your child--a robust son, by the by--is presently in the care of a nurse whose compensation, you will be gratified to know, is made possible by your generous monetary donations for Miss Devlin's medical fees. However, I regret to say that when those funds are depleted, Madame will have no choice but to turn the child over to the orphanage. She has already expended a great deal of time and trouble in the matter of Miss Devlin's death and the interring of her corpse, the hiring of a nurse, and the fashioning of a nursery for the child.

As I have said, Miss Devlin wanted to care for this child (how, I have not the least notion) without your knowledge of its existence. However, in view of her death and the babe's impending removal to a home for orphans, Madame and I concluded that you would perhaps appreciate being informed after all.

If we do not hear from you within a fortnight from the date of this letter, we will assume you have no interest in your child's future, and shall subsequently turn him over to a home for indigent orphans. There he shall be either adopted by strangers, or raised under strict supervision until the age of sixteen, at which time he shall be expected to make his own way in the world. For myself, despite my falling out with your father, I find it troubling to think of a Neville wandering the streets or working as a common laborer. I would not wonder should you feel the same.

Madame DuFoire and I shall try our best to keep word of these unfortunate circumstances from spreading, as your reputation in Parliament is of utmost concern to us both. However, in light of the servants' propensity for gossip, I greatly fear the story will out, no matter what our intentions. The only *sure method for containing gossip, in my experience, is fattening the purses of those involved, and as expediently as possible. I make this suggestion only for your sake, as I repeat: we are quite concerned and fearful for your reputation here in London.*

I am certain you will understand my relating all of this to you in writing, as you made it quite clear some time ago that I was no longer welcome in your home. I await word from you.

Ever at your service,
Lord Whittingham

"My *father*," Lena whispered, clutching the parchment so tightly her fingernails made an impression.

"Aye, the blackguard," Thorne muttered. He was hesitant to touch her just now, though he wanted desperately to reassure her.

She regarded him soberly. "Does he speak truth, Thorne?"

"The liaison is fact," he said slowly. "My paternity, possible." He watched her face for signs of anger, recrimination, or hysteria. There were none. More yet, she surprised him by laying a gentle hand against the silk ruff of his shirt.

"Each of us has a past, husband, and our deeds in those pasts have consequences." Her hand glided upward to smooth his brow. "I should know. Isn't our beloved Catherine the consequence of my own past?" Tears filled her eyes. "Thorne, my love, you have embraced my daughter as your own. Don't you think I would do the same for a child of yours? Don't you see? God...fate...choose whom you will, is offering me the opportunity to return your generous gesture in kind." She stood on tiptoe to touch her lips to his. "We must hurry to London, and see how matters truly stand. Shall I make ready now?"

Staring at her, Thorne shook his head. "I must have unwittingly performed some heroic deed in my past...or I'll eventually be called upon to do so...otherwise, I could not possibly deserve your love."

Lena's eyes suddenly darkened in the way they did whenever her lust was aroused, and Thorne took her into his arms and seared her tender white throat with his lips. She shivered, clinging to him tightly as he took possession of her mouth, but when he slipped a hand down her bodice and caressed a pebble-hard peak, she breathlessly extricated herself from his grasp. "My lord, you do have a way of making me forget myself and everything around me."

"Good," he said huskily, and enfolded her in his arms again. "Then you won't notice that I'm smuggling you up the service stairs to our chambers."

"Wicked, wicked boy," she said with a soft moan and a smile. "You know very well you're tempting me...oh, Thorne...no, love, we mustn't...shouldn't we be packing for a night away?"

"Aye." Sighing ruefully, he kissed her nose, then drew back and smiled. "A son," he marveled. "To think that only a few months ago I doubted I'd ever have children, and now I've two." He stroked her hair. "We've rushed headlong into family life, wouldn't you say, my love?"

"Aye, and in rather unorthodox fashion at that. But I haven't a single regret. And Thorne, just think--Catherine shall have a playmate now, something neither of *us* was fortunate enough to have."

"Except-" Thorne began, but Lena was already amending her statement.

"-when we had each other," she finished tenderly.

* * *

"So this is a bawdy house," Lena breathed, as the coach drew up to the gate.

Thorne tried hard to keep a straight face. "That would be one term for it."

"But it looks like the residence of gentry, doesn't it?" Another inch and her nose would be pressed flat against the window.

"I'd no idea you would be so impressed."

"But I'd always thought such places were quite dingy and rundown-"

Thorne bent over, his face in his hands.

"Well, 'tis just that I pictured-" She broke off as she saw his shoulders shaking. "Really, Thorne! I do have a brain, you know, and the curiosity that comes with it. Besides which, I'm quite aware of their existence. Bawdy houses, I mean."

He raised his head, his eyes swimming with unshed tears of laughter. "And why is that?"

"Because my father always supported such establishments," she said wryly. "Even before my mother died."

"Ah." Thorne sobered, wiping his eyes. "Begging pardon, my lady, I was momentarily addle-pated. Forgive me."

Her lips upturned slightly. "You're forgiven. Shall we go in now?"

He gaped at her. "We?"

"Yes, we. I'm coming with you."

"The devil you are!" Thorne scowled. "I had doubts enough about allowing you to make the journey with me! Poor Dobson nearly burst a blood vessel when he learned our destination."

One chestnut eyebrow rose delicately. "'Allowing' me?"

"You know what I mean."

"I've nearly as much at stake here as you, Thorne."

"No, Madelena, you do not." He shook his head. "Aside from this child he alleges is mine, your father bears a grudge for me, as you saw by his letter. And considering how matters stand between you and him, I'll be hanged before I let him near you. Nor will I have any wife of mine seen entering or exiting an establishment such as this."

Gazing out at the tall scrolled-iron gate, Lena merely sighed and took out her fan.

Dobson opened the coach door and let down the step; satisfied with his wife's docile turn, Thorne alighted.

* * *

Escorted without waiting to Madame Claire's private salon, Thorne found Lord Whittingham lounging in a high-backed chair before the fire, his stubby fingers interlaced over his paunch and his Italian-leather-shod feet propped on an ottoman.

"Neville! I hadn't thought to see you quite so soon."

The oily voice raised Thorne's hackles, but he was careful not to show it. "Your letter was most intriguing," he allowed, and Lord Whittingham chortled.

Madame Claire entered the salon. "M'lords," she said graciously, and took a seat. "*S'il vous plaît, asseyez-vous.*"

"I'd prefer to stand, Madame, thank you all the same. When may I see the child?"

Her glance sidled toward the earl as both tried to hide their surprise.

"Patience, man, patience." Lord Whittingham sounded slightly disgruntled. "There is business to be gotten out of the way first. Have you my letter?"

"I have," Thorne replied, but made no move to produce it.

Lord Whittingham frowned. "Well, if I remember correctly, I mentioned the difficulty of keeping the servants quiet."

"Only a mention, as you say. I vaguely recall it."

The earl squirmed slightly in his chair. "And what are your thoughts on the matter?"

Thorne shrugged. "Actually, I haven't given it any."

Lord Whittingham took his feet off the ottoman and sat upright in his chair. "You forget, Neville, we're not in the country here. Rumors spread throughout London like wildfire, a man's reputation can be ruined in a matter of hours." The black eyes glittered. "Parliament, though its members aren't monkish by any means, is less than understanding when one of them openly flouts the rules of genteel society, particularly one who is landed gentry and holds a seat in the House of Lords." The mustachioed mouth took a smug curve.

Thorne smiled, too. "Those members of Parliament who are not monkish generally use common sense. Few announce themselves in broad daylight or by their true names." He glanced at the proprietress. "Wouldn't you concur, Madame?"

Lord Whittingham waved the question away. "Servants are not all stupid, and many recognize a nobleman when they see him."

"Aye, and in a house such as this, they're paid handsomely enough to wear blinders...no?" Again he directed his question at the madam. She sighed, evidently beginning to lose patience as well, no doubt having thought like Lord Whittingham that this entire matter would be resolved quickly and cleanly.

"There are always those crafty servants who let the cat out of the bag but never get caught holding the bag," Lord Whittingham reminded him sharply. "*They* are your Achilles heel here."

Thorne sat back, assuming the face he wore at the gaming tables. "And just what will it take to deflect Paris' arrow?"

Lord Whittingham looked like a toad whose sticky tongue had just reeled in a fly. "Keep in mind that Madame has many servants in her employ, not to mention the 'ladies.' One never knows what might be said in the privacy of a bedchamber...and you are not by any means the only influential patron of this establishment."

"Yes, I can see that."

"*Touché*," Lord Whittingham murmured with a dead-eyed smile.

"Surely you've a figure in mind, then?"

Madame Claire interjected, puffing her chest out self-importantly. "You must remember M'lord, that my time and trouble have been quite consumed with the *bien-être* of both the mother and the child."

Lord Whittingham, momentarily distracted by her generous décolletage, dragged his attention back to Thorne. "I can vouch for that. Madame DuFoire went *far* beyond what was required of her in the care of Katherine Devlin."

"She was well paid to do so," Thorne reminded him flatly.

"Those funds are quite depleted," Lord Whittingham said crossly. "So of course I have a sum in mind, a rather meager one, but it should cover costs, the major of those being silence."

"Numbers, please."

"Fifty thousand."

"Pounds, of course."

"Of course."

Thorne smiled.

"What, you find that amusing?"

"I have never found extortion amusing."

"You and your father," Lord Whittingham said with a sneer. "Ever the ones to hold morality dear. Yet you've begotten a child out of wedlock, with a whore, no less!"

"I know my sins, and one or two of my father's as well," Thorne said coolly. "But neither of us could be accused of extortion--or *child molestation*, or *attempted incest*."

The madam gasped, while the earl's swarthy face paled. "Your father was a liar if he told you such about me!"

"My father told me *naught*," Thorne retorted. "Even when I asked why you no longer visited, he was unwilling to sully your name. I, however, have no such scruples."

"Nor have I," chimed a feminine voice from somewhere behind them.

Thorne's blood froze.

Lord Whittingham strained to peer around the high back of his chair. "Who is that? Who speaks?" he demanded. "Step forward and tell me who gave you bloody permission to intrude!"

Lena glided into the room, halting in partial shadow. "No one gave me bloody permission, Papa. I bullied my way in. You understand the concept, surely."

Lord Whittingham nearly twisted himself in half as he leaned over the arm of his chair. "*Maddie?...is that you?*" He squinted at the tall, willowy woman who had just moved into the warm circle of light. "It cannot be--oh, sweet Jesu, '*tis* you!" He half stood, wild eyes darting to Thorne, whose expression had gone from inscrutability to feral watchfulness. Looking back at his daughter, he groped for the seat of his chair, clutching at his chest, and fell onto the plush velvet as if the wind were knocked out of him.

Madame Claire, jaws agape, made neither move nor sound.

Slowly, Lena approached the group. Lord Whittingham, ashen and perspiring, seemed unaware of the look that passed between his daughter and his other caller.

"I'd given you up for dead, Maddie," he said, his voice cracking. "I searched for you constantly, everywhere I went-" He broke off, leaning forward to peer more closely at her. "God, you've the look of your mother, girl...now more than ever..." He made as if to rise, already reaching for her.

"*Dare not!*"

Stunned, Lord Whittingham froze in mid-move. His look of sick fascination for Lena turned to confusion as Thorne became his focus.

"No, Thorne, this is *my* cause!" Lena turned to her father. "I warn you, Papa, that if you value your life, you won't lay a hand on me, not even in greeting." She eyed the scar on his forehead. "And this time I'll need no fire-iron to make good my warning."

"You dare to threaten me?" Lord Whittingham heaved himself to his feet. "You are yet my daughter!" His eyes were black coals burning in the furnace of his now florid face. "By *God*, Madelena Hargrove, you will tender me the respect I am due!"

"Which is none at all!" she declared in a ringing voice. "Respect must be earned, Papa, not demanded. You'd have done well to keep that in mind years ago. So, you thought me dead? I doubt that. Likely you *wished* me dead, 'twas what you gave others to believe, rather than reveal your sick little games...how *dared* you fondle me, mere child that I was, as if I were your whore, and then beat me about the head when I cried for help! No doubt you killed Mama, but if she died at her own hand, as you say, I don't wonder--'twas better borne than your cruel perversity!"

"This is calumny!" Lord Whittingham cried hoarsely. "You vicious, lying little trollop, I'll be damned if I let you defy me another moment!" His eyes bulged from their sockets; spittle flew from his lips. "By God, I'll have you hauled forthwith to-"

He broke off with a painfully loud gulp, finding his throat suddenly in a vise and his field of vision engulfed by a pair of ice-blue eyes.

"*Touch her*," came Thorne's growled warning, "and *I will kill you where you stand*."

Madame Claire gasped a "*Mon Dieu*" and crossed herself. Lord Whittingham merely gagged, until Thorne relaxed his grip. "Remember your place and my rank, Neville," he managed to croak then, his face a mottled shade of port. "Madelena is *my daughter*!"

"And she is *my wife*." Hissed through Thorne's teeth, the words slashed the air like a fine-bladed sword...and drew blood, if the earl's sudden pallor was any indication.

* * *

Seeing the malignant promise in Thorne's eyes, Lena shivered; she would never have believed him capable of such a look. Whether out of some odd sense of obligation to protect her father, or merely for reassurance that her gentle husband lurked somewhere behind that deadly gaze, she moved to Thorne's side and hooked her arm through his.

Whittingham stared at the two of them, and, as comprehension slowly dawned, seemed to age before their eyes. His sickly pallor exaggerated the sagging jowls, the heavily veined beak of a nose, the lines and dark pouches under his eyes.

"You're just like her," he whined, "your accursed mother. Begrudged my gaming and every twit that ever warmed my bed--yet she wouldn't warm it. Said I was a Cretin, a beast. But I put her in her place soon enough, and showed her a thing or two in the bargain. She never issued *me* another ultimatum, by God..." his voice trailed away as he registered his daughter's stare of repugnance.

Madame Claire hastened forward and laid a firm hand on his sleeve. "His lordship is tired and out of his head at the moment," she said nervously, wincing as he tried to throw off her hand. "But let us keep in mind our true *affaires* here." Lena saw her give Whittingham's arm a quick, hard squeeze. "You may see the *enfant* now, M'lord. *Venez, puis*."

She led her visitors up a winding staircase and into a room that had been transformed into an attractive nursery. Whittingham lagged behind as if he'd lost heart in the proceedings, but Madame Claire's silk skirts rustled briskly in the stillness as she swept across the room to an ornately carved crib.

Lena held Thorne's arm tightly as they approached the sleeping babe. She saw the tic in Thorne's jaw and knew that despite his outward calm he was in turmoil, and her heart ached for him.

She looked down at the babe. A soft cry escaped her.

He was beautiful. Utter perfection. *Like my Catherine*, she thought, and felt her heart swell as she imagined the two of them together. By all appearances the boy's age was relevant to the time of conception claimed in Whittingham's letter. Deep-auburn hair framed his tawny face in tiny curls.

Smiling upon him benevolently, the madam stroked the babe's cheek, and suddenly he opened his eyes.

Eyes, Lena noted with quickening heartbeat, more intense and vividly blue than those of anyone she had ever met in her life, with the exception of two people: Robert and Thorne Neville.

A chill went up her spine as Thorne's muscles went rigid beneath her hand, and she knew at that moment that he acknowledged the babe as his own.

Yet he said nothing. He seemed dazed.

"Is he not a *parfait spécimen* of *noblesse*?" the madam asked, her tone wheedling. "See the broad brow, and the healthy bloom of his cheeks...have you ever laid eyes on such a child?"

Lena saw Thorne blink, felt the leap of his pulse.

"Aye," he said slowly, "but only in a dream."

* * *

Thorne blinked again, disoriented by a wave of dizziness. Of course! *This* was the babe Katy had laid in his arms.

"M'lord, are you unwell?"

The madam's plaintive voice invaded his consciousness. He shook his head slightly and focused upon Lena, who was watching him anxiously.

When? When, what night, had he dreamed it?

"Thorne, what is it?" Lena whispered.

He stared at her blankly, straining to recall. Shortly before Catherine was born...yet Catherine was not the infant in the dream. *Not yet*, Katy had seemed to say upon presenting him with the child...dear God, a premonition of her death, then. *She was entrusting the babe to me before she died.* He shut his eyes for a second, then pinned them on the madam. "Have you some form of proof that this child is mine?"

Sensing that Lena was about to protest, he stilled her with a quick squeeze of her arm, and felt her stiffen. Just then Whittingham stepped forward, rubbing his bruised throat.

"Are you blind, Neville?" he rasped. 'Tis in the *eyes*, man! This is no time for bluffing, your son's welfare is at stake here!"

"I asked for proof," Thorne repeated coldly. "Any barrister will tell you that there is not a court in the land that would deem eye color testimonial to a child's paternity."

- 271 -

Claire DuFoire looked about to cry; Whittingham trembled with suppressed rage. "Then the child will be transferred to Sheffield House for Indigent Orphans this very eve, Neville. And lest you have it in mind to go there and adopt him, you should know that Sheffield House maintains a waiting list for infants, and the orphanage's policy is quite strict. The child will go to the very first couple on the roster, no exceptions. No title of peerage will allow a client to take precedence over one ahead of him, and there are several already waiting. I say again, no exceptions."

Thorne shrugged. "Do what you must. I've no wish to support the bastard child of a whore."

* * *

The coach had just begun to roll when the earl came storming across the portico and down the walk. "I could ruin you," he croaked desperately.

The horses were halted; Thorne leaned his head out the window. "Not before I'd ruined you, my lord. Your reputation precedes you, and I know of at least two very young girls in Whitechapel who would come before the magistrate with tales of your latest sick escapade."

It was an impasse never to be breached. As Lena looked on, her father spat on the coach, then turned on his heel and marched back up to the house.

* * *

"Lena, what is it?"

He sounded so calm, so gentle. She stared blindly out the window, tears threatening to overflow, and searched her memory for anything that might have indicated such a flaw in his personality. A psychosis, perhaps? She'd read of a woman with two distinct personalities. And then came a thought so awful her heart skipped a beat.

Vengeance.

She had deserted him. She had borne his half-brother's child. And she had deceived him about her identity. Was this his revenge?

But suddenly he was beside her, and try as she might, she could sense no threat from his nearness; only a solid, reassuring warmth.

"I can see you're quite put out with me," he said quietly. "Why?"

Tears plummeted to her overskirt. "Because apparently the man I thought I knew, the man I have loved all my life, my champion up to this very afternoon...never existed."

"What man is that?"

"Oh Thorne," she cried, turning to face him. "Don't persist in this farce, you know I speak of you!"

He frowned. "I know it now. What do you mean, I never existed?"

"The man I saw in that nursery this afternoon bore no resemblance whatsoever to the man I married, but was so cold and cruel that he made my skin crawl. How, Thorne, *how* could you deny your own child? You know as well as I that he's yours, yet you looked so awfully *glad* to hear he would go to an orphanage! Why? Because of what his mother was?" Her voice caught on a sob. "Which, by the by, you said outright in his

- 272 -

presence...will you tell Catherine, then, that I was a whore? Is this your revenge upon me?"

Without knowing quite how, she found herself clamped fiercely to Thorne's side in a one-armed embrace, her head cupped firmly in his other hand and her face upturned to his. "*Never*," he said hoarsely, "*never again* refer to yourself in that way...do you hear?"

Looking into his face, Lena saw all the compassion that was nowhere to be found when they had stood beside the infant's crib--as well as pain, adoration, and a deep abiding love. All for her.

"Answer me, Madelena."

"Very well, I shan't ever again." Fresh tears trickled down her cheek.

He pressed kisses to her eyelids, her wet cheeks, and then her mouth. "Forgive me," he murmured against her lips. "Forgive me for deceiving you."

"Deceiving me?"

"'Twas not my intent to deceive *you*," he said gently. "Remember, I hadn't planned on your entrance. Had you not distracted me so, I'd have been far more convincing in my role."

"Your role?" She struggled to sit upright, her heart beginning to race.

He nodded. "As the arrogant nobleman, the sort who refuses responsibility for anything that doesn't meet society's approval."

"Which is *exactly* what you did."

"Aye, but I'd have done it much more impressively without those tortured dove-eyes of yours upon me all the while."

She grabbed his hands, and the pitch of her voice rose with her excitement. "You're saying 'twas all an act?"

He nodded.

"Then you *do* believe the babe is yours?"

"Without a doubt."

"I knew it!" she crowed. "I felt it the instant you did...so now tell me, why the charade?"

"Because I refuse to purchase my son, Lena--from anyone, much less my own father-in-law, brigand that he is. But make no mistake about it, love, I've every intention of securing him and raising him under my roof."

Lena squeezed his hands. "Soon?" she asked breathlessly.

Thorne nodded toward the window. "We're approaching the city now."

She uttered a little cry of delight, realizing they were indeed headed in the opposite direction of home, but then turned to Thorne with a stricken look. "The waiting list..." Tears surfaced again. "Your son must be awarded to strangers, 'tis the policy of the orphanage!"

Thorne drew her to him. "No, my love. Hush now, and listen."

"Moments ago, you mentioned how glad I looked when Lord Whittingham told us the child's destination. There was a reason for my gladness, Lena, the very reason we left Madame Claire's house as quickly as we did." He drew out a handkerchief and gently blotted her cheeks. "You see, it so happens I know of a way to circumvent the orphanage's official policy."

"You do?" She gazed hopefully at him through her tears.

"I do indeed." A smile played about his lips. "'Sheffield,' you might recall, was my mother's family name. Sheffield House, as you might have soon guessed, was a part of her dowry...also her passion, her life's greatest work...and *her legacy to me*."

Lena stared, slack-jawed, as Thorne's smile broadened.

"Aye, my lady...I am owner, benefactor, and policy-maker of Sheffield House for Indigent Orphans."

EPILOGUE

The pair of them stooped on the broad flat boulder at beck's edge, heads together over their find, the boy's auburn hair afire in the setting sun, the tips of the girl's chestnut-colored braids brushing her lap. Taking a smaller child by the hand, they placed the tiny green frog in her open palm. She examined it warily, then shook her tawny little head, at which point her brother quickly rescued it from certain calamity.

"Can you believe, Thorne, that Rob and Cathy are nearly six years old?"

There was a catch in Lena's voice, and Thorne knew she was thinking again about the governess who would soon take up residence at Wycliffe Hall.

From his prone position on the picnic cloth, he reached for her hand. "Aye, and I've the gray at my temples to vouch for it."

She laughed then, and Thorne smiled, his eyes closed against the lowering sun. Even after six years, her laugh never failed to turn his thoughts toward a lustier vein, and he found himself craving the privacy and cool sheets of their bed.

Squinting, he watched her nestle their sleeping toddler more closely to her bosom. He brushed a hand against little Thomas' dark silky curls and on up Lena's arm, then swiftly sat up behind her and touched his lips to her nape. "'Tis time we made another babe," he said low. "What say you to the end of our picnic?" With an eye on Robert, Catherine, and Sophia, he discreetly cupped a breast. His long fingers gently massaged the pliant fullness, then sought out its distended peak. He chuckled quietly as Lena gasped and involuntarily arched her back.

"Aye," she breathed, leaning against him for a moment. "You do play me like a fiddle, Thorne Neville."

"Rob! Cathy, Sophie!" The hoarseness of Thorne's voice betrayed his own arousal, and it was Lena's turn to chuckle.

"Papa, come see!" Rob called. "We've a frog, and we want to take him home!"

Catherine stood up and made a beeline for her parents, tugging four-year-old Sophia along behind her. "Can we, Mama? He's just a wee thing."

Thorne grinned, noting Sophie's dubious expression.

"Leave the poor thing to find its mother," Lena chided. "Would you like it if someone caught you and took you away from your family?"

Catherine's small brow furrowed. She dropped Sophie's hand and ran back to her older brother. "Let him go, Robby. His mama will be looking for him." She watched, hands on hips, until he reluctantly released the creature.

"The little minx is more like her mother every day," Thorne said with a smile, and, as Lena's mouth dropped open, took the opportunity to cover it with his.

"Ha-ha-ha!" It was their younger daughter's delighted peal of laughter. "Wobby, Caffy, wook! Papa's kissing Mama!"

"Ugh!" her brother said. "Papa, come fish with me!"

Thorne dropped a kiss on Thomas' lolling head, leaving Lena with a quick squeeze and a murmured promise, then swept Sophie up onto his shoulders and strolled toward the older children.

"Too late for fishing today, Rob, time for us to be on our way." He ruffled the boy's hair, pulling him fondly against his side, and nodded toward the western sky. The sun appeared precariously balanced on the topmost limbs of a huge ash tree--the very tree, as the children knew well, on which were carved their parents initials, in a testimony to a love that had begun when they were but five years older than Catherine and Robert. "Look there. Sol is diving into the Irish Sea. Dusk will be at our heels before we reach the Hall."

"There's William!" Catherine cried, pointing into the forest, her eyes shining. "I shall ride fore of him!"

Lena shaded her eyes to see their young stable master through the trees, easing his mount down the ravine. She laid Thomas down gently on her shawl and gathered up the picnic cloth, then shook off the breadcrumbs and stray strawberry caps and folded it over the china and flatware already packed in the basket.

"M'lord, Milady." William dismounted and bowed. "I come to tell ye my Celeste has just took a roast suckling pig off the spit, and she's having a rare fit, afraid no one'll be home to eat it. About to drive old Bridey mad, she is." He whistled into the deep shadows behind him, and Raven appeared, saddled but without a rider.

Thorne winked at Lena. "Well, I'm not about to miss Celeste's roast suckling pig...indeed I've a little suckling in mind myself," he murmured. "Ride fore of me, and I'll keep you abreast of the matter." As Lena smothered a laugh, he said more loudly, "William can handle Rob, Cathy and Sophie...can't you, Will?"

"Aye," the young stable master said. "Else they'll handle me. Be it one or t'other, we'll all get where we're going." The children ran to him with excited squeals, but suddenly Robert dropped back. "Must you be such a child, Cathy?" he scolded, then to the amusement of his parents whirled about, his vivid blue eyes dancing. "Papa! You and Mama and Thomas can race us home!"

Lena laughed, wrinkling her nose at Thorne. "The lad is more like his father every day."

She emitted an un-matronly squeal, clutching Thomas tightly as Thorne swept her up with dizzying speed onto Raven's back, then mounted behind her. Thomas awoke to protest, but finding himself perched atop "Raben's" back, he settled delightedly against his mother as his father encircled them in his arms and took the reins.

* * *

Arthur paused on the flagstone walk in the south gardens to light his favorite brier, where he spotted the horses rounding the bend in the Northampton road.

"Bridey!" he called through the kitchen door, open to the delightful spring air. "Look lively, they're on their way!"

Bridey shuffled out the door. Side by side, they watched two horses and seven riders canter up the road against a backdrop of pine-covered hills and crimson sky.

"What a time you'll have in the kitchen when Sir Richard and Miss Bernice and their families arrive. This old Hall will be overrun with children."

"Aye, as it should be!" Bridey's grin was comical with two of her front teeth missing. "'Twon't be any hardship though, what with Hilly and Susie and Celeste to help me. Saints Peter and Paul, but that girl can cook--as good or mayhap even better than old Lizzie can! But I never said that, mind ye," she cautioned with a snicker.

Arthur smiled. "Aye, she's a fine girl, a good wife to our William." He puffed on his pipe, then glanced sidelong at the old cook. "'Tis rumored there's to be a <u>wee</u> Will or Celeste before the year is out...perhaps you've heard?"

"Perhaps," she said through the side of her mouth. "Now, I've soup to stir." She shuffled back into the kitchen, chuckling.

Arthur folded his arms across his chest and drew on his pipe, watching the approaching riders with a heart full of pride--his family, as he thought of them, just as Thorne had wanted. The children called him "Grandpapa," and were forever clamoring for his attention. He wished his Anna were standing alongside him now, but he knew she was aware and with them in spirit.

The memory of those dreadful months before the children had come to Wycliffe Hall had dulled over the years, as so many joyful times had come along in their stead. He had watched the love of Lena and the children work its magic on Thorne, and knew within the first year of the marriage that he was a changed man. Nevertheless, Arthur also knew that it was the very trials Thorne had endured with Gwynneth, Hobbs and Caroline that had taught him that love was *not* an ill-afforded luxury: that it was instead the binding ingredient for a full and happy life. And surely, Arthur mused, old Robert Neville, looking on from a higher plane, could see the error in his well-meaning but misguided advice, and would be proud of his son, and glad for the direction his life had taken.

He waved as one of the children spotted him, and watched with a smile as the horses and riders entered the stable yard, the children squealing and shouting with the boundless energy of youth. His mind wandered back to another warm evening, some seven years ago in July, when he and Thorne had sat in the relative coolness of Duncan's public alehouse. At that time Thorne had spoken the words which, though referring to his upcoming first marriage, seemed so much more appropriate now.

"My course is set," he had assured Arthur with a smile, "and I embark happily on life's journey, my mate at my side through fair weather and foul, for as long as she'll have me."

And Arthur, smiling in return, had replied, "Bon voyage, my friend and liege...and God go with you."

About the Author

Daughter of an avid reader and journalist, Linda cut her teeth on the English classics. She began writing fiction as a teenager, and was surprised to find it both cathartic and in demand by her peers as entertainment. A few years later, an office colleague introduced her to the English translation of the *Angelique* series by French husband-wife team Serge and Anne Golon. Linda has been a fan of historical romance ever since. A quilt artist and volunteer caregiver as well, she lives with her husband, son, and three cats in Kentucky.